SMOKE AND IRON

VOLUME FOUR OF THE GREAT LIBRARY

RACHEL CAINE

Allison & Busby Limited
12 Fitzroy Mews
London W1T 6DW
allisonandbusby.com

First published in Great Britain by Allison & Busby in 2018.

Copyright © 2018 by RACHEL CAINE LLC

A CIP catalogue record for this book is available from
the British Library.

First Edition

ISBN 978-0-7490-2201-3

Typeset in 10/15 pt Sabon by
Allison & Busby Ltd.

The paper used for this Allison & Busby publication
has been produced from trees that have been legally sourced
from well-managed and credibly certified forests.

Printed and bound by
CPI Group (UK) Ltd, Croydon, CR0 4YY

RACHEL CAINE is the number one internationally bestselling author of more than fifty novels, including the bestselling Morganville Vampires series. She lives and works in Texas in the USA.

rachelcaine.com   enterthelibrary.com
@rachelcaine   rachelcainefanpage

To Tez, who cheers me on even
when I'm too tired to run

EPHEMERA

Text of a letter from Red Ibrahim in Alexandria to Callum Brightwell in England, delivered via secure messenger.

My most honoured cousin in trade,
I am advised by my daughter Anit that you have engaged in a dangerous game with the Archivist Magister of the Great Library.

I do not think, given your history and your legendary cunning, that I need to remind you of the danger this brings, not just to you but to all of us. While we sometimes use the Library in the pursuit of our trade, we must never allow ourselves to be used in turn. An ant cannot direct a giant.

You have placed your son in the gravest of danger.

As one loving father to another, I beg you: call off this plan. Bring your son home. Withdraw from any further engagement with the Archivist. I will likewise have Anit deliver her captives back into your custody, and you may do as you like with them, but pray do not continue to involve my family in this foolhardy venture.

The Archivist may talk most pleasantly with you. A viper may learn to talk, but it is still full of poison.

Blessings of the gods to you, old friend.

Reply from Callum Brightwell to Red Ibrahim, delivered via secure messenger.

My son Brendan can well care for himself, but I thank you for your concern. Should the worst occur, I still have his twin Jess. He's not presently pleased with me for sending his brother in his place, but I expect that will pass.

If you plan to lecture me, you might have taken greater care with your own sons – both lost to you now, advancing the cause of your own business. Don't lecture me on how to protect my own. As to your daughter, she entered into this arrangement on your behalf, and with your full authority; you may take up any misgivings you have with her, not me.

I expect you to uphold the agreement as she has made it. Anit and I are of like minds in this, and as she is the heir to your vast empire of commerce, you should listen to her. She's clever, and as ruthless as you, in many ways.

And you wouldn't like to make enemies of our families.

I think upon calm reflection you will see the wisdom of gathering the Library's favour as chaos gathers around us. The world is more unsafe now than it ever has been in living memory. Being allies with the Archivist means that their guard will be lower when we decide to turn these tables to our advantage, as we might at any time.

Peace be upon you, my friend. Let's see how this plays out.

PART ONE

JESS

CHAPTER ONE

It had all started as an exercise to fight the unending boredom of being locked in this Alexandrian prison cell.

When Jess Brightwell woke up, he realised that he'd lost track of time. Days blurred here, and he knew it was important to remember how long he'd been trapped, waiting for the axe to fall – or not. So he diligently scratched out a record on the wall using a button from his shirt.

Five days. Five days since he'd arrived back in Alexandria, bringing with him Scholar Wolfe and Morgan Hault as his prisoners. They'd been taken off in different directions, and he'd been dumped here to – as they'd said – await the Archivist's pleasure.

The Archivist, it seemed, was a very busy man.

Once he had the days logged, Jess did the mental exercise of calculating the date from pure boredom. It took him long, uneasy moments to realise why that date – today – seemed important.

And then he remembered and was ashamed it had taken him so long.

Today was the anniversary of his brother Liam's death. His older brother.

And today meant that Jess was now older than Liam had ever lived to be.

He couldn't remember exactly *how* Liam had died. Could hardly remember his brother at all these days, other than a vague impression of a sharp nose and shaggy blondish hair. He must have watched Liam walk up the stairs of the scaffold and stand as the rope was fixed around his neck.

But he couldn't remember that, or watching the drop. Just Liam, hanging. It seemed like a painting viewed at a distance, not a memory.

Wish I could remember, he thought. If Liam had held his head high on the way to his death, if he'd gone up the steps firmly and stood without fear, then maybe Jess would be able to do it, too. Because that was likely to be in his future.

He closed his eyes and tried to picture it: the cell door opening. Soldiers in High Garda uniforms, the army of the Great Library, waiting stone-faced in the hall. A Scholar to read the text of his choice to him on the way to execution. Perhaps a priest, if he asked for one.

But there, his mind went blank. He didn't know how the Archivist would end his life. Would it be a quiet death? Private? A shot in the back? Burial without a marker? Maybe nobody would ever know what had become of him.

Or maybe he'd end up facing the noose after all, and the steps up. If he could picture himself walking without flinching to his execution, perhaps he could actually *do* it.

He knew he ought to be focusing on what he would be saying to the Archivist if he was called, but at this moment death seemed so close he could touch it, and besides, it was easier to accept failure now than to dare to predict success. He'd never been especially superstitious, but imagining triumph now seemed like drawing a target on his back. No reason to offend the Egyptian gods. Not so early.

He stood up and walked the cell. Cold, barren, with bars and a flat stone shelf that pretended at being a bed. A bare toilet that needed cleaning and the sharp smell of it was starting to squirm against his skin.

If I had something to read . . . The thought crept in without warning, and he felt it like a personal loss. Not having a book to hand was worse punishment than most. He was trying not to think about his death, and he was too afraid to think about the fate of Morgan or Scholar Wolfe or anything else . . . except that he could almost hear Scholar Wolfe's dry, acerbic voice telling him *If only you had a brain up to the task, Brightwell, you'd never lack for something to read.*

Jess settled on the stone ledge, closed his eyes, and tried to clearly imagine the first page of one of his favourite books. Nothing came at his command. Just words, jumbled and frantic, that wouldn't sort themselves in order. Better if he imagined writing a letter.

Dear Morgan, he thought. *I'm trapped in a holding cell inside the Serapeum, and all I can think of is that I should have done better by you, and all of us. I'm afraid all this is for nothing. And I'm sorry. I'm sorry for being stupid enough to think I could outwit the Archivist. I love you. Please don't hate me.*

That was selfish. She should hate him. He'd sent her back into the Iron Tower, a life sentence of servitude and an unbreakable collar fastened tight around her neck. He'd deceived Scholar Wolfe into a prison far worse than this one, and an inevitable death sentence. He'd betrayed everyone who'd ever trusted him, and for what?

For cleverness and a probably foolish idea that he could somehow, *somehow*, pull off a miracle. What gave him the right to even think it?

Clank.

That was the sound of a key turning in a heavy lock.

Jess stood, the chill on his back left by the ledge still lingering like a ghost, and then came to the bars as the door at the end of the hall opened. He could see the hinges move and the iron door swinging in. It wasn't locked again when it closed. *Careless.*

He listened to the decisive thud of footsteps against the floor, growing louder, and then three High Garda soldiers in black with golden emblems were in front of his cell. They stopped and faced him. The oldest – his close-cut hair a stiff silver brush around his head – barked in common Greek, 'Step back from the bars and turn around.'

Jess's skin felt flushed, then cold; he swallowed back a rush of fear and felt his pulse race in a futile attempt to outrun the inevitable. He followed the instructions. *They didn't lock the outer door. That's a chance, if I can get by them.* He could. He could sweep the legs out from under the first, use that off-balance body to knock back the other two, pull a sidearm free from one of them, shoot at least one, maybe two of them. Luck would dictate whether he'd die in the attempt, but at least he'd die fighting.

I don't want to die, something in him that sounded like a child whispered. *Not like Liam. Not on the same day.*

And suddenly, he remembered.

The London sky, iron grey. Light rain had been falling on his child's face. He'd been too short to see his brother ascend anything but the top two steps of the scaffold. Liam had stumbled on the last one, and a guard had steadied him. His brother had been shivering and slow, and he hadn't been brave after all. He'd looked out into the crowd of those gathered, and Jess remembered the searing second of eye contact with his brother before Liam transferred that stare to their father.

Jess had looked, too. Callum Brightwell had stared back without a flicker of change in his expression, as if his eldest son was a stranger.

They'd tied Liam's hands. And put a hood over his head.

A voice in the here and now snapped him out of the memory. 'Against the wall. Hands behind your back.'

Jess slowly moved to comply, trying to assess where the other man was . . . and froze when the barrel of a gun pressed against the back of his neck. 'I know what you're thinking, son. Don't try it. I'd rather not shoot you for stupidity.'

The guard had a familiar accent – raised near Manchester, most likely. His time in Alexandria had covered his English roots a bit, but it was odd, Jess thought, that he might be killed by one of his countrymen, so far from home. Killed by the English, just like Liam.

Once a set of Library restraints settled around his wrists and tightened, he felt strangely less shaken. Opportunity was gone now. All his choices had been narrowed to one course. All he had to do now was play it out.

Jess turned to look at the High Garda soldier. A man with roots from another garden, maybe one closer to Alexandria; the man had a darker complexion, dark eyes, a neat beard, and a compassionate but firm expression on his face. 'Am I coming back?' he asked, and wished he hadn't.

'Likely not,' the soldier said. 'Wherever you go next, you won't be back here.'

Jess nodded. He closed his eyes for a second and then opened them. Liam had faltered on the stairs. Had trembled. But at the end his elder brother had stood firm in his bonds and hood and waited for the end without showing any fear.

He could do the same.

'Then let's go,' he said, and forced a grin he hoped looked careless. 'I could do with a change of scenery.'

They didn't take him to the gallows. Not immediately, anyway. And though he half feared he'd never see the shot that would kill him from behind, they reached the end of the hall and the unlocked door without incident. *Lucky that Captain Santi isn't here to see that breach of security,* he thought. Santi would have had someone's head off for it. Metaphorically speaking.

And now he wished he hadn't thought of that, because it added another possible execution method to his imagined deaths.

It was a long march through quite a number of checkpoints, each strongly manned with soldiers and automata; the sphinxes watched him with red, suspicious eyes and flexed their lion-claws. Of all the automata he'd faced before – lions, Spartans, once a hawk-headed Egyptian god – these were the ones that most unnerved him. Something about the human pharaoh's face made them especially inhuman. They'd have no trouble tearing him apart in these close quarters, coming as they would from either side.

Jess added it to his preferred ways not to die and was grateful when the route took them out through an iron gate and into dazzling sunlight. Dying in the sun was always better than dying in the dark, wasn't it? He sucked down thick Alexandrian sea air in convulsive breaths and turned his face up to the warmth; as his eyes adjusted, he realised he was being marched through the small ornamental garden that led around to the side of the giant Alexandrian pyramid that held the Scholar Steps. Too brief a walk, one he didn't have much time to savour, before they passed into the darkness of another doorway near the base of the vast, looming structure.

Then he knew exactly where he was. He'd been here before.

The guards marched him through a long lobby guarded by gods and monsters in their niches and down a hall inscribed with hieroglyphs to a final door. Another, larger sphinx sat in an alcove, and a warning growl sounded until the soldier in charge held up his wrist to show the gold bracelet there. The sphinx subsided, and the door opened.

Jess stepped into the outer office of the single most powerful person in the world.

His guards didn't follow him in. When he looked back, they'd already turned to walk away, and the door was swinging shut.

There were guards, of course; these wore the distinctive red-slashed uniforms of the High Garda Elite, sworn to the personal protection of the Archivist, and they took custody of him without a word. Jess almost missed his old escort. He'd trained as a High Garda himself, had worn the uniform, had eaten in the same dining hall as those men. The Elites were more akin to fanatics than to soldiers. They had separate quarters. Separate training. And they were dedicated to one man, not to the protection of the Great Library.

The Elites hardly gave him a glance as they formed a tight cordon around him and marched him through the outer office, where an assistant's desk sat empty, and then through a set of massive double doors decorated with the Library's seal.

He was escorted to a heavy, ornate chair and pushed into it, and the guards immediately withdrew to stand in the shadows. They went as immobile as automata.

Jess raised his gaze to find that the head of the Great Library wasn't even bothering to look at him.

The old man looked different, Jess thought. Greyer, but somehow stronger, too, as if he'd taken up a new exercise regimen. His hair had been cropped close now, and his skin had a darker hue than before, as if he'd spent time out in the sun. Sailing, perhaps. He must have a ship or two at his disposal.

The Archivist signed official documents with quick scratches of his pen.

Jess expected to at least have the old man's attention, but the Archivist said nothing. He simply worked. In a moment, a young woman walked in with a silver tray, and put a small china cup of strong coffee on the table next to Jess.

'Can't drink it, love,' he said with a shrug of his shoulders, and twisted to show her his bound hands.

The Archivist sighed without looking up. 'Remove his restraints, will you, please?' The order was directed at no one in particular, but a guard immediately stepped forward to press his Library bracelet to the shackles, and they snapped apart. Jess handed them over, and the guard took up his invisibility game again. Jess picked up the coffee cup with a fleeting quirk of his lips at the lovely assistant – she *was* beautiful – and it was only after he saw the hurt in her eyes that he realised he should have remembered her.

And *Brendan* Brightwell certainly should have remembered her. He couldn't forget, not for a second, that he was now intent on carrying on an impersonation of his twin brother, and his brother, God help him, had carried on a secret affair with this very same young woman. Whose name he couldn't remember, no matter how he tried.

Get your head in the room, he told himself. He wasn't Jess any more. Couldn't be. Jess Brightwell was a dead man in Alexandria; he'd come here to set plans in motion, and he'd done it the only way he could: as his brother Brendan. His life now depended on everyone believing that he was his twin, as unlike him as it was possible to be. Sarcastic, sharp, brash, always ready with a grin or a joke or a knife in the ribs.

He returned his focus to the Archivist Magister, the head of the Great Library of Alexandria, as the old man – still without looking up – said, 'Explain why I shouldn't have your head taken off here and now, prisoner.' He frowned down at the document he was marking and put it aside to take up another.

Jess held onto the brash smile that was his brother's shield. 'In here? You'd be days cleaning the carpets.'

'Don't be obtuse.'

'Well, then. You'd just be robbing yourself. I'm here bearing gifts. Valuable ones, at that. And I have much more to offer.'

'Heretics and criminals have nothing to offer me,' the Archivist said. He still hadn't given him real attention.

'You must not have read my father's message.'

'Your father is a heretic and a criminal. Did you miss my point, boy?'

Jess drank the coffee. It was strong, and familiar as home. 'Not at all,' he said. 'But we're both aware the Great Library has dealt with far worse than my da to get what it wants.'

'And what do you and your book-dealing father imagine that to be?'

'The thing that will destroy this place.'

The Archivist finally put his pen down and looked at him directly – a cold stare, empty of pity or mercy. This was a man who'd sentenced Scholar Wolfe to torture once, and Thomas, too. Who'd killed countless innocents who'd stood between him and the Library's goals, and showed no sign of ever caring.

'Go on,' he said.

'The Library has rested for nearly four thousand years on the supremacy of alchemy, and the Obscurists who practise the highest levels of it. Everything you do rests on some aspect of their power: the automata who keep cities in fear. The portals you send your armies through. But most of all, the *books*. When only the Library is the source of learning and knowledge, you have a stranglehold on the world.'

'I might argue with your sinister interpretations, but not your facts,' the Archivist said. 'The Library *is* the source of learning and knowledge. The automata help keep order. The Translation Chambers are an efficient way to move our people from one point in the world to the next. And your point is . . . ?'

'That one simple invention brings it all down,' Jess said. 'Something so blindingly simple that it ought to have been invented thousands of years ago, if it hadn't been deliberately and continuously suppressed by the Library. And you.'

The Archivist sighed and made a point of going back to his papers. 'If you insist on talking in riddles, then this conversation is over, and I'll send your body back to your father for a proper burial. It's the least I can do.'

Jess sat back and smiled. 'We have a working model. In fact, it's churning out copies of things that have been secret for a thousand years – you remember the Black Archive books my brother and his friends stole from you? At this very moment, your power is being eroded one page at a time. If you'd like to ignore that, please yourself.'

The old man was good at this, Jess thought; not so much as a flicker, a flinch, a twitch. But the card had been played, and he'd done it as well as he could do it, and all he could do now was sip coffee and pray that he hadn't just signed his own death warrant.

The Archivist put down his pen. 'I'll do you the honour of acknowledging that this is of some interest to me. It is of advantage to the Library, long may it survive, to take control of this machine so that it may be properly administered. It's to no one's benefit to unleash such a technology on a world unready to handle it responsibly. Surely even your father can see that?'

'My da's not one for social responsibility,' Jess said, and showed teeth. 'He's more interested in the financial benefits. What do you offer for him to destroy it? Has to be more than he stands to gain, mind you.'

'Blackmail?'

Jess shrugged. 'You're the learned man. I'm just conveying the offer. For a price – and a very, very large one – my father will destroy his press, shut down all operations, and hand over the plans *and* the man who drew them up.'

'Thomas Schreiber.'

Thomas's name from those bloodless lips made Jess want to abandon this plan and kill this old lizard now, before more harm could be done to his friend. He spent a pleasant few seconds thinking of how to accomplish it. It was thinly possible that he might be able to lure a guard, snatch a gun, and put a bullet in that evil head before anyone could stop him.

Assassination was always possible if one didn't care about getting away with it. Or surviving.

He held himself still, smiling, though the hate that surged in him physically ached. The old man was tapping his fingers silently on his desk, and whatever he was thinking, none of it showed in his face until he said, 'What's your father's price?'

That was it, then. Jess had been balanced on the edge of a cliff, and now a bridge had appeared in front of him. Narrow, death still very much a possibility at any misstep, but a chance. *A chance*.

'Oh, it's *very* high,' Jess said. For the first time in his life, having an identical twin was proving to be a good thing. A lifesaving thing, in fact. He copied Brendan's brash grin and loose, easy posture, and crossed his legs. Took in a deep breath of familiar air. He'd missed Alexandria down to his bones, and it helped steady the shaking anger he kept tightly locked. 'It might ruin a medium-sized country. But you'll pay it, because it will bring an end to this business once and for all. I already brought you one Scholar you wanted so badly, and the Obscurist too, for free. As a sign of good faith.' Wolfe's betrayal was a burden he'd have to endure for a lifetime. The desperate look in the man's eyes . . . The Library's dungeons had broken him before, and only time and love had put him back together again. This time? This time there might be no repairing what Jess had done to him.

'Yet you didn't deliver your brother along with them.'

'Well, family's family. My father might. But not yet. Early days.'

The Archivist studied him, and those sharp eyes, faded with age but every bit as dangerous as they'd ever been, missed nothing. The old man's skin might be rough and lined, his hair dulled, but he was a killer. A survivor. A ruthless and morally bankrupt absolute ruler. 'You know, the resemblance between you two really is remarkable. Without the scar I couldn't tell you apart.'

Brendan's shrug was higher than Jess's, and more fluid. 'Really? Because we're nothing alike. My brother's a bookish idiot and always has been. I'm my father's son. I'm not sentimental.' Brendan's smile stretched his lips. 'And you have my father's assurance he sent me. But that's your business, whether you believe me or not. Please yourself.'

The Archivist smoothly changed tack. 'You realise that I do have bargaining leverage, boy. I have *you*.'

'And my father has another son. Not much benefit to angering him, either.' Jess took a sip of coffee to give himself time, and listened to the Archivist's silence. Silences, he'd learnt, had layers to them. Some were tense, on the verge of violence; some were slow and calm and peaceful.

This one had edges.

Jess moved his gaze away from the Archivist and studied the office as if he'd never seen it before – he had, once, but he'd been younger then, and desperately afraid. Brendan, having never seen it, would take it all in: the lush carpets in Egyptian motifs, the shimmering wall of glass that offered a view of the blue waters of the Alexandrian harbour and the boats sailing on it. The oversized automaton statue of the hawk-headed Egyptian god Horus, standing with one foot forward. It would be ready to protect the Archivist at the slightest threat, in addition to the waiting Elites.

Jess sipped coffee, but he tasted only bitterness. His pulse threatened to race, but he breathed deeply, the way that his friend Khalila had taught him, and felt the pressure slow. *Wait it out*, he thought. Brendan would.

At last the Archivist said, 'Tell me, Mr Brightwell, have you ever heard of the Feast of Greater Burning?'

Jess's skin went cold, and he felt muscles tighten in his back. Tried to keep it from his face. 'Not familiar with it,' he said, because he was fairly sure Brendan wouldn't have known. 'You're inviting me to dinner?'

'Our ancestors here were not known for the savagery of many other cultures, but the occasional sacrifice was known to occur. We give many offerings during the Feast of Greater Burning, and these days, they are symbolic and ceremonial. A thousand years ago, the feast was a practical way to both continue tradition and dispose of . . . particularly troublesome individuals. If you understand my meaning.'

'You're threatening to burn me alive? Don't dance around it, sir. I'm not likely to faint. Or beg. Kill me, and deal with my father. More to the point: don't.'

The Archivist had been unnaturally still and composed, but he slapped his hand on the shining surface of his desk with a report like a gunshot. He didn't move like an old man, Jess thought. There was real strength behind the blow. 'Don't presume to threaten me, boy, I am the *Archivist of the Great Library*! I command the respect, wealth, and loyalty of the world!'

'You did once,' Jess agreed, and it sounded quite calm. 'But the world is changing. And this is your only chance to control it.'

The Archivist went as still as the Horus statue looming in the corner. Those eyes caught the light from the windows and turned an eerily hollow shade. *Got him*, Jess thought. The one thing that every Archivist for nearly a thousand years feared was change, and it was upon this one whether he liked it or not. With a working press to print copies of books, people would no longer be beholden to the alchemically mirrored copies from the Great Library. They could *own* books, not merely borrow them. They could *write* books without the oversight of Scholars and the censorship of the Library. The Library had started as a preserver of knowledge, a beacon of light, but through the centuries and millennia, it had become a centre of power.

Power rotted from within.

If the Library was going to survive at all, the one thing the Archivist needed to stop was the printing press.

Jess sighed. 'Let's not pretend you don't want what my father has. You've killed a hundred Scholars to keep the secret over the centuries. We're willing to trade it to you, with all the plans. But if you're not interested, I expect we can sell the idea elsewhere.' He stood up.

The Horus statue turned its gleaming golden head in a sharp, birdlike gesture, staring down at him.

'Careful,' the Archivist said softly. 'If I made you disappear, no one would ever find your bones.'

Jess put both palms flat on the man's desk and leant forward. He had some satisfaction in knowing he was ruining the shine. 'If you make me disappear,' he said, 'you'll be the last Archivist of a ruined Library. If you think that's an empty threat, unleash your metal god.' He heard the rush of human footsteps as the guards came forward, but the Archivist lifted a hand and they stopped.

Silence. Edges, and humming tension. When a full ten heartbeats thudded past, Jess stepped back to his chair and settled in, as if he was at home. 'We can be powerful allies,' he said. 'Burners are rising all over the world against you. Kingdoms are on the verge of rebellion. Your High Garda troops are stretched too thin to protect your vital outposts. We can help.'

'I do not deal with smugglers and thieves.'

'You've dealt with rulers and kings for years. My father's crown is shadows, but it's real enough. Think of it in those terms, and swallow your pride if you don't want to lose all . . . this.' Jess gestured around at the office and the great central pyramid in which it stood: the home of the Great Library of Alexandria, in a city devoted to its glory, in a country made incredibly rich by it, protected by armies and tradition, automata and alchemy.

It was all more fragile than it seemed, and they both knew that.

The Archivist made a small gesture, and the Horus statue's head returned to its neutral position . . . but once you'd seen it move, Jess thought, you'd never forget it again. The point had been made.

Mutual destruction.

'What does he want in return for such . . . consideration?'

'Books,' Jess said. 'Rare and valuable. It's nothing to you; you've got vast storehouses of things no one's ever seen.'

'How many?'

There it is, Jess thought. They had an agreement. Now they were only arguing terms. He relaxed a little, but only a little. 'For the press and plans? One hundred thousand rare volumes, and I'll inspect each one.' He smiled. Brendan's cynical smile. 'Believe me, I'd rather be doing something else. It's my brother who's the bookworm.'

'That will take weeks,' the Archivist said.

'Are you in a hurry?'

That earned him a sharp glower. 'Your answer implied you have more to barter.'

'Well, the press and plans are worth that much, to be sure, but the mind of the one who built that wonder . . . that's worth more, even if it's just to ensure he doesn't build more.'

If the Archivist was aware of it, he kept his own counsel. 'Schreiber is valuable to us.'

'Then that's another hundred thousand books. And the others?'

'What others?'

'Captain Santi. Khalila Seif. Glain Wathen. Dario Santiago,' Jess said. He tried not to think of their faces. Tried to care nothing about them, as Brendan might have done.

The Archivist flipped a dismissive hand but then thought

better of it. 'Santi deserves punishment,' he said thoughtfully. 'An example should be made of him. Dario Santiago's family is royal. Pardoning him could earn us the renewed loyalty of Spain and Portugal.'

'And Khalila?' Jess tried to keep his voice calm and light. Difficult.

'The Seif girl made her choice. She can rot with her father and brothers in prison, until their execution.'

Jess's chest began to burn as if he was holding his breath, but he was pulling in plenty of air. Khalila, *Khalila*, executed without a thought for her brilliance and compassion. 'That leaves Wathen.'

'Drop the Welsh girl into a well somewhere and be done with it. She's not important.'

You bastard. You cold, stupid bastard. She's your next High Commander.

And suddenly, the burning in his chest turned to ice. He'd done it. It was agonising, playing to this man's vanity, drawing him into a discussion that dismissed people he loved to death and torment . . . but now, with the casual admission that murder was acceptable, the Archivist had shown his flank, and he was vulnerable. *A fish on the line*, Jess thought. *Don't let him wriggle off.*

He nodded casually and tapped his fingers on his thigh. 'I'll convey all this to my father. He'll want terms for the ones you want.'

'You may use my personal Codex, if you'd prefer. It is not monitored.'

Brendan's grin hurt his lips this time, but he deployed it anyway. 'I'm not a fool,' Jess said. 'I'll manage my own affairs. If we deliver Santi, Khalila Seif, Thomas Schreiber, return Dario to his relatives, and dispose of Wathen, what do you offer in return for all that?'

'Besides the two hundred thousand rare volumes you've already demanded? You go too far, young man.'

'I am my father's son, after all. A fair offer buys you what you want. It's simple commerce.'

'I am not in *commerce*.' The Archivist managed to make it sound like a mouthful of filth, but after a hesitation, he donned a pair of thin spectacles and opened a book on his desk. He appeared to scan its contents, though Jess doubted he had to check; a man in his position would know precisely what he had to offer, and what its value would be.

A moment later, the Archivist clapped the book shut and said, 'I've wasted enough time on these fools and rebels. Two hundred thousand rare original books from the Archives, plus a full High Garda company's shipment of weapons sent for the use of your father, including Greek Fire. And the High Garda turns a blind eye to anything the Brightwell clan does from this point forward, so long as it doesn't involve outright threat to the Library. Does that suffice?'

Despite everything, Jess found himself unable to reply for a long few seconds. *The Archivist Magister is selling weapons and Greek Fire as if it's nothing. And guaranteeing protection to black market smugglers.* The betrayal of the Library's principles ran so deep, offended Jess's soul so much, that for a difficult few breaths he couldn't master his distaste.

He rose again, slowly this time, and nodded tersely. 'I'll tell my father,' he said. 'I expect an answer within the day. Where should I wait?'

The Archivist had already moved on and was taking another book from the stack on the corner of his desk, and a pen. He made swift notes without looking up. 'My assistant will take you to more comfortable accommodations,' he said. 'For now, you are my guest. A guest with no privileges, and no freedom, you understand. I hold you hostage for your father's good behaviour. And make no mistake, if I see any signs of betrayal, I *will* kill you.'

Jess bowed slightly. A touch mockingly, as his brother would have. 'Of course.'

CHAPTER TWO

He didn't allow himself to relax until the assistant – what in God's name was she called? – led him from the office and into the anteroom decorated with ancient friezes from Babylon, where her own desk sat. Less well polished, that wood, and stacked with work. She wore a gold band of service, and yes, she was lovely; he could certainly see why Brendan had been so taken with her. Graceful as she motioned him to a seat and opened a book on her desk – one that no doubt contained orders from the Archivist that he'd just written out.

He studied her while she wasn't looking. The rich skin tone told him she was of Egyptian heritage, mixed with something else he couldn't define; he remembered the thick braid she wore down her back, and the cheekbones and pointed chin. *I need to remember her name. N something. Naomi? Nallana?*

It came to him with sudden clarity, and he used it. 'Neksa, about the way I left . . .' This was a bridge he needed to test. Carefully.

'You left exactly the way you intended,' she said in a brisk voice very different from the warm one that Jess remembered from their first encounter, the night he'd realised his brother had taken a lover from the Library's staff. 'Without any warning, and without a word.' She looked up, and those sharp eyes seemed to cut right through him. 'Though I thank you, at least, for a decent note to tell me you regretted it. I wish I could say it lessened the sting.'

Brendan had written a letter? An *apology*? Clearly, his brother felt more for this girl than had been obvious. 'Sorry,' Jess muttered. He wanted to say something else, but it was risky, and the further he pushed Neksa away, the better for both of them. 'Had to be done.'

'I suppose,' she agreed. She opened a drawer in her desk and removed something that she extended to him. It was a wooden box, carved with the symbol of the Great Library on the top, and when he opened it, he found a copper bracelet sitting on a bed of soft red velvet.

He shoved it back at her. 'I'm not joining your cult.'

'And we wouldn't have you,' she said. 'If you don't agree to put it on, your accommodations will be the sort that are far less pleasant. Did you imagine you'd be granted the same freedom this time?' That, Jess felt, was a double cut. Probably well deserved, that rejection.

Jess gave her a look he well remembered from Brendan's childhood – petulant, with a bit of aggression – and plucked the bracelet from the velvet. He slid it onto his wrist and winced when the alchemy embedded in the metal closed the bracelet and shrank it to fit close to his skin. He'd need an Obscurist, or the alchemical key that Neksa probably kept well hidden, to remove it.

'Tight,' he said. 'Can't you loosen it—'

'Of course not,' she said. 'I don't suppose you're brave enough to chop your hand off for comfort?'

Jess was honest enough to admit that he wasn't. At least, not without far more dire circumstances. He bowed slightly. 'After you.'

He followed as she led him through the corridors of the Serapeum. It was jarring to realise that the hallway they entered was *not* the same he'd passed through to get here, and it preoccupied him trying to make some sense of it. He had the strange, unmistakable sense that the office was no longer where it had been when he'd been brought into it. Was that possible? Or was there some strange, confusing Obscurist field that scrambled his memory of the directions?

The thick sea air closed over him as they passed out into an unfamiliar courtyard, and he felt that strong sense of *home* again. This place had quickly become something special to him. He'd made his first real friends here. He'd found purpose.

And now this was a hostile environment, full of traps. He needed to remember that.

Neksa took him through the gardens that surrounded the base of the huge pyramid, and Jess looked up at the sun-gilded marble facing of it, the fire of gold at its top. They were on the public side of the pyramid now, where a steady stream of people entered the vast reading and study rooms. On the other side, the side he'd entered before, were the Scholar Steps. Thomas Schreiber's name had been carved there, and Khalila Seif's, and Dario Santiago's . . . if they hadn't been chipped into oblivion yet. Likely. Jess imagined that would have been first on the Archivist's list, to erase them from Library history.

Scholar Christopher Wolfe's name was years gone already. The Library *seemed* permanent. But the steady, quiet editing of its own history showed its vulnerability.

He concentrated on following the sway of Neksa's braid out of the shadows, through the lush, blooming gardens, and out to the busy street. That took them past a lounging statue of an enormous sphinx, and the automaton turned its pharaoh's head to regard them with flickering reddish eyes. Jess's skin prickled with a flood of adrenaline, but he kept his pace measured and tried to control his heartbeat, too. This was the beast that would be set on his trail if he violated his parole. And while he *might* be able to disable the thing, it could easily disembowel him with a swipe of its claws, or take to the air with its wings to crush him down. Worse still, that human-shaped mouth hid a nightmare of razor-sharp teeth. Better to never see those, or hear the shrill, eerie scream.

The bracelet he wore was both protection and threat.

Neksa stepped confidently into the wide, white-stoned street and gestured for an oncoming steam-powered carriage, which hissed to a stop next to them. Neksa gave an address and they scrambled in. They sat on opposite sides, staring at each other, as the vehicle lurched into motion, and the wonders of Alexandria began to scroll past.

Neksa finally said, 'You'll leave when your business is done here.'

It was not quite a question, but Jess treated it as one. 'I will,' he said. 'I owe it to my father.'

'And you owe me nothing.'

Jess looked away and fixed his gaze on the broad shape of the Lighthouse Tower, where his friends had once held offices. 'I owe a lot of people a lot of things,' he said, and wasn't sure if he was speaking for himself or his brother. 'No idea how I'll be able to pay all those debts.'

She shook her head but didn't answer otherwise, and they rode in silence, clanking past the Lighthouse and around a shallow curve that took them into different streets. Alexandria held a wide, wild variety of architecture: Greek, Roman, Egyptian, a few styles from further afield. They passed a lush Chinese palace surrounded by carefully tended gardens, and then a manor house that could have easily passed for English.

They were, Jess realised, passing a diplomatic district. His pulse sped up as he spotted an ornate Spanish palace behind heavy iron gates, because he knew who lived behind that facade. Dario had told him that he had a cousin serving as an ambassador in Alexandria.

Dario's family was stuffed with royals and lords and ladies. Hardly surprising they'd end up in positions of power here, too.

Jess noted the location, and the carriage took another turn into a much drabber section . . . perfectly respectable but very small homes, decorated with a variety of bright colours. The carriage drew to a halt, and Neksa handed the driver a slip of paper – a promissory note from the Archivist, most likely. After they stepped out, the driver clattered her carriage onward, and Neksa led him up the worn steps to a door that swung open when she pressed her hand to it. 'It's keyed to your bracelet,' she told him. 'And, of course, the lock can be overridden at any time by someone of higher rank. You will be watched, monitored, and tracked. We will search your quarters regularly.'

'I expect nothing else,' he said. The single room they stepped into had blank white walls, plain furnishings that seemed comfortable enough. A bed in a doorless alcove that could be curtained off for privacy, a long reading couch, a desk and chair. The kitchen held the rudiments necessary for cooking. There was a bathroom in yet another curtained alcove.

The windows were small and barred from the outside, and there was no other door.

'Adequate,' he said. 'And how far am I allowed to go?'

'You don't. You wait until you're told differently. The Archivist has told me you'll be put under lock and key in the prisons if you set foot outside this door. Do you understand?'

'What am I supposed to do for food?'

'You'll get food brought to you. Beyond that, it's not my concern.'

'So this is another holding cell, is that it?'

'A much better one. Count your blessings, Brendan.'

For a long second, they stared at each other. She was looking for something in him, he realised. Some spark.

He didn't have it to give her.

Neksa looked away, took in a quick breath, and said, 'If you need something else, write it to me in the Codex.'

'Books,' he said. 'I'll need books.'

'There is a shelf of Blanks next to the bed,' she told him. 'We're not cruel.' There was an accusation buried in it, and then a bit of a frown followed it as she tilted her head to study him again. 'When did you become such a reader, Brendan?'

A second of inattention, and he'd slipped. Jess was a reader. Brendan was not. 'Just wanted to do a bit of research for Da.'

She nodded, but that little notch of a frown remained between her eyebrows. Jess stared her down, and she finally looked away again and then left without a goodbye. The door shut behind her, and Jess sank down on the couch. Allowed himself a deep, shaking breath.

It was alarmingly easy to become his brother . . . but the little things mattered. Neksa was now on her guard, even more than she had been. If *she* began to doubt he was who he claimed, he'd end his days screaming in a dungeon, or worse.

He put his aching head in his hands, because that made him finally face the rest of it: Scholar Wolfe, locked in his own private hell again because bringing him here had made this charade possible. And Morgan, *Morgan*, back in the Iron Tower, where she'd be once more enslaved, not even her body her own.

This has to work, he told himself. He couldn't use the Codex that had been provided to him; it was obvious that Neksa would see every pen stroke he wrote in it, watch it appear in real time in her own mirrored volume. And with the bracelet locked on his wrist, he couldn't slip away to send messages.

They were all locked up, in their own ways. Dario, Khalila, Thomas, Glain, Captain Santi . . . all prisoners headed for Red Ibrahim's ship, which would carry them here to Alexandria for sale to the Library. That was the bargain Jess's father had made with his fellow master smuggler. Red Ibrahim would exact his own terms from the Archivist, in his own time.

Every one of his friends, *every one*, was inches from death, or prison.

How did I ever think this was going to work? Not that he'd had much richness in choices; he'd known that his father would betray them back in England, and this had been the last-ditch effort, once that happened, to keep some elements in play. Wolfe, for one; he hadn't brought Scholar Wolfe here by chance. He'd been afraid that, of all of them, the Archivist would have ordered Wolfe killed instantly. He and Dario had agreed that delivering Wolfe gift wrapped was the only decent option of a set of very bad choices. Jess was acutely aware that it meant, at best, sentencing Wolfe back to a prison that had destroyed him before.

No, no good choices.

Delivering Morgan had been more strategic, because of all of them, Morgan had the most chance of turning the tide . . . but that meant sending her back to the last place she wanted to go: the Iron Tower.

Standing here, an inch from death, Jess didn't feel especially sure that it was a plan at all.

But it was all they had.

Jess opened a Blank and summoned up a map of the city. He found where he was, near the diplomatic district, still within easy walking distance of the Serapeum, Alexandria University, and the closely guarded precincts of the Great Archives.

He was near where he'd last visited the Alexandrian Greymarket – Red Ibrahim's criminal enterprise. But that shadow gathering never lingered anywhere; it was a constant game of cat and mouse with the High Garda, a dangerous one. He had no notion, and no way to find out, where the Greymarket might convene again, not without tapping into family lines of communication. And that he couldn't do, with the Library monitoring his every move.

And Dario, damn him, hadn't come through as agreed. Jess had been watching everywhere for a sign – especially as he'd passed the embassy – but Santiago, as always, had proved to be reliable only when it suited him.

That was unfair, but it felt exactly true in that moment.

Jess fell asleep, despite the urgent flood of worry he couldn't seem to shut off. How long he slept he had no idea, but suddenly he was sitting straight up, ready for a fight.

He'd have blamed it on a bad dream, but he knew it was more than that. Something was wrong. The sudden shock of adrenaline made him want to rush to his feet, but he knew better. Any move without information could be the wrong one.

A small handheld glow flickered on, and he saw a man of about thirty-five standing not ten feet from him, leaning against the small kitchen table. How he'd managed to enter a locked door and barred windows Jess had no idea, but the most important thing was that the man was not holding a weapon and was putting a finger to his lips, then circling the same finger in the air around them and touching his ears.

There were some sort of monitors here. Listening. That was a warning.

Jess stopped and looked around for something with which

– and on which – to write, but the only thing he saw was the Library-provided Codex on the table. He went back to studying the man, and now that he was getting control of his first impulse to fight, he thought the man looked a bit familiar. Only a bit, and he didn't think he'd seen him before . . .

Then it hit him. He was looking at a Spaniard with some passing family resemblance to Dario Santiago. Taller, thinner, lacking the devilish goatee that Dario had decided to sport.

Jess thought hard for a few seconds, then slowly signed out with his fingers, *Are you from Santiago?*

The man seemed startled, then pleased, and he replied, just as slowly, *Yes. Dario taught you to sign?*

Dario's sister had been born deaf. Most of his family, Dario had said, had learnt to sign. And Jess had considered it a useful skill to pick up, in slow moments locked in a Philadelphia jail. It had kept him and Dario occupied, at least.

He did, Jess said. *Why are you here?*

Helping. The man spread his hands wide and shrugged. *Dario asked. What can I do?*

Dario, of all of them, was the one whom Jess had trusted the least . . . until recently. He was gaining a brand-new appreciation for the Spaniard's ability to play this game of deceit.

But could he trust this man? In truth, he couldn't even be sure Dario had sent him. And Jess's own sign language was nowhere near fluent enough to conduct an in-depth interrogation . . . not that they had time for it. However this wraith had got into the house, he'd need to be out before the Library detected anything out of the ordinary.

You doubt me, the man signed, and gave him a grin that was so effortless it was hard not to return it. Jess felt the familiar mix of irritation and – reluctantly – liking. *Smart of you. Dario said you would doubt. He said to tell you to trust me . . .* Here, the man faltered, thinking through his signs, then spelling the word out carefully. *Scrubber.*

Ah. That old, familiar insult that Dario had been levelling his way for more than a year. At least now it had a tinge of fondness to it. And only those who knew Dario would know that name.

Can you help me? Jess asked.

Escape?

No. Get messages out without detection.

The Spaniard nodded. *Give me names.*

The Spanish ambassador.

The man's face relaxed, and he almost laughed, and then he gave Jess an elaborately ornate bow. *Your servant. I am Alvaro Santiago.*

You're the ambassador?

That's me. Alvaro shrugged, as if to say, Why not? This time, Jess had to stifle a laugh. *Safe for me to come. Even if caught, not likely to be punished.*

That was a neat checkmate of a move, though Jess had never imagined an ambassador who could move with the quiet skill of a criminal. He'd always thought they came with escorts of rattling guards.

What do you need? Alvaro asked when Jess hesitated. *Who else to contact for you?*

This was another conundrum, but Jess only spared it a second's hesitation before he signed back a response. *Elsinore Quest. Mesmer.*

I will find her.

Him.

Ah. Fine. To come here?

No. Tell him to intercept me the next time I'm taken to the

Serapeum. Jess hesitated. *He'll require payment. A large one.*

Alvaro gracefully waved that aside. *I trust you to repay all debts. Why a Mesmer?*

Only a feeling, really, but he had the definite feeling that the next interview with the Archivist would be far, far more difficult, and Elsinore Quest had a skill set that might come in quite handy. But Alvaro didn't need to know that. *Not important*, Jess signed back.

Alvaro doubted that, clearly, but he shrugged and let it go. *Anyone else?*

Red Ibrahim. Smuggler.

The ambassador cocked his head, clearly not recognising the name. Why would he? Royals and the smuggling royalty almost certainly didn't share social circles. When Jess spread his hands, not sure how to indicate an impasse, Alvaro nodded and signed, *Then I will find him.*

Criminal, Jess signed, with a little extra emphasis. Funny, this was one of the first words that Dario had taught him. *Be careful. Dangerous.*

The ambassador waved that away with airy disregard. Too noble and too arrogant to believe he could be at risk himself, Jess thought; he'd spent too much time being respected for his birth and station in life. Dario had been forced to learn his limits. Maybe this Santiago would as well.

Just don't die, Jess thought. He'd hate to have that on his conscience and, perhaps just as importantly, lose his only real ally. He'd have to thank Dario later for setting this up. That would be unpleasant, but credit was due: his noble friend had thought of a sideways move where he'd only been looking straight ahead.

Dario kept reminding him that this was a game of chess, and he was annoyingly right.

Alvaro was watching him expectantly. *Anyone else?* he signed, and Jess shook his head. He had few enough people to trust now, and the tighter the circle he drew, the better. Not even Alvaro could get into the Iron Tower.

When you speak to Red Ibrahim, remember to say that I am Brendan, Jess replied, twisting his fingers around the spelling of his brother's name and nearly botching it, but the meaning must have come across because Alvaro nodded briskly, stepped forward, and offered his hand for a silent shake. The ambassador inclined his head at a precise, regal angle, gave Jess a smile that was a copy of Dario's confident/arrogant expression, and walked directly to the door. When he saw Jess's frown, he smiled even wider.

The Archivist relies too much on his Obscurists. There are alchemical scripts all over this house. Every word you say will be transcribed into the record. Remember that. I'll have people watching the door at all times. They'll convey a message if you sign to them. Trust no one else.

With that, he opened the door and strolled out, bold as brass. Jess walked as far as the entrance but remembered the bracelet on his wrist, the one he couldn't remove. They'd tethered him in place quite effectively. Alvaro had no such restriction.

Jess watched him calmly walk away, and within a few steps, men glided out from the shadows and corners to surround him. Alvaro had an expert personal guard, one that many kings would envy.

There was no sign of the promised watchers from the Library. Perhaps they'd been drawn away, or bought off.

And what now?

Jess had no answers.

He waited for half an hour, then an hour. He lit the chemical glows throughout the small living space and examined every corner, drawer and inch of it before he poured himself a glass of water from the kitchen tap and sat down at the table. There was a Codex provided, and a shelf of Blanks. At the very least they'd given him that. He could request any book from the Archives, and it would be mirrored into the Blank, and he'd have something to read.

Except, of course, that Brendan probably wouldn't do that. Brendan didn't read for pleasure, only for purpose. In many ways, it was going to be the most difficult part of carrying off this impersonation.

Jess compromised and called up anything on the subject of censorship. The first entry was an obscure treatise written by a Scholar named Liburn on the absolute necessity to restrict the reading material of the general public – apparently, too much reading, and reading too widely, could cause people to aspire above their station. Women, especially, were considered vulnerable to an 'excess of learning'. It was a rank piece of ignorance. He thought about Khalila Seif and the crisp opinion she'd have on that, and shook his head as he wiped the text and tried to think of something else, *anything* else, that his brother might read.

While the page of the Blank was clear, a curious thing happened: a new section of handwriting appeared. He didn't notice at first; he was intent on searching through the list of approved texts on the Codex. But when he glanced over, he immediately recognised the hand that had written the words.

She didn't give her name, no doubt in case anyone else should see this, and he had no idea at all how she was able to make her message appear not in a Codex, where it properly should go, but in a Blank, where as far as he was aware it ought to be impossible.

But then, the impossible was just another challenge to Morgan Hault.

The paragraph read:

You can't write back to me; this communication is one-way only. I pray you have the chance to see this. Don't worry, it will only appear once and fade in an hour. It's the best I can do with the time and tools I have. I am well, and, yes, wearing a collar, and I like it no better than you'd expect. I hope that in a few days I might be able to make contact with the man we discussed. He is our best hope. I am monitoring the Codex of the Archivist's assistant; her security is far lower than her master's, which is how I know how to find you. I will watch out for any danger and alert you in the same way as this. Keep a Blank with you at all times. I love you.

That was all business, until the last sentence, and the simple declaration of it stopped him cold for an instant. He'd sold her into slavery in the Iron Tower as part of this terrible bargain, and he'd never forget that. If anything went wrong . . .

Stop, Jess told himself, and closed the Blank. He kept his hand on it, as if he was holding her. *Morgan is strong. She'll survive.*

Now he just had to keep his end of the bargain and stay alive, too.

EPHEMERA

Text of a letter from Khalila Seif to her father, undelivered.

Beloved Father, I pray this reaches you, and that Allah's infinite mercy has found you first, and freed you from your imprisonment.

This is my fault, though I take comfort in knowing you would never have had me do anything but what I have done. My actions have been driven by love, loyalty, friendship, and pure respect for the mission of the Great Library, which I know you also cherish.

It seems impossible that such pure things could have led us to such a dark place, but as you once told me, when you fight evil men, good intentions can't protect you. But the fight must be made, and I am making it.

We have a plan to save you, and with faith and prayer and hard work, I believe it will succeed. I hope I will do you honour in this.

Please tell my brothers that I pray for them as well, though not as much, because they would be the first to tell me you deserve prayers more. And send my love and grieving regrets to my uncle for the loss of Cousin Rafa.

He was betrayed by the very people he trusted without question, and that, more than anything else, tells me that we must win this fight even if it costs my life.

Inshallah, I will see you soon, Father.

PART TWO

KHALILA

CHAPTER THREE

The clouds were the colour of lead and pressed flat on the horizon, erasing the line between heaving sea and sky. Khalila stood at the railing and watched the oncoming storm. She was aware of the wind whipping wildly at the long lilac dress she wore and was especially glad of the extra hairpins she'd put in her headscarf, which she'd wrapped carefully and tucked beneath the neck of her dress. It held in warmth, which was a blessing from Allah, because the gusts had an edge of pure ice to them that worked its way through any small opening to bite at her skin. Far too cold out, so far from the safety of land.

A weight settled around her shoulders, and she shot a grateful smile towards the young man who'd brought her a heavy coat. It smelt of thick sweat and wet sheep, but there was no denying its insulating power. 'Thank you, Thomas,' she said, and the German nodded and leant on the railing. That *almost* made them of a height. He seemed calm, but she didn't trust it. Thomas, of all of them, had been the most devastated by the betrayal of the Brightwell family that had landed them aboard this ship; he couldn't reconcile it. In Thomas's rather innocent world, family was always to be trusted, and he counted Jess – and by extension Jess's twin, Brendan – as a true brother.

'You're thinking about him,' she said.

'How can you tell?' Thomas managed a thread of a smile.

'Your face,' she said. 'I know how you feel. When I see Brendan Brightwell again, I'll kill him. Betrayal is a serious thing, in my part of the world.'

She watched Thomas's hands flex on the iron railing. His deep-seated innocence had been battered, if not broken. 'Mine too,' he said. 'God help them if we come face-to-face with any of the Brightwells again, then.'

'Yes,' she said. 'Even Jess, if he had some part in it.' She had a strong suspicion that Jess had *everything* to do with this, and for that, she wasn't sure if she could ever forgive him. If Jess had arranged all this, he'd hurt Thomas, of all people, and she felt a great, banked fury for that. Thomas met her gaze for a second, then gave her a quirk of a smile, very different from the usual full-souled one she loved. 'The storm looks bad,' he said. 'She'd be a fool to sail into it.'

'Anit is not a fool,' Khalila said. 'But she will want to deliver us quickly to Alexandria. We are not an easy cargo, and we've already been delayed. We're lucky to have this much freedom, to breathe the air and walk the decks.'

Thomas shrugged and gestured at the heavy, heaving sea. 'Where else could we go?'

She didn't miss the dark look in his eyes or the way he lingered on those waves, as if he was thinking about the peace that might be had under them. Khalila silently slipped her hand into his and held it. She knew her fingers were freezing, but Thomas's were warm, and he didn't seem to mind. Together, they watched the lightning stitch through the clouds ahead. The thunder was inaudible over the boom of the sea against the metal hull of the ship. Even in these conditions, the huge cargo ship sailed smoothly, though Khalila kept her other hand on the railing; that might change soon, if that storm came at them. She supposed she ought to have been properly frightened of the weather, but there was a wild beauty in it as well. A power that showed, clearer than anything else, the magnificence of Allah's creations.

But the wind was still cold enough to steal her breath away.

'Do you think they're all right?' Thomas asked her then. Like her, he was watching the lightning. She saw it dance in his pale eyes. 'Wolfe and Morgan?'

'Yes,' she said. 'I believe they will be.'

'I wish I could be sure. All I can think about is . . .' He didn't finish, but she knew what he would have said; he would have been thinking of his time trapped in the dungeons of Rome, at the mercy of the Great Library. They'd nearly broken him there. Nearly.

Thomas shook his head, violently, as if trying to throw something out of it. Bits of sea spray glittered in his stiff, close-cropped blonde hair like a cap of jewels. He was growing in a thick, short beard, too. 'Why did Jess let this *happen*?'

Khalila had her own suspicions, strong ones, but she kept them to herself. Worse to guess and be wrong. 'I doubt it was at all his choice,' she said. 'I think he'd have moved heaven and earth to be with us, fight with us. Don't you?'

She saw something else flicker in his eyes then, but it was too brief for her to recognise it clearly. 'The Jess I knew would do that.'

'Then believe that he'll find us now.'

Thomas said nothing else, and she let the silence stretch warm between them. Before she'd met Thomas and her other year-mates in training at the Great Library, she'd never have believed she could befriend someone so unlike herself; he was so *huge* and strong and . . . well, solidly and mysteriously German. But he was brilliant and sweet and funny; of all of them, his loyalty was as unbreakable as she imagined that thick skull to be. She cherished him. She cherished all of them, in ways that continued to unfold in new and surprising directions.

'Isn't this adorable?' a new voice said from behind them, and Khalila glanced back to see that Glain Wathen had joined them. Another tall person, but Glain had a narrow Welsh cast to her features that gave her the beauty of a precisely honed knife. 'Is it a private love affair, or can anyone join?'

For answer, Khalila held out her other hand. Glain snorted and linked arms with her instead. She rocked and balanced easily on the deck and stared into the storm without a trace of fear. A great deal of appreciation, though.

'Dario's down below puking his guts out,' Glain said. She sounded uncommonly cheerful about it. 'Santi's sleeping. He said to wake him if we sink, and not before.'

That sounded like the very practical High Garda captain. Rarely disturbed by any impending doom. If there was something to do, he'd do it, but otherwise, he saved his strength . . . though, Khalila thought, he'd been darkly quiet since they'd been taken aboard this ship. He wasn't speaking about his feelings or about the loss of Scholar Wolfe. She understood, in part; she loved Scholar Wolfe like a dour brother or a quarrelsome uncle; not quite a father, but most definitely family.

They were all family now. And she was proud of that.

'Dario said that he needed to talk to you,' Glain said. 'Go on. I'll keep the great lump here from falling overboard.'

'I won't fall,' Thomas said. Glain glanced at Khalila, quick as the lightning flickering on the horizon, and Khalila knew they'd both caught the inference.

He wouldn't fall, but he'd definitely thought of jumping.

It was part of the reason Khalila had spent so much time up here on the freezing decks; she wanted to keep an eye on him and make sure his anger and despair didn't turn even darker. She didn't think he'd do something so unforgivable, but she could understand the wild impulse. He felt betrayed, alone, lost. Hopeless.

She fought that herself. But she had faith – faith in her friends – to sustain her, as well as her unshakeable faith in the plans of Allah. They had all survived this far. All was not lost.

She had to believe it and make *them* believe it, too. At least Glain seemed completely unbothered by their current circumstances as unarmed prisoners, surrounded by enemies and ocean water.

'Try not to pick any fights,' she told Glain. 'Here.' She stripped off the warm, stinking coat and draped it over Glain's shoulders; she instantly regretted it when the wind sliced through the fabric of her dress and began to claw at her skin. Still, she paused long enough to plant a gentle kiss on Thomas's cheek – one he kindly bent down to allow. 'Watch Glain's back for me,' she whispered. It would keep him solid.

'I know what you're doing,' he whispered back. 'But I will.'

'And shave your beard,' she said, in a louder tone. 'It's like trying to kiss a bear.'

He laughed, and she was glad to hear it; it wasn't quite the old, happy laugh she remembered, but it was a start.

She fought her way across the decks, past surefooted sailors moving about unknowable tasks, and when she arrived at the door that led below, she glanced up and at the lighted bridge. The brawny, scarred captain stood there, and several of his officers, and with them the slender form of a very young woman. Anit, daughter of Red Ibrahim, and at least for now, their captor.

Anit did not spare her a glance. She was intent on charts, and the words of her captain. Khalila stood for a few seconds watching them, trying to memorise the faces of those framed in that light.

The girl finally looked up, as if she felt Khalila's regard. Anit looked away first.

Interesting. Some guilt? Or just disinterest?

Belowdecks the tossing felt worse, and the air was thick with the smells of rust, mould, and – as she approached the tiny cabin that Dario shared with Thomas – vomit. Khalila eased it open. 'Dario?'

She winced at the sound of him spewing into a bucket. From the sound of it, the bucket badly needed emptying. She looked in to find him collapsing back on his bunk. Dario, even in the worst of times, always prided himself on his neat appearance, but just now he was pallid, with messy hair and a stained shirt that clung as if he'd gone swimming in it. She could smell the rank sweat even over the sick.

'*Cristo*,' he groaned, and she didn't know if it was meant as a prayer or a curse. 'This is no place for you, flower, but since you're here, pray God bring me a dagger and let me get it over with.'

'Hush,' she said, and draped a towel over the slop bucket. She carried it to the small toilet in the corner and emptied it, and rinsed it in the basin before setting it back near his bunk.

'You may look like a delicate thing, but you have the cast-iron stomach of a born sailor,' Dario said. He looked feverish, eyes reddened and cheeks flushed, but his skin had a translucent pallor she didn't like. 'Stay a moment. I need to talk to you. And I wouldn't have called for you to act as my nursemaid, you know that.'

'Well, I can't imagine Glain emptying your slop bucket,' she said, and settled next to him on the bunk. She took his hand and felt the tremor in it. 'You're dehydrated. You need water. I'll fetch some.'

'Not now.' He studied her for a few seconds. 'You know, don't you?'

She smiled a little. 'Know what?'

'About Jess.'

'I have a guess,' she said, and the smile went away. She felt cold inside now. Hard as ice. 'Why didn't you tell me, Dario? Why did you . . .'

'I couldn't. We told Morgan, of necessity; we needed her help for him to carry this off at all. But you've too honest a face, madonna; if he'd told you that he planned to impersonate his brother and go to Alexandria in Brendan's place, you'd have given the game away when they came to take us. We needed you to fight like your life depended on it.'

She'd come dangerously close to killing Brendan, she remembered that; she'd been intent on cutting down as many of the Brightwell soldiers as she could, trying to keep from being taken prisoner. And Brendan – that had been *Jess* – had been one of those she'd have been happy to run a sword through. 'You still should have told me.'

Dario shook his head. 'We're far down that river now. Jess is in Alexandria, and his credentials assure him access to the Archivist. He'll have delivered Morgan to the Iron Tower, where she has her own plans.'

'And Scholar Wolfe?' She was hoping to hear that Wolfe, too, had been privy to this, that he had some brilliant scheme to make this gamble worthwhile.

'Wolfe didn't know,' Dario admitted. 'If he had, Santi would have sensed something was off. And we couldn't risk Santi refusing to cooperate. Wolfe would have approved of this. We were certain of that.'

Whatever doubts she had about it, they were not useful now. 'And Thomas?'

'Are you serious? The worst liar in the world? Though I admit, I thought he was going to tear Jess in half before the fool escaped.'

The Translation tag Jess had used would have deposited Jess – and Wolfe and Morgan – into the centre of the Great Archives, inside the stronghold. It was, she had to admit, an audacious plan. It might even be a good one. But the risk was fearfully high – not just for Jess, but for all of them. 'Is Jess's plan to kill the Archivist?' If he did, Jess couldn't survive it, but it would undoubtedly be a victory of some kind. But someone near the throne would rise to fill the office, and likely it would be someone just as bad; she shuddered to think of that rat-faced Gregory, now Obscurist, assuming the job.

No, until the Library saw the error of its ways and chose a new course of its own will, until the Curia and the Archivist were replaced with leaders who understood the damage their repression had done . . . until then, assassination accomplished nothing, except to force the Library to crush down with more force.

She hoped Jess knew that.

Dario shrugged a little. 'He'll do whatever he thinks best, as he usually does. It's aggravating, especially since the little scrubber usually turns out to be right.'

'Stop calling him that. You love him, too.'

Dario sighed and closed his eyes. 'You mentioned water, didn't you? I could do with that, my love. I don't want you to see me in this state.'

'Nonsense,' she said, and gave him a full smile. 'I love seeing you in this state. It means that for once, you're human and have given up your delusions of grandeur.'

'I do *not* have delusions of grandeur. I am, in fact, grand.'

She laughed, but once that bright moment faded – and she let it fade – she said, 'Once you're better, we *will* have a talk about how much I despise dishonesty. You may consider that a warning. I will not be lied to, Dario. Not even for what you believe is my own good.'

'If I survive the night, I will look forward to your lecture,' he said. 'And I know. If the stakes of this hadn't been so high, the choices so few . . . but I should have known you would figure out our plan eventually. There is no one like you, Khalila. No one on God's earth.'

She wanted to kiss him in that moment but settled for a quick, gentle stroke of fingers across his forehead. 'And no one quite like you,' she said. 'Allah be praised for that.'

He caught her hand as she tried to draw away. 'Wait. Back in England you said . . . Well. I was hoping that you'd changed your mind and . . .'

'Decided to marry you?' She asked it in a brisk way and managed to keep her voice steady. It was what he'd asked her in England, just before the soldiers had broken in on them and everything had fallen apart. *Of course*, she thought. *He asked because he was afraid we would lose each other then. That one of us might be lost for ever.* 'What did I say, Dario?'

'You said you might,' he said. 'I was hoping for a more definite answer. Given that we might still be facing our deaths. Or at least I might be, if I keep vomiting my stomach inside out.'

'Consider I'm giving you reason to survive.'

'Is that a yes?'

'That,' she said, 'is a very definite *might*.'

He let go. He didn't want to, she could see it, but she appreciated that he knew when to back off. And besides, she could see the nausea twisting in him again. She quickly rose and headed for the door as he groaned and wrapped his arms around the bucket.

Khalila found washcloths and soap, and once he'd emptied whatever small amount he had left to surrender in his stomach, she stripped off his shirt and helped him scrub off the sweat. A fresh shirt came out of a supply laid in for the crew – not Dario's usual quality, but he could hardly complain – and she brought him water and made him drink until he finally collapsed to the pillow again. His colour was better, and though his hair needed a thorough washing, he seemed more himself.

'I love you,' he sighed. 'God help me.'

'If you love me, tell me what you were planning to accomplish by getting us captured and loaded on this ship,' she said. 'Because you're in no shape to carry it off now, and someone must.'

'Why do you think I had anything planned?'

'Because I'm not an idiot, and neither are you. Jess had his plan, Morgan had hers. What was yours?'

Dario swallowed, closed his eyes, and said, 'Slight . . . problem with my plan. It was a bargain with Anit, and I've since determined that she's gone back on it. She wasn't supposed to deliver us to Alexandria, but it seems now she's intent on doing just that.'

'Where were you planning for us to go, then?'

'Cadiz. Where we'd be met by envoys of my cousins.'

'Your . . . cousins?'

'The King and Queen of Spain,' he said. 'Well, I did tell you I was grand, didn't I? The plan was that they would pay a wonderfully great ransom for all of us, Anit appeases her father, and we'd have royal support to continue on our journey. Spain and Portugal have broken with the Library, as have Wales and a few others. I think they will gladly give us everything we need.'

Khalila realised her eyebrows were raised – probably at the casual mention of Dario's cousins – and left them that way. 'And do you have an answer for how to put us back on that original plan?'

'Not presently,' he admitted. He put an arm over his eyes. 'If only I could *think* instead of spewing . . .'

She patted him on the shoulder. 'Lucky for you, you're not the only one with a brain. Rest. Leave it to me.'

That got her an uncovered pair of brown eyes and an unexpected hint of vulnerability from him. For all his confidence – or arrogance, less charitably described – Dario knew the risks of this game they were playing. And the penalties. 'Please be careful, madonna,' he told her. 'For the love of Allah, be careful.'

'For the love of God, rest,' she said, and smiled to soothe his pride, then went to see the one person she least wanted to face.

CHAPTER FOUR

When she tapped lightly on Captain Niccolo Santi's door, she was told immediately to enter. Not asleep as had been assumed, then. He was fully dressed, and clearly not as bad a sailor as Dario . . . not that she could imagine Santi being bad at very much. He had a drawn look and a shadow in his eyes, but he nodded briskly and indicated that she should take a seat on the single bed in the room. She refused politely and put her back to the wall; it helped to steady her. Santi rode the waves without a sign that he even thought about it.

'I've been waiting,' he said. 'I should have guessed it'd be you. Were you elected, or did you volunteer?'

This wasn't the Santi she knew: the one easy in his skin, who treated them all with a kind of paternal exasperation at worst. Santi was the kind one, the one who wore his responsibilities with ease, while Wolfe snapped and barked at the best of times.

This Santi was sharp, aggressive, and she didn't like it. Khalila ignored the question and said, 'I'm surprised they haven't locked you in.'

'I'm clearly not that dangerous. After all, I let them take me back at the Brightwell castle,' he said. 'I let them take Chris.' She felt the self-directed anger behind that. Searing.

'Captain—'

He pushed that away with a slash of his hand. 'What do you want?'

She ached for him, but there was no healing his toxic guilt. He knew what waited for Wolfe in Alexandria at the hands of the Archivist Magister. Santi would sooner have died than see that happen. 'Forgive me,' she said. 'I have something to tell you.' She took in a breath. 'It's about Jess.'

That sharpened his focus. He was a fiercely smart man; she watched him assess all the possibilities before he said, 'My God. What did that fool do?' But he was already far ahead of that. He answered his own question. 'He realised the Brightwells would sell us out before it happened. But instead of involving all of us, he made his own dice throw. Not alone, though. Dario, at a guess. Not Glain; she'd have come to me. Thomas would have had none of it. You – well. I think you would have known better, too.'

He knew them so well. Khalila let out a slow breath, took in another, and said, 'Dario and Jess, at the start. They involved Morgan, as I understand it. For practical reasons . . .'

'Your next words had better assure me that Wolfe knew what they were doing. That they didn't drag him off as a prisoner *without telling him*.'

She swallowed and tried to think of some neutral answer, but that took too long. She saw the bitter ignition of rage in his eyes . . . and then he was moving.

'Captain? Captain, wait! Where are you going?' Because Santi was stalking towards the cabin door.

He didn't answer.

She managed to glide into his path and put her back to the door. For a heart-stopping second she was afraid he might just thrust her out of the way, but he came to a halt, glared at her with brutal intensity. 'Please don't go after Dario. He's very ill. *Please*.'

'I don't care.'

'Captain,' she said. 'Imagine for a moment that Scholar Wolfe knew the Brightwells would most certainly betray us, and there was no possible way out of that trap. Don't you think he would have advised us to use that as an opportunity? To turn a defeat to a *chance*? That is all that Dario and Jess did. They overturned the table, because there were no winning moves. As a military man, you know that – sometimes – it's the only option!'

He didn't like it. She watched the blind fury struggle against his good sense, and finally he slammed the heel of his hand hard into the steel bulkhead beside her and wheeled away to put his back to her. When he finally faced her again, he was more composed. 'Jess is in Alexandria? Posing as his brother?'

'Yes,' she said. 'I believe so.'

'He'd better have a care when I see him again,' he said. 'But that can wait. Why tell me this now?'

'Because the plan that Jess and Dario concocted was for Anit to betray her father and convey us to Spain, where Dario has allies who will help us. But she's lost her courage, it seems. We're headed straight for Alexandria. I think you know that if we're handed over in chains . . .'

He nodded sharply. 'If we reach Alexandria, we're dead,' he finished. 'Most of us, in any case. They'll execute me and Glain out of hand. And you, along with your relatives they already have, to keep your country in line. Dario . . . he might escape. Thomas they'll keep. He's valuable to them.' It was a quick, concise analysis, and deadly accurate. It matched precisely her own.

'We need to take this ship,' Khalila said. 'And we need all of us to do it. Including you, Captain.'

'Just the five of us against the entire crew?'

'Four,' she said. 'Considering Dario's condition. We are outnumbered. Yet Anit has left us free, and I find myself wondering why on earth she would do that, knowing how dangerous we can be. I think she can't disobey her father – no doubt the captain and his men would report her in an instant if she tried – but, at the same time, I think she wouldn't be disappointed if we are able to force the issue.'

Unlike Wolfe, who would have snarled at her and called her a fool, Santi gave that serious thought. She knew he was doing what she'd already done: analysing each of the points of vulnerability, and the fortifications and arms that protected them. 'Obviously, if we take the bridge, we can steer the ship,' he said. 'But we can't take the bridge.'

'We can take Anit.'

'She's a child.'

'Old enough to run her father's operations and command the hundred or so sailors who crew this vessel,' Khalila replied. 'Which is, to me, old enough to be taken hostage. I'm not saying we hurt her, but since she conspired in the first place with Jess and Dario, and changed her mind . . .'

'Fine. We take the girl hostage and force the ship to Cadiz. What does that get us, precisely, besides a safe haven? I'm High Garda. I'm telling you that Alexandria has never been taken.'

'In the last thousand years, who's *tried*? The last serious threat were the Mongols, and they were defeated by the Ottomans before they ever came close. Tell me, Captain: have the real, physical defences of the Library ever been tested? *Truly* tested?'

'There are always four full companies inside the city, with the Elite unit stationed at the Serapeum. That's not even counting the automata. No one is taking that city without tremendous losses on both sides. Which I would have told you *if you had consulted me* before embarking on this plan!'

'Morgan's job is to take care of the automata,' Khalila said. 'Why do you think Jess included her? From inside the Iron Tower, she can take down a great many of the defences the Obscurists have always maintained . . . And you, Captain, you know the other captains. Three out of four commanders around Philadelphia agreed with you. There's a very real possibility of a High Garda rebellion, isn't there? If the opportunity for reform seems real?'

'The difference is that those three commanders stood aside for us *in the field*. They would never do that in what we consider home. They'll defend it. No matter whether they like me or agree with me, they will fight for the Library.'

'The battle is coming to Alexandria. Whether we do it, or the massed armies of the kingdoms already denying treaties do, or it happens in twenty years when Thomas's press has eroded the power of the Library beyond repair . . . *the Library will fall*. We are talking about how to protect what is true and good about it before that happens. If you love the Library as I do, we *must* gain control of it and begin to make it what it truly should be: not a tyrant kingdom, but a spiritual and intellectual leader. That is its truest purpose.'

She needed him to believe it. Captain Santi was their best hope to achieve military victory in Alexandria; with any luck, it could be done with a minimum loss of life. But to save Alexandria, they first had to take it. She had to make Santi believe it was at least possible, or his heart would break before they ever made landfall. Captain Santi was the strong, quiet centre of their group. If he broke now, they would all shatter. This was a thing, she believed, that Jess and Dario did not understand.

But she did. And so it fell to her.

She watched him think through it, step by step. He knew the risks. The points of failure. The slim odds they could ever be successful.

But he also had to know that if they wanted the Great Library of Alexandria to survive and uphold its beautiful ideals . . . then those who truly loved it would have to take these risks.

We are not destroying the Library, she wanted to say to him. *We are saving it.*

But he would have to reach that conclusion himself. Without Santi, they would not find the strength. Without Jess, no inspiration. Without Thomas, there was no real future. Without Glain, no protection. Without Morgan, no audacity. Without Wolfe, no challenge to do better, *be* better.

Without Dario, no subtlety.

Without her . . . but she didn't see her role. It would have been prideful to imagine she could not be spared, but she knew she could not spare even one of these others.

Santi said, 'You have the gift, you know.'

'What gift?'

'Silence,' he said. 'You let people think. And yet, you also lead from silence. I've met a few like you.'

She felt a slight heat in her cheeks and raised her chin against the urge to deny what he'd said. 'Were they worthy of your trust?' she asked.

'Oh yes,' Santi told her. 'Every one of them.' He sighed. 'The path to Alexandria leads through allies, connections, and communications with those I can trust. I make no guarantees that we'll ever see the city, or survive it if we do. But you're right. We need to land in Cadiz and build allies.'

'Then we take the ship?'

'We take the ship,' he said. 'God help us.' He nodded at the small bunk. 'Sit down. It's too suspicious if we gather in numbers, so I'll need you to memorise plans, timing, all of it. You'll set everyone in the right place and time.'

She sat, smoothing her skirt with restless fingers. She was aware that by coming here, and staying for long, she'd be inviting gossip. But let them talk, if they intended to. Better the crew assume she and Santi were lovers than that they suspect they were conspirators. 'One thing,' she said. 'Give me a chance to talk to Anit first.'

He stared at her for a long moment, then said, 'If you insist on doing that, you have to be prepared to fail. Are you? Prepared to fail?'

'You mean, am I prepared to take action? Take her prisoner? Slip a knife in her ribs?'

He nodded.

'Anit made her choice,' Khalila said. 'And, yes. I am prepared.'

CHAPTER FIVE

Anit was no kind of fool. She'd been hardened in the same fires that Jess Brightwell had been; she understood full well how brutal the world was, and what place she had in it. She was quiet and thoughtful and noticed *everything*.

Anit was also wary of her own captain and crew. Khalila understood that very well. Women watched their allies as much as their enemies, if they wished to prevent trouble and keep their power. Especially if all of their subordinates and peers were men. Unfair, perhaps, but practical.

If this was to work at all, Khalila thought, she needed to play upon the fact that Anit had grown up guarded, alone, and under constant pressure from the men around her.

The fact that Anit would unwillingly, perhaps unconsciously feel kinship with another young woman.

It didn't take long for Khalila to come up with the correct approach. She waited until midmorning, then changed to a black dress and moved with deliberate speed towards the metal stairs that led up to the bridge, where Anit stood. She was, of course, instantly intercepted by two stout men: sun-weathered, hair bleached nearly blonde, covered in blurred tattoos. 'No access,' one of them said. 'Go away.'

'I need to speak with Anit,' Khalila said. 'Please.'

'No access.'

'Tell her it's a private matter.'

'Don't care,' the first sailor said, and shoved her back. 'Move on. Now. Before I feed you to the fish.'

'Not without my express permission you don't.' Anit's voice came from the door to the bridge, and when Khalila looked up, she saw the girl watching them. Assessing. 'What kind of private matter?'

'The kind I don't prefer to talk about with them listening,' Khalila said. 'Please.'

Anit came down the steps, waved the sailors a few steps away, and waited with her arms folded. She was in no danger; there were at least ten men only feet away who, though intent on their own business on deck, would certainly come running at her call.

And, of course, Anit could very likely defend herself.

'You have something to ask?' Anit prompted.

'I assume you have a woman's monthly supplies,' Khalila said. 'There are none in my cabin. I'm afraid I've already stained a dress.' She pitched her voice loud enough that the sailors could hear, and smiled as she saw them draw back. She could never fathom how men failed to come to grips with the workings of a woman's body.

'No one provided you with—' Anit let out a frustrated sigh. 'Of course they didn't. They didn't even consider it. Glain must need some as well. Please come with me. I'll give you what I can from my own stores.' She glanced at the sailors and rolled her eyes. 'No need to accompany me,' she told them. 'I'll be fine.'

Anit led her off to the large cabin she occupied on the ship, and as she opened cabinets and took down a box of menstrual pads, she said, 'So what is it you really want to talk about?'

'Oh, I do need these, believe me. I have no doubt I'll be

bleeding in a day or so. But you're right: I also needed to talk about our situation.'

'Situation.' Anit found a small canvas bag and began to load it up. 'I've doubled the supplies. You can share with Glain.' There was a small hesitation in her voice, something that set Khalila on alert. She put her hand lightly on Anit's arm and felt the girl tense. *Careful*, she told herself. She could easily turn this wrong.

'Why did you change your mind?'

Anit's hands suddenly stilled, and she looked up at Khalila. For a moment, Khalila was sure the girl would answer, but then her look flattened, darkened, and she thrust the bag into Khalila's hands. 'You should go.'

'Anit . . .' Khalila took a deep breath. 'I understand that your father ordered you to change our agreement. No one blames you. I don't blame you. But it's clear you're taking us to Alexandria. You know what will happen to us.'

'You should go,' Anit said. 'Now.'

'Not until I know what he threatened, to make you betray your agreement. I know your word means everything to you.'

'I can have you removed.'

'Yes. You can call your sailors. You can lock us in our rooms. Drop me overboard, should you wish—' The flinch and widened eyes from Anit made Khalila press on. 'Is that your father's orders? To put us over the side?'

'Not all of you,' Anit said. 'Only the one with no value to the Archivist.'

'You mean Glain.'

'Yes.'

'When is it to happen?'

'I have my orders, Khalila.'

'I'm not asking you to go against them. I'm asking you to tell me when they plan to kill her so we can come to her defence. That leaves you entirely out of it.'

Anit looked away and said, 'I didn't want this. We had an agreement. But . . . my father has made promises, important promises. I can't go against him on this.'

'I understand,' Khalila said. 'When will they take Glain?'

Anit didn't meet her eyes. 'Tonight. They'll drug your food and drink so there's no interference.'

'Will they drug all of us? Or only Glain and myself, since we share the cabin?'

'Just the two of you,' Anit admitted. 'But if you don't eat it, they'll know I warned you.'

Khalila nodded. 'I'll eat it. But all the same, the others might accidentally see it happen and come to her rescue.'

'They'd best be prepared to fight,' Anit said.

'Which among us is the most valuable?'

'Thomas. And Captain Santi.'

Khalila cocked her head and frowned. 'Santi? I'd have thought he'd have gone over the side with Glain. He's no one to ransom him. What value does he have to the Archivist?'

'It isn't about ransom,' Anit said. This time she did meet Khalila's eyes, but only for an instant, and then she turned away and wrapped both arms around herself, as if feeling the chill. 'The Archivist wants to punish Wolfe. He can use Santi to hurt him.'

The depth of depravity in that made Khalila feel sick. That someone so powerful should use that power so cruelly . . . and so randomly. There was a deep, personal anger there, one that she was glad she couldn't understand. 'All right,' she said. 'Thank you for these. I appreciate the kindness.'

'We must all be kind,' Anit said. 'While we're still able. Khalila? I never wanted any of this.'

Khalila knew she shouldn't ask, but she had to. 'Will you help us?'

'No,' Anit said, and smiled. 'But somehow, I know that won't stop you.'

Khalila left and was glad of the strong blast of wind on the deck, even as it bleached the heat out of her. She needed to feel something bracing. She'd been ready to take Anit hostage, if need be, but she thought Anit *wanted* to help. And under just the right circumstances, she might be free to do so.

All that remained was to work out how those circumstances needed to occur.

But first, they'd need to save Glain's life.

She remembered little of the evening. Eating the drugged meal had been hard, but the worst had been watching Glain consume it too, all unknowing. Out of an abundance of caution, Santi and Thomas had elected not to eat or drink at all, though they made a good simulation of it.

Glain hadn't noticed.

By the time the meal was done, Khalila already felt the drag of the medications and sent Thomas a half-panicked look as Glain yawned. Dario had eaten only a little of his own food, probably because of his still-unsteady stomach, but he also yawned. It was hard to say whether it was a sympathetic response or the drugs at work in him, too. *Did Anit lie to me? Did she tell them to drug us all? At least Santi and Thomas will still be effective.*

But that also might mean they'd be watched, and prevented from acting.

Glain collapsed into bed almost immediately when they

reached their cabin, but Khalila tried hard to keep herself awake, hour after hour . . . pacing, praying, resorting to pinching herself when her legs failed to support her any more. At the last, she crawled into her bed, and the drag on her eyelids became irresistible.

Khalila woke with a pounding headache, a dire thirst, and the ship tossing like a toy boat in the teeth of the storm . . . and when she crawled out of her bunk and checked, Glain was not there.

Glain was not there.

'No,' Khalila whispered, and swept the covers aside, as if somehow the young Welsh woman could have been hiding underneath them. She dragged herself to her feet and threw on a fleece-lined robe that Anit had loaned her, cinched it tight, and staggered outside into the teeth of the wind. Her hijab nearly tore loose, but she clamped a hand to it as she tried to see what was happening.

The deck was nearly deserted, only a few sailors struggling about their tasks. She didn't see Glain.

She didn't see any of her friends.

Khalila ducked back into the shelter of the hall and hurried to the cabin that Thomas and Dario shared. Empty. She tried Captain Santi's room.

And found all of them gathered there.

Dario rose immediately and came to her as she stood panting and shaking, unexpectedly weak. He tucked a stray lock of hair that had come loose back under the cover of her hijab; she hugged him fiercely and felt such an intense relief that it made her knees threaten to buckle. She tried to speak, but tears choked the words. She lingered on every face, especially Glain's; the Welsh woman sat nursing a drink, paler than normal. She had a bandage around her head and another winding her forearm.

She wasn't the only one with injuries. Every one of them had visible bruises or bandages, or both. Dario winced when she squeezed too tightly, and she instantly released him and held him at arm's length to study him.

'I'm fine, madonna,' he told her, and fitted his hand to her cheek in such a natural, gentle motion that she closed her eyes for a moment to control the racing of her heart. 'We're all fine.'

'Speak for yourself,' Glain growled. 'I've got a nasty hangover and my ears are still ringing from hitting the damned railing.'

Khalila felt breathless. She knew the kind of fight each one of these people could put up, and the fact that they were *all* injured . . . it meant she had missed something truly violent.

Santi said, 'Sit before you fall, Khalila.' He moved a chair forward, and she gratefully took it. Dario's chair, she thought; he stayed on his feet. She wasn't certain that he'd conquered his seasickness, but at least he was able to stand upright and not look as though he might spew. Small victories.

'What happened?'

They told her in bursts. First Santi related watching their cabin, with Thomas as backup. The arrival of four sailors to retrieve Glain in the dark of night had been foiled, but more had come, and then others had joined the fight.

Glain had been dragged out by Anit's crew and towed towards the side. Dario had managed to grab Glain just as she'd been pushed over the railing, limp and unconscious. He'd suffered bruised ribs while unable to fight back, but he'd grimly held on to her arm and kept her dangling above the waves, until Thomas's strength had come to save her.

Then they'd surrounded Glain, who'd begun to revive in the cold wind and rain, and kept her safe until Anit ordered the attack to stop, for fear of killing her father's valuable prisoners in order to dispose of a useless one.

'Useless.' Santi shook his head. 'Even half-unconscious, she fought like a devil. She's worth her weight in gold.'

'Captain,' Glain said. 'I fought like a drunken rag doll. But thank you for the kindness.'

'You've taken too much of Wolfe's judgement to heart. I've been a professional soldier all my life, and I can only think of half a dozen I'd pick to have by my side in a brawl. You're in that number.'

Glain, Khalila thought, looked as though she'd been sweet-talked by a lover. Her eyes sparkled. Her cheeks blushed. She craved a good fight the way most yearned for love or money. 'I'm honoured,' Glain said. 'And thankful you all came to my defence. I'll return the favour, anytime.'

'We know,' Dario said. He looked at Santi. 'Will they try it again?'

'We're not giving them a chance, because we're going to take this ship.' Santi unrolled a rough map, hand drawn but to Khalila's eye highly accurate; it showed the ocean, the coast of Spain, and the opposing coastline, with Alexandria marked by the Horus eye symbol of the Great Library. Cadiz he'd marked with a star. 'We're off the coast of Portugal now, making for the Strait of Gibraltar; the ship's sailing into the teeth of the storm because there's no alternative, and Anit's been given some deadline to meet. The storm helps us; it keeps the majority of her crew at their posts and makes communication more difficult. But she'll be on her guard for it, too. Anit's locked herself into the bridge with her captain and officers. They're armed, and we're not. In less than a day, we're sailing past Cadiz and headed for the entrance to the strait. We'll lose our opportunity.'

'Weapons?' Glain asked.

'All the pistols and rifles are locked in a cabinet on the bridge.'

'And the locks?' Dario asked.

'Jess might have been able to pick them, but I don't think any of us could. Morgan might have been able to do something with an Obscurist power, but we don't have that, either.'

'Is there a workshop on this ship?' Thomas asked.

'I suppose. Why?'

'I can find us weapons,' he said. 'Nothing with bullets, they won't be so careless, but they will have other things I can adapt. Explosives, possibly. Welding tools. All these can be useful.'

'Right,' Santi said. 'Dario, you go with—'

'I'm the only one uninjured,' Khalila said. 'I'll go with him. Together, we can work faster.'

'My flower, do you know even the slightest thing about workshops?' Dario asked her, which was patronising enough to make her send him a sharp, dangerous look.

'My uncle was a Library inventor for thirty years, and I apprenticed with him,' she said. 'When you call me *flower*, you imply I can't fight. We both know that's untrue. With a sword, I am far better than you.'

Dario winced. Good. Knocking him back occasionally would keep him at least a little humbled. 'I retract the insult, however I meant it,' he said. 'Though I'd feel better if I came with you.'

'No. Glain?'

'Happy to assist,' Glain said. 'I was starting to feel useless sitting here. Besides, if you're making weapons, Thomas, best you have someone to test them out for you.'

'No,' Khalila said. 'You're still at risk.'

'And to take me, they'll need to overpower the two of you. Not bloody likely. Besides, I'm not drugged, and I'm not going down without taking them with me.'

Thomas nodded. He didn't seem displeased. He usually didn't, when Glain was near. Khalila suspected he admired the young woman a great deal more than he was willing to show, especially considering that Glain herself showed no interest whatsoever in any romantic partners of any gender. In any case, they made a good team, the three of them.

That left only Dario and Santi together, which worried her; both could take care of themselves, of course, but Dario's ribs were bandaged, and the captain looked battered. She exchanged a look with him, but the captain only nodded. 'Go,' he said. 'And Scholar? We all need to agree on engagement rules.'

'I think we know what they are,' she said. 'We are in this to the end now. There is only one engagement level, though I prefer not to use fatal force when less will do, and to use threats when force is not necessary. Diplomacy when that will suffice most of all. Agreed?'

'Agreed,' he said, and smiled tightly.

It was only later that she wondered just when Santi – and all the others – had agreed that she was in charge. And when she had become so comfortable with the idea.

The workshop proved to be a toy box for Thomas, full of scrap metal he quickly sharpened for them into crude – but deadly – daggers and swords. 'The edges won't last long,' he warned them as they tested the balance and weight of the blades. 'I could make properly done ones if we had a day or so. But they will do for short, dirty fighting.'

'My favourite,' Glain said, and slipped one of the daggers into her belt, then another into her boot. 'Any chance of a projectile weapon?'

'No. Everything I could reconfigure would require smithing,

and we don't have time. I considered the riveters, but they're too heavy for our purposes, and tethered with steam hoses.'

'Still not impossible,' Glain said, and tried the weight of the rivet driver. Khalila doubted she herself could have managed it, but in Glain's hands, it looked quite at home. 'There were two connectors on the bulkhead outside of the bridge. One must be for steam. I'll chance it.'

'And the charges?' Khalila asked. Thomas held up a small box in one hand and a quart-sized glass bottle full of green liquid in the other.

'The powder charge in this box will fuse the lock on one of the bridge doors so it can't open,' he said. 'The Greek Fire will cut open the other.'

'Careful with those,' Glain said, and Khalila understood her nervousness. There was enough Greek Fire in that glass to ignite half the ship. 'You trip, and we all end this voyage on the bottom.'

Thomas gave her a faint smile. 'I'm large. Not lumbering.'

No one had happened on them in the workshop, which was a bit of a miracle, but someone would *surely* notice Thomas – who was very noticeable – toting a bottle of Greek Fire. Swords and daggers could be concealed, and Khalila now carried a belt full of blades beneath the fleece-lined robe, out of view. She sighed and hunted up another wooden box that fit the bottle, and padded it with rags. Thomas latched it shut and hefted it, along with the other items. It didn't look innocent, but at least it didn't look as openly guilty.

Glain didn't bother to conceal anything, and there wasn't much use arguing with her.

The first man to spot them in the corridor heading for the cabins was, happily, one of the sailors Khalila disliked the most;

he'd threatened to disembowel Dario, for one thing. He seemed instantly suspicious and opened his mouth to say, 'What do you think you're doing around—'

He never reached the end of that question, because Glain stepped forward and slipped a dagger neatly between his ribs. Khalila caught her breath, because every instinct in her shouted that it was unnecessary . . . but she knew better. They were outnumbered and about to enter a very dangerous fight – one that would determine more than just their own fates.

He could have given an alarm. Glain had stopped it.

The sailor was dead within seconds, and nearly silently. They dragged him into a storage locker, and they slipped quickly back to Santi's cabin, where the captain and Dario waited.

'About time,' Dario said, and pulled them in. He checked the hall and closed the door. Khalila stumbled into him as the ship took a breathtaking lurch; the storm was worse again, though she couldn't imagine how much more violent it could possibly get. 'Did you find anything?'

For answer, she unfastened her outer robe and began to remove swords and daggers. A pair for each of them, and a few spares. She'd been clinking as she walked and gained almost half again her weight from all the metal. It was a relief to lay it down, except for the sword and dagger she kept. These she belted on outside the fleeced robe this time. Let them notice. She no longer cared. They all looked warlike and piratical now, especially Dario, who seemed most suited to the occupation by looks. And Glain, toting the industrial rivet gun on her shoulder.

'Plans, Captain?' Khalila asked. He was looking thoughtfully at the weapons.

'Questions,' he said. 'No one found you in the workshop?'

'No one,' Thomas said. 'Lucky.'

Santi didn't seem to believe it. 'Even on such a stormy day, that seems odd.'

'We did kill a man on the way back,' Glain offered. 'Quietly.'

He nodded at the point but still looked troubled. 'I don't know if this is some kind of trap, but we don't have much choice. If we wait, we'll be into the strait, well past our port.'

Khalila said, 'If we *don't* take action Anit will simply carry on as her father commands. She has nothing to lose from it. But . . . I do believe she's hoping we will find a way. She may have even kept her crew away from the workshop. She's not a fool. She'd guess how we'd proceed.'

'Agreed,' Dario said. 'That girl's a fiendishly good chess player.'

'Then we move,' Santi said. 'Khalila, you have steady hands. Set the explosive charge to fuse the bridge door we don't intend to enter. When we hear the blast, we'll burn through the other side, quietly. Hopefully, the crew's attention will be drawn the wrong way.'

'And what's she to do if it draws everyone straight to her?' Dario asked. 'I'd better go with her.'

'No,' Santi said. 'We'll need the four of us when that door does open, because even if Anit doesn't fight us, her captain and bridge crew will. There are seven of them. I can't spare you, Dario.'

'I'll rejoin you as soon as I can,' Khalila promised. 'I'll be all right.'

Thomas put the small box in her hands. 'There's a small, self-starting fuse,' he said. 'The charge will stick to the door; it's magnetic. Put it over the lock, just here—' He demonstrated on their cabin door. 'Pull the tab to start the fuse. You can leave it to do its job then.'

'How long is the fuse?'

'About ten seconds,' he said. 'Long enough to get to safety.'

She took a deep breath and nodded. *Steady. Steady and calm.*

But the ship was pitching wildly, and she put the box under one arm and held tight to a handhold as the ship groaned like a living thing, rolled sharply to the left. Kept rolling, as if it intended to overturn . . . and then, suddenly, righted itself.

'They should be steering into the storm, not putting their starboard side to it,' Dario said. He looked wretched again, but grimly determined. Khalila watched as a chair skidded from one side of Santi's cabin to the next. She was grateful that the Greek Fire was cushioned, but Allah preserve them all if Thomas dropped that box.

'How do you know?' Glain asked. 'You're a terrible sailor.'

'I do read,' Dario shot back. 'Try it sometime.'

'Stop bickering,' Santi said. 'Focus. We can't wait. This ship is making the turn towards the strait. We're out of time. Khalila splits off once we reach the deck, makes her way to the port side of the bridge, where she places the charge and comes to us as soon as possible. As soon as we hear that explosion, we breach the starboard door, and we do what we must to steer this ship to Cadiz. Use the least violence we have to, but don't hesitate. Understood?'

'Yes,' they all said, in unison.

'Then let's go.'

Khalila looked at Dario for an instant that seemed like an eternity, then quickly placed a kiss on his cheek.

That was the only goodbye she would allow herself.

CHAPTER SIX

What seemed simple enough became vastly more complex the moment the door opened to the deck of the ship. When she'd last been up here, Khalila had been admiring the oncoming storm's distant beauty. In the heart of it, there was only brutality. The wind hit like hammer blows, and the rain drove needles into her exposed skin; the deck pitched and yawed, wallowing in the deep waves. Water surged over the metal decks and threatened to drag her over, until Thomas clamped a hand on her and held her tight against the pull. She gasped in gratitude, though she was worried that he'd not be able to anchor her and keep a good grip on his very dangerous box . . . and then she realised, as she blinked away stinging salt spray, that Glain had a hand on his other arm. They'd all linked, instinctively.

The crew had strung ropes around the deck. Anchors to cling to, when the sea broke across the deck. She broke Thomas's grip and lunged for one of those. The others could brace one another, but she was going to have to make her own way now.

If anyone called after her, she couldn't hear in the roar of the storm. Lightning broke the sky on the port side, a spear forking from heaven to drive into the sea, and the thunder slammed into her like a physical blow. She'd gone a few feet from the others, and already she'd lost sight of them. *Good cover*, she told herself. Her heart was racing and her mouth was dry, and she was terrified. Her dress, soaking and heavy now, threatened to trip her. She moved down the rope as quickly as she could, heading for the port side of the ship. When she touched that railing, she ducked under the rope and followed the railing towards the stern of the ship. The bridge was up a set of stairs.

Another, more distant shock of lightning illuminated the steps before she passed by them, and she lunged for a handhold and had begun to climb up when the door at the top swung open and a sailor muffled in a thick rainproof coat stepped out.

They stared at each other in surprise.

Khalila moved first. She backed down to the pitching deck and shoved the box inside the sodden fleece of the robe she wore.

Then she drew her sword, and as the sailor shut and secured the waterproof door at the top, she waited with the blade concealed behind her.

'What are you doing here?' he shouted at her over the roar, and came down towards her.

Forgive me, she thought, in the instant before she lunged.

Her balance was off, and the ship plunged into a trough in that second, throwing the sailor forward and her blade lower than she intended. It slid into his stomach, not his heart, and she felt a blind second of panic as he screamed – but no one could hear it. She tugged the sword free and lunged again, and this time, her aim was true. She felt the sword scrape lightly against a rib, then slip deep towards his heart.

He took one step towards her and collapsed.

Her heart hammered so loudly it was almost as deafening as the storm, and she gasped for breath against the shock of what she'd done. It had been necessary, she knew that, but even so . . . Khalila shoved the bloody sword back into her belt with cold, trembling hands and hurried up the steps. She opened the box, set the magnetic charge, and even as she adjusted it to the right spot on the door, just as Thomas had shown her, she wondered how anyone could possibly hear even this explosion in all the howl of the storm.

It didn't matter. She had to proceed, regardless. She pulled the tab, igniting the fuse that Thomas had put inside the device, and turned to go down the steps.

Someone crouched there, blocking her way. Another sailor, looking at the man she'd killed. He hadn't noticed her yet. She slipped down towards him, and as he rose, she braced herself on the slick railings and kicked out with both feet, sending him crashing into the port-side railing. *Ten seconds.* She needed to be clear of the stairs, but he was still blocking her path.

He turned like a cat to grab her as she tried to dart past him onto the deck.

Time to use the dagger, which she tried to do, but this man was warier and faster, and he caught her wrist in a crushing grip and twisted. She lost the blade. No space to draw the sword, but there was more to a weapon than just the edge; she grabbed a handful of the thick fleece gown and used it to cushion her hand against the blade as she shoved it upward, and the rough pommel of the sword collided sharply with his chin. His head snapped back, more in surprise than in real harm, and she stepped forward to put her right foot behind his left, and twisted into his grip instead of away.

He went down, mouth an open O of surprise, and hit the deck hard. He rolled for the knife, but she found it first and dropped on her knees to bury it in his throat.

She rolled away, praying she had time and Thomas had been precise in his mixtures. She was only a few feet away when she felt the shudder of the explosion through the metal, and a brilliant bright-red jet of fire burst out from the door to cook the falling rain into a puff of steam.

Khalila scrambled up, staggered as the ship lurched again, and almost fell into the guide rope. She slipped and clung for her life. The winds were so strong that they pummelled like lead fists, and she couldn't pull in breath against the full force of the blast. Bright sparks swam in her vision, and she prayed for another burst of lightning; there was nothing to see now but darkness and flying rain.

And then she saw the glow from the bridge above. Couldn't make out anything within it, only the indistinct light. She was halfway to the starboard side. Halfway to the other set of stairs.

She fought her way against the wind until she fell across another obstacle in her way. A dead man. A sailor, by Allah's mercy, not one of her friends. She climbed over him and realised that she'd found the stairs. She pulled her sword free and scrambled up.

The opening at the top was a melted mess of metal and still-bubbling Greek Fire, though someone – likely Thomas – had thrown down a counteragent to prevent the stuff from eating through the hull of the ship and sinking them all. She jumped over the flickering green flames and into the bridge . . . into the middle of a stand-off.

Anit looked like a delicate toy in Thomas's hands, and Thomas . . . well. He looked dangerous, and so did the blade he held to the girl's throat. There were two of the bridge crew down, wounded or dead; the remaining, save the helmsman, who'd stayed at his post, were backed up to the sealed port exit. Through luck or design, none of them had High Garda guns, which could have ended this very badly.

Khalila stopped where she was, sword at the ready and breathing hard. Santi's focus didn't move from the captain, though Dario's did, in a flicker, to sweep her for injuries. He must have been satisfied she was all right, since he didn't move towards her.

She felt weak now, and the cold had set deep. Rain coursed down her face from her soaked hijab.

But she held firm as Captain Santi said, 'Surrender or we kill the girl, and probably all of you. You know we can do it.'

One of them laughed.

There was a loud puff of air, and a red-hot rivet appeared in the steel beside the man's head. Anit glanced over. Glain, it seemed, had found the connection for the steam hose below, and she seemed very content to try her aim again on the next one to doubt their sincerity.

No one laughed again.

The ship's captain, a burly, scarred man who had survived far worse than this, finally said, 'All right. Maybe you could kill us. But you need us if you want to sail this ship and survive the next five minutes, and you know that.'

'And just where do you plan to sail it after you let Red Ibrahim's daughter be killed under your command?' Santi asked. He seemed cool and calm, and utterly in charge. 'Alexandria? Her father doesn't sound the type to let you explain what happened. From what I've heard, he's the type happy to take your tongue out first.'

'With all of you dead, he'll only hear one side: ours. She's all you've got, you fool, and the numbers are on our side. Your only choice is to give up.'

'It's not,' Santi said. Khalila knew that tone, light and careless. This was Santi at his most dangerous. He lifted a half-full bottle of green liquid – the leftover Greek Fire. He pulled the stopper. 'If I pour, it eats straight down, through every layer of the ship, until it bores through the bottom. Won't take long. And my friend Thomas has the only countermeasure. Do you think you can take it from him in time?'

The sailors froze, and everyone looked to the captain, who struggled to seem unimpressed. 'You'd go down with us.'

'It's better than what waits for us with the Archivist,' Santi said. 'Agreed, my friends?'

'Agreed,' Thomas said, in a voice pitched so low it was like an earthquake.

'Agreed,' Dario said.

'Of course.' Glain.

'Yes,' Khalila said, last of all. 'We're not afraid of death. If we were, we would never have begun this.'

'Stop,' Anit said sharply. Not to them. To her captain. 'They mean it. They'll send us all down together. *Give up.*'

'Your father—'

'I will deal with my father. This is on my head. *I command you to obey!*'

Whether it was Anit's direct order or the threat of Santi and that jug, the captain hesitated only a moment before he nodded and ordered his men to their knees, hands on their heads. He joined them. The helmsman hadn't released the wheel; he couldn't, Khalila realised. He'd been tied to it, to avoid being tossed away in a sudden lurch.

'Change course,' Thomas said to the helmsman. 'We head for Cadiz.'

The man murmured under his breath as he spun the wheel. 'I'll need the exact heading,' he said. 'From the charts.'

Santi stoppered the Greek Fire and handed it to Glain, and

pulled a chart from the rack at the rear of the room. He unrolled it on the table and read off coordinates. The helmsman's face was not made for deception, Khalila thought, and she glided up behind him and put a knife to his throat. 'Put us off course, and I'll kill you,' she said very quietly, just for him. 'I know you're thinking of it. Don't. You can all live through this. Anit will take the blame, and none of you will be punished. Do you believe me?'

'Yes,' he said. 'I'll get you to Cadiz.'

'Then we have no quarrel,' she said, and released him. The relief that spread over his face, as she stepped to the side to watch him, convinced her he meant what he'd said. '*Salaam alaikum*, brother.'

'*Alaikum salaam*,' he replied, with a wary nod.

'You find friends in the oddest places,' Dario observed. He'd drawn close to her, and she noticed that in the press of the moment, his nausea had receded, maybe for good. He seemed to be riding the sharp slip of the waves much more easily now. 'How did you know he was Muslim?'

'A sailor without tattoos?'

'Oh. I forgot. Tattoos are haram.'

'Yes,' she agreed. 'But that aside, he was reciting the shahada while Santi held that bottle. In case he might die.'

'The shahada?'

'The profession of faith.'

'And with all that was happening, you thought to notice.' He didn't make it a question. 'Honestly, flower, sometimes I find you quite frightening.'

'Good,' she said, and stretched up to kiss his cheek, just a modest and soft brush of lips on skin. 'You really must wash. You smell like death.'

'Bathing will have to wait until I'm sure one of these fine new friends of ours won't knife me in the tub,' he said. 'Thomas? I think you can let the poor girl go now.'

'Oh,' Thomas said, as if he'd forgotten he held Anit. 'Sorry.' He released her, and Khalila noted that despite the apparent ferocity with which he'd held the girl, she had not even a reddened mark on her neck.

And, more significantly, the girl didn't look angry. 'Thank you for not crushing me,' Anit said. 'I suppose I deserved it.'

'Before we start that conversation, please tell your captain that I'm a man of my word,' Santi said. 'And he'd best be a man of his, because I will keep this bottle ready until we're off this ship.'

'He isn't in charge here, Captain. I am. And I tell you that we have a bargain. This ship sails to Cadiz. Whatever comes there, I will bear the responsibility for my father's anger.' Anit, Khalila thought, was *pleased*. She'd hoped for an opportunity to change her mind.

Which they'd given her. *We are pawns in her game*, Khalila thought, but she didn't mind. Red Ibrahim's daughter had a dangerous road to walk, and she travelled it bravely. Let her have her victories where she could.

Their own victories would be longer in coming.

As they steered on, the storm's fury seemed to lessen a little. Allah's will, Khalila thought, though she knew he had far too many concerns to be directing the wind and fury in their favour. Their success, or failure, would depend on their own grit, luck, and intelligence.

And Santi's very credible threat.

'Leave my bridge,' the captain said. 'I follow the orders of my mistress. I'll see you safely where you're bound. But my bridge is my own.'

'From now on, you'll have to consider me crew,' Santi said, and folded down one of the built-in seats. 'I'll be here until we're safely in dock, because while I trust the word of Red Ibrahim's daughter, I don't trust *you*.'

'He stays, we all stay,' Khalila said, and settled wearily in the corner. She was shivering now, soaked, and the ebb of adrenaline that had carried her through this was making her feel sick. Now that the crisis was over, she was forced to remember that she had killed two men today.

She closed her eyes and began to pray for their souls as the ship carried them on to the shore of Spain and whatever might come next.

EPHEMERA

Text of a report by Thomas Qualls, Master of Cells, to the Artifex Magnus. Not submitted to the Codex, and marked as private correspondence.

I have enclosed the last round of direct transcription of Scholar Christopher Wolfe's interrogations. There is little point in wasting your time reading it; there is no variety in his responses to questioning, whatever the particular tools we chose to employ. He rarely speaks at all now.

As I told you six months ago, I believe we have long since gathered all useful data from this prisoner regarding his invention, his process, his research, and each and every associate who might have factored into the development of the device in question. He has been steadfast that his lover, Captain Niccolo Santi, has no knowledge of, or responsibility for, the invention, building, or operation of the device, and in fact has never seen this machine, or even been told of its existence. As I've told you, I don't think it's worth killing a High Garda captain.

I don't know why you hate this Wolfe so much, but I assure you that if your plan was to break him, he is long past broken. You have destroyed his invention, destroyed his research. Erased all his writings from the Library's records. You have done everything short of killing him, and that is no favour. I am, as you're aware, not a merciful person, or a kind one; I would not last long in this job if I had even a shred of such fine qualities.

So understand this when I tell you I have had enough. I will not subject this prisoner to more pain.

There are limits, and he has reached them. So have I, surprisingly.

Therefore, I have personally released Scholar Wolfe, and I have seen the Archivist in person and explained my decisions. The Obscurist Magnus has also been told. The Archivist was not happy with this, but he agreed – based upon my extensive knowledge of other prisoners kept in our Roman cells – to allow me to exercise this one, small, almost meaningless act of mercy. Or, at least, he didn't dare stop me, given the rage of his Obscurist.

Leave Wolfe alone, Artifex.

I have resigned my post, and there is nothing you can do to punish me. I will retire in comfort and wealth. But I will be watching, and I promise you, if Christopher Wolfe is ever imprisoned again, I will take steps to make sure you regret it for the rest of your life.

We both know how deep the rot extends in our beloved Library. And if I need to expose it to the burning light of day . . . I will.

PART THREE

WOLFE

CHAPTER SEVEN

It was the smell, in the end, that was the worst of it. Not that the Great Library kept a filthy prison, but the stench of terror and despair was harder to wash away than more organic stains. This facility used stones that had been quarried for similar purposes five thousand years ago, long enough that the walls had been well soaked in pain and horror, and exhaled it constantly.

And he knew the miasma of it so intimately, horribly well.

He could ignore the darkness, the bars, the discomfort. But not the smell. And so, after the bars had closed around him, Christopher Wolfe had gone a little mad. A day of shuddering, flinching, imagining that every noise was a torturer coming for him again. A night when he wouldn't close his eyes, for fear the past would smother him.

The morning of the second day – which he calculated not by sunrise, which was invisible down here, but by the changing of the guard watch – he had grown more accustomed to the stench of the place, and the darkness and the confinement, or at least he'd mastered his dread of those things a bit. He reminded himself that if he was right, his job here was not to wallow in useless self-pity, but to do something more.

If he was right, of course. *If* this was some plan that Jess and his miserable twin had conjured up. *If* this was not simply betrayal, but betrayal to a purpose.

The question then was what he was expected to accomplish, locked up here. Morgan, he could understand. But if this was a plan, by rights one of them should have whispered at least a hint to him before it was too late.

Then why would it profit any scheme – and he sensed Dario Santiago's Machiavellian hand behind it – to send him back to a hell he'd never have agreed to return to? Wolfe had worked hard to keep his trauma silent and secret from the younger members of their little band, but Jess, in particular, had been privy to details. The young man knew at least the edges of that particular knife, if not the terrible wounds it had left.

No way to solve this puzzle without information, he told himself, and concentrated on the one he could solve: the security of this prison.

Here in this passage, he saw more of the dull metallic gleam of moving sphinxes than he did human High Garda. *An overdependence upon automation*, he thought. The sphinxes could be got around. Jess had worked out how. Even Dario had managed it.

Human guards were more difficult, if less lethal. They adapted. The sphinxes at least operated upon a set of rigid orders.

But surely his feckless students hadn't put him here just to escape; no point in that. No, there was a purpose behind it, just as there was behind putting Morgan back in the Iron Tower.

That was when he heard the murmurs from another cell. He recognised the words, and they were echoed from other locations – one farther to his right, and one almost directly to his left. Prisoners at morning prayers.

And suddenly, Wolfe knew *precisely* why he'd been placed here. It started with prayers but would hardly end there.

He sat cross-legged on his narrow bunk and ran through where, precisely, these prisons were located. They'd not taken the precaution this time of moving him to another city. He was in Alexandria, in the cells buried far beneath the Serapeum. Holding pens for those sentenced to death. *Ignore that*, Wolfe thought, as he felt a small crack run through his resolve. *Just another problem to be solved.*

He listened. Sat for the better part of an hour and simply listened, pinpointing coughs, shuffles, rustles, the distant sounds of moans and sobs. *This place is full of dissidents.* Normally, it would not be; the Library's opponents ranged from Burners – who normally killed themselves rather than end up here – to smugglers, who were usually killed quickly.

This prison, he realised, had been packed with individuals the Archivist thought might go against him. *We did this*, he thought. *Our small act of rebellion, rescuing Thomas from Rome, echoing across the entire Library system . . . it forced him to tighten his grip, eliminate those who could do him harm.* He had no doubt that the individuals jailed near him were Library sworn . . . Scholars, librarians, High Garda soldiers.

The core of the Library, now seen as its enemies. Tyrants turned on their own, in the end; it was the only way to keep power.

The prayers ceased, and Wolfe stood up and went to stand at the bars of his cell. They were heavy, cold iron, and he thought of a thousand ways to break them. All required things he didn't currently possess, but that had never stopped him for long. 'My friend next door,' he said. 'Are you by any chance a relative of Khalila Seif?'

There was a moment of silence, and then a guarded reply. 'Why do you ask?'

'Because I know her well,' Wolfe said. 'And a more brilliant, clever student I've never taught. She's that rare combination of a great mind and an even better heart.'

He heard the release of a breath. It sounded shaken. 'That's my sister,' the man said. 'My younger sister. I'm Saleh. She's well?' The young man – he was young, perhaps a few years older than Khalila – sounded shaken. 'She's not here?'

'Safe I can't guarantee, but last I saw her, she was well, and far away from here.'

'I pray she stays far away, too.' He hesitated a moment, then said, 'My apologies. I've given you my name and not asked yours.'

'Christopher Wolfe.'

'The rebel Scholar.' Saleh's voice had turned brittle. 'The one who brought all this on us.'

'Blame can wait. Survival first,' Wolfe said. He had no patience for fools, now or ever; the only thing he'd ever done to deserve the blame was to invent a machine the Library didn't want. Everything, *everything*, followed from that. His imprisonment. His release, and erasure from Library records. His penance as lowly instructor. His determination to never allow the Archivist to destroy another bright mind. 'Tell me who's here with us.'

'My father, uncle, and older brother are farther down the row,' Saleh said. 'Arrested on suspicion of treason against the Great Library. Which is nonsense, of course. We were arrested to force Khalila to come back.'

'Who else is here?'

'A Scholar Artifex, Marcus Johnson. Le Dinh, Scholar Medica. Captain Ahmed Khan, High Garda. Two or three Scholars from the Literature ranks, one a beloved author whose recent works are considered heretical. A host of librarians, for various crimes including concealment of original works and Burner sympathies.' Saleh paused to think. 'There's one at the end of this corridor I don't know. He never speaks. My father tried sign, but there was no response. But that only accounts for this one hallway.'

'How many other High Garda confined in here?'

'Six more. Ahmed's the only one of significant rank, though.'

Wolfe had forgotten about the bars around him now, the chill in the stones, the evil smell of the place. He found a small chip of stone and used it to begin scratching out a list on the wall. 'Start methodically,' he said. 'Are you at the end of the hallway?'

'No.'

'Then tell me who is next to you.'

When he was done with Saleh, he engaged the woman to his right, Ariane, who'd been listening. She was High Garda and delivered her account in a crisp, calm voice that he quite liked. It reminded him for a terrifying second of Nic, and he had to pause and push that need away. *Niccolo is safe*, he told himself. *And on his way. Your job is to be ready when he arrives.*

The word spread slowly down the hall, and passed back to him, as he drew a complete map of the prison hall, with names attached. By the time the meagre ration of lunch arrived, he'd memorised the placements and rubbed away the map.

'Eat it, don't throw it,' advised the High Garda soldier who handed him the tray of food. Meat, bread, cheese, figs, a small portion of sour beer and a larger one of water. 'Throw it, you get nothing else today or tomorrow. Doesn't take long for people to learn the lesson.'

Wolfe glanced up at him and had a second of doubt. Did he know this man? Recognise him? It was possible, but he couldn't be sure, and the soldier gave no indication at all of knowing him.

'I'll throw it when I'm tired of the food,' he said.

That got him a bare thread of a smile, and the young man – he was young, nearly as young as Wolfe's students – tapped fingers to his forehead in a mock salute. 'That's why you're a Scholar,' he said. 'You get right to the bottom of things.'

I do know him, Wolfe thought. He couldn't place the boy in proper context; surely they wouldn't put one of Santi's people on duty here? Unless, of course, there was more going on in Alexandria than he'd previously suspected – eminently possible, considering the shocking number of Scholars and librarians imprisoned. Perhaps the stronghold of the Great Library was no longer holding quite as strongly. An interesting theory to chase.

Wolfe ate his food slowly, not to savour its taste – it had little – but because he was involved in assessing the residents of this prison for their potential value in any escape attempt. The Artifex Scholar would certainly be useful. The writers could certainly come up with distractions. He was most concerned about Khalila's father, who suffered from a delicate heart, which these conditions certainly hadn't improved.

He was still deep in thought when he scraped the last of the watery meat from the bottom of the bowl.

There was a message written on it, barely visible now and disappearing fast. It said, *Lieutenant Zara sent me.*

Wolfe paused, closed his eyes a moment, and took in a deep, slow breath. Brightwell had not, after all, abandoned him here without a word, without a plan. Santi's lieutenant – not a woman he cared for a great deal, but competent nonetheless – had been alerted to his plight. And knowing Zara, she had plans.

Now he had a messenger, and possibly even an extra ally.

Wolfe used his thumb to scrub the rest of the message from the bowl and put the tray through the slot outside the bars after downing the ale and most of the water, which he desperately needed.

When the young man came back to collect the dishes, Wolfe finally placed him in his proper context. A lieutenant, one who'd been in charge of the Blue Dogs in Santi's squad. Troll. His nickname was Troll. A competent young man, and fearless, which would be an asset here. Wolfe nodded. Troll glanced down in the bowl, gave that thread-thin smile again, and left without a word.

Wolfe sat back on his bunk and began to methodically catalogue every item in this bare, depressing cell for its usefulness.

Because soon, he'd need every possible asset to find a way out of this.

CHAPTER EIGHT

He woke in the dark, disoriented, and for a moment he reached out to touch Santi's sleeping form, only to hit cold stone. Memory struck a second later, along with the stench of the place, and he groaned and tried to put himself back to sleep. He'd be better off unconscious.

'Oh, wake up, you waste of skin,' said a voice that did not sound like it came out of his nightmares . . . or did it? The lines had blurred considerably recently.

'You're not real,' he mumbled, and turned over to face the cold stone wall.

'The woman in the cell next to you is named—what is her name, boy?'

'Ariane, sir. Ariane Daskalakis,' said a second voice. 'Lately a lieutenant in the High Garda.'

'Tragic, the talent that is being wasted in these dark days. Very well, Wolfe, sit up and talk to me, or I'll order Daskalakis here shot right now.'

He sat up. No denying that this was real now. He could see only a faint outline of the man standing beyond the bars, but he knew it was no spirit haunting him. The hiss of a glow igniting in the man's hand threw a faintly greenish light over both of them, and Wolfe threw up a hand to block the glare as his eyes struggled to adjust. *Getting old*, he thought. *I'd have blinked that away easily a few years ago*. It was an idle observation. He was currently unlikely to get much older.

'Artifex Magnus,' he said. 'I should have expected to see you, I suppose. You never could resist a chance to gloat.'

'Do you really imagine that's why I'm here?'

'Well, I doubt you're here to kill me quietly in the dark. You've never been that kindly disposed.'

The Artifex gave him a cynical grin. 'I've never liked you, that's true. You're an arrogant, insufferable bully who believed he could do anything without penalties. As brilliant and driven as you are, you could have risen to sit in my chair, if only you'd kept your haughtiness under control. But still, this is a pity, the depths you've sunk to.'

'Can we dispense with the pleasantries and get to the point? What brings you out of your warm, and no doubt very comfortable, bed?' Wolfe looked beyond the old man, into the shadows. No guards, just a very nervous young Scholar who clearly looked frightened out of his wits and wouldn't look directly at Wolfe at all. Odd. 'And unescorted?'

'There will be no records that I came here,' the Artifex said. 'The automata will have no memory of it. I came to ask you a question. It's important.'

'You really could wait until visiting hours.'

'If you were ever allowed to see another friendly face, that might be clever. But since you're going to rot in this cell until you die screaming, I'd think you'd settle for an old enemy.' There was something strange about the Artifex's tone now. Wolfe couldn't quite pin it down.

'I doubt I'll ever be that desperate,' Wolfe said. But he was, of course. And the Artifex knew it.

'One question. Answer it honestly, and no one dies tonight.'

Wolfe didn't answer directly, but he inclined his head just a touch. There was a very real danger that if he didn't comply, Ariane might be killed. Or Saleh. It would be one of his neighbours, close enough that he could hear the damage done.

'I knew you were smarter than you seem. Do the Brightwells really have a working press?'

'Oh, yes,' Wolfe said. 'And it's better and faster than anything I've seen before. Better by far than what I built. Better than the first attempts Thomas made, too. It certainly will do the job.'

'The job,' the Artifex repeated.

'The job of destroying the power of the Great Library to censor and withhold information. Which is what you've feared all along.'

The Artifex stepped closer and wrapped his free hand around a bar of the cell door. 'Do you understand what you've done, Wolfe? What you're so arrogantly destroying?'

'Yes,' Wolfe said. 'We've finally opened a door you've kept padlocked for a thousand years. And there's power in what we have. Power you can't take away.'

'You're worse than the Burners. If this machine spreads, it will tear the Library apart, piece by piece. Destroy something that has united the world for so many thousands of years.' There were tears – real tears – in the old man's eyes now. 'You think you're fighting for freedom. Freedom is *dangerous*. Give humankind freedom, and they will inevitably fall into chaos and war, religious zealotry and senseless violence. We have *kept the peace*. And we've done it by giving the people what they need, when they need it. Not what they *want*. Want is nothing but blind and selfish greed.'

'Don't wrap yourself in virtue,' Wolfe said. 'You've killed

tens of thousands in the consolidation of your power – and that's what it is: raw power. The power to decide for hundreds of millions of people what is good for them and what isn't. They don't need your godlike guidance. They need to *grow*.'

'Cancer is a growth,' the Artifex replied. 'Is cancer a good thing?'

'If you've come to debate with me, for the love of the gods, leave me to die in peace,' Wolfe said, and stretched on his bunk to put his face to the wall. 'You're a sick man in a sick, dying system. And something healthier must replace it.'

'Christopher.'

Use of his first name made Wolfe turn over and stare. 'We aren't friends. You don't have the right.'

'We were. Once. Long ago. You remember. I was a mentor to you.'

Unwillingly, he did. And wished he could block it out. 'What I remember is that you didn't hesitate to send me into a trap when it benefited you. I nearly died.'

'It did benefit me,' the Artifex acknowledged. 'And you, as it turned out. You came out of it covered in glory and awarded a Scholar's gold band. Do you think that happened by accident?'

'I think I earned it,' Wolfe snapped, but suddenly he was no longer as certain as he sounded. The Artifex, even before he took the title, had always been a game player. 'And it landed you the wealth you wanted, didn't it?'

'It did, at that. Christopher, my point is that we have benefitted each other before. We could do so now. All I need from you is information.'

'What, you don't mean to torture it out of me this time?' Wolfe kept his tone dismissive and acerbic. 'How generous of you. And unusual.'

'Torture didn't avail us well last time. I see no reason to think it would be any better this time. So I offer you a bargain, and, Christopher, you'd best listen closely, because you will not get a better one.'

'Get it over with. I'm tired.'

If his contempt threw the Artifex off, it wasn't at all visible.

For answer, the Artifex took a folded sheet of paper from his pocket and slid it across the floor. Wolfe frowned at it, then picked it up and unfolded it.

Written on it in the Artifex's hand was *I will protect Santi if you take your own life.*

It fair took his breath away, for a moment. But when he spoke again, his voice stayed steady. 'And why would you want me to do that? I thought the Archivist had an entire elaborate execution planned.'

'Because I don't trust you,' the Artifex said. 'I don't trust that you're some helpless prisoner. I don't trust that the Brightwells mean what they say. And I most *specifically* don't trust that there is no plan to turn all this to your advantage. I believe that with you dead and gone, your students will lose their way, regardless of what orders they've been given.'

Wolfe shrugged. 'Flattering, that you think I have such vast control. But it's not much of a bargain, considering that you don't have Nic.'

'Oh, but I do,' the Artifex said. 'And I promise you, if you don't accept this bargain, I will see that he suffers every torment you can possibly imagine in your place. I'll even have you brought along, so you can see it first-hand. I know you, Christopher. And I know what will destroy you. Do the right thing. I will give you three days. If you aren't dead by that time, then we'll begin this terrible journey together.'

Wolfe balled up the note and threw it back through the bars. 'Are we finished? Because I'm bored with your company.' His tone remained just the same, but there was a crack inside him, an earthquake shift of horror. *Did* he have Nic? Had the entire plan – whatever it could have been – come completely apart? It was all too possible. He rolled over towards the wall without waiting for an answer, and the Artifex didn't speak again. After a long few moments, Wolfe heard footsteps receding, and the burn of the glow went dark.

He lay there shaking in the dark, staring hard into it. *He doesn't have Nic. And he won't. I know my little band of students better than that. Whatever plan is in motion, it can't depend on me kneeling to the Artifex. Or dying in this cell.*

He wished he could believe it. He slammed the heel of his hand into the wall again and again, until he felt the skin break and smelt hot blood, and cursed the moment he'd ever laid eyes on any of the students of his Postulant class.

EPHEMERA

Text of a letter from Obscurist Eskander to Obscurist Magnus Keria Morning. Not submitted to the Codex, and marked as private correspondence. Destroyed upon her death.

I have loved you for years. Half my lifetime now, I have known that there is no one else for me, and never will be. And I know that you are at peace with our life in the Tower, and I will never be.

But I swore to you long, long ago I would never break the seals of this place, never walk out of these doors and find my freedom . . . not if it meant more pain, more slavery, more destruction to the Obscurists I'd have to leave behind. My freedom would come at too high a price.

It's strange that I now have to remind you of your own duty.

Keria, I know you are angry. I know you are raging; I can feel it through the walls of this tower. But no matter how deep your pain, how right your anger, if you strike at the Archivist and lose, imagine what will happen to these Obscurists you now have sworn to protect. Imagine how a shallow, predatory man like that, who values his own life above all others, will react. If you kill him, you might cut out a cancer . . . or simply spread it everywhere. All that holds the Great Library together now is belief. Shatter it, and we are all at risk.

The Library has been forced to live under bad leaders before. Let him age, and wither, and die. We will outlive him.

All we can do now is to protect our son, who has been so terribly wounded.

And to do that, you have to swallow your anger, and wait. Wait until it's time for revenge.

I read over this, and I realise that though it's all true, I had meant to say this in kinder ways. But you know that I love you. And I love our son, lost as he is to us.

It's odd to me, of all people, to be counselling you about caution.

With love,

Your hermit.

PART FOUR

MORGAN

CHAPTER NINE

Morgan's first mistake was almost her last.

Being parted from Jess and Wolfe was something she'd expected, but she still hated it; worry about what would happen to them distracted her too much, and when the Obscurist's carriage had come to collect her from the Great Archives, she'd had to resist the urge to fight. She could have easily got free, but that wouldn't have advanced their cause. She had to be inside the Iron Tower to do that.

The last place she ever wanted to be.

The carriage had been reinforced with scripts to keep her powers blunted, and the first thing the Obscurist who'd come for her had done was lock a golden collar around her neck. She'd felt the alchemical formulae written inside it connect with the power in her, and the collar had sealed itself shut.

But that still wasn't a mistake. It was an advantage. They believed they had her under control. And in the days since, she'd bided her time and pretended to be cowed. She'd sent a message to Jess, but the Obscurists were slow to trust her again; they kept her locked in a room, and when she broke the wards on the door, her collar shocked her into unconsciousness for several hours. When she woke, the wards were up, stronger than ever.

They'd also taken away her Codex. There wasn't a writing

utensil or scrap of paper left in the room, and apart from a food tray slipped through a slot in the door, she'd been left completely alone for four days.

On the fifth day they let her out, but only to meet with the Obscurist Magnus.

He had her summoned to the lush gardens near the top of the Tower – an entire floor devoted to beauty and growth, and windows that were open to the outside to permit the warm sea breezes. No point in trying to throw herself out of them; they would snap shut well before she reached them. She'd experimented with that more than a few times during her last internment here.

She took a seat near a pool filled with blooming lotus flowers, and a servant – another Obscurist, but a very lightly talented one – brought a cup of hot tea and sweet pastries. Tea seemed like a miracle to her; they'd denied any to her from the moment she'd been locked away. Morgan poured a cup and took her first sips just as Gregory came into the garden, and the sight of him drove it all home to her in a way the collar and the familiar sight of the garden had not: she was a prisoner here, again.

And he looked so damned smug about it.

Gregory had always struck her as a would-be tyrant, and now he wore the robes of the Obscurist Magnus, the second-most powerful (or, perhaps really third) person in the Great Library. Everything about the way he approached her, from the superior smile to the arrogant thrust of his walk and the toadies scurrying in his wake . . . it all showed how much he enjoyed his newfound power. Wolfe's mother had died in this garden. There had been a lot of damage, as Morgan recalled; she could see the repairs now that she looked for them, and the new plants.

Gregory had commissioned himself a new set of robes. These were far more elaborate than what Wolfe's mother had been content to wear, fine as those were. He was a petty, selfish man. The Archivist had set about raising men and women to the top of the Library who believed more in power than learning, more in arrogance than humility. Gregory was only the latest of a rotten breed.

The smell of blooming flowers seemed overpowering, and her stomach lurched as she realised that if she couldn't leave this place under her own terms, she'd never leave it at all. Worse: she'd be tasked with the job of accepting Gregory's match for her. Bedding a man she couldn't love. Birthing a child that, if sufficiently gifted, would be kept just as much a prisoner – or seeing it taken from her and sent away to the orphanage if not gifted enough.

To a stranger's eyes, the Iron Tower might seem luxurious. Elegant rooms, fine food . . . the Obscurists went begging for nothing, except their freedom.

But it all left a rotten, wretched taste in the back of her throat, and for a perilous moment she was afraid she might spit out her tea. She drank down the rest in a gulp and set the cup aside, came to her feet, and met Gregory as an equal.

'I knew we'd get you back, Morgan,' Gregory said. 'All that drama and death, and for what? You end up where you belonged from the beginning. And don't worry. I've learnt a thing or two about controlling unruly residents. Keria wasn't willing to face the fact that you represent both a huge gain for us and a huge risk. I am.'

'So you're going to lock me away,' Morgan said, and shrugged. The collar felt heavy and thick around her neck. Gregory seemed to waver in the heat – when *had* it got so warm in the garden? –

but she was sure his smile grew wider. 'Or try, more likely. I've escaped from this tower more than once. I'll do it again.' Her voice sounded strange. Hollow, as if she heard it through a long metal tube. *Voice communication*, she thought. Thomas would be fascinated; she wondered if she should mention it to him. She vaguely turned, as if she expected to find him standing nearby, and then realised that no, Thomas was not here, Jess was gone, their little company of friends and allies was shattered into bits, and suddenly the grief and loneliness overwhelmed her. She wanted to weep. *Jess*, she thought, and felt empty to her core. *Jess*. She needed him here. She needed him to tell her that it would all, finally, be all right.

Nothing seemed right. Not the light, which broke into rainbows around her. Not the heat, which seemed as thick as a blanket on her sweating skin. Not the sound of Gregory's quiet laughter, as much nightmare as reality.

When he touched her, it might have been gentle, but his fingertips seemed made of hot coals and rough as granite, and she flinched back. *What is it? What's wrong with me?* She struggled to piece thoughts together; they wanted to fly apart, spin into broken colours and sickening shards. *The tea. He put something in the tea.* Something to make her vulnerable, make it harder for her to access her power. She felt the suffocating, deadening effects of the Iron Tower, and the collar weighing her down, and for just a moment she felt a grey wave of despair. *I can't. I can't do this. I'm going to die in here.*

She reached out. Not for Gregory. Nothing so obvious. She didn't need to destroy him, even if she could manage it. She just needed to be sure she could defeat what he'd dosed her with.

It hurt like ripping away a piece of herself, and she gritted her teeth on a scream as the pain built, and built, echoing from the walls of the Tower and the collar, and then, a fresh red rose blooming just behind Gregory caught her attention.

She pulled and felt a hiss of energy flowing from the rose. The bloom faded, shrivelled, and the life pulled out of the stem, the leaves. Tempting to pull more, faster, destroying the entire bush, but she stopped with just the one stem.

The petals drifted down, wrinkled and dead. Blackened.

The power she'd taken in broke through the drugs. She was still trapped. Still at Gregory's whims and mercies.

But she was not helpless.

Because he seemed to expect it, Morgan allowed her eyes to roll back and let her body go limp. Gregory caught her on the way to the ground, and she felt herself being lifted, carried, and the hissing, buzzing complex web of life inside the garden faded away into iron and stone and the bright, burning shadows of other Obscurists and servants.

Let go, she told herself. *Let him think he's won. Unless he believes it, he'll just put you right back in that locked room. Let him win.*

She rolled into the dark and found it a welcome shelter.

CHAPTER TEN

Waking was a painful process that came in a rush of headache, nausea, and an ache that went so deep she wondered if she might truly be ill. The light filtering red through her closed eyelids seemed far too bright, and she groaned and rolled over, trying to hide from it. Failing miserably.

'Oh hush,' said a strangely familiar voice. 'Open your eyes, Morgan. You're not the first to ever have a hangover.'

The voice had the lingering traces of an accent – Scots, Morgan thought – that gave the woman's Greek a lilting, teasing sound. Morgan didn't respond for a second or two, and then carefully opened her eyes a slit. Quickly shut them again. 'Close the window?'

'No.' That voice was far too cheerful. 'I like the light. And since we'll be sharing this room, you'll just have to make do, won't you?'

Annis. The voice finally fell into proper place, and Morgan opened her eyes wide this time, blinking until the glare resolved into a bright aura around a woman with grey-threaded red hair, a rounded face, and a tilted smile. The lines near her eyes and mouth showed she laughed often, and deeply.

Annis was one of the least talented Obscurists confined to the Tower – someone who had barely passed the threshold of entrance and was capable of only the most rudimentary of alchemical work. It had never put a dent in her happiness. *Born happy*, others said of her. *She'll laugh when she dies.*

She was certainly smiling, if not quite laughing, at Morgan's pain.

'I'm not hungover,' Morgan said. It came out as a feeble, annoyed protest, which she hadn't meant. 'I was drugged.'

One of Annis's eyebrows rose sharply. She was braiding her long hair in quick, efficient swipes, and now she neatly tied off the end and began coiling the waist-long braid into a crown atop her head. She slotted in pins to hold it without so much as glancing in a mirror. It was impressive. 'Drugged?' she repeated. 'I suppose you drank Gregory's special tea, then.'

'He does this often?'

'Often enough,' she said. Not smiling now, and in no way amused. 'When he thinks he might not get his way. Funny thing: give the man all the power he wants, and he still feels weak. Almost as if there's a hole in him that can't be filled.' Annis's look had turned sharp now. Assessing. 'Feeling better?'

'Some. Don't suppose you have any headache remedies?'

'Of course.' Annis turned to a cabinet and came back with a glass of water and a single pill. 'This should settle you.' When Morgan hesitated, Annis made a face. 'I'm not one of Gregory's lackeys. I was Keria Morning's friend. And I'll not be loyal to the man who all but jumped into her still-warm shoes.'

Morgan took the pill and chased it down with the water. 'Then we might be friends,' she said. Through the pain of her headache, she sensed a very definite hiss that gave away the presence of alchemical scripts near her. No, *around* her. She could see them, when she concentrated, though it nearly split her skull in two: bands of symbols that ran in spirals up the walls of this room. Expertly done, but not expertly enough to be hidden from her.

She concentrated on the one point of weakness: the symbol that relayed the information gathered by the scripts to the transcription automata. She reached out to stroke her fingers over the barely perceptible writing and thought about sending a surge of power through it to disable the connection . . . but no. If she did, that would alert him that she'd recovered her power. And they'd simply repair it.

Annis, she realised, was talking to her. 'I'm sorry. What did you say?'

'I said that you're also not my friend, girl. You're my charge. I'm completely responsible for your behaviour. That's a neat trick, don't you think? I'm his most vocal doubter. If either of us steps wrong, we're both in it.'

'He can't kill us.'

'He can't kill *you*,' Annis corrected. 'Me, I'm of little enough use to him. Too old to bear another child, and the least of all in this rusty prison. Killing me would be easy. So by all means, factor that into your thinking.'

It was the last thing Morgan wanted to do, honestly. Having another person depending on her choices made her feel claustrophobic. 'You were friends with Keria Morning? Really?'

'Aye. When I came here, she was the first to make me welcome and the last to make me feel inferior. I knew she had a destiny, that one. I'm sorry it had to include dying for her son's folly, but that was as she wished it.'

'You think it's folly to fight for the heart of the Library?'

'I think the Library is too huge a beastie to turn with the poke of a few spears.'

Morgan almost laughed at that, dire as it was; the image of the Library as a lumbering beast the size of an ancient dinosaur, but composed entirely of books, was too strange. She liked Annis.

That was going to make things much, much more difficult.

The headache pill was already starting to lift the throbbing fog from her brain, and without that to focus on, she began to notice other things: the cool, incense-scented air that tasted just a little bitter on the back of her tongue. The luxurious comfort of the bed on which she rested – only the finest for the Obscurists, of course. It was a fancy cage, indeed. Most accepted it without much protest, though from her previous confinement here, she could name only a few who were truly content.

Annis, though truly happy, was by no means *content*. She had a sharp mind, a sharp tongue, and a spirit that would never come to terms with this prison, however sweet it seemed.

'Annis,' she said. 'Do you know what's happened to . . . to my friends?'

The older woman stopped in the act of wrapping a colourful knitted scarf around her neck and turned to stare at her. 'No. Why? Weren't you captured alone?'

'I wasn't captured,' she said. 'I was—' She remembered the scripts in the walls and held up a finger, then slowly turned it to the wall. 'Oh, my head is still making me sick. Do you have another of those pills?' As she said it, she shook her head. Annis looked mystified, but then nodded.

'Why, yes. Yes, I do.' Annis wasn't much for deception; that sounded as artificial as a first-year actor in a play. 'Let me get that for you.'

She stood up and then looked around uncertainly, and mouthed, *What are you doing?*

Changing a script, Morgan mouthed back. *Keep talking.*

Annis looked completely thrown by the request, but she found something to chatter about – food, it sounded like, and her favourite dishes – while Morgan summoned up that tiny hoarded store of power from the dead rose and began to examine the complex formulae that surrounded the room. *Clever*, she thought. But not clever enough.

It took a single, focused burst of power to rewrite the variable to be switched on and off at will, with a simple voice command.

Morgan blinked, let the alchemical formulae fade, and said, '*Silencio*.'

'Did you just tell me to shut up in Spanish?' Annis asked. 'Because I'll have you know I'm excellent with Spanish, don't you try to throw me off—'

'They can't hear us now,' Morgan said. 'I don't dare leave it off for long, but whenever we want to talk without eavesdroppers, just say that.'

'Handy,' Annis said, and blinked. 'You could honestly see the scripts? In here? Weren't they hidden?'

'Very hidden. But I have a gift for that sort of thing.'

'Obviously.' Annis took in a breath and blew it out. 'All right, then. What do you want to tell me?'

'That I came here because I wanted to,' Morgan said. 'And I warn you, if you go to Gregory, it won't stop me. I'll just find another way.'

'I wouldn't give Gregory the sweat off my back. He was a horrid, power-hungry bully all his life, and he's turning into a monster as fast as he can. Your secrets are safe with me.' Annis considered her for a long moment before saying, 'Why would you come back here of your own free will?'

'Because the best place to start taking away the Archivist's power is here, where his power really rests. Without the Iron Tower, he's got very little.'

'He has the High Garda,' Annis said. 'Which is no inconsiderable threat in itself.'

'If he truly has them.'

'Hmmm. And he may have overstepped, you know. He's called for a Feast of Greater Burning,' Annis said. 'The public execution of his political enemies. And I've heard that many otherwise loyal High Garda soldiers aren't well pleased to be doing his dirty work.'

'How would you hear that?'

'My girl, I've made it a point to, ah, intimately befriend the guards when they seem so inclined. And they seem happy to talk under those conditions. Especially since they know I can't tell anyone outside these walls. Oh, don't give me such a blushing look. I've always enjoyed the pleasures of a good bed partner, and heaven knows, we've got little else to do for entertainment.' Morgan started to laugh in uncomfortable delight but managed to keep it to a muffled giggle. Annis's grin widened. 'So. You're right that if you somehow break the links of the Iron Tower to the Archivist, the High Garda might not be as firm an ally as he imagines. No one likes what he's doing.'

'I like it even less. It's a terrible, cruel waste. And thinking that he might put Scholar Wolfe on that pyre . . .'

Annis shut her eyes briefly and then opened them again. The shine had taken on a hard quality. 'He has Keria's son? You're sure?'

'Yes.'

'She died to protect Christopher, you know.'

'I know. I was there.' Morgan swallowed hard. 'I wanted to like her. But I only ever knew her as my jailor. Seeing her with Wolfe . . .'

'She never wanted to give that boy up,' Annis said. 'She hated that he was taken away. Once she became Obscurist, she bent the rules regularly to keep children with parents as long as she could, even when there was no hope that they would test as talented. She wasn't a monster, Morgan. She was a woman trying to do her best, under tremendous pressure.'

'What about Wolfe's father?'

Annis fell uncharacteristically silent. She rose and walked to the tall mirror in the far corner of the room, adjusting the fall of the warm robes she wore. 'He broke her heart.'

'Is he still here? In the Tower?'

'Oh yes, he's here, though he's not been seen in many years. Self-imposed exile, though I suppose Gregory will make it more official than that and lock him in for good one of these days.'

'Is he as powerful as they say he is?'

'Aye.' Annis turned slowly to regard her. 'And that's what you really wanted to know, isn't it? About him?'

'I'm just curious,' Morgan lied. 'What's he like?'

'Like? Like a wild, mad bastard who never accepted his fate. He loved Keria. Too much, I think. When he turned down the chance to become the Obscurist and she took it instead . . . that was the end of them. That, and how she let their son be sent away, or at least, that's what he came to believe. We all thought he'd come crawling out, sooner or later; few seal themselves away and mean it, you know. But he did. He shut the door and never left those rooms again.'

'You're sure he's still alive?'

'Dead men don't take deliveries of food and supplies, have their clothes cleaned, and all the other mundane necessities of life. But he's put wards on his doors that only Keria could break – and I know others, including Gregory, tried.'

Morgan was desperate to ask exactly *where* Eskander's room was located. The Tower was large and complicated; she'd explored some of it before, but hardly all, and though the whispers about the Hermit of the Iron Tower had come to her attention, she hadn't been interested then in following them.

She'd pushed Annis enough, though. There was no doubt Gregory was forcing the older woman to spy on whatever Morgan did, and while Annis would likely cover for her out of sheer dislike for the Obscurist, if it became too obvious, she wouldn't have too much of a choice.

'I'm going to turn the ears back on,' Morgan said. 'Pretend they're not there. But don't mention Eskander or anything we talked about. All right?'

Annis nodded. 'You said there's a word to speak to turn it off. What turns it on again?'

Morgan said, '*Presta atención.*' *Pay attention.* 'Thank you for the medication, and letting me rest. I think it's starting to help. I think I might be a little hungry.'

Annis stumbled a little but finally said, 'Well, then, we'll be having something to eat. Come on. I'll refresh your memory on just how good the cooks are here.'

She seemed relieved when they left the room, and whispered, 'So they're listening? God help me, I say the most indecent things.'

'Pretend they're always listening,' Morgan said. 'And if you want to have private conversation . . .'

'Yes, I understand. I told you, I'm brilliant with Spanish.' Annis winked at her and led the way to the winding stairs. 'And with Spaniards, too.'

Morgan was sure that was at least partially true.

CHAPTER ELEVEN

Annis escorted her to the Iron Tower's dining hall, where Morgan forced herself to smile at Obscurists who welcomed her back – some even meaning it – and ate her food in silence. She'd choked down most of it when a hush came over the large room – and over the fifty or so Obscurists gathered in it – as a High Garda soldier wearing the symbol of Iron Tower dedicated service strode in, scanned the room, and headed straight for the table Morgan and Annis shared. Others in the room averted their gazes; in such confined spaces privacy was paramount, just as gossip was king. The soldier was a man of native Australian heritage, with solid features and deep-set eyes. He nodded to Annis, who silently took her cup of tea and left the table, leaving Morgan quite alone in the midst of a crowd.

'Captain wants you,' the soldier said. 'Now.' His Greek was excellent – better than Morgan's – and she nodded and got up without a word. Resisting would only bring more of the guards, and this wasn't the time for a meaningful fight. Besides. She was curious what possible interest a captain of the Iron Tower High Garda could have in her.

Her answer was even less clear when she was presented to the captain, who proved to be a tall, severely dressed woman. Skin the colour of the bark of an olive tree, and a prominent nose that looked to have been broken at least once. In her middle age, with threads of grey beginning to dust her dark, sleek hair. The High Garda captain's office was on the ground floor of the Tower, temptingly close to the exits, but it wasn't the time to consider running, either. So when the captain nodded to a chair in front of the plain desk, Morgan took it.

'Morgan Hault,' the captain said. 'That's your name?'

'It is.'

'Mine is Captain Nofret Alamasi.' The captain had a Codex open on her desk, and Morgan suspected that what was written there contained reports of her prior behaviour and misconducts – and escapes. 'I am known for two things, Morgan. I am not friendly, and I am loyal to the Great Library beyond question. Which is why this is my posting. The last High Garda captain had a tendency to befriend Obscurists. I do not have that failing. If you keep faith, I will treat you as an honoured guest in this tower. If you break it, you will be a prisoner.'

'I'm already a prisoner,' Morgan said. 'We all are.'

'It doesn't have to feel that way unless you make it so.' The captain closed the book. 'I wanted to see your face, and for you to see mine, when I give you this message: if you seek to escape this tower again, I will confine you to a single room, feed you through a slot in the door, and you will never see the light of the sun again. Are we clear?'

'Clear,' Morgan said. 'Captain Alamasi. How long have you held this posting?'

Alamasi gave her a level stare before she said, 'Not long. Why?'

'You might look into how long your predecessors lasted. Your new Obscurist Magnus is not a patient man, and he isn't a good man. You'd do well not to put your faith in him.'

'I don't,' the captain said. 'I put my faith in my orders. Which

I will carry out without fail. You may count on me to do that. I don't need warnings, and I don't need conversation. I've warned you. And that's all the grace you'll get.'

Interesting. It sent Morgan's mind careening down a path she hadn't thought of before, and she was a little distracted when she said, 'Yes, Captain. I understand.'

The captain nodded at her waiting soldier, who ushered Morgan out again, up into the lifting chamber that rose through the levels of the Iron Tower. He was returning her to her room, she realised, and not to the dining hall. She didn't object.

Annis was waiting for her, and when the door swung open, the older Obscurist jumped from the bed where she'd been sitting to stand in awkward silence, looking from Morgan to the soldier. Not sure of what her response should be.

'It's all right,' Morgan told her. 'I've just met the High Garda captain. She seems nice.'

The soldier gave her a look that told her he *almost* appreciated the joke, and then he turned and marched away, leaving her to Annis's care.

'Christ above, I thought they were marching you off to . . .' Annis didn't finish the thought. 'Well, at least you're safe. Just a warning, then?'

'A warning,' Morgan said. 'I've got nothing but warnings since I stepped into this tower. What exactly are they afraid I'm going to do?'

'What aren't they afraid you'll do? Here. Orders came for you.' Annis handed her a Codex. The first page held a message from Gregory in the man's cramped, inelegant hand. It said, *Tell Morgan Hault to report to the Master Copyist. She will serve there until I decide she can be trusted with more vital duties.*

Serving under the Master Copyist was one step above kitchen

duty – mind-numbing work, hand-copying scripts developed by more gifted Obscurists. It was reserved for those who were too low powered to do anything more creative.

'Annis,' Morgan said thoughtfully. 'You work under the Master Copyist, don't you?'

'For my sins,' Annis said. 'Why?'

'We are going to the same place.'

'No!' Annis looked horrified. 'He wouldn't! *You*? What a waste of talent that is!'

'I expect it's to teach me humility and make sure that I understand how to obey,' Morgan said. 'I don't suppose it'll be very effective at either, but I'll copy for him. As much as he likes.'

'Will you, now.'

Annis's regard this time was steady and interested, but Morgan didn't satisfy her curiosity. She simply couldn't afford to do so. Annis might be an ally in what was to come. Or she might be a dire problem.

Either way, Morgan didn't intend to involve her any further than necessary.

Settling in as a copyist was ridiculously simple, and it gave her time to construct advanced formulae in her mind, which she wrote out on a mental Codex in letters of fire while her hand copied down simple mirror scripts, over and over, for inclusion into the bindings of Blanks. There were about fifty Obscurists set to the task, all copying the same mindless string of symbols and imbuing the scrap of paper with a brush of talent to link it to Aristotle's universal liquid. He'd been right about this, if wrong about many other things: there truly was an undercurrent of power in the world, one that those with specific skills and gifts could access to shift the nature of a thing from one state to another.

I could write one symbol down, pour power into it, and kill everyone in this room, she thought. For just a moment, she could feel the trembling possibility of it in her fingertips, a dark power like shadows brushing her skin. *I could take all this away from the Archivist. Every one of his Obscurists.* It seemed so simple in that moment, so breathtakingly easy, that when she realised what she was thinking of doing she flinched and ruined the script she was copying. The Master Copyist – a nasty little beetle named Fratelli – looked sharply in her direction, and she disposed of the ruined paper in a bin beneath her desk and pulled another slim scrap onto the copy surface.

She wasn't here to kill anyone. She was here to save them. Her power had been twisted and came from darker places now, but that didn't mean she had to give in to the impulses it fired in her mind.

She copied the script. Flawlessly. And the next, and the next, until the Master Copyist's attention wandered away.

Then she began to alter the scripts.

It would have taken a sharper eye than his to realise what she was doing, and fooling the older man who sat beside her to double-check her work was even easier. All of the scripts appeared to work perfectly; when he brushed his thumb across the inked symbols, they rose from the paper in glittering images.

But there was one tiny difference in the scripts from the standard she was supposed to be duplicating . . . and each script stored a single letter into a message she was composing. It took a great deal of concentration, and more than two hours to do even the brief message she intended, but at last she wrote the final symbol, and imbued it with the last piece of punctuation. Then she tapped pen to paper, a seemingly innocent gesture, and all the scripts flared into power at once in a single burst.

Somewhere in Alexandria there was a Codex that Brendan Brightwell had been assigned, and if she knew Jess, he had already picked it up and read through it, and some of his essence had marked it. Her message sought that essence and directed itself not to the Codex – which was sure to be monitored – but to the nearest Blank to it.

She indulged herself by wasting a total of seven letters at the end to say *I love you.*

Unnecessary, but she couldn't resist. She felt a wild, sudden yearning for him, for his easy smile and the clarified light in his eyes when he looked at her. She needed to hear his voice to tell her that however unlikely it seemed right now, it would succeed. Her breath seemed to swell in her chest, like tears, and she closed her eyes for a moment and imagined herself somewhere else, far from here, with him in a place of sunlight, silence, warmth.

A hand rapped sharply on her desk, and she opened her eyes. 'Stop lagging,' the Master Copyist snapped. 'Keep writing.'

Morgan bit back the impulse to suck the life out of him in one convulsive, wonderful pull, and put her pen back to paper to draw the same symbols, over and over and over.

The day was almost done when a hand fell on her shoulder, and she looked up into the face of the Obscurist Magnus. Gregory. Her skin tightened, and she resisted an urge to strike his grip away. *Did he know? Is he better than I thought?*

But there was no awareness in the Obscurist Magnus's face that she'd been slowly, carefully manipulating the simple task she'd been set. No, this was something else.

And she felt needles of alarm sweep through her at the sight of the cold focus of his gaze.

'Come,' he said. 'Walk with me.'

Across the room, Annis was just rising from her copy desk;

the older woman caught sight of Gregory, and there was no mistaking the alarm on her face, but she did nothing but avert her gaze and hurry off. No help from her.

No help from anyone, as the room quickly emptied, and Morgan debated whether or not it was time to mount a resistance. *Not yet.* Of course not yet.

She silently stood and joined Gregory as the Obscurist walked out of the copy room and down a winding set of stairs that wrapped around the vast walls of the Tower. It was dizzying, this method of descending, and she tried not to look down. She'd always had a hidden fear of heights, though she knew there were alchemical barriers in place beyond the railings; after the first few times Obscurists had hurled themselves from the highest floors, precautions had been put in place. If she was bent on suicide, she could have easily unravelled them, but she wasn't. Though pushing Gregory over was an interesting thought.

'Where are you taking me?' she asked him.

'To meet someone,' he said. 'Someone special.'

She almost, *almost* bolted then; Gregory took an unhealthy interest in the darkest secret of the Iron Tower: the breeding of Obscurists. She'd accepted when returning here that they would assign her a partner in the hopes of producing a talented child to add to the thinning ranks of the Obscurists. She'd accepted that they'd *try* to force her into it.

She never, ever intended to cooperate . . . though the fact that Gregory had so easily drugged her on arrival was worrying. She'd need to develop defensive scripts to repel any other attempts. *I should have done that already*, she thought. She felt cold and alone, descending these steps.

Gregory stopped on the landing for the seventh level, which held the Obscurists' opulent library. An entire wall of Blanks waiting to be filled with requested content, and an array of Codexes to use to select it. But more than that, the Obscurist library also contained an entire wall of original volumes and scrolls, some so ancient and fragile that they were kept in cases with alchemical formulae designed to slow their destruction.

For a disorienting moment, Morgan imagined Jess here. She could vividly see him sprawled just there on that tufted couch, an original volume in his hands. He'd secured reading material even in their Philadelphia prison. He'd have found this a rare delight.

But the young man sitting on the couch – not sprawling – was reading a Blank, and he quickly put it aside and rose at the sight of the Obscurist Magnus.

Then he looked at her, and she stared back without a single flicker of expression. She didn't dislike him, not at all; his name was Benjamin Argent, and he was a kind, smart, intelligent soul.

'Morgan,' he said, and extended his hand. He was taller than she was, and slender, and she thought she could see both resignation and resentment in the brief eye contact they shared before both looked away. 'You're back.'

'Evidently.'

'I didn't expect to ever see you again.' His tone was neutral, but she easily read what he meant: *I hoped I'd never see you again.*

'It came as something of a surprise to me, too.'

Gregory was smiling at them both. A cold, knowing smile. He said nothing, but the silence said everything he needed to convey to her – no, to both of them. Morgan knew that Ben already had a lover within the Iron Tower, but not the one that had been chosen for him. Ben had politely, calmly, pointedly refused to submit.

'I have a question for the two of you,' the Obscurist said.

'Do you recall the last time an Obscurist was executed for disobedience in the Iron Tower?'

It was such an unexpected question that Morgan glanced at Ben, mystified, and he seemed just as puzzled. 'No, sir,' Ben said. 'Punishments, yes. Execution, no.'

'Exactly,' Gregory said. 'Obscurists have been exempt from execution for a very long time. We have always been a rare breed, and over the past thousand years there have been fewer and fewer of us. A few hundred years ago, Obscurists were free to come and go from this place, you know. Free to marry whomever they wished. The folly of this became obvious over time. We are, and always will be, a valuable resource. So every possible effort is made to rehabilitate Obscurists who fail to comply with their expected duties. Correct?'

'Yes sir,' Ben said. 'I'm not sure what you—'

'The rules have changed,' Gregory said. 'And none of this is for your benefit.'

He cut the young man's throat.

It was so sudden, deliberate, and shocking a move that for an instant, Morgan didn't even understand what she was seeing. A flash of a knife Gregory had held casually at his side. A sudden, violent burst of red across Gregory's robes (*plain robes, he planned this, he wore things he could afford to have stained*). The sharp, copper smell flooded over her, and she felt trapped in it, off-balance and slow with horror.

She looked down, still not comprehending what had happened. Benjamin had collapsed, his lifeblood pumping out and soaking the rug he lay on. He was gasping for air, and she thought wildly, stupidly that she should *do something, anything*, and her shock broke with an almost audible snap inside.

The rush of anguish, horror, and fury mixed with the red

taste of blood in the air, and she reached for power, *any* power, to use to strike back.

'No, no, no,' Gregory said. 'None of that.' He touched her collar.

The agony that hit her was like nothing she had felt before. She screamed and collapsed next to the dying young man, and felt his warm blood on her skin as she writhed uncontrollably. She could feel his life seeping away, and she couldn't touch it. Couldn't manage more than a tortured gasp for breath.

She was barely conscious when Gregory leant over her. His blood-flecked face was framed by black sparkles as she fought to stay conscious. 'Consider this a lesson,' the Obscurist Magnus said. 'I know you're thinking of ways to undermine me. The first time you defy an order from me, *any* order, someone else will die. I told you. The rules have changed. You and your friends did that.'

She gasped for air that seemed thick and liquid in her lungs. Gregory's voice seemed smeared and far away, his face receding down a long, dark tunnel.

You and your friends did that.

And then she tumbled away into the black.

EPHEMERA

Text of a letter from Brendan Brightwell to Jess Brightwell, sent via ship from England to Alexandria. Lost, along with the ship *Valiant Isis*, in a storm off the coast of Spain.

I'm as bored as bored could be, Brother. Being you is dead boring. I've been given stacks of books, and I'm forced to make some show of actually reading them, since I'm supposed to be you.

You are impossible. How do you ever live with yourself?

I'm sorry to have to tell you that no one misses you. Well, certainly not Da, who rubs his hands together in glee when he thinks about the vast amounts of geneih he's about to make from the Library, and the equally vast amounts of other currencies that are pouring into his banks from every corner of the earth. Your Thomas's press is something of a nine-day wonder. Every unpleasant character from Shanghai to the American colonies has sent emissaries to have a look, and he's got quite good at demonstrating the thing. God help us if it breaks, but Thomas left thorough instructions. I'm sure that – as you – I'd be forced into pretending to fix it.

Do overthrow your tyrant and finish this soon. Since you don't have half as much of a fondness for wine, or food, or casual ladies, I'm forced to do without most of the things that make life worthwhile.

Books, Jess. Really?

Release me from the hell soon, or I might just release myself.

PART FIVE

JESS

CHAPTER TWELVE

For a long few days, Jess waited for word. *Any* word would have been better than the frozen silence from the Serapeum; he'd expected to be summoned for more interrogation, threatened, or – most unlikely – delivered to the Great Archives to begin choosing books for the trade with his father. He waited for any further messages from Morgan, but none arrived. No word from Dario's cousin, either, though he could see from his front door that there were always men and women posted to watch him. Whether they were Library or Spanish spies, he had no way of telling.

Might as well get on with it, then, he thought that morning, as he watched the sunrise and drank sweet, black, thick coffee. He stood in his doorway and leant there, marking the positions of each watcher. They were as bored as he was. He'd given them no reason at all to raise their alarms, after all. That was intentional.

Jess held one hand down at his side and, with deliberation, spelt out his message in sign: *Send Quest now.* Santiago had told him that he'd have someone watching for any such communications; Jess could only hope that the agents weren't asleep on the job at this early hour. At least the ambassador had seemed like a serious, competent man. Perhaps he inspired others to be just as alert.

He repeated the sequence of letters five times, just to be sure;

it took the entire leisurely drunk cup of coffee, and the entire sunrise, to do it without making it seem obvious. He was praying that none of the High Garda spies could read sign, or at least, not the specific Spanish sign dialect that Dario had taught him.

After he'd thrown the dregs of the cup into the street, he turned and went back inside, shut the door, and waited on Elsinore Quest.

Quest never arrived.

The High Garda did.

His first warning was when the door smashed open and a flood of uniforms rushed through it; he was thrown against the wall with shouted warnings ringing in his ears, and while his face was pressed tight to the rough paint, he listened to them tear apart the house.

'What's this?'

A soldier yanked him back by the collar, slammed him into the chair at the kitchen table, and held up two tightly wrapped packets in thin metallic foil, each about the size of his hand. Jess shrugged. The soldier carefully slit one open and peered at the brown sludge inside, then sniffed it.

'Smoke bomb,' he reported to his commander, who stood watching. She nodded sharply. 'Expertly made.'

'Of course it is. We gave him access to a Codex. He likely has dozens of toys made by now. Tear it apart. Find everything.' She turned her gaze to Jess. 'I don't blame you. I'd do the same. But others might not be so forgiving.'

'I was bored,' Jess said. 'What else was there to do? Couldn't go out for a stroll, could I?' He finished it with Brendan's best, most charming smile, the one his brother deployed to great effect, and watched it have no impact at all.

'Pity you didn't show a little good faith and patience, Brightwell. You might have lived through this.' She shook her head. 'Odds are, I won't be seeing you again.'

The urge to just *run* felt dirty and overwhelming, and for a few seconds he allowed himself the fantasy. He could fight. He might even make it to the safety of the Spanish embassy; from there, he could be out of Alexandria on a friendly ship. When he closed his eyes, he could feel the cool salt spray on his face.

And where could he go to escape the guilt?

Running meant leaving Scholar Wolfe to die screaming in the Feast of Greater Burning. It meant leaving Morgan locked in the Iron Tower, forced into a life she never wanted – and that she'd gone back to voluntarily, out of sheer faith in his ability to pull this off.

Run, and you're the worst kind of coward, he told himself. The part of him that was so very good at impersonating his twin, Brendan, argued back, *Run, and I'm a pragmatist. It was always a risky plan. It isn't going to work if I'm locked up here, without access, without influence. I can make another plan.*

Jess closed his eyes and, in a moment, opened them again. If running was the intelligent thing to do, then he would have to be a fool.

It took the High Garda less than five minutes to strip his little prison down to bare floor and bare walls; they were well trained indeed. They found almost all the things he'd hidden: the carefully sharpened knives, the concoctions he'd brewed from spices and oils to create stinging, blinding fogs; the small, crude still he'd made to brew pure alcohol. The captain set it on the table with raised eyebrows. 'That's for personal consumption,' Jess said. 'I told you I was bored.' It wasn't, of course. Alcohol was an excellent base for many things, including firebombs. Hardly as effective as Greek Fire, but then, he couldn't make Greek Fire out of fruit, sugar and yeast, all of which they'd provided him as part of his kitchen supplies.

'Clever little criminal,' she said. 'The worst kind. Get up. Let's go.'

He shrugged. They didn't shackle him, which he found interesting, but they closed around him in a cordon and took him out of the house to the street.

They parted to reveal not a High Garda carrier, but a large, formal carriage with the seal of the Great Library on the side and glimmering gold on the brightwork.

'Archivist wants you,' the captain said. 'Inside.'

Quest, you bastard, Jess thought. It was too late now. If the Spanish spies had got the message, if they'd passed it on, then Quest had been slow to respond, and there was no longer any use wishing. He knew that this meeting with the Archivist would be something far less cordial than the last.

This would be the real interrogation.

And he would have to survive it without help.

'Coming?' he asked the captain, as he climbed into the carriage. She shook her head. He held out his hand. 'You've been fair. Thank you.'

For the first time, she let a tiny smile crack her hard surface. 'I'm not fool enough to shake the hand of a skilled pickpocket,' she said. 'Good luck, Brightwell.'

She slammed the door, and he heard the locks engage.

Trapped. *Doesn't matter*, Jess told himself, though he felt the coil of wire in his guts pull tighter. *Whatever comes next, you can outwit it.*

He had to believe that. If he didn't, this would be over quickly.

The interior of the carriage reminded him, quite darkly, of a carriage he'd entered at ten years old, when he'd first watched a vile man rip apart and eat a book he'd have given his life to save. Ink-lickers. Jess shuddered when the memory crawled up his spine; he hadn't encountered that particular book vice in years, since the Library had been intent on stamping it out. It seemed a uniquely English obsession, so far, and by far the most disturbing one he could imagine. At least as it related to the written word.

He tried not to think about what was coming as the carriage rolled smoothly on. There was no point in trying the locks; they were clearly alchemical, and he was no Obscurist. With time, he might find a way to force them.

He didn't have time.

The carriage had gone for a few minutes when the trap slid back on top of the coach with a bang that made him jump and look up; silhouetted by the sunlight, the driver was just another uniformed Library servant. Jess hadn't looked at him twice before climbing in; he'd been utterly unremarkable.

More remarkable now that he said, 'Right, let's go on with it, boy. We don't have much time.'

Jess blocked the light with his hand, and the features came into shadowy focus. 'Who are you?'

The man sighed. 'Truly, I have the curse of a forgettable face. Or the benefit, in my line of work.'

'*Quest*?' Jess felt a jolt of astonishment, with a healthy dose of chagrin; he'd completely missed the obvious. Then again, so had the High Garda, even the commander. Quest had a gift for blending in . . . and a rare nerve, to do it so boldly.

'Well, you did quite generously hire me for a small fortune, young man. Or have me hired, at any rate. I trust I can do as fine a job for you as I did for your Scholar Wolfe in the past, but without quite as much trauma, perhaps. What is it you require?' Elsinore Quest was a skilled Mesmer, capable of convincing almost anyone of almost anything; he'd helped Scholar Wolfe unearth the buried and agonising memories of his time under Library captivity, in order to pinpoint where Thomas Schreiber had been taken. An ugly task at the time, but a very necessary one.

'Can you mesmerise me on the move? While driving?'

'It's not ideal, but it will have to do. I only have this very special position for a few more blocks, mind you, and then I'll have to exit the box and the regular driver will be restored quite peacefully, and won't remember a thing of leaving his post. Don't worry. You won't remember it either.'

Jess opened his mouth to ask details of that particular feat, but Quest continued. 'Your very fine Spanish friend relayed me quite a huge pile of Alexandrian *geneih*, or I promise you, I'd not be wearing this rotten livery and taking such a ridiculous risk, so you must trust me that I know my business. What is it you wish me to do for you?'

Jess told him. Quest was quiet for a long moment, and Jess had the sharp premonition that payment or no, Quest was about to disappear from his post atop the box without another word. Not even *no*.

Then the man sighed. 'I suppose it's possible. Very well. How long do you want it to last?'

'At least the rest of the day. How long will it take to achieve the proper—'

'Shhh,' Quest said, and there was something soothing about his voice now. Quiet and still. He was tapping a finger lightly against the roof of the carriage, and Jess's attention was drawn by the rhythm. 'Just a little further, Mr Brightwell. Just listen to the sound of my voice. Listen and relax. Listen and relax, and we will have a chat about all of this, a wonderful and calming chat about your brother.'

Jess found himself collapsing back against the seats.

And then he didn't remember anything else.

CHAPTER THIRTEEN

It couldn't have been more than a few moments before he opened his eyes, but he felt as if he'd slept a full night. All the dull aches drilled into his bones by the stress and worry were gone.

He looked up through the open trap of the door and saw a silent driver in livery. *Something about the driver.* He'd forgotten what he'd observed, and it no longer seemed important. He yawned and stretched and thought, *Well, if I'm going to my gruesome death, at least I'm doing it in a damn cheerful mood.*

The carriage rolled swiftly on through the streets; lesser conveyances moved out of the way, pedestrians stepped back, and even the larger, lumbering steam wagons that moved goods through the city made respectful space for their passage. *Well, this is posh*, he thought. *And when did the Archivist become an emperor?* Ages ago, most likely, a bit of grandeur and arrogance at a time. Power formed like pearls, in accretion layers over time. Pharaoh's reign had passed, though a ceremonial Ptolemy still acted as a figurehead and kept Egypt's rich history alive. Gradually, inevitably, all of the devotion that the old god-king demanded had landed on the Library.

And now it formed a crown on the head of the most corrupt man ever to hold the office of Archivist.

Da had always said that the corrupt were easier to do business with than the honest, at least; if that held true, today would end in huge profits. And if it went badly, he could always sacrifice himself to remove the old man from the board. Better a bloody, costly victory than a slow defeat for the family. He didn't have a weapon, but he'd make do. His father had taught him early on in life that anything, even a tightly rolled piece of paper, could be effective enough as a weapon. Speed and ruthlessness were the key components of any attack, and he'd need to have both of those if he intended to kill the Archivist; the High Garda and automata would be on him in a second, maybe two, and he had to make it count. If that was what the day required.

No sense in raising his pulse now. He couldn't control what was to come, so he closed his eyes until the steady hiss of the steam engine changed pitch. The carriage was slowing, and the drive was over.

Pity. It was a perfect day outside.

The carriage didn't pause at the checkpoints, which parted without question; the prowling sphinxes there glared in at him with reddened eyes, their eerie human faces reminding him of someone and no one at all. The sphinxes used at the checkpoints were larger than their more common counterparts, and the wings folded at their sides were not at all ornamental. They could fly for short distances, the wings were sharp as knives, and he'd heard rumours that their bites were poisonous. He believed it. The aura of menace coming off these things was especially intense.

There was, he noticed, also a large number of High Garda Elite manning the checkpoint – twenty, by his guess. If there were as many stationed at every side of the Serapeum's pyramid, the Archivist was uneasy.

Good. An uneasy negotiator was an easier mark.

The carriage deposited him in a secured courtyard – more automata prowling – and the driver ushered him out with icy politeness.

Neksa was waiting for him. He felt a lurch in the pit of his stomach, seeing her again. Sweet, lovely Neksa.

'At least if I'm going to die today, I get a last look at true beauty.' He didn't even think about the words before he said them, but they sounded right. Felt right. He paired them with an extravagant bow.

As he straightened, Neksa slapped him. Hard enough to rock his head back and inscribe a hand-shaped burn on his cheek, and he blinked back his surprise and somehow managed to hold onto the slipping grin. 'Suppose I deserved that.'

'Suppose you deserve a great more,' Neksa snapped. 'You are here for the Archivist, not for me. If it was up to me, I'd put you on a boat back home and drill holes in the hull as a going-away present.'

Well, you do care after all, love. He followed her stiff back and swaying hips through a small door at the back of a water garden thick with lotus and found himself in one of the many claustrophobic passages within the pyramid itself. He'd never been inside it, and he marked it for later, though he hadn't seen how she'd managed to open it. Likely it was keyed to the band around her wrist, which would clearly list her privileges and restrictions. Wouldn't work without her being alive and wearing it, of course; the Library wasn't stupid.

If he wanted to use this way again, he'd have to make Neksa an ally . . . or a prisoner. Though he didn't relish that last, but he didn't rule it out.

The looming, arching walls were inscribed with hieroglyphs nearly as fresh as the day they were chiselled, millennia ago, and he resisted the urge to trail his fingers over those sharp edges. History was everywhere in Alexandria. It was in the air he breathed, the stones he walked on. The Great Library had survived the march of time. It gave him some hope that he might survive his day inside it.

Neksa reached the distant end of the corridor – which, he noted, had no branches and he strongly suspected could be locked off at either end with either the airflows blocked, or lethal gas introduced. Stepping through to the next room was disorienting, since the next chamber was a huge vaulted gallery filled with twenty-foot-high gilded statues of gods, all marking a path that led to the other side. Horus guarded the end of the row, facing towards them; the giant hawk-headed god stood staring straight ahead with a flail clasped in his right hand. All the gods had been decorated with gold and silver, but Horus's body had been crafted of pure black stone, and the craftsman had taken a Roman approach to showing the perfect musculature . . . an odd effect, and more than a little unsettling.

He was unsurprised when the god's eyes lit red as they approached and the golden hawk's head tilted down to regard them. The flail in its hand was razor edged. It would cut them both in half with a single swing, and Jess watched for any twitch of movement that would signal that was about to happen. *Dive for the floor, roll, hope for the best. At least you won't suffer long if you're slow.*

Neksa, without pausing or slowing her stride, held up her hand to show her bracelet, and he did the same. Horus tracked their progress with unnerving intensity but didn't move, and once they were past the tree trunks of his legs, he allowed himself a little breath of relief. He'd been so occupied with Horus he'd failed to check the other gods in the rows, but he had little doubt that they, too, were automata, which meant anyone invading this place would come to a bad, red end.

Not the sort of place you took by force of arms, the Serapeum.

'Impressive,' he said. Neksa ignored him. 'In London we never see the like of these particular automata. Are they new?'

'Stop talking,' Neksa said. 'Or you'll get to inspect them all too closely.'

She sounded sincere, and he went quiet, absorbing the next hallway, and the next. It was a labyrinth in here. He wondered if the hallways themselves were, in some form, automata; perhaps they moved and reconfigured on a schedule, to foil people like him memorising the layout of the place. They all seemed the same, and confusingly indirect to the purpose.

For what it was worth, though, he kept a mental map until they'd arrived in an anteroom he recognised . . . one with four High Garda Elite on duty. They all looked strong and razor edged. One – he presumed the one in command – nodded to Neksa briskly and fixed a dark stare on him. 'Against the wall,' the commander barked. She was a small woman, with the fair hair and skin of the Nordic regions, and greenish eyes that looked as cold as sea ice. Scars on her neck, her hands, and a particularly large one on the side of her face. She looked like she ate fear for breakfast.

He put his palms against the nearest wall and leant. She searched him efficiently and thoroughly, finding nothing, and when she snapped her fingers to indicate she was finished, he turned and leant back on the wall to give her an appraising look. She ignored him and returned to her post.

Neksa was already seated behind her desk and was writing in the Codex there.

'Well?' he asked. 'Was I summoned to admire the decor?'

He might as well have been a bug for all the attention they gave him, and the minutes stretched by until Neksa suddenly rose and threw open the double doors to the Archivist's office.

A man strode out, followed by a small army of retainers. He wore too-ornate Obscurist robes as if he still hadn't quite worked the stiffness out of them . . . and then the newcomer's face went florid with rage and he pointed. 'Arrest him!'

The Obscurist's retainers moved forward instantly, but the High Garda commander stepped into the path and shook her head mutely. That ended the matter.

'What are you doing? That's Jess Brightwell! He's a wanted criminal!'

'Understandable mistake. I'm the other Brightwell son. Brendan. My brother does indeed resemble me. Makes for an uncomfortable visit here, I'll tell you that.'

'Visit?' The Obscurist barked it out in bitter amusement. 'I don't care who you are; your whole family should be burnt to the ground. You're enemies of the Library, all of you.'

'*Allies* of the Library, you mean,' Brendan said and bowed slightly. 'Though I'll grant you, it's a strange turn of events for us too. I've got no love for my feckless brother. If I lay hands on him, I promise, you can have him, sir.'

'It's *my lord*. You are speaking to the Obscurist Magnus.'

'Oh.' He cocked the eyebrow with the scar in it. 'Thought the Obscurist Magnus was a woman. My error, *my lord*.'

He couldn't resist mocking the man, even though he knew how dangerous it was.

The Obscurist gave him a thin, angry smile. 'She was,' he said. 'Dead and forgotten now.' He took a few steps past, then made a show of turning around as if he'd only just thought of something. 'Please tell your beloved brother that his young lady

Morgan is in good hands. I've matched her with our brightest Obscurist. I'm sure their children will be *most* gifted.'

It was obvious enough that the idiot thought that might goad him into some fit of temper, but he'd chosen the wrong Brightwell for that.

Brendan shrugged. 'Well, doubt I'll be talking to Jess anytime soon, seeing as how he's cut ties with me as well as you. But I'm sure he'd thank you for your consideration.'

Whatever the Obscurist had been looking for, the bland answer didn't please him. He stalked off without another word.

Neksa said, without looking up from the paperwork she was shuffling on her desk, 'Don't keep him waiting.'

Brendan nodded and noted the slight tremble in her hands, the colour in her face. *She still cares*, he thought. He hardly deserved it, of course, and he wondered what she was so worried about. His father's power protected him . . . and if it didn't, there was absolutely nothing he could do to prevent coming to a bad end.

He reached out and touched her on the cheek. For an instant, she froze, and her eyes moved to lock on his. 'It's all right, love,' he told her. 'I'll be all right.'

Her mouth opened, but she said nothing.

He walked into the Archivist's office.

There was no one inside. Just the desk, the silent automata, and a chill in the air that might have just been his imagination.

His breath went cold in his chest. His fingers went numb. And he realised that the cold wasn't his imagination at all.

'Sit,' a voice said, and for a disorienting moment, he thought it was the statue of the goddess Bast speaking to him . . . and then he realised that something very wrong was happening. The air smelt sickly sweet, too thick, too heavy in his lungs. He felt himself moving, not to a chair, but to collapse to a sitting position on the carpeted floor like a dropped puppet. *This is wrong*, he thought, and the word rang in his head like a silver bell: *wrong, wrong, wrooooooong* . . . It smeared into a silver mist and was gone, and he sat, waiting, for the goddess to speak again.

'Tell me your name,' the voice said.

'Brendan Brightwell,' he said.

'Again.'

'Brendan Brightwell.'

'Again.'

'Brendan Lyell Sinclair Brightwell,' he said. He felt free now, floating outside his heavy, inert body. 'Son and heir of Callum Brightwell.'

'Did you come here with a valid offer from Callum Brightwell?'

'Yes.'

'Do you intend to deceive us?'

'No.'

'Do you intend to cheat us?'

Brendan felt himself grinning. 'I'd be foolish if I didn't try,' he said. 'Though if you make it profitable enough, I'll play straight. Father's orders.'

He heard another voice, low and in the background. An angry old man. *Cheat me, will they? I'll see them all hanged.* Hanged, like Liam, on a dirty gibbet in London when Brendan was just a boy. He remembered watching. It had been an object lesson in the price of failure. His brother Jess had tried to turn away, had cried. But Brendan had watched, dry-eyed, and he'd won his father's approval that day. It wasn't that he hadn't loved Liam, though the boy was much older than he and Jess; it was that he understood, as Jess never had, that death was the cost of play. Great rewards required real risks.

Why was he thinking of Liam? Hadn't thought of him in ages. But now he remembered his elder brother ruffling his hair, sneaking him treats when no one was looking, especially when he'd been exiled to his room in punishment. Liam had died younger than Brendan was now.

He felt a trickle of wetness on his cheeks but couldn't raise his hands to wipe it away.

'What is your name?' the voice asked again.

'Brendan Brightwell.'

'And the name of your brother?'

'The live one, or the dead one?'

Whispered conversation he couldn't follow. 'The live one.'

'Jess,' he said. 'Jess Brightwell.'

'Do you love your brother?'

'Of course.'

'Would you betray him?'

Brendan fell silent. Remembered Liam on the gallows, waiting for the drop. In that last moment, Liam had looked straight at him.

'Yes,' he said. 'If I had to.' It broke something inside him with a sharp, cold snap. 'Don't make me.'

'Where is your brother?'

'I don't know.'

'At your home?'

'I don't know.'

The voice took on a dark amusement. 'But you'll tell me where your home is, won't you?'

'No,' Brendan said. 'Before I left England, I took the precaution of having that particular memory blocked by a Mesmer. I can't lead you to my father, or the press. Or my brother, if that's who you want most.'

'Why did you come here?'

'To make a deal. Simple as that.'

'Do you intend to betray the Archivist or the Great Library?'

'No,' Brendan said. 'Not unless my father decides there's a better deal elsewhere.'

Honest answers, every one. Silence ticked by like a leaking tap, *drip drip drip* of seconds, minutes, and he waited, frozen in place. His legs were going numb. He wasn't sure he could stand up even if the goddess allowed it.

Then it all began again.

And again.

And again.

His voice had gone hoarse by the time silence fell at last, and his skin felt raw from the cold. He was so tired it was all he could do to hold himself upright, and he was pitifully grateful when the voice of the goddess finally said, 'We're finished here.'

A fresh blast of air hit him in the face, fluttering his hair and clothes, and he pulled in a breath of something that ached sharply in his lungs. He felt weak, and then exhausted beyond any reasonable measure, and pitched sideways onto the carpet as if his muscles had been cut. He gasped in the cool, clear air, and as the fog began to subside in his head he knew what had happened. *Gas. He'd been drugged.* But not only that. There had been a compulsion as well, something centring in the bracelet he wore. An Obscurist who'd trained as a Mesmer – and a powerful one – had been manipulating him. Trying to pry the lid off his brain and stir around in there.

The sense of nausea that swept over him made him glad he'd collapsed; if he'd been upright, no doubt he'd have ruined the carpet. It subsided before it grew too desperate, and he slowly rolled over on his back as a door at the rear of the room opened to admit the Archivist and an impressive retinue of armed guards.

'You bastard,' Brendan gasped, and tried to get up. He failed but kept trying until he finally managed to climb to his feet and stagger to the nearest chair. He fell into it with sick gratitude and cradled his pounding head in both hands. 'What was the point of that?'

The Archivist seated himself behind his desk and fussed with the placement of his Codex, blank paper, pens . . . and then sat back and tented his fingers together as he stared at Brendan. 'I had to be certain,' he said. 'You and your brother are so startlingly alike. I needed reassurance that I was not dealing with the wrong Brightwell. That would have been a fatal error.'

'Well, you aren't,' Brendan snapped. 'And if you *ever* do anything like this to me again, the deal's off and I'm gone, and my family *will not take it well*. Understand?'

'Of course.' The Archivist's tone was smooth as melting butter. 'I wouldn't dream of subjecting you to it again. You are now a respected business partner – one I shall have to treat with care. I commend you for your honesty, young Brightwell. I much prefer to have loyalty and limits stated up front, especially when embarking on such a partnership. Now. How quickly can your father deliver the plans for this printing machine?'

'Thought you *had* plans for it,' Brendan said. 'Wasn't that what you threw the German lad in prison for, drawing them?'

'The Black Archives where such things are stored became a liability. We . . . closed them.'

'Meaning?'

'The contents of the Black Archives are gone,' the Archivist said. 'Better that dangerous information be lost for ever than inflicted on an unready world, don't you agree?'

Brendan shrugged. 'The more you burn, the rarer the volumes

we sell. So that means our printing machine is the only version there is? Interesting. The price might have just gone up.'

'I expected nothing less from you,' the Archivist said. 'But the price will remain as we agreed. If I find your father has broken trust with me, if these machines appear *anywhere else*, I will have you executed in a way that will burn in the memory of anyone tempted to cross the Library again, and I will hunt down every single member of your family, however remote, and do the same to them. Your father. Brother. Mother. Every cousin. Babes in arms. Are we understood, Brendan Brightwell? But if you keep your agreement, I will keep mine. Believe me.'

In Brendan's experience of men who thought themselves honest (and rarely were), the phrase *believe me* was a clear signal they intended to do the opposite of what they said. But he nodded. The black storm inside his head wasn't lessening, and he felt an unsettling tremble in his muscles, but for the purposes of this meeting, he'd have to manage through it. 'We'll require immediate payment in Alexandrian *geneih*, of course. English currency isn't worth much at the moment, given the Welsh rampaging all over our country.'

'Already done. The funds have been sent to the bank your father specified. He has been in contact directly, of course.'

That woke prickles of alarm down Brendan's spine. If the old man was negotiating directly now, what did that make him? Nothing but a hostage. And, most likely, an object lesson.

'Then are we done here? Because I'd like a stiff drink and something for my headache.'

'I wouldn't drink,' the Archivist said. 'It would probably kill you just now, and that would be an awkward situation. Best thing to do is to stay awake, stay active, and let it work out of your system. In fact, I'll help with that. Your assistance will be helpful today.'

'With what exactly?'

'Captain Wahl will tell you. You may go.' The Archivist brushed the back of a hand at him, as if sweeping him away like an annoying bug. And just like that, he was forgotten.

That was one of the more annoying things about this evil old bastard, Brendan thought: he could sincerely threaten to peel your skin from your bones one moment and treat you as beneath his notice the next. And for a moment, Brendan seriously thought about using the dagger he'd lifted from the High Garda captain while she'd been searching him and burying it right in the old man's eye, just for the sheer justice of it.

But that didn't seem like a wise waste of his life.

The female captain, the one with the ice-cold eyes and Nordic heritage (and scars), stepped forward and fixed her unsettling stare on Brendan's face. 'You're with me,' she said. 'Step a toe out of line, and I'll leave you dead for crows. Understand?'

'Charming,' he said, and gave her his best grin. 'I'm sure we're going to get along wonderfully.'

CHAPTER FOURTEEN

Captain Wahl ushered him out of the Archivist's suite through yet another different path, this one avoiding the Hall of Gods altogether; the Archivist had a frankly annoying number of ways to avoid his enemies, and every path seemed designed to end in disaster for someone bent on disturbing the old man's calm. Wahl's route marched him through a series of nondescript rooms, each looking the same; he supposed they were waiting rooms but could see no signs directing visitors to them. *If you have to ask*, he thought, *you shouldn't even be here.*

'Captain,' he said, as they passed through the seventh of such rooms, occupied by empty chairs and shelves of Blanks for the entertainment of non-existent occupants, 'exactly what are you planning for me?'

'If you're worried I'm marching you to execution, I'm not,' she said. 'But I do have full authority to leave you dead in the road if you try to escape.'

'Yes, you made that very clear; thank you for clarifying. I meant, what is it you want my expertise *for*, exactly?'

She didn't bother to answer, only lengthened her stride, which made Brendan simmer; his brother Jess enjoyed vigorous exercise as well as bookish pursuits, but Brendan only liked to run when chased. And her pace seemed designed to punish him for his lack of enthusiasm.

They came through a doorway guarded by two automata into a stone courtyard; this one wasn't decorated with winsome gardens or floating lotus flowers. It was utilitarian, a rally point for soldiers, and Brendan took quick stock of it, noting the access points, the defences, and where he stood in relation to the Lighthouse of Alexandria, which was plainly visible. He'd need to sketch a map later, but he had a facility for details. And plans.

Since Wahl seemed unwilling to part with details, he watched *her*. She seemed comfortable and assured, but there was something about the ten guards travelling around them, spreading out once they achieved the street outside the Serapeum, that made him wonder. She had them on a ranger patrol, looking for threats. Not looking at *him*. That seemed odd, if he was counted as any kind of threat.

They encountered nothing, and they made quick time as they jogged through the streets. People and vehicles made way for them, and he felt the heavy weight of stares and knew gossip would be flowing in their wake. *Stupid way to travel*, he thought, though at least he wasn't out of breath yet. *City's full of High Garda carriers. This is doing nothing but flaunting the Archivist's power.*

'Where are we going?' he asked her again, more loudly this time. They'd passed the University districts, headed down from the Lighthouse, and now they were in one of the poorer, more anonymous sections of town, crowded with merchants and cheap, temporary housing that looked ripe to fall at any moment. Cleaner and brighter than London, but he knew the type of neighbourhood well. It was where deals were made, both legitimate and criminal.

'I wanted you because you're said to be connected in the smuggling trade. You might be able to convince your brothers in crime to give up peacefully.'

'We call them cousins, and *wait*, are you mad? We're going to raid a smuggler's den? You should have brought more bodies. These won't even provide a good shelter to hide behind once they fall.' She sent him an impatient glance and increased the pace, which was annoying. 'I'm very serious, Captain. These aren't just idiots hiding secret book collections in their private homes! These are hard people who survive in the hardest city on earth for their trade. You do *not* go after them like this!'

'This is just my personal escort, Brightwell,' she said. 'My army is already waiting.'

'Where?'

She whistled, and the entire contingent of Elites shifted from a jog to a smooth, quiet walk as they approached a corner. Brendan's nerves prickled, but he couldn't see anything out of the ordinary.

'Up,' she said. 'Look up.'

He did, and felt his heart shrink in an instinctive spasm of dread, because there were sphinxes perched motionless on roofs. Large ones. And as he looked down, he realised that they were on the ground, too, crouched motionless in shadows.

'Where are we going?' he asked her.

'Straight ahead. The building with the blue trim.'

That was a generous description; the trim might have been blue an age ago, but it was a weathered, flaking, indeterminate colour now, on a building that sagged as if it might melt completely in the next rain. A ramshackle thing made for knocking down, at least to the casual eye.

But he recognised the precautions.

The windows were, of course, barred; that was no surprise in such a neighbourhood. But they were also dark, and he thought they were almost certainly covered by steel plates. The door looked old, but it would be reinforced and highly armoured. Inside, the place would be a fortress, with dozens of tunnels for escape.

It was large enough to be a major storage point for Red Ibrahim's business, though the old fox would be careful to keep visible traffic to a minimum.

'Well?' Wahl raised a fist, and her escort came to a halt along with her. 'Go and make them surrender. That's why you're here.'

'They'll kill me.'

She shrugged. 'I assume you're hard to kill. But if you want to stay here and refuse, we'll find out fast.'

'Do I at least get a weapon?'

'Besides the dagger you lifted from me earlier? No.' She pulled her sidearm and aimed it straight at his chest. 'Go on. I'm almost sure the sphinxes won't tear into you.'

He felt sweat break out at the back of his neck. This was a death sentence, and it was blindingly clear to him in that moment that they intended to have him killed, but with the excuse that he'd been killed *by smugglers*. A neat solution to the Archivist's puzzle of how to get rid of his annoying visitor, while also claiming innocence to his newly made ally.

He took two steps towards the building. A sphinx's wings unfurled somewhere above him with a faint, metallic ring, and he glanced up.

He was aware of a flash of light from the building he was facing, and then a hammer blow to his chest, and being lifted off his feet and thrown like a toy. Fragments of images crowded in, all chaotic: a massive red fireball rising to the sky. A sphinx falling out of the sky and crashing to the pavement. Two High Garda soldiers cut to pieces by flying metal in splashes of vivid crimson.

He landed on his side and rolled until a hard wall crushed him to a stop, and for a moment just panted for breath and waited for his dazed eyes to come back into focus.

When they did, he saw a slaughterhouse. Half of Wahl's soldiers were down, blood on the street and splattered on dirty walls. There was nothing left of the building they'd been approaching but crumbled walls and burning rubble.

Those of them still standing were in a white-hot fight for their lives. Sphinxes were tearing apart surrounding buildings, trying to get at those firing from shelter, but as soon as an automaton succeeded in forcing its way in, it was faced with hails of hellish gunfire. He saw three sprawled, motionless machines. Red Ibrahim's people had a way to kill them effectively enough, though he heard tortured screams from a building on the left where a sphinx had ripped through the roof and descended on unprepared residents.

Innocents, perhaps. But probably dead in seconds, if so.

'I found the traitor!'

He hardly heard the shout; it sounded like a whisper in his blast-numbed ears. He looked around, dazed, and then happened to look *up* and saw a man with a red scarf over his face aiming a rifle down at him.

He rolled away at the last instant, bullets peppering the ground and building around him. None of them found their mark, but some came far too close, and then he saw something falling towards him. It was just a shape, indistinct, and he put his hands up to protect his head.

He caught a thrown bottle of Greek Fire that, by all rights, should have reduced him to burnt bones on a molten street, and once he realised what he held, he nearly dropped it anyway, out of sheer surprise. The cap popped loose and rolled away, and the liquid sloshed and rippled with half-seen flames. He steadied his hands and pulled it down to rest on his chest, which was all he could do at that moment. No throwing it back without splashing it all over himself.

More bullets rattled down, and he curled carefully on his side and hugged the wall, with the deadly bottle as protected as he could manage. If a bullet hit him, he'd likely survive. If it hit the flask, he wouldn't.

He stayed where he was, acutely aware of the deadly weight held against his chest, and stared at the dirty wall in front of his face as an eerie silence finally fell. A beetle wandered up the scarred surface as if all the danger around it meant nothing. *Lucky you*, he thought. Though the beetle would burn just as surely as he if this glass container cracked.

'Brightwell?' Wahl's voice was breathless. He turned his head at an awkward angle and looked up at her. One side of her face was bloody, and she had a half-dozen bullet dents in the black armour over her chest. 'Surprised to find you alive.'

'Surprised myself,' he said. His voice sounded as shaky as his hands felt. 'Mind taking this?'

She spotted the Greek Fire and took in a sharp breath, but she retrieved the cap and made it safe before picking it up. He rolled over on his back and sucked in a couple of deep, cooling breaths before climbing to his feet again. As he leant against the wall, he counted the soldiers standing and realised that most of those who'd been in her escort were down.

A sphinx was systematically ripping apart something that had once been human at the far end of the street. It was damaged, with one wing gone and one leg dragging uselessly, but that didn't make it any less horrific.

'You were right,' Wahl said. For the first time, she seemed to have a flicker of humanity in her eyes. Not for him, of course. For the men and women of her squad. 'We should have brought an entire company. Not even the sphinxes can stop murderers who don't mind destroying their own headquarters. We can only hope we can find one still alive to question.'

He didn't tell her that Red Ibrahim certainly knew she was coming and that the building had likely already been emptied of everything of value. That the ones fighting were almost certainly hired mercenaries, with no connection back to his real organisation.

If she had been better at this, Brendan would have buried the dagger in her and found a spare piece of shrapnel to shove into the wound. Blamed it on the explosion. But she wasn't. She had no real understanding of how smugglers worked, and that was a good thing. Better to keep her in charge than someone like Jess's Captain Santi, who almost certainly wouldn't have made these mistakes.

He thought, *I hope I don't have to kill you, Captain Wahl.*

But he knew full well he would if it came to that.

Family first.

CHAPTER FIFTEEN

Wahl walked him to the door of his sad little house, and Brendan walked inside, grimaced at the wreckage of the place, and wearily slammed the door. His head ached fiercely, he had bruises in places he'd never been bruised before, and he reeked of smoke and blood. He couldn't recall feeling this tired in a long time. All he wanted to do was sleep now, and the sight of the rumpled small bed drew him like a magnet. He toppled onto it facedown and felt darkness descend frighteningly quickly.

In two hours, Jess Brightwell opened his eyes.

On waking, you'll remember everything, he heard a voice say. It took him a moment to place it, but then he remembered the carriage ride to the Serapeum, and Elsinore Quest. *You will remember that you are Jess Brightwell. You asked me to mesmer you into believing you were your twin, and so I did. It shouldn't last more than a day at most. You'll come back to yourself as soon as you sleep, and remember all the events of the day as if you did them yourself. You'll remember that you asked me to do this, most especially. I insist you remember that, because I don't wish to end up at the wrong end of your knife.*

Jess felt sick, and for a moment he stayed where he was, flat on the bed, until he felt comfortable in his skin again. His heart was racing, skin flushed and prickling with alarm, and, *blessed*

Heron, he ached from the abuse his imaginary brother's body had taken. Quest's mesmer skills were incredibly well honed, to convince him that he was Brendan to such an extent; he'd thought differently, acted differently. Even moved differently. He'd even flirted with Neksa.

But it had all worked. He'd feared interrogation, though he'd expected it to be physical rather than at the hands of an Obscurist and mind-altering gas. Thank God he'd asked Quest to specifically shield the part of his memory that had to do with his father's location. He'd feared the Archivist would decide to torture that last bit out of him, and though torture hadn't been involved, the question had most certainly been asked, and an answer compelled.

But Brendan – the Brendan that Quest had created in him – had been able to swear to a great many blatant lies with perfect sincerity.

Whatever Alvaro Santiago had paid the Mesmer on Jess's behalf, it wasn't half enough.

Jess stood up. He felt every wound that Brendan had collected and recalled in sharp detail the nearly deadly day he'd had. Including the gentle, intimate touch on Neksa's cheek . . . *which she'd allowed,* or at least been too shocked to protest. He wasn't certain yet whether that had been inspired or a terrible mistake. Time would tell.

He opened the tap at the sink and washed his dirty face in icy water, then stood for some moments staring into the mirror. The difference between himself and his twin was so small, and yet so large it was like walking a high wire above a furnace. Exhausting. *Maybe I should have Quest convince me I really am my brother for the duration. Could be restful.*

But no. He'd need both sides of his personality to get through this, because now that the Archivist believed him . . . somewhat . . . there was much to do.

He checked the Blank, but once again, there was no message from Morgan. *It isn't safe for her yet*, he told himself, but the worry gnawed harder. Morgan had been confident she could find a way to get around the Iron Tower's restraints. What if she hadn't? What could have happened to her in there? He found himself staring at the page for far too long before he slammed the book shut, ate a meagre meal he didn't taste, and fell into a troubled, dream-crowded sleep.

He woke up to a pounding on the door and squinted at the window. Wasn't yet light outside, and it took all his control not to bury his head under the pillow and seek sleep again. Not that it would matter, he knew; they'd just come in and drag him out of bed if he tried.

A fresh High Garda Elite contingent stood outside, glittering with sharp edges in the dull predawn light. Jess wondered what had happened to Wahl.

'Come with us,' the man in charge said, and turned to head down the path. The rest of his soldiers waited for Jess to step out, and he debated it for a long few seconds before closing the door and following. They closed in around him. No carriage today; they'd brought a sturdily armoured carrier. *Good.* The more the High Garda was worried about Red Ibrahim's retaliations, the less they'd pay attention to their prisoner. He didn't doubt they still considered him one.

The carrier was standard: bench seats along both sides, hanging straps for those who didn't earn a seat. Jess was given the seat closest to the metal barrier and the driver – and the farthest from the exit. No one seemed inclined to make conversation, and he was still regretting getting out of bed and not insisting on coffee. He put his head back against the metal as the carrier's doors slammed, the engine hissed and gears engaged, and they glided rapidly towards their destination.

He expected to emerge at the Serapeum and be led through yet another confusing tangle of corridors, but instead, he found himself at the Alexandria Colosseum. An old Roman import, still maintained and in use; the vast structure could hold as many as fifty thousand, and while the old blood sports had been long outlawed, the more civilised contests remained popular. 'We're taking in a football game?' he asked. He'd played it with other children in London, a ragged, barely serviceable ball kicked back and forth and chased to grimy landmarks that served as goals. Hadn't played it since he was twelve, and had never attended a game, though they had been as popular in London as anywhere.

But there were no happy sport fans here. The place was deserted, and the perimeter iron fences had automaton guards. It felt eerie and as ghostly as the departed spirits of the Caesars.

The High Garda surrounded him in a tight cordon, and he was pushed forward . . . to a guarded entrance.

And a downward-sloping ramp, lit by greenish glows on both sides.

The descent was harrowing. The place smelt like centuries of death and blood, and a stomach-turning electric feeling crawled his nerves. *Nothing good has ever happened here*, he thought. These weren't the changing rooms for the teams, or the public galleries. This was ancient, and awful.

It was also in use.

The ramp levelled out into a long, broader hallway, still lit with the same glows that, though bright enough, cast a sickly pall over pale stone and iron doors, all tightly shut. The High Garda captain pushed one open and said, 'In.'

If I go in there, I'm never coming out. The whole place

screamed at him to fight as hard and as dirty as he could, and stay alive for another moment.

But that was a fight he couldn't possibly win, and he had little choice but to limp inside.

The door slammed behind him, but he hardly noticed. He was too surprised by what spread out before him.

He stood on an overlooking gallery, and beneath it was spread a neat, orderly, modern workshop, with hundreds of tables and Scholars and mechanical technicians moving among them. Automata, half-built or under repair, occupied most of the space: sphinxes, both large and small. Lions. Spartans. Something in the back, veiled behind cloth, that looked more massive than any of the rest, but he couldn't make out any details except a ridged back.

The Archivist waited at the railing.

'The mission yesterday was not what I'd hoped for,' said the Archivist. 'Though I understand I can't legitimately blame it on you.'

'Did you blame it on Captain Wahl?'

'Captain Wahl understands that failure is not acceptable for High Garda Elites,' the old man said. 'Don't worry, I won't ask you to be our stalking horse for the next raid. Your father was informed of the . . . difficulties. He was very plain that you were to be treated as a guest.'

'I'm sure he asked very nicely.'

'In his way.' The Archivist looked out over the workshop. 'This used to be the space where condemned criminals were held before they were brought into the amphitheatre to fight for their lives. Savage times. We've put it to better use.'

'Thought I was going to the lions,' Jess said, in Brendan's slightly sarcastic tone. 'Is this supposed to frighten me?' He leant on the railing beside the old man. There were, of course, guards, guards everywhere, and off to his left and behind them sat a massive automaton lion, ready to spring if he made the slightest mistake. Tempting, to think about tossing the old man over the railing. He imagined how easy it would be.

But it wouldn't save anyone else, either.

'Caution you to mind your step,' the Archivist said. 'The rigorous questioning you went through has established your identity. Whatever doubts I have now are simply to do with the general untrustworthiness of your . . . type.'

'Criminals?' Jess let loose a fierce grin. 'Reasonable. But we're in business. And I'll keep my word because it's in my da's best interests.'

'Perhaps. As you know, it's unwise to cross me. I made the promise to empty France of its pernicious rebels, and I did it. Destroying your entire family would be a wave of my little finger.'

'And I could shove you off this balcony,' Jess said. 'But I won't.' He leant back from the rail and faced the Archivist fully. 'When do I see the books?'

'Soon. But first I thought you'd be amenable to telling me more about this smuggler operating so effectively under my nose. Since he and his band almost took your life yesterday.'

Risks of doing business, Jess thought. That applied to his danger yesterday and what he was going to do now. 'That will cost you. It's no small thing for me to betray someone like him.'

'If you are loyal to me and to the Library, you will be protected. You won't need to pander to your rivals any more. All I want is for you to—'

The Archivist paused at a cry of alarm from below in the workshop, and Jess had a bare second to glance in that direction and take in the sphinx that had launched itself into the air, gliding on metallic eagle wings. Its back legs were not a lion's; they were knife-sharp talons.

It was coming straight for them.

The Archivist's guards reacted with admirable speed, as unexpected as it was; a hail of gunfire shattered the air.

It bounced off the armour that coated the sphinx. This was no ordinary automaton, Jess realised. And when he took his riveted gaze from it and looked back at the workshop, he saw that the Scholar who'd been standing by that table was still watching, unafraid. Unmoved.

This is an assassination. The Scholar had been waiting for this opportunity. And now, all Jess had to do was stand back and allow it to happen. Most of the workshop below was in chaos, technicians and Scholars scrambling for safety. There were a dozen guards in the room, and they were all focused on firing on the sphinx circling above, to little effect. No one would fault him for saving himself.

But if there was one thing that would earn him his freedom to do as he pleased, it would be this. No more questions. No more doubts.

Much as he wanted to see this old man's guts strewn on the floor, he needed to save him.

He reached a lightning-fast decision, grabbed the Archivist, and shoved him away from the banister an instant before the sphinx's talons sheared through the metal and cracked the stone floor. He kept the old man moving, running, dodging, on the gallery as the soldiers poured more fire into the attacking automaton. *Off switch*, he thought. *Must be an off switch!*

He turned and threw himself back at it, hand grabbing for the neck of the thing as the smooth bronze face contorted, the needle-sharp teeth snapped at his arm. His searching fingers slid on smooth, featureless metal.

No off switch. Not there, where it should be. Unless the

Scholar had deliberately removed any chance of shutting the evil thing off. *I'm dead*, he thought. Time seemed to stretch. He saw the sharp claws extruding out of the lion paws; they were an instant away from gutting him, and if those teeth got a good hold it would rip his throat out in a bloody spray.

In that moment, he remembered something. It came in a sudden rush of light, colour, sound, smell . . . as vivid as if he was there again, standing in Thomas's filthy cell beneath the streets of Rome. Drawings etched on the walls and on dirty scraps of paper.

A beautifully detailed automaton.

Thomas designed this thing. His plans.

And a circled notation with two words.

It might be nothing. It might be everything.

Jess gasped in a breath and whispered '*Pax Romana.*'

The sphinx blinked its red eyes, stopped, then pivoted and soared up to a perch at the highest point in the workshop, on a stout wooden scaffold. It perched and settled with a hissing ruffle of metal wings.

The light went out in its eyes.

'No!' the Scholar cried below, the one who'd set the thing in motion. He was only a few years older than Jess, but in that moment terror made him sound like a child. 'No! He has to die! Why—'

He picked up a sharp knife from the bench beside him and ran, but it was a useless effort. Whether he was on the attack or running for his life, it didn't matter; he was shot dead in two steps and collapsed heavily to the floor. There was a hole the size of an apple in his head, and when Jess looked up, he saw one of the High Garda was lowering a rifle.

The Archivist was pale and sweating, and as Jess turned towards him, the old man stumbled and caught himself against a wall, then slid down it. That was the face of a man who'd seen his own death, and clearly, and didn't care for the warning.

Jess crouched beside him and tried to check his pulse, but the Archivist struck his hand away. 'Don't touch me,' he said. 'What did you do?'

'Nothing,' Jess said. He hoped that the Archivist, in the press of the chaos and fear, hadn't heard the whispered words. From the wonder in his eyes, he hadn't. 'I thought it was about to gut me like a fish. Thing must be broken.'

'Broken,' the Archivist repeated, and looked past him at the now-still automaton. Its eyes were dark and empty. It might have been an inert statue, and perhaps now it was, after those words. Jess's heart felt like it was exploding in his chest with every fast beat, and he smelt the rank, burning stench of his own sweat now.

'Yes, yes, of course, you're correct. It was malfunctioning.' The old man gulped in several shallow breaths, and some colour crept back into his face. 'It couldn't defeat the safeguards I had put in place. There was no real danger. It could never have actually harmed me.'

Jess felt a bitter burn of a laugh deep in his throat, but he swallowed it. 'Didn't know that,' he said. 'Thought I'd best look after my family's interests.'

'So you did, lad. So you did. Whether there was any risk or not, you showed extraordinary courage. I won't forget it.' The old man held out his hand, which was trembling, though his voice had taken on its veneer of calm again. Jess grasped it and pulled him to his feet.

If he expected more effusive thanks, he was disappointed; the Archivist turned and stalked to the High Garda soldier who'd put the bullet in the Scholar's head, snatched the rifle away, and flung it into the corner. 'You. What were you thinking?'

The soldier was a young, muscular woman who had the look of South Asia to her features, and she clearly didn't expect to be attacked for what she'd done. She took a half step back, shot a wide glance at her commander, then raised her chin and snapped to attention. 'Sir, I acted to prevent the danger from reaching you.'

'The danger? That idiot was half a room away. How do you think we'll learn anything from a man with half his brain on the floor?'

'Sir—' the High Garda captain began. It was a mistake. The old man hated having seen his mortality, and his own fear. Would have been far wiser to keep out of his notice.

'Quiet!' The Archivist's shout was full throated and vicious, and the captain froze. All the soldiers went to attention, instinctively. 'Is that how you train your *best soldiers*? Because these are the best, are they not? Or are you trying to have me killed as well?'

'No, sir.' The captain's face was rigid, his eyes glassy and narrowed. 'I would give my life to—'

'I only saw one life being thrown in the way of that thing, and that was a *criminal's*. You're demoted, Captain. Get out of my sight.' The Archivist spun towards the woman who'd fired the shot. 'You have an hour to depart the city, or I set a sphinx to hunt you down. *Get out.* I won't have you in that uniform. Go back to whatever backwater province the Library found you in.'

Whatever resentment they felt, whatever shock, the soldiers took it without expression now. Both nodded and left through the door Jess had entered.

Another soldier took a solid step forward. He briskly opened his Codex and wrote inside it. 'We will escort you out of here, sir.'

'You will *not*. Get another team in place to take me home. You're all sent back to the High Garda. If any of you had been fit to be Elites, you would have prevented this from happening at all.'

It was a breathtaking, petulant show of power. The Archivist had just destroyed the careers of a dozen people who had risen through the ranks and were accounted the cream of the High Garda Elites . . . for what? The worst of it was a failure to wound, when all their training had been instructing them to instantly kill anyone who raised a hand to him. The whole thing was petty and brutal.

That, Jess thought, *is how you destroy the loyalty of the High Garda.* He knew how passionate these soldiers were about their duty, about their ideals . . . but here stood the man who personified those ideals, and he was as flawed and petty as any other. If he'd been a good leader – and he must have been, once – he'd long forgotten how to inspire.

He could only punish in the hopes of keeping his uncertain grip on the reins of power.

'Sir,' Jess said, and bowed when the old man's sharp gaze pierced him. 'Do you want me to write a report to you about the Alexandrian smugglers?'

'Yes. Go. You may requisition the appropriate supplies. Neksa will see you are given approval.'

'Then I'll be on my way.'

'Yes. Jess?'

It was a good job that Jess was looking away at that moment; the situation had rattled him, and Jess *nearly* answered to it.

But the extra beat gave him a second to set himself before he looked up, innocent and grinning, to say, 'Got me confused with my brother again, Archivist. But I won't hold it against you.'

'Yes.' The Archivist's eyes were as cold as death. 'Yes, of course. Brendan.'

Then he turned and walked out, waiting for a bullet to find

him, or a sphinx's claws. The sound of his boot heels seemed very loud. Very final.

Then he was down the hallway and up the ramp and in the clean outside air, and he gasped and took a moment to lean against an ancient stone column and thank whatever gods were looking after him these days.

No. Not gods.

In the moment when he knew he was about to die, it hadn't been a god who'd come to him. It had been a memory of Thomas.

What made him finally move was not the frowning faces of the guards protecting the carrier, or the angle of the sun; it was the knowledge that Thomas depended on him. So did Wolfe, and Khalila, Glain, Dario, Captain Santi.

And Morgan.

He looked up and found the black spire of the Iron Tower. Birds circled it, though none landed; whether that was Obscurist power or the material the thing was made from, even they had the good sense to avoid it.

He walked towards the gates and past the carrier, and though the guards surely would have shot him dead yesterday, today they let him pass. He owed consideration to the dead Scholar below, with his useless attempt at rebellion. And he couldn't waste the gift that man's blood had given him: the trust of the Archivist and the freedom to move without constraints.

It was time to start a war.

EPHEMERA

Text of a letter from Dario Santiago to Khalila Seif. Destroyed by Santiago without delivery prior to their departure from England.

As you well know, lovely flower, I am rarely at a loss for words, but you have a way of turning my own flaws against me, and my own virtues, too. Though which of those my eloquence might be, I leave to you to decide.

I'm setting this down on paper because I know that in the moment, when I am looking at you and I know that the course of my life rests on the words you will say . . . I don't know if I will have the courage to speak my mind. No – not my mind. My heart. You know I protect that particular organ with more care than any other; I hold everyone at a distance, partly because I genuinely find it hard to care for people, and partly because I was hurt often when I was young. Always by those closest to me.

I say that not for sympathy – why would you have any for that? Everyone has been hurt – but because I need for you to see that I want the opposite with you. What began as flattery and, yes, a casual kind of lust, has become something entirely different. I treasure you. I honour you.

I know that you are nothing I deserve, and everything I want in my life.

And so, I intend to ask you to marry me. I will do it at the very worst moment, because I am hopeless and stupid in such things, and I fully expect you will tell me with all kindness that you would rather become a nun than marry me. (Does the religion of Islam have nuns? I apologise. I should know this by now.)

But I will ask. And when I do, please know that I stand before you an honest man, with my heart for the first time wide-open. I know you can pierce it with a word.

But better dead at your feet than never having tried.

There, my eloquence is back.

Perhaps this will go better than I expected.

PART SIX

KHALILA

CHAPTER SIXTEEN

Khalila wrote letters to the families of dead men while sitting in a lush hotel waiting room in Cadiz, after begging sheets of paper and a good pen from the desk clerk. Outside of the hotel's windows, a storm still raged, but the force was slowly dying. The ship that had delivered them would be departing soon, seeking cover in the last of the gale.

The captain had been paid very well to report that all of the prisoners had been killed during a rebellion and thrown into the sea . . . and Anit would make certain that he kept his promises. Whether the Library would believe the captain's report or not, the truth was unprovable at the moment, and that would sow confusion and buy time. But the clock should be moving quickly, and instead, here they were: waiting.

'You shouldn't bother with that now,' Dario said from where he watched her write. She was currently writing in Portuguese, to the family of a sailor from Lisbon. 'There'll be a lot more men lost before this is done. And the sailors on that ship would have killed us, you know.'

'And I would hope they'd seek forgiveness for it,' she replied. 'But I am not responsible for their souls, only for mine.'

'Of course.' He didn't understand that, she thought, but at least he respected it. And she respected him for it. 'At least it keeps you occupied. I should have known his envoy would be late. Typical royal punctuality.'

'The weather is foul out there, and you're too impatient. Have some of . . . what is this, again?'

'*Tortilla de patatas*,' he said, and cut himself a broad slice of the round egg dish. 'Eggs and potatoes. Delicious.'

'And that?' She pointed at something that resembled a bread tube. He cut off a piece and handed it to her. She forced herself to chew and swallow. It was better than she'd expected. She'd eaten a bite or two of the tortilla, enough to keep hunger at bay but not enough to feel she was sated. She didn't want to be comfortable, not while writing the news of a person's death. It seemed wrong.

'Bluefin tuna. You like it?'

'It's good. But I'm not very hungry.'

'I'll be happy to finish it.' His tone was light, but he was restlessly shifting and staring grimly at the lobby doors. 'I hate wasting time. While you're scribbling and I'm nibbling, God only knows what's happening to the others.'

'Thomas and Glain? Captain Santi?'

'You're deliberately misunderstanding me.'

'Apparently.' She signed her name to the bottom of the letter, folded it, and put it into an envelope she'd already marked with the family's address in Lisbon. 'You're usually less concerned about the fate of Jess Brightwell.'

'That's because my ultimate survival generally doesn't depend on him.'

'Dario.'

'*Mi amor*, it isn't that I don't care what happens. He's a good ally. A fine one to have at your side. I even count him as a friend. Is it wrong to say that in other circumstances, I doubt our paths would have crossed except when he steals me blind?'

She shook her head. Dario was in a foul mood, scowling now at the doorway and toying with the pearl earring dangling from his left earlobe. He'd traded someone aboard the ship for it, or else won it at dice. She preferred not to know. It did suit him, though. So did the clean, new clothes he was wearing – black shirt, black trousers in a particularly attractive cut that she really shouldn't have noticed. A flash of red lining in his coat. He looked accustomed to the best, and the only thing spoiling it was his unmistakable anxiety.

Khalila said, 'No, you aren't wrong. It only shows that Allah's given us a great gift in blessing us with such interesting people.'

'Allah hates a thief, I've heard.'

'So does God, I believe. And yet, here we are, in debt to one.'

Dario's scowl deepened, and he sighed. 'Don't remind me, flower.' He paused for a moment, then burst out, 'If the fool's gone and got himself killed—'

'Then we will have to make it our mission to rescue Morgan and Scholar Wolfe,' she finished for him. 'And bury our dead friend with honour. Yes. I'm sure that is what you were about to say, since you are an honourable man at heart, Dario.'

He sent her a quick, apologetic glance. 'Am I?'

'For the most part, you aspire to it, and that is all anyone can ask. Now, would you do me a service and take these letters to be posted?'

'Anything to keep me occupied,' he said, and took the handful of envelopes. 'You wrote for all of us? To all the families?'

She felt a hard pull of guilt inside and blinked. 'As you said, those men would have killed us all or sold us into the hands of the Archivist without a second thought. But that doesn't make it right. And the families deserve to know.'

'I'll never understand you,' he said. 'I doubt Santi writes letters to the families of soldiers he kills in battle. Only those he loses from his own side.'

'You're right, I don't,' Captain Santi said. Khalila had glimpsed him coming down the stairs from the third floor, where they'd taken rooms; no doubt Glain was still on duty there to guard their space 'But she's not a soldier, and it's a good habit, remembering that every life we take breaks dozens more. It keeps us from killing when there are other options.'

'Fine, then, I'm outvoted and half a monster . . .' Dario's voice trailed off, and the silence made Khalila look up and follow the direction of his stare. '*Dios Mío*, he hasn't just sent someone, he's actually come himself. That's why we've been cooling our heels so long.'

'Who's come?' Santi asked, and she could see him changing his stance subtly, bracing for a fight if one was brewing.

'The king,' Khalila said softly. She could see the cordon of sharply dressed soldiers who surrounded the golden carriage and who now peeled away to form an armed wall on either side of the hotel doorway leading between the carriage door and the entrance. She stood up and belatedly rubbed ink from her fingers against her dark dress, thanking Allah she hadn't chosen the sky-blue fabric today. The deep purple hid all sins. 'Did you expect this?'

'Well.' Dario didn't seem to quite know how to feel. 'We were close when we were children, but I didn't expect him to stir out of Madrid. Still, the king's train to Cadiz, coach to here . . . he's only put himself out a couple of hours at most. I wouldn't put too much emphasis on it.'

The hotel front doors burst open, held back by two soldiers who despite their shimmering, perfect livery looked well capable of killing everyone in seconds, and then the King of Spain swept in.

He was *nothing* like Dario. For one thing, he was a plain young man, very nearly ugly, with narrow, close-set eyes and a nose that flattened too broadly . . . and yet, the smile he aimed at them was wide and warm and erased all such shallow thoughts. As he strode towards them, she realised he was a short man, shorter than she was in her flat boots, and he wore gold shoes with significant heels to raise him significantly above his natural height.

But he strode like a giant and dazzled like a gem, and when his gaze flashed to her, she felt like the sun had burnt through clouds.

'You must be Scholar Seif,' he said, and came straight towards her, ignoring Dario. 'It is my delight and honour to meet you.'

She bowed – just a little, enough to show her thanks, not enough to show subservience – and it must have been correct, because the king's smile grew even wider and warmer. 'Sire, I'm not certain I'm at all worthy of your time, but I do appreciate your words.'

'Not worthy? Nonsense. You and your friends are moving the balance of the world. Did you not realise how significant that is?'

He was, she realised, not simply flattering. There was real intent in those sharply intelligent eyes, and a message despite his warmth. She felt some of the dazzle lift, just as Dario said, 'Honestly, Cousin, could you please *not* sweep the love of my life away on your glittering golden wings?'

Without breaking his smile, but somehow markedly shifting it, the king turned on one heel to face Dario. 'You have never shown any weakness in the area of the ladies. But I do congratulate you on finally choosing one who is so considerably better than you deserve. She's having a good effect, I hear.'

'It's not my business to rehabilitate him,' Khalila said. 'Nor the business of any woman. Should he improve himself, then it is his own doing, and not mine. Respectfully. Your Highness.' She added that quickly, in case the king of the country in which she stood might take offence.

He laughed. 'I'm not the kind of man who lops off heads for speaking truth,' he said. 'And you *have* improved him, like it or not. God knows we've all been struggling to accomplish that for years. When we were children together, I had to bloody his nose to get him to stop calling me names. I didn't think I could ever beat him hard enough to make the leopard actually change his spots.'

'I should have fought back,' Dario said. 'Would have, if you hadn't been—'

'The king?'

'Smaller.'

'Ha, Cousin, I know you better. Please, Scholar, don't stand on ceremony with me. I'm happy to be simply Ramón Alfonse, as long as I'm with friends. I do consider you friends. Even you, Dario.'

Dario managed not to *quite* roll his eyes. 'Family, at least.' He sobered. 'But we have important things to discuss, Ramón, do we not? Most notably, whether or not we are all about to be crushed under the heel of the Library.'

'If you are asking if we are officially at war, well.' The King of Spain snapped his fingers, and a retainer stepped up to proffer a rather official-looking scroll, which he took without looking and handed to Khalila, not to his cousin. 'In a sense, we are.'

Khalila unrolled the stiff paper, heavy with seals and redolent of the sweet beeswax that had formed them. She was holding something that would be an important piece of history, she realised: a withdrawal from the ancient Treaty of Pergamum, the foundational document that ensured the neutrality of the Great Library. And not just by Spain; Spain, it appeared, was a latecomer to the agreement, following Wales, England, Portugal, Turkey, Russia, Japan, the exiled queen of France, and the United Colonies of America. It was a stunning list, and she gasped without meaning to do it, as Dario leant in to take a look.

'I see Spain was reluctant to join the party, Cousin,' he said. Which was not what she was thinking at all.

She was imagining the chaos that would ensue from this, and she felt sick. The Library would, of course, be withdrawing its Scholars and librarians from these countries and locking down their Serapeum . . . but they couldn't strategically turn their backs on such a large part of the world. Russia alone was enough to rip the fragile fabric of the Library's grip on power. And Japan and Wales were known to hold learning in such high regard that any attempt to cast these rebel countries as barbarians would be worthless.

Spain and Portugal were conservative lands. England was proud in defeat. And while France's queen in exile might be expected to support any such measure, for the American colonies to break with tradition meant something dire had changed.

The Library had burnt Philadelphia, and America would not forget it.

Santi, as usual, was practical in his analysis. 'Dramatic, but these are all lands that don't touch Egypt,' he said. 'Easy to be rebellious at a distance. We still need a better way in.'

'Or a navy,' Ramón Alfonse said, and bowed slightly. 'Captain Santi. Spain and Portugal have the honour of offering you ships and men to your cause. But first, we must agree on what the goals of this battle will be.'

'No,' Santi said. 'I don't want to lead a foreign army against my own people. I'm trying to save the Library, not destroy it.'

'And where, then, are your troops? Besides these good people.' Ramón gave Santi an appraising look. 'I am compassionate towards you, Captain Santi. I understand your point. But remember, regardless of who fights by your side, should you be successful, a new treaty may well be forged with the Great Library.' Ramón gave Santi an appraising look. 'And for all your undoubtedly high principles, I believe you're interested in saving someone in particular *from* the Library, first and foremost.'

Santi could hardly argue that point, but he didn't let his expression show it. 'The Spanish and Portuguese navies are the envy of the world, no doubt, but don't you think they'll expect you to use them? We need a better plan than an attack they can anticipate without getting out of their chairs. Your ships will be a vital part of that, without any doubt, but we need a much different approach if we want to win control of the Library without unnecessary bloodshed.'

'Well, I am no strategist; I leave that thorny problem in your capable hands, Captain. My job is to end the Library's oppressive grip upon knowledge to the benefit of my people. That last part is the most important, of course.'

'Are you in communication with the Russian Tsar and the Emperor of Japan?'

'As it happens, I am. But I hardly think the lobby of the Cadiz Grand Hotel is the proper venue for that discussion. Come.'

The king turned and abruptly headed for the door. His soldiers didn't seem at all surprised; a core of them closed ranks around him, but another part split off to rush up the stairs, and a third portion moved to take posts around the three of them: Dario, Santi, and Khalila.

One of the soldiers stepped smartly up to Dario and bowed slightly. 'Don Santiago, His Highness Ramón Alfonse is pleased to see you moved to more secure and comfortable accommodations in Madrid. Please follow me.'

Santi said, 'And if we don't wish to go with you?'

The soldier was a thin-faced man, hardened, with eyes as lifeless as a doll's. 'Then, Captain Santi, you will be taken to more secure and less comfortable accommodations here in Cadiz. While I have no wish to kill you, I will obey the orders of my king.'

Khalila didn't want the full focus of that man's eyes, but she raised her chin and didn't blink when she received it. 'I am a Scholar. So is Scholar Santiago. Captain Santi is of command rank within the High Garda. You understand what you are doing, do you?'

'Spain's recently declared its independence from the Library, Scholar,' he told her. 'And that makes you a foreign refugee, at best. Don Santiago is welcome to travel with the king to Madrid, as are you, as his guests. But do not imagine wearing the symbol of the Library gives you any special consideration.'

It was no more than she should have expected, she knew that, but the vicious precision with which the man said it indicated years of pent-up resentment, a vicious satisfaction at a minor revenge. She felt a shiver go through her and hoped it was not something he could see. *We didn't think of the resentment. Or the glee with which people would view the Library's vulnerability.* Once the chill passed, she felt heat. Anger, building to fury. *You will not destroy the Library. You will* not.

'We're happy to be my royal cousin's guests,' Dario said. 'Of course. Are we not?' His tone was butter smooth, but the quick glance he sent her and Santi was loaded with warning. They all knew Santi was on a hair trigger; the last thing he wanted was to become enmeshed in royal politics when every moment wasted was another his lover spent in a cell in Alexandria, moving fast towards execution.

But Santi nodded agreement, however hot the look was in his eyes. And in a moment, the guards returned from upstairs, leading Thomas and Glain. Thomas looked like he was in the mood to fight, but he calmed when he saw the rest of them standing unharmed. 'What is this? They're packing our bags. Such as we have, of course.'

'We're going on to Madrid,' Dario told him. 'It's all right.'

But was it? This had the feeling of a trap closing around them, for all that they'd hoped for something like it. 'Should we do this? Are we sure?'

'There are no right moves, at this stage,' Santi told her. 'Everything will go wrong. Egos will get in the way. Politics. Greed. We have to find a way through, whatever happens.' He took in a slow breath. 'But you two would be far safer staying in Spain and organising the unification of countries against the Archivist. You're both natural politicians. Make them call for the Archivist's removal, and the replacement of the Curia with new leadership, as a condition of signing a new treaty.'

'And you?' Khalila asked.

'Let me and Glain go on to Alexandria.'

'The days when one or two people could save those we love are long gone, Captain.' Surprisingly, it came from Glain herself. She looked calm, though she was watching the soldiers around them with sharp focus. 'To cripple the Archivist's power, you have to make people believe he's vulnerable. That's already started. Wales openly defied him, and they still conquered London and brought England to its knees; he threatened them for storming the Oxford Serapeum, but he couldn't stop them, either. That hurt him, and this hurts him more with every country that declares its independence. We need to take advantage of it.'

'And Dario? Is your cousin going to commit real troops to fight a real war?' asked Santi.

Dario shrugged. 'Let's find out.'

Not that they had much choice.

CHAPTER SEVENTEEN

The royal coach was, as might have been expected, luxurious, and large enough for twice their number; Ramón Alfonse dismissed all but two of his guards from the interior to make them comfortable, and offered water and juice. Dario looked over the selection with a frown. 'Nothing more relaxing than that?'

'A king is offering you refreshment from his own hands, and you criticise? Really, Cousin. You haven't changed at all.'

'I have. I no longer think that I'm the most important thing in the world. I've met people who've convinced me of that. I thought you'd be pleased.'

'Oh, I am,' the king said, and poured a crystal glass full of orange juice at Khalila's request. He passed it to her with a smile. The carriage they travelled in was so well insulated that she could only barely detect the hissing of the carriage engine and the sound of the wheels. No sense of motion at all. 'We all thought that you'd never grow out of your arrogance, but we'd hoped you'd learn to point it in a useful direction. I suspect these friends of yours have helped.' A glass went to Thomas, who took it carefully in his massive hand. It looked like a child's teacup in comparison. 'You, sir, you are an inventor who understands the automata?'

'Yes.'

'And, if I heard correctly, who also can reproduce the

written word using some sort of machine? Tell me, does it copy script quickly? I've seen automata that can do such things. A French inventor built one, but it was meant as an aide to scholars, and was slow enough that the Library felt it was of no particular interest.'

'They take this machine seriously. Once the letters are set on a tray, a page can be printed again and again, without limit.'

'Quickly?'

'Yes.'

The king's eyebrows rose, and Khalila watched him take a long, meditative sip of his juice. 'Well. I'd heard rumours, but this is the first confirmation. And does such a machine actually exist?'

'Yes.'

'Is it in use now?'

'Yes.'

'Then the dogs have been unleashed, and we don't have time to waste. If I intend to stop the High Garda from using every Serapeum with a Translation Chamber as a potential invasion point, I need to act quickly to preserve the kingdom.' He drummed his perfectly manicured nails on his knee and looked off into the distance. 'And, of course, We will require the plans for such a machine, in exchange for Our assistance.'

His tone had shifted. So, Khalila noted, had his pronouns; she could almost *hear* the weight of them. This was the King of Spain speaking, not Ramón Alfonse.

Dario had missed it. 'Cousin, before we give up anything—'

'It's customary to call me Your Highness,' the king interrupted. 'We permitted you landing and shelter. It aligns with Our interests to support you in your quest to, shall we say, reform the great institution to which you owe your true loyalty.

But this is not an *exchange*. Crowns negotiate only with crowns.'

'Which means?' Captain Santi asked.

'When great kings fall, the world trembles. Who is the Archivist's successor, when you achieve your goal?'

'I'm no kingmaker, Your Highness.'

'You have no choice. And you must take that seriously. I don't know your Scholar Christopher Wolfe. Would he be capable of holding the centre in such a time of crisis? Of not only leading a Library caught in the throes of change, but dealing resolutely with the heads of every nation on earth? Because Spain will not come to the new Archivist as a supplicant. We will come as an equal. All the reverence and history the Great Library has behind it means nothing if it cannot defend its own existence.'

Santi was silent, and Khalila could see he'd never asked himself such a question. It took a long, charged moment before he said, 'Wolfe is fully capable. But he will never want it.'

'Then who? Who leads the Library if you succeed? If you don't know, your quest is nothing but disaster. The Archivist is a fixed star in the heavens. Remove him, and you had best install a great light to keep the sky from falling.'

'So says the King of Spain?'

'So would say a friend,' Ramón Alfonse said. 'Sadly, a king has no friends once he takes the crown. It may be put aside from time to time, but a king is not a man. A king – and an Archivist – is a country.'

'There are tens of thousands of truly great Scholars still loyal to the true ideals of the Library,' Khalila said. 'We will find someone, sire.'

'No. You will not. There is nothing rarer than an honest politician, dear Scholar, and that is what you will need to prevent the greatest disaster of this – perhaps of any – age.'

The king was quiet for a moment, and then he said, 'I think you began this effort of yours for noble reasons, but the road to hell is paved with good intentions, as the Scholars frequently quote. So be sure what you are doing. And be ready. Spain is an ally, to a point. But Spain will not fight for the same goals that you seek.'

The silence in the carriage was profound after that quiet statement. Khalila felt a little sick. She thought herself an intelligent person, but he was right: none of them had fully considered the effects of what they'd set in motion. It had started as a means to save friends, and now . . . now it was larger than they'd ever imagined.

'King Ramón Alfonse,' she said. 'Does Spain believe in the burning and destruction of the Great Archives? Of the wholesale loss of millions of original works?'

She'd struck him from an unexpected quarter, and she saw him blink. 'No. Naturally, that is abhorrent to any person of any land.'

'But it will happen. It is inevitable. If we count politics above the preservation of knowledge, that is the outcome. We know, because it happened for a thousand years before the Great Library created the Archive system and the Blanks. Tens of thousands of precious, unique works, all gone because a king decreed that destroying them was *useful*. That denying knowledge to others was a tactic of war. Those are the days we fear, and they are coming. Unless we succeed, and *you help us*, then you will one day look on a world with no respect for knowledge and no tools to tell truth from a lie. Is that what you want?'

'Of course not. But the Library can't survive on reputation alone. It needs strength, and it needs a leader who can mend all this damage. It's been a long time coming, but the worst will happen quickly. You must be ready, Scholar Seif.' The king's gaze swept across the rest of them. 'You must not wait to find your new Archivist. When you present Spain with a name, you will receive our full support.'

It wasn't Scholar Wolfe; she knew that. Wolfe didn't have the temperament or, she thought, the desire.

Then who?

She didn't know. And she had the sick, falling feeling that none of them did.

The carriage suddenly picked up speed with a lurch, and they all swayed from the change. The king turned to the guard beside him and said, 'What's happening?'

The guard slid open the compartment window that separated them from the driver, conversed, and slid it closed. 'Your Highness, we're informed that High Garda troops have arrived via Translation at the Cadiz Serapeum, and they are fortifying the building, along with the librarians. We believe the same is occurring in the Madrid library, and several others throughout the country.'

'Then Spain must choose,' King Ramón Alfonse said soberly. 'We must take every single Serapeum. If they surrender, they will be given safe passage to Alexandria. If they resist, take the fight forward until resistance is done. Give the orders.'

'Wait,' Khalila blurted out, and instantly wished she hadn't when all eyes turned to her. '*Wait!* If you start this war, it erupts everywhere! And at what cost?'

'To the Library? Everything. To us? We risk becoming the burning wasteland that was France, after their rebellion. Or, more recently, Philadelphia. But the Archivist cannot fight on so many fronts, and so we stand little risk of punishment. As King of Spain, I must do this.' The king stared at her with such intensity she felt an instinct to look away . . . but she did not. 'This is the path you've paved for us.'

'Then let us try something else first,' she said. 'Let us talk to them.'

'Talk?' He sat back, a frown forming now, and looked at Dario. '*Talk?*'

'She's right,' Dario said. 'There are doubts in the ranks. We had help getting away in America. And what loss to you if we can persuade at least one of the Serapeums to side with us?'

'I don't like your chances, but it's your funeral Mass to schedule.' Ramón Alfonse tapped the barrier, and it slid open. 'Counter that last order. Take me to the train. Then you may deliver our friends where they believe they need to go, and assign a full company of soldiers to guard them. I'll expect them in Madrid in one piece. If they fail, or God forbid are murdered, then my original orders stand: take the Library properties with all speed.'

'Sire,' the driver said, and closed the window again.

'There.' The king arched an eyebrow at them. 'I wish you luck, my friends. And if not luck . . . then I will exact vengeance.'

CHAPTER EIGHTEEN

Talking their way into the Serapeum had seemed like a reasonable idea in the heat of the moment.

Standing on the blocked road that led to the building, surrounded by grim, determined Spanish soldiers, it seemed a great deal more like suicide.

Khalila, to calm her nerves, walked away from the low, intense discussion between Santi and Dario and Thomas and found Glain, who was sitting on the back of a troop carrier. She had a rifle in her hands, efficiently loading it, then fine-tuning the optical scope. She'd put on Spanish armour, since it was all that was available, and she looked as at home in that as she did in High Garda gear.

'What are you doing?' Khalila asked.

Glain, without looking up, said, 'I'm making sure that I'm ready for what happens when everything else fails.' She looked calm, but then, she usually did; the High Garda had done that for her, smoothed away her old flares of temper and given her purpose and direction. Glain had been born for soldiering, far more than anyone else Khalila had known. They had nothing in common, and yet, strangely, they had so much, too. 'Did you finish your prayers?'

'I did.' Khalila sat on the back step of the lorry and stared out at the street. They were looking at the sweep of the Cadiz Serapeum, which had been designed by the famous architect Gaudí; it was a fabulous structure in the shape of a coiled dragon, with shimmering blue tiled scales and a snaking roofline that outlined the dragon's back. Beautiful, and somehow very suited to this odd, lovely country. The rain was still falling in a steady, relentless mist, but at least the winds had passed, and the temperature was a bit warmer. She was still grateful for the heavy coat that the palace guards had pressed on her.

She was also grateful for the weapon in the coat pocket. A Spanish pistol, heavy and full of brutal promise. She preferred swords, but she'd studied with pistols as well. She could do what was needed.

'I think we're going to need prayers,' Glain said. 'The king was right. We've opened the gates of hell, you know. And what comes out now is our fault.'

'Is a fire the fault of the man who drops a match, or the one who spilt the oil all over the floor, knew it, and left it there?'

'Scholar arguments. I'm practical. We started this, and now it's a war. We need to prepare for that.'

'You don't think we have a chance?'

Khalila looked directly at her friend. Glain's hair had grown out and was curling at the ends. Not a conventionally attractive young woman, but then, Glain had little time for appearances or romance, though in her own way she did love those around her; it was only that the love she felt was expressed as loyalty, fidelity, and friendship.

'I think we haven't begun to understand the costs of what we're doing,' Glain said. 'But you point me at what needs to be done, and I'll do it. I'm a soldier. You, Khalila: you're a politician.'

Khalila laughed. 'I am not!' But she was, of course. She'd grown up moving through a political family, in a highly developed political society in Saudi Arabia. And the politics of the Great Library had simply seemed familiar.

Glain sent her a look that was part wry amusement, part exasperation. 'When they talk about who will lead the Library, you realise that the Curia will have to go, don't you? Not just the Archivist. They've all been complicit in what he's done, all these years. At the very least, they're weak. At the most, they're as bad as he is. So we have to find not just his replacement, but the heads of all the specialties, unless they break ranks and join with us – and even then, we'll have to be careful of spies and traitors. Some of them will want us dead, even in defeat.'

As usual, Glain and Santi had the same view of the tactical situation, and Khalila had to admit that it was . . . not encouraging. 'We need to preserve. That's our first objective. Protect the books.'

'It's what we swore to do,' Glain agreed.

'But we also should protect our brothers and sisters who might not understand what they're fighting for. We didn't. Not until it was too late.' Glain nodded, but it didn't look like wholehearted agreement, either. 'You don't want us to do this.'

'I don't want any of us putting ourselves out as easy targets,' Glain replied. 'There's brave, and then there's stupid.'

'Which am I?'

'That depends.'

Khalila turned to meet her eyes over the rifle. 'But you'll look after me.'

Glain pulled in a breath and slowly let it out. 'Stupid, then.'

She stood up. 'Don't tell them until I'm gone.'

'Khalila—'

She shook her head. 'We can win this with force, or we can try to win it with the power of an idea. I want to try that first. I *need* to do that first, for my soul.'

Glain muttered something in Welsh that Khalila only vaguely understood, but it sounded grim. 'I'll see you buried according to your faith, if it comes to that. And shoot the brains out of anyone who hurts you. That's all I can do, for *my* soul.'

'I know that, Sister.'

Glain's grin came like a burst of sunlight, and was just as quickly gone. '*Chwaer*,' she said. 'If you want to be accurate. Though I don't suppose you'll ever learn to pronounce it properly.'

'*Chwaer*,' Khalila said back, with what she thought was a surprisingly good attempt. 'Don't let them stop me.'

She stood up and walked around the lorry, keeping it between her and Santi, who'd be the first to spot her movement and guess her purpose. She was aware of Glain moving behind her – finding a good vantage spot, she thought. Something high.

There was an automaton pacing in front of the gates of the Serapeum. It was a sphinx, which meant they'd likely brought it from Alexandria; it froze when it saw her and turned its pharaonic head in her direction. She didn't pause. She walked steadily forward. The sphinx didn't attack, but it crouched lower, those baleful red eyes glowing brighter.

'I have come to talk,' she said. 'I am Khalila Seif, Scholar of the Great Library, and I come to talk.'

She heard a shout from behind her in the distance. It rang down the street, from wet cobbles and the looming stonework of the buildings rising on both sides. She was afraid and trembling, and she wanted very badly to turn and run back to the safety of her friends.

Dario was calling her name in a sharp, panicked voice.

'Let me in,' she said. 'At the very least, you gain a hostage. One the Archivist wants very badly.'

For a moment, the sphinx only crouched lower, and she could see the hard cables that served as its muscles flexing beneath that bronze skin. *I know what to do if it attacks*, she told herself. She remembered Jess's instruction and felt a little steadier. A little stronger. She could freeze that automaton in place with a touch and walk in looking as powerful and mysterious as an Obscurist.

If it didn't take her hand off first, of course.

'Khalila!' Dario's shout was closer. He was running towards her. She heard the crack of a rifle shot and a yelp and backward-pedalling footsteps. Didn't dare take her attention from the automaton, but she prayed Glain hadn't deliberately wounded him. No, she'd have placed a shot neatly at his feet and forced him back to cover. He'd think it was a Library sniper. Hopefully. That would keep all the rest back as well. 'Khalila, love, *get out of there!*'

'I'm coming inside,' Khalila said to the sphinx, and took another step.

It rose from its crouch, turned, and glided towards the gate.

She followed, and as she passed the barrier of that open courtyard wall, she pulled in a breath that smelt of rain, iron, and rust, and a phantom hint of blood. There were gardens surrounding the Serapeum, thick with late-blooming flowers and trees whose turning leaves still clung to branches. It was a beautiful place. She imagined what it would be like after a battle to take this place. Churned, broken, and destroyed.

No. This cannot happen.

Ahead, the sphinx moved with a silky lion's stride to the closed, thickly barred gates . . . which silently opened. The automaton paused outside of them, watching her, and as she passed it, the thing bared needle teeth in an unmistakable threat.

She stepped inside, the gates slammed together behind her with incredible speed and force, and she very nearly cried out at the ring of the iron . . . but she stopped where she was, just a foot or two inside the sacred Serapeum grounds, and caught her breath. Her heart was speeding faster now, and she allowed herself to take in where she stood in the small respite.

This close, the form of the building *did* look like a resting dragon, with the wide entry hall its long, narrow head, and a pair of slitted yellow windows above glowing to give the illusion of eyes. A terrifying symbol of power, this construction; on a day less grim, on an occasion less dire, it might have looked beautiful, but the clouds and rain had stripped all ornaments away to show the pure menace beneath.

And I have walked in alone.

They let her wait for a long few moments before she felt – rather than saw – someone approaching her from the side. She turned her head without moving any other muscles that might get her unnecessarily killed and saw a uniformed High Garda soldier training a weapon on her. A turn to the other side confirmed what she already knew: there was another there as well, angled so that her merely ducking wouldn't kill them in a crossfire. She suspected there would be a third somewhere invisible up higher in the building's serpentine roofline.

Khalila folded her hands and waited for the real negotiations to begin.

It took another few moments before the door opened in the dragon's mouth and a small, old woman in Library robes descended the steps with the help of a cane. She was of Japanese ancestry, and her robes reflected the cultural style of that land; her cane, Khalila noticed, was carved with the shape of a dragon's head.

There was no mistaking the gold band around the woman's wrist.

Khalila bowed low, and the Scholar matched it to a careful degree less deep. She carried an umbrella in her other hand, though she didn't offer to shelter Khalila with it. The older woman's eyes were calm and unreadable.

'Scholar,' Khalila greeted her.

'Scholar,' the other woman said. 'You demonstrate disregard for your own safety. How did you know we wouldn't simply have you killed?'

'I didn't,' Khalila answered. Quite truthfully. 'I hoped.'

The woman was motionless for a long stretch of seconds – long enough that the chill began to eat at Khalila's nerves. But then she said, 'I am Scholar Murasaki Shirasu. I am aware of who you are, of course. Not your scholarly accomplishments, which are slight, but your actions, which loom much larger.'

'I'm honoured to have come to the attention of the great essayist Murasaki at all,' Khalila answered. 'As to my accomplishments, I am too young to claim any.'

Murasaki gave her a slow smile. 'Humble and elegant,' she said. 'And you do not rise to the bait. Come inside, Scholar Seif. Let us warm ourselves with tea, and you may present your case not just to me, but to the High Garda as well. I doubt you will ever leave us again, but that was, of course, your choice.'

Khalila didn't answer, because she couldn't think of anything that wouldn't betray her uncertainty.

She followed Scholar Murasaki into the dragon's mouth.

CHAPTER NINETEEN

The first thing the High Garda did the instant she crossed the Serapeum threshold was relieve her of her pistol, of course; she had expected as much. She had not quite expected to be facing so many drawn weapons – ten, at her count, though those were only the ones she could see – and she raised her arms and stood very quietly for the search, which was so thorough even Glain would have been impressed. Scholar Murasaki ignored all of it and walked across a wide, intricately inlaid wooden floor to seat herself in a carved wooden chair next to a stand that held a chained, oversized Codex.

The smell of the place overwhelmed Khalila for a moment with helpless longing. *Books.* The crisp, lightly spiced smell of pages, as constant in the air here as incense. The entry hall was immense and rose in a rounded, organic bubble. It was topped with a huge blue curved window with grey that spiralled in like smoke. Gorgeous and odd. This entire Serapeum was a delight.

I can't let this be destroyed. We have few enough things to feed our souls.

'Clear,' the soldier said, and stepped back. He was a blonde young man who topped her by a head and twice over in breadth. Unlike the angry man in Philadelphia, he hadn't insisted on the removal of her hijab, but then, Spain was a deeply cosmopolitan country, with seeds of the culture of Islam in its arts, architecture, and food. She felt more at home here than she ever had in the Burner camp.

'Is she the one with Obscurist powers?' asked a dark-skinned woman wearing librarian robes. She sounded anxious, and she was hiding in the back, behind the row of weapons. *As if I might bite*, Khalila thought.

'I am not,' she replied. 'My friend Morgan Hault is the Obscurist, and she has been taken to the Iron Tower in Alexandria. Scholar Wolfe is, we assume, in prison and awaiting execution. You have nothing to fear from me, I assure you. I come only to talk.'

'About what?' That brought someone else out of the shadows: a tall, scarred man with shockingly red hair shaved close to his skull. One of the scars ran a white ridge through the left side of his head. No librarian, this one; he wore High Garda armour and uniform, and command like a mantle. 'Because if you're here to talk to us about giving up the Serapeum for the Spanish to loot, you know better.'

There was something of an opening in what he said, she realised. He didn't simply condemn her and order her arrested. *He was listening*.

So was Scholar Murasaki. The gravity of the situation suddenly descended on her, freezing her in place, and she took a moment to compose her thoughts. *Think. What will convince these two very different people?*

'I have never been here before,' Khalila said. 'To Spain, or to Cadiz, or this Serapeum. Yet the moment I stepped inside, it was familiar to me. It was *home*. I look at you, and I don't see enemies. I see those who value what I do: the preservation and distribution of knowledge. The delights of discovery and the honour of guardianship. You are the Great Library; you are its heart and soul, spirit and blood. And I would rather die than see you, and this place, desecrated when I can prevent it.'

They didn't say anything at all. There was no reaction. And Khalila closed her eyes. 'There is a rot at the heart of what we love. It is not the knowledge or the preservation of it. It is the notion that *only we* can decide what is worthy, what is not, what is progress, and whether or not it should proceed. For thousands of years, the Archivists have *told* us that all we have here is all there can be. But it isn't. I saw. I know.' She turned to Murasaki, whose face was thrown into stark, aged lines by the light cascading in from above. 'Do you know the poet Murasaki Hiroko?'

'I do not. There is no such poet.'

'But there was,' Khalila said softly. 'I saw the manuscript, Scholar. She wrote poems to her lover, but her lover was another married woman, and at the time the Curia deemed them unfit for distribution. When she protested, they told her to destroy the work. She refused, and wrote more poems calling for the end of censorship by the Great Library. I read them. They were rotting in the Black Archives. If you don't know of her, it is because she was simply . . . erased.'

She felt the shift of tension – the wrong way. 'Nonsense,' the red-haired captain said. 'No such thing. The Black Archives are a fable told to frighten children and interest conspiracy-minded crackpots.'

'It was vast,' Khalila said. 'Storey upon storey of shelves, all filled with works the Library deemed seditious or dangerous. Confiscated from the Scholars who wrote them. Locked away, to rot in darkness and silence, all those books silenced. *I saw it.* I was there. I read Murasaki Hiroko's poems, and they were . . .'

Her voice faltered and broke and she took in a gulp of air. 'They were searing, and angry, and brilliant. They were beautiful. And now they're gone.'

This time, the silence felt heavy, and it lasted a second too long before Scholar Murasaki said, 'Gone. But you claim they were in the Black Archives.'

'They were,' Khalila said. She had tears in her eyes now. 'Where they'd been kept for almost five hundred years. But once we had been there, seen them, the Black Archives were no longer secret. And the Archivist ordered them all destroyed rather than let them see the light of day.'

'You're lying,' the captain said. 'The Library does not destroy books. We're not Burners.'

'But we are,' she said, and let the tears come, the grief cascade out of the locked box she'd kept it in. '*We are*. That is the ugly, filthy truth; the Library decides, in secret, what should be read and what shouldn't. What should be destroyed if it poses a danger. I watched those books *burn*. Hundreds of thousands of books, row upon row, all turning to ashes . . .' She couldn't speak. She tasted tears and struggled not to cry. 'We saved what we could. It wasn't enough.'

'What you're alleging is heresy,' the Scholar said. For the first time, she sounded shaken. 'Heresy at the highest levels of the Great Library.'

Khalila wiped her tears with shaking hands. 'I told you what I saw. I will swear to it under any oath you say. You may question me as much as you like; I will tell you the truth: I saw the Black Archives burn on the Archivist's command. There is no greater sin than—'

'What *you* are saying is heresy!' That was from the librarian who'd been hiding in the back but who pushed forward now. Her eyes were bright, her cheeks flushed, and she levelled a pointing finger at Khalila. 'You and your friends, you betrayed the Library. You abandoned your posts. And you've been declared outlaws and enemies! You took refuge in a Burner city, of all places! Why should we believe anything you have to say, especially when you claim the Black Archives actually exist?'

'Have you never had a doubt?' Khalila ignored the librarian, because now she focused on the High Garda captain. 'Have you never been given an order you thought was wrong? Never arrested people without understanding what they'd done to deserve it? Never seen Scholars vanish, their work mysteriously gone? I've seen the prison under Rome. I've seen how the Library treats those it fears.'

He didn't reply, but she could see the flicker in his gaze. She'd hit a mark – how deeply, was the question.

'Is Captain Santi still alive?' he asked.

'Yes. Do you know him?'

'I did.'

'Do you respect him?'

'I did before.'

'You still should. He has never compromised his beliefs.'

'He's in open rebellion against the Great Library!'

'No. He is seeking to spread the knowledge that has been denied to us by generations of Archivists. He seeks, as I do, to preserve the ideals of the Library, from which we've long ago strayed. We seek to bring the light of knowledge back to what is now a dark room. And I came here to ask for your help.'

Murasaki stirred. 'We cannot support rebels.'

'I am not asking that at all,' she said. 'I'm asking that you preserve this place. Use it as it was always meant to be used.

Open it. Don't listen to the orders of the Great Library, which tell you that the people around you are your enemies, that *we* are your enemies, that the King of Spain stands outside to destroy everything you love; he doesn't want to do that. He wants to see this place remain exactly as it is.' She turned back to the High Garda. 'Are your orders to advance on Madrid?'

He didn't answer for a long moment, and then he said, 'Not yet. First, our orders are to find you, Santi, and the others, and send you through the Translation Chamber to Alexandria, where you'll be held for trial.'

'None of us will get a trial,' she said. 'I've seen the orders. Glain is to be killed immediately. Santi and I, we would be sent to join the prisoners for the Feast of Greater Burning, where my father, brothers and uncle are already imprisoned. And Thomas – Thomas will be made to work for them until they decide he's of no use any more. And none of us will be remembered. No journals of our lives. No mention of our works. We will vanish . . . like the books of the Black Archives.'

None of them spoke. She took in a deep breath. 'I pledge this to you: I will die here in this place before I let anyone, *anyone*, plunder this beautiful library. And King Ramón Alfonse knows that.'

'Brave words, Scholar,' said the High Garda captain. 'But all it takes is a single shot to kill you, and your promise means nothing. Spain stands at our gates with troops ready to take this building. Are you asking us to trust that the king will hold back out of the goodness of his heart?' He shook his head. 'I'm not in the business of taking the word of a young woman barely out of training on the motives of a man she doesn't even know.'

'If I can sign Spain to a new treaty, will you break with the Archivist?'

There was a moment of silence, and then Murasaki said, 'You mean, break with the Library.'

'No. I mean the Archivist. Because we mean to replace him. The Library will live on. Your vow is to the Library. Does it matter to you who sits in that office?'

'It might,' she said. 'It might a great deal. And you cannot guarantee that the one who takes his place won't be as bad, or worse. Can you?'

'Scholar Murasaki, I can promise you that you will be part of that choice.' It was a rash promise, but Murasaki was a widely respected Scholar, one who had refused a post on the Curia to take leadership of the Cadiz Serapeum. *We could hardly find a better, more impartial person to take the Archivist's robes, if it comes to that.* 'You are a woman of great standing and reputation. If you join with us, if you believe in our cause—'

'You can't trust the word of the Spanish king,' said the librarian who'd pushed forward. Khalila didn't recognise her, and there was something about her that put her on edge; the glittery eagerness of the woman's eyes, the tense set of her shoulders. 'Kings lie. They'll promise peace, and as soon as they have the chance, they'll loot this sacred place and kill us all. We can *never* trust these power-hungry savages, surely you know that, Scholar . . .'

'I come from what some call power-hungry savages,' Murasaki said evenly. 'And I know King Ramón Alfonse very well. He will not willingly destroy one of the jewels of his kingdom unless we force him to do so. Our lives and our books are safe; Scholar Seif is quite correct. The question is, will the High Garda obey commands to retrieve these fugitives and send them to Alexandria? Or will the High Garda choose to do as it is sworn, and guard this place against any harm?'

'You're talking treason,' the High Garda commander rumbled.

'I am asking a question,' Murasaki said, with glacial composure that Khalila herself didn't possess – not inwardly. This had become a thorny knot of a conversation, and she didn't dare inject herself. She'd set it in motion. Now she could only stand back and see how it ended. 'And the question is, to whom do all of us owe our loyalty? To an Archivist who seems willing to provoke wars to get his hands on his enemies . . . or to the Library?'

Khalila imagined, quite vividly, that this debate might end with her own blood on the floor, and felt a little faint . . . but also, oddly, a little thrilled. Finally, they were engaged in the world. Affecting it directly. And that felt . . . powerful. It felt important.

'You took an oath, same as I did, Shirasu,' the commander said. 'Whatever we think of the man, he is the elected head of the Library.'

'Perhaps I do not remember my oath all that well, my friend. What was the wording of it? Did it swear my allegiance to a man?'

The commander stroked his beard. Khalila knew Murasaki was ruthlessly correct: the oath was to the Library, not to the Archivist who headed it. But he still had an answer. 'It's up to the Curia to remove him, then. Not to the head of one Serapeum far away from Alexandria.'

'The head of my discipline rose to the level of Curia through corruption, as did most of them,' she said. 'Favours for favours, payments, patronage and favouritism. I'm not blind, Fergus. I know the corruption of which this young woman speaks. Do you think we punished France solely because of its rebellion against the Library? It was a convenient excuse to loot an entire country of its treasures, which became a river of gold to enrich the Library's flagging treasury. I know that because I saw it.

And for many years, I have regretted that silence.' She smiled slightly, and it softened the severe lines of her face. 'Fergus. You told me yourself of your discomfort when the previous High Commander was removed and replaced by someone you didn't think was half so worthy.'

'Aye,' he agreed. 'Captain Chu was a pompous ass and only as good as the lieutenants under him, that's true. But he's not bent.'

'When a strong gale constantly blows, everything bends,' Murasaki said. 'And even the most honest make accommodations, and soon they are not honest at all.'

Khalila's attention was drawn back to the librarian, who was edging closer to the front now. Her body seemed stiff, and her face shone with sweat in the reflected light from the window above, though the temperature inside was cool enough. She wasn't registering objections any more. Her gaze was fixed on Murasaki, and she was heading straight for the Scholar where she sat in her chair.

Khalila saw the librarian's hand come out from the pocket of her robe, and knew she had seconds to act. She didn't know and couldn't see what it was the woman held – knife, gun, something else – but she lunged forward, grabbed the woman's hand and twisted it.

It was a bottle.

Liquid splashed onto the woman's robe in a long, slick stain from chest to hips, and the smell of it hit Khalila an instant before she felt the drops that had hit her exposed hand begin to burn. She grabbed a thick fold of her skirt and wrapped the skin tight to stifle the fire; so long as it was starved of oxygen it couldn't spread and burrow, though the pain was a sharp, stabbing agony that made her gasp in breaths.

She was lucky.

There was no saving the librarian.

The woman screamed as her robe erupted in a rush of green fire that greedily wrapped around her. Everyone scrambled out of the way. Murasaki came to her feet and shouted orders Khalila couldn't hear.

The Greek Fire caught with a vengeance as the commander – Fergus – shouted orders. The librarian continued to scream as her skin turned red, then black under the flames. She turned in wild circles, and where she stepped, fire took hold. It was chaos.

And then Murasaki herself took a gun from a soldier and put a bullet in the woman's heart.

The body collapsed to the inlaid marble floor, hissing and burning, until a High Garda soldier dressed in thick padding ran to the rescue and sprayed a thick, suffocating foam over the body.

Khalila tried to be still. The stench, the smoke, the horror of it was all too much, and around her others were screaming, crying, running away into the other parts of the vast complex. She composed herself, tried to breathe shallowly, and waited for Murasaki to realise what had just happened.

It didn't take long.

The old woman handed the pistol back to the soldier, who seemed rightfully ashamed of his lack of action, and exchanged a long look with her guard commander. These two, it seemed, truly were friends of long standing. There was very real regard; it burnt in the look. Fergus was breathing heavily, fury in those blue eyes; Murasaki, for her part, seemed as calm as ever. 'So,' she said. 'We knew it could happen.'

'Excuse me?' Khalila said. She felt off-balance now. 'You *knew* someone would try to kill you?'

'I have been living on borrowed time since word began to

spread of Christopher Wolfe and his arrest and . . . erasure.'

'You know Wolfe?'

'I know him very well. He was a brilliant man, if somewhat unlikeable. It came as a blow to many of us when he was taken from the rolls of the Scholars. We never knew what heresy or crime he had committed to earn it, but most who knew him were certain it was wrong. Tell me, does he still live?'

Khalila wanted very badly to be able to say yes, but instead, she could only say, 'I hope he does. He's in the hands of the Archivist now, along with my friend—' She almost said *Jess*, but Jess's safety in Alexandria depended on discretion. 'Morgan, who would have been sent to the Iron Tower. I don't know what's happened to Wolfe, but we are going to find him. You have my word.'

'I do not know you, or the value of your word, Scholar Seif, though nothing you have done causes me to doubt it.' Murasaki turned her focus back to her High Garda commander. 'Well? What do you say?'

He sighed. 'I say if the Archivist is desperate enough to assassinate you – and she was his creature, no doubt about that; we've long established as much – then we don't have much of a choice. He sees you as a threat.'

'He should. I came here of my own accord to avoid being a rival to him. But I could easily change my mind.'

'You should lock down your Translation Chamber,' Khalila said. 'Before they send troops to take this place away from you. He might order it destroyed.'

'You think he would? Destroy it?'

'I think the Archivist will do anything to preserve his power, and Scholar Murasaki has a powerful reputation. If she sides with us, it will hurt him badly. He won't take the chance.'

Fergus nodded and snapped his fingers. A lieutenant stepped forward. 'Kali, lock it down. And keep the Scholars and librarians in the interior. I don't want them put at any more risk than we must. Lock down the Codexes, too. All of them. The slower Alexandria gets word of this, the better.'

'Yes sir,' the woman said, and cut her eyes towards Khalila. 'And about them . . . ? Our orders . . .'

'We're not the Archivist's personal guard, and these people don't threaten our Serapeum. We're not leaving these grounds.'

She saluted and turned to give orders to soldiers, who scattered on their missions. Which left the still-smoking corpse, Murasaki, Fergus, Khalila, and the lieutenant alone in the vast room. Smoke had risen up to stain the windows overhead and swirled there like storm clouds.

'Lieutenant, please have a squad of troopers make the body safe and store it,' Murasaki said. 'Find out her funeral preferences. I will personally pay for her burial, and transportation to her family if that was her wish.'

The lieutenant silently saluted and left.

Fergus said, 'Are we really doing this, Shirasu?'

'We've talked about it more than once. I don't think we have any choice if we intend to keep faith with our vows,' she said, and turned to Khalila. 'You're injured, child. I'll summon a Medica.'

Khalila realised she was shaking from the pain, but at least it wasn't growing worse. If she uncovered it now, she was afraid the Greek Fire would find new breath and spread. 'I'm fine,' she lied. 'Scholar Murasaki, I need to know what you intend to do.'

'I would have thought it was obvious,' Murasaki said. 'I will continue to serve the people of Cadiz and the people of this country. If necessary, we will protect this place and these books with our lives. And I will reject, by force, any attempt by the Archivist to take control of this Serapeum. You may tell King Ramón Alfonse that while we continue to serve the Great Library and its ideals, we do not support the Archivist. Nor will we fight on his behalf.'

Khalila bowed her head. 'Thank you.'

'Thank Scholar Wolfe,' Murasaki said. 'The Archivist's injustice to him is the only evidence I needed.'

'One more thing,' Khalila said. 'A favour.'

'You saved my life. I think I might owe you this.'

'Use of your Translation Chamber.'

'To go where?'

'Alexandria,' Khalila said. 'Not to the Serapeum. The High Garda compound.'

Murasaki's brows climbed. 'Are you so eager to be killed?'

'We have friends there,' Khalila said. 'And a plan. If it happens as I hope, you may follow us home, honoured Scholar, to help us restore the Library we both love.'

There was a long silence – too long for comfort – and Murasaki finally inclined her head a regal degree. 'This I will do for you,' she said. 'But, Scholar, be warned: this is not a game for children, or amateurs. You have taken on something so much larger than you know. I hope you are not crushed under its weight. I believe that if you live long enough, you might do great things.'

Khalila bowed and put her hand to her heart. 'You honour me, Scholar. May I leave to gather my friends?'

'And how do you know you'll not be leading them into a neat trap?' Fergus rumbled. He was still frowning; maybe it was simply the way his face fell even at the best of times. 'Easy for us to take you all and offer you up to the Archivist.'

'Yes,' Khalila said. 'It would be. But I think there is some honour, and some wisdom, left inside the Library, Captain.'

She turned, took a deep breath, and walked out of the jaws of the dragon into the wider compound, past waiting High Garda who did nothing to stop her. The gates opened, and she dared to hope that finally, something was going their way.

Then she was almost knocked over by Dario as he threw his arms around her.

'That was stupid,' Dario told her as he pressed his lips against her forehead. 'If you hadn't come back—'

'You'd have gone to your cousin,' she said.

'No. No, flower. I'd have fought every one of them to get to you.'

She sighed. 'Then we are both stupid. I'd do the same for you.'

'Your hand!' He frowned down at it, cradling it carefully. 'Let's find a healer.'

'In a while. First, let's find Captain Santi.' She pulled back and looked at him directly. 'I've found us a way home.'

EPHEMERA

Excerpt from the personal journal of Niccolo Santi. Not yet available in the Codex.

I sit with my journal and my pen, and I find nothing to say. I look back on other pages, and I understand why; every page is full of Christopher. The things he does that annoy me, or amuse me, or delight me. The joy of sitting together in the quiet between missions, when we still had those to look forward to together. He has always been a sharp ball of thorns, and difficult to hold on to, but that has never stopped me from loving him.

In the silence where he should be, I hear nothing.

I wait.

I try to lock away the rage I feel for this stupid Brightwell boy and his stupid plan that has sent the man I love into another dark hole in the ground, endless nights of fear and pain and anguish. There is nothing in the world worth Christopher's suffering. Not to me. Let the Library rise or fall; it only matters to me if he is alive, and safe, and sane.

If that is heresy, then I will be happy to die a heretic.

If he comes broken out of that place – and he must

come out of it – then I will take every bruise, every hurt out on Jess Brightwell.

God help me if this takes Christopher from me for good.

PART SEVEN

WOLFE

CHAPTER TWENTY

'All right,' Wolfe said in a low whisper, leaning against the wall that separated him from Ariane, on his right. 'Ready?'

'Ready,' she whispered back.

'Twenty-two guards on this level,' he said. 'Four hallways, with four guards always assigned to each one. Two walk, and two rest. Each guard is armed with a standard High Garda pistol, rifle, and two knives. There are six automata: one on each hallway, and two that roam at random. Guards change in six-hour shifts, but each hallway changes an hour after the one to its right. All right. Repeat it.'

Ariane repeated it. Where she faltered – she was not well, and he worried that she wouldn't be strong enough to keep this up, soon enough – he patiently reminded her, until she'd recounted it exactly three times. Then she moved on to teach the sequence to the person housed to her right.

This was the routine now, every day, noting details and adding to them, and sharing so that every person had the same information, should any opportunities come.

But it wasn't enough. Not yet.

Wolfe wanted to sleep, to be rested for what was coming . . . but once he stretched out, as always, relaxing brought the memories. He'd fought them every night, sometimes all night; lack of rest made them more vivid and compelling, but the vicious circle was hard to break. His hands trembled. His skin itched so fiercely that he rubbed scars until they bled. Hunger, thirst, the constant, gnawing chill . . . those he could stand. But the memories were the worst.

Please, Nic. Help me. Help me one more night. He slowly closed his eyes and summoned up Nic. First his smile, the one that came so rarely in public and so easily in private. The rich, dark colour of his eyes, the soft silk of his hair. The scrape of a beard Nic could never quite shave clean for more than an hour or two.

His neck. Powerful shoulders. Scars. The shape of his chin and his hands. Everything about him, built memory by memory, until Wolfe could feel his warmth, his strength, as a barrier between him and the pulling darkness. *What are you so afraid of, Christopher?* Santi's voice, quiet and gentle in the night. *Your scars have healed. They can't break you now. You are made of scars, and so am I, and together, we can forget them all.*

I'm not afraid, Wolfe told him. *Not now.* He twined his fingers with the warmth of Niccolo Santi's hair and kissed him, and the warmth of that let him drift away, lost in the feeling, until the nightmares lost their way and sleep found him.

It didn't find him for long, because he woke in a convulsive rush and sat up with his heart pounding and nerves jumping. He'd heard something, something more than just the random noise of a prison.

There was someone inside his cell.

Dark as it was, he could hardly make out the shape, but he was certain it was a human shape, wrapped in black.

'Quiet,' a voice whispered. Barely a thread of sound. 'Hush now, Scholar. Crying out will do you no good.'

The voice was too soft to identify, but he knew it on some deep, visceral level. *I'm imagining things*, he thought. *I've lost my mind. No one can get in here, past the guards, past the automata.*

For a wild, random moment, he thought he knew who it was, and he whispered, 'Nic?' But of course it wasn't Niccolo Santi, conjured up by his longing.

'No.' The voice was just a whisper. 'You know who it is, Scholar. You always know when I arrive, don't you?'

He stopped breathing. Like a child, hiding in the dark from the monsters, that was all he could do. There was nowhere to run. No one to call on for help.

'You know,' the shadow said. 'We're old friends, you and I. I've been with you in your darkest moments. I've cleaned your wounds. I've listened to you weep. Remember?'

'No,' Wolfe whispered. 'No. You're not here. You're not—'

A cold finger touched his lips. Cold and thin as bone.

He closed his eyes.

'I'm not here to hurt you,' the voice said. 'I am here to ask you a question, Scholar. You remember how I asked you questions, don't you? Sometimes it was very gentle. Those were the good times.'

That had only made it worse, the times when the questions had been kind and soft, and there had been a cup of tea and a sweet pastry and a bath. Fresh clothes. Wolfe remembered it so vividly every scar began to ache.

Kindness made the inevitable cruelty so much worse.

'Do you know who made me do that to you, Scholar? It was your old friend the Artifex. He's always been afraid of you. You, you see, would have become the Artifex, and he knew that. He's still afraid of you taking his place. Is this his doing now?'

Wolfe shook his head. His throat had gone painfully dry. *I'm talking to a phantom*, he thought, but the finger touching his lips felt so real. So cold, but so real.

'The Archivist,' he said. 'It's the Archivist who wants us all dead. He's old. His grip is slipping on the throne.'

'More than you know,' the whisper said. 'Be patient. This will be over soon. They've left you alone, but the questions are coming. And I will be coming back to ask them.'

He knew that was true; the questions always came, and always, always, the grey, pale shadow was there to ask them. He was going mad, completely mad, and this was an impossible nightmare.

The cold finger left his lips. The chill lingered like a fog.

'You let me go,' Wolfe whispered. 'You said you'd let me go.'

'I always keep my promises. You remember, don't you?'

He did. *He remembered*. And that was more frightening than the idea that this was a ghost, a phantom, a madness. 'Qualls.' The name alone made him feel faint, and he had to brace himself against the wall. 'No. You're gone. *Gone*. You let me go.'

'Did I?' Qualls gave out a terrible, chilling chuckle, a scrape of iron on stone, of screams echoing from far away. Even in full light, the man had always been terrifying. Something about him was dead, and it showed in his eyes, his smile, the not-quite-human way he moved. 'Very well. Go. The cell door is open . . . if you have the courage to run.'

And then he was gone, as quickly as that. A shadow in shadow.

No, Wolfe thought. *He was never here. Couldn't have been here. I'm broken.*

Santi's voice whispered, *Broken bones heal twice as strong*.

Wolfe held his head in his hands, shivering, sick, shaking from the onslaught of memory, and finally, he realised there was a way to know if it had ever happened at all.

He slipped out of bed, went to the cell door, and pulled.

It opened without a sound.

Wolfe froze, shocked into stillness. He'd never expected this, never thought it would move.

He was here. Qualls was here.

He went weak against the bars. *Go. I can run. I can escape.*

But something inside him twisted and screamed in terror at the thought. *I won't make it.*

He heard a soft growl.

Red lights glowed in the darkness: the eyes of the sphinx, moving forward with slow, deliberate pads. Wolfe leant against the bars and tightly wrapped a hand around the bars to hold the door shut. If the sphinx pushed . . .

The growl turned to a hiss, and the light grew brighter, until quite suddenly it flared into a red glare bright enough to dazzle his eyes. He blocked the worst of it with his left hand while keeping his right firmly around the bars, and slumped down. Hoped he looked as desperate and dejected as he felt.

'I can't sleep,' he said to the thing. 'Please. Help me. Tell them I need something to help me sleep. A bit of wine, a drug, *anything*. For the love of the gods—'

In the harsh red light, he saw a lion's paw swipe at the bars at the level of his fingers. *If I let go and it isn't locked . . .*

But he had to let go or have his fingers severed. He snatched his hand back just in time, and leant all his weight against the door as he covered his face. Through the cover, he sensed the sphinx was pacing back and forth in a restless figure eight. A paw rang sharply against the bars again, and he flinched. Pretending to cry left him perilously near the real thing, but he held himself back from plummeting off that cliff. He'd spent months in a cell like this, huddled and broken. He wouldn't go back to that.

'Please,' he said, in a voice he allowed to tremble and break. 'Please, for mercy's sake, let me *sleep*.'

It sounded true because it was. A wail came from deep within him, and he let it out. A tormented, ugly sound.

The sphinx hissed, and then he heard it take up its slow, steady pace moving down the hallway. The other cells were deathly quiet now, no rustles or moans, snores or cries. Everyone was aware of what had happened.

Wolfe moved to the corner of his cell closest to Saleh's and whispered, 'Noise. I need noise. Pass the word to the other end of the hall.'

'Done,' Saleh whispered back. Word passed quickly. Coughs and sneezes began at the other end. Snoring. A voice counting out loud.

Freedom was there, in his grasp. He knew the guards and the automaton routes, but even so, an escape would be impossible without tools and help. He couldn't do this. He couldn't.

He couldn't run and leave the others here.

You have to try. All of us agreed we would, if the chance came.

He reached out for the door and pulled.

It didn't open.

It was locked.

Had it ever been unlocked at all?

It happened before. You imagined Santi was with you the last time. You imagined he was taken to be questioned. You imagined you could hear his screams. You kept crying for them to stop hurting him. It had all been very real, in those dark months. He had needed someone so badly that he'd created Santi out of whole imagination . . . but even that desperate delusion hadn't been able to block out the very real pain.

You're imagining things again.

No, that couldn't be true. The door had been unlocked, hadn't it? He'd felt it move under his hand. *And you heard Santi's screams back then, but he was never there.*

But why would he imagine Qualls? His torturer? What sense did that make?

Wolfe put a hand on the wall to steady himself. The rough stone felt damp and slick under his palm, and very real. He concentrated on that, on the texture of what he could feel, the smell of the place. *This is reality.*

The door had felt real as it moved, too.

He was coming apart, just as he had before, in a cell like this under the Forum in Rome. Qualls had been there. Imagining him was a sign that his healed, twice-strong bones were cracking. That he couldn't hold.

Wolfe collapsed to the floor and rolled over on his back, staring at the black ceiling. Opened his mouth and started to scream without making a sound. He felt tears streaming down from the corners of his eyes, and the ache inside felt black and empty and bottomless.

I'm not strong. I'm broken. I can't save anyone. I can't even save myself.

As he lay there, he heard the whispering tread of the sphinx again, saw the muted red glow of the eyes turn to regard him, but he didn't move, and the monster didn't lurk. When he was sure it was past, he rolled up to his feet and crawled into the bed. He knew he wouldn't sleep, but it was more comfortable than the cold stone, at least by a small margin.

He felt Santi's phantom warmth settle beside him, felt his lover's arms around him, and heard Santi whisper, *I'll be with you. When you think you can't endure, I will help. Believe in me, if you can't believe in yourself.* No, that was a memory, not a phantom; when he'd come back from Rome a broken, shaking shell of a man, that's exactly what Nic had said to him.

There was no Qualls. Qualls was a spectre, a ghost, a terrible memory screaming under the surface. A phantom, to drag him into the darkness.

He deliberately summoned up Nic in every line, every texture, every memory he could find, and held him close. Nic would keep him safe.

It was a trick, a fidget, a lie, but it let him slide away into a dark, dreamless, whispering sleep at last.

CHAPTER TWENTY-ONE

Morning brought a certain sour satisfaction with it. Wolfe woke alone, curled on his bed, and though there was never any morning light to help mark the hours, the glows had been brightened again. He heard the normal shuffle of men and women in their cells, and before he rose, he quickly ran through the map in his mind, placing each of them in the three-dimensional model he'd built, then adding the guards one by one, in as much detail as he could. Last, the automata.

The imaginary visit in the night seemed like a vague dream to him now, and he was glad of it. It was a bitter taste in his mouth to think he could be so fragile. They hadn't even used torture yet, only deprivation and the boredom and routine of prison.

But the counterpoint to it was the sure and certain knowledge that come the Feast of Greater Burning, they were going to die, and horribly. So in a sense, the torture was ever present, and none of the guards had to sully their hands with prisoner blood. Not, he thought, that most would blink at the job.

'Wolfe!'

A tap on the bars from Saleh's corner, and Wolfe rose and walked there. 'What is it?'

Saleh let out a breathless laugh. 'What do you mean? What happened last night?'

He'd forgotten that he'd spoken to Saleh in the depths of his delusion. Or at least had hoped that the conversation had been imagined as well. Wolfe took a moment to think how best to say it, but he didn't have a chance before they heard a sharp cry from somewhere down the hall. Hard to pinpoint where it was coming from, but it only took seconds for word to be passed down the row.

'That's my father,' Saleh said. He was trying to sound calm, but Wolfe could hear the tightness underneath it. 'They've taken him out of the cell. Where are they taking him? For what?'

'I don't know,' Wolfe said. 'Focus, Saleh. He's valuable. They won't execute him out of hand, no matter what he does . . .' His voice trailed off, and he blinked.

Because it was true. Only a few of them, of course; the patriarch of the Seif family was one, Scholar Maria Kent was another, located down a level on the east hall. One or two others who stood high enough to be counted as truly exceptional prisoners that the Archivist would want to make a public show of destroying.

'They've taken him away,' Saleh said. He was trying to sound calm, but the worry gave his voice a tremble it didn't normally have. 'What are they going to do to him, Scholar? Is this because of my sister? Because of *you*?'

It was, without any shadow of a doubt. Wolfe knew he bore a great deal of responsibility, if not guilt, for what was happening to the Seif family; he'd have to carry that, too, without flinching.

'Yes,' Wolfe said honestly. 'It's why I'm here, to help you.' *Please, all the gods of Egypt, let that be the plan.*

'Then *help*! My father is an honest man, a Scholar, loyal always to the Library. You can't let them hurt him!'

Wolfe closed his eyes for a moment, then opened them.

'You're right,' he said. 'I can't.' He raised his voice. 'Guard! I need a guard!'

The man who came at his call wasn't alone; he was paced by one of the sphinxes. Their stares were equally warning. 'What do you want?' the soldier asked.

'I want to speak with the Artifex Magnus,' he said. 'Immediately. It's important.'

'We'll get to you,' the soldier said. 'Wait your turn, Stormcrow.'

'All right. I will. And I'll be sure to tell the Artifex what you said when he finally sees me, so that he knows who to blame.'

'Blame for what?'

'My old students are planning an attack,' Wolfe said. 'A daring and potentially ruinous one for the Library that will happen in just a very few hours, now. I know when and where. But by all means, continue uselessly interrogating prisoners who have nothing to do with it. I'm sure that's highly effective.' His contempt, he'd long ago learnt, had a special sting to it, and he deployed it now to good effect. It wasn't an act. He really did find these High Garda Elites to be contemptible. They'd long ago compromised their true loyalty to pin it to the person of one man. When they'd lost their path wasn't material any more, and all the excuses in the world meant nothing. They were corrupt, and on some level, they knew.

'Why should I believe you?'

Wolfe shrugged. 'Then, don't. As I said: I'll make sure the Artifex hears the full story. Including how you failed to report an imminent threat against the Library. Never mind. I'm happy to wait.'

He turned away from the bars and stretched out on the bunk. He even added a tuneless hum.

It only took fifteen seconds, counted in fast pulse beats, for the soldier to turn the key in the lock. 'Out,' he snapped. 'Now. If this is a trick, you'll suffer for it.'

'Of course,' Wolfe said. 'Naturally.'

He sat up, fought against a wave of very real nausea and dizziness, and forced himself to his feet. He would show none of it – none of the exhaustion, the fear, the screaming panic. He'd had years of experience now at concealing it from everyone except those who mattered to him.

A broken bone heals twice as strong, he told himself. Santi had taught him that mantra the night he'd stumbled in the door of their house. He could still hear the soft, insistent whisper of it if he chose. Santi had bathed him, dried him, clothed him, held him through the night to whisper it in a constant, bracing refrain, because Wolfe had been unable to speak or explain where he'd been.

Stay with me, Nic, he thought, as the shackles closed around his wrists. *I need you more than ever.*

As they passed Saleh's cell, Wolfe locked gazes with the young man and nodded. Saleh nodded back. He'd keep things moving forward here; there was no doubt. Khalila's brother could be counted on.

Even if Jess Brightwell's could not.

'Scholar? Scholar Wolfe?' One of the librarians – Kima, he remembered her from his circuits; she'd been the senior at the Serapeum in Leeds – leant against the bars and held out her hand. He brushed her fingers with his, which resulted in a warning to Kima and a push between his shoulders to quicken his pace. He passed every cell and marked every face. They were all watching. Trusting him to do *something* to redeem them.

One thing about being a Research Scholar, as he'd been for

almost all of his lifetime: he knew things that those who had no such background couldn't imagine.

And he knew the Alexandria Serapeum better than even the guards who patrolled it. If he could get there, he knew exactly what to do.

But first, he was going to have to spin the most fabulous, compelling tale he could to take to the Artifex, and then to the Archivist. It would have to be the best lie of his life.

He knew what it would have to be.

Brendan Brightwell is not who you think he is. You've been misled.

That would certainly set the Archivist's teeth on edge. As lies went, it was just bold enough to work.

EPHEMERA

From a treatise by the Medica Phlogistes written in 1733. Interdicted from the Codex to the Black Archives upon review in 1881.

Although there are a great many of my very learned colleagues who disagree with me on every point, I contend that while the number of Obscurists is, without a doubt, decreasing over time, there is no evidence that the trait that makes an Obscurist so valuable – the ability to sense and manipulate the universal fluidic energy that lies beneath everything – is not latently present in all of us. A gifted metalworker is not thought to possess the Obscurist talent, and yet, he is able to fashion metal in ways that no one else can duplicate. A Scholar able to tell a story in a unique and involving way . . . is that not also such an expression? And many Medica know full well that we have a touch of the talent, and we can use it to enhance our cures and treatments. In many religions, this is known and accepted as fact.

Why, then, do we treat Obscurists as such a special and prized breed?

The answer lies not in our desire for the innate value

of their talents, though we value the skill of the Medica, the metalworker, or the writer.

The answer is that we value them out of proportion because we simply need them to operate a system that has not been changed in thousands of years. That is, namely, the Codex and the Archives. If the Obscurists were no longer necessary to make those core functions of the Library work, how much more could be accomplished in our world? How much better and faster and stronger would the Library now be?

We have fettered ourselves to a system that is bound to fail, and is failing now.

I am only a Medica, and not even Medica Magnus, but I will say this: we must see beyond our present needs to our future state.

If we do not, there may be no future for us at all.

PART EIGHT

MORGAN

CHAPTER TWENTY-TWO

It took weeks for Morgan to work out what clever thing Gregory had done to cripple her abilities. Elegant work, masterful . . . and, she strongly suspected, not his doing. Someone else had written the script, which by itself was useless; the targeted Obscurist had to have a particular innocuous drug in her system for the script to take any effect.

There was nothing she could do about the script, which he'd built into the crafting of her collar.

But the innocent companion drug? That was a point of failure.

She and Annis both looked up at the quiet knock, and Annis whispered, 'Ready?' Morgan nodded, and the older woman stood and went to open the unlocked door.

The kitchen server brought the tray and set it down silently on the nearest table.

'Good, I'm famished, and the wee girl here needs that soup; she can't seem to keep anything else down,' Annis said. Her winning smile and warm charm disarmed whatever wariness the server might have had, and he smiled back, and instead of bolting from the room, as he'd probably been directed to do, he took the time to uncover the dishes and show Annis the contents.

'Lovely,' she said. 'Just lovely, the work you do. Food is home, as I'm sure you know, and I thank you for it.' She put a gentle touch on the young man's wrist, staring straight into his eyes. 'You're so tired, dear lad. Why don't you sit for a moment?'

If this was going to work without violence, it had to work in that moment . . . and it did. The server, without a question, slipped quietly into the chair next to the table. Morgan watched in fascination as Annis weaved a silken, unbreakable web of words, lulling the man into a relaxed, trance-like state. She'd known Annis's Obscurist powers were slight, but in this one area, she truly excelled.

Morgan sat up slowly when Annis gestured, but didn't come closer.

'Now, my friend, is there any special seasoning in these dishes?' Annis asked.

'Yes.' The young man's voice was flat but calm. Annis sent Morgan a nod. All was well. 'Salt, pepper, curry powder, cardamom . . .'

'That's in my dish, yes. And in my friend's soup? Was there anything added to hers that is not added to someone else's?'

The answer came slowly, but firmly. 'Yes.'

'And what is it?'

'I don't know. It's from a bottle we were given. It isn't harmful.'

Annis's glance at Morgan had taken on a hard look, but her voice remained quiet and gentle. 'Of course not; you'd never do such a thing. None of you would. And who assured you it was harmless?'

'The Obscurist.' The young man frowned a little this time, as if the mere mention of the title disturbed him.

'I see. Tell me, do you like him?'

'It doesn't matter. I'm loyal to the Tower and the Library.'

'Yes, I know that. And it is to your credit – what is your name, young man?'

'Friedrich,' he said.

'Well, Friedrich, you have done nothing at all wrong in following the Obscurist's orders; of course you haven't. That liquid you add is as harmless as water. So it really doesn't matter which bowl you add it to, does it?'

'No. But I was told—'

'If it's harmless, it doesn't matter, isn't that right?'

'Yes, that's right.' His frown cleared.

'And could you do me a favour, my friend Friedrich?'

'Of course, Obscurist Annis.'

'From now on, when you reach for that bottle, you will pour it instead into the food *next* to the one designated for Obscurist Morgan.'

'But I have orders . . .'

'The liquid is harmless, remember? So it doesn't matter which food it goes into. You'd never do anything to harm any one of us, isn't that right?'

'Yes,' Friedrich said, and then more strongly, 'Yes, that's right.'

'Then from now on, you will just add that liquid to my bowl, or if I am not eating at the same time as Obscurist Morgan, then to anyone else's food. That sounds perfectly fine, doesn't it?'

'Yes.'

'So what are you going to do at the next meal?'

'Add the liquid to someone else's bowl. Yours first. But any one other than Obscurist Morgan's if you aren't there.'

'Wonderful. Now. Friedrich, I know you work very hard, don't you?'

'I like my work.'

'Of course you do. But you must take time off sometime!'

'I work five of the seven days,' he said. 'Two of the days I leave the Tower and go to my parents' home.'

'And when you are gone, who takes your place?'

'Millicent Thorpe.'

'When will she next be taking over your position?'

'In two days.'

'Well, that's lovely,' Annis said, and her voice had taken on a lazy, slow reassurance again. 'You should look forward to your time off, Friedrich.'

He nodded but didn't answer.

Morgan snapped her fingers and scribbled out a message on a scrap of paper. Annis took it, read it, and said, 'Friedrich, one last thing: when I say the magic word, you are going to forget we ever had this conversation, but you are going to do as we agreed and never again put that liquid into Obscurist Morgan's food, all right?'

'All right.'

'And when I say the magic word, you will stand up and go about your duties. You will only remember that you delivered the food as you are supposed to. You understand that?'

'Yes.'

'Good. Are you listening, Friedrich? The magic word is . . . *forget*.'

And with that, the young man straightened, stood up, and walked straight to the door. Morgan watched him leave with a little feeling of awe. When the door shut, she turned that stare on Annis. 'That was . . . unbelievable. When you told me you could do it, I honestly didn't believe you. I didn't know an Obscurist could affect a mind so directly without some kind of script, and drugs!'

'No, no, it isn't about being an Obscurist at all. This is merely mesmerism, something anyone can learn if they've a mind and a bit of a talent, though it's sure that the Library tries to keep

Mesmers pushed away from the legitimate trades. You'll find them more in criminal circles than anywhere else, as someone who has a little bit of talent and a lot of time on my hands, knows well. I know a great many obscure and only partly legal things.'

'Thank you, Annis. I don't know how to—'

Annis waved it away. 'Please. You think I'm doing it just for you? The more I can do to spite Gregory, the better I like my life here. It's what Keria would have wanted. She'd have torn his head off for what he's doing, and I'd have held him down. Here.' She picked up the plate of fragrant, steaming rice scented delicately of saffron and topped with a rich, red sauce. 'Hope you enjoy curry as much as I do. It's lamb and potato vindaloo.'

'Sorry about the soup,' Morgan said. She took a cautious mouthful of the curry and nearly choked as it set her tongue burning like Greek Fire. 'God!'

'Delicious, isn't it?' Annis gave her a cheery grin. 'Food of champions, my girl, and no mistake. Eat up. You'll need your strength for what comes next.'

Morgan wiped her tearing eyes and kept at it, and after the first fiery shock, the taste of the vindaloo made her wolf it down in happy mouthfuls. Still searingly hot, but she could get used to it, she thought. 'How soon will the drug be out of my system, do you think?'

'I'm not sure. It was damn clever, how he drugged you obviously the first time and then secretly from then on. I'd say at least a day; they've been dosing you for a while, and I'd rather not try it before time, since you said it hurt badly enough to put you down when you last tried to work any aggressive uses. I can explain away headaches and nausea, but fainting spells mean they might send you to the Medica, and for all we know, the Medica's going to dope you with the same again.'

'Frightening – but realistic – thought. All right. I'll give it a day.' She chewed her lip. 'Did you speak to Natasha about the additions to the Codex monitoring scripts?'

'Aye. And she handed me my ass for it. Not my business, above my skills, all that.' Annis shrugged. 'But I did manage to gather that the monitoring has been redone, again, which means they're looking for you to try a contact. I wouldn't.'

Damn. Jess was alone out there, and she had no idea what kind of trouble he was in . . . or what was happening to Scholar Wolfe. Just as they couldn't know her situation, she supposed. What kind of a conspiracy couldn't coordinate efforts? One doomed to fail. And she *had* to be the one to solve that problem, not Jess. If he grew desperate enough, he'd do something brave and foolish, and she needed to keep him from it by holding up her end of the job . . . but neither of them had counted on the Iron Tower using drugs to control her.

Annis was right, though. Using her powers in any way that Gregory hadn't specifically authorised would result in paralysing agony right now, and that alone would give away her intentions.

'What about doing something without powers?' Morgan asked.

'Such as?'

'Trying to see him.'

Annis knew very well who *him* meant, and her faded red brows shot up in sceptical arches. 'Not wise,' she said. 'Besides, he won't see you. He doesn't see anyone. Not even Gregory can break the wards on his door, you know. Not even Keria could do that.'

'Did she try?'

'I don't know, but I think it's more that he built them with a personal key that only she possessed. She was the one person Eskander trusted fully, and she was the one person who could have done it with or without his permission, given time. But she always asked before she went to him. And he usually allowed it.'

'Were they in love?'

Annis thought about that. She spooned up her soup quietly for a while, then put the utensil down and reached for a glass of water. Annis was careful about the water, and they knew it, at least, was safe to drink. 'Oh yes, desperately,' she finally said. 'But love is never as simple as you'd think, is it? Or as easy. At least it isn't in here; no idea how it is out there. They understood that love was a trap, a weapon to be used against them. Eskander never wanted to be here, not a single day. And he fought it, over and over. Then, when their son was born, he stopped fighting . . . but when Wolfe was taken away from the Tower, put into the orphanage, that was the breaking point, I think. Love can't heal all. It can't repair broken hearts. And I think in the end they were both shattered by it.'

It seemed a breathtakingly sad story, and it made Morgan shiver a little; she loved Jess, or at least, she thought she did. Or was it only that he seemed so taken with her that she'd accepted it as fate? She *did* care for him, and deeply. But the more time away, the more she saw herself clearly . . . the less sure she was that she was what Jess needed, or wanted. Or that he was right for her, either.

Maybe they would end up like Eskander and Keria. Or maybe this would turn out differently. She closed her eyes and imagined Jess, and his image came vividly; ink stains on his fingers, that quiet, odd smile of his, the sharp intelligence of how he analysed things. The sudden bursts of precisely calculated speed and violence when he needed them. She'd never met someone with so little fear, and she wondered if he knew how afraid she was, every day. There was something both reassuring and intimidating about being with him.

And she did want him. Thinking of him made her remember the way his hands felt against her skin, his lips on hers.

Love is never as simple as you think. Annis was right about that. And in this moment, she couldn't properly sort her feelings, except that she wanted Jess more than she'd ever wanted anyone else. Was that love? The kind of love that lasted? She didn't know. And for now, it didn't matter.

Nothing mattered except contacting Eskander, and in a way that didn't alert Gregory to her intentions.

'Did you get the plans?' Morgan asked, and Annis nodded and reached beneath her robe into a hidden pocket – one she'd sewn herself – to retrieve a thin, folded sheet of paper.

'Had to do it small,' she said. 'But it's accurate enough. He's warded every way in, though, as you can see; I've marked them down. The only one that – as far as I know – isn't warded is the window, and it doesn't open. Won't break, either.'

'What about this?' Morgan put the empty plate back on the tray, and pointed to a tiny square high in the wall of Eskander's rooms. He had three rooms, as large as the chambers that Gregory now occupied and likely just as opulent: a bedroom, a bath, and a sitting room. The square was on the wall of the room Annis's tiny script had designated as the bedroom.

'Too small for any human to pass,' Annis said. 'And screens on both ends welded in place. It's the air venting. There's another here . . .' She pointed to one located in the sitting room on an opposite wall. 'But I don't see what possible good they could do.'

'What's the nearest access point to this vent? One we can reach?'

'There isn't one. They connect directly back to the central air-processing hub; for him, that would be on the twelfth level.'

'So theoretically, if we get into the air-processing hub, we could talk to him,' Morgan said. 'Directly. With no one overhearing.'

Annis blinked and looked at the paper, then frowned in thought. 'That's two floors away,' she said. 'And I can't be certain no one else would hear, if you're shouting loud enough to be heard that far away.'

'Who said anything about shouting?' Morgan smiled. 'I'm talking about sending down a resonant crystal, with the matched component on our end.'

Annis looked blank. 'I took a fancy to mesmerism, not engineering,' she said. 'Explain.'

'Sympathetic vibration,' Morgan said. 'There is an entire department of Obscurists on Level Four who are working on crystals that are sympathetically linked, and you may speak into one and listen from the other.'

'Long-distance talking?'

'You didn't know?'

'I don't pay much attention,' Annis admitted. 'The engineers from Artifex are always sending over blueprints for some nonsensical invention or other, and few of them prove to work. It's not my area. It all sounds crackbrained to me.'

'Oh, it should work,' Morgan said. 'All we have to do is obtain a raw pair; the script to link them together should be simple enough, once I know what the frequency is to vibrate them.'

'And how do you propose we steal such a thing?'

'We don't. We find an Obscurist working there who wants out of this iron trap we're in, and we work together.'

'No, no, no, we can't do that. The chances of betrayal double with every person you tell!'

Morgan gave her a long, serious look, then took the older woman's hands. 'Annis,' she said. 'It's why I came here. It's why I've risked my life and my freedom to enter this Tower. To make sure that no one is ever locked in it again against their will. There will be risks. And we have to start taking them *now*.'

Annis's hands tightened on hers, and the woman's cool, translucent skin seemed to pale even further . . . but then she nodded. 'Well, then. You'll be wanting to know who in that section might be helpful.'

'I would.'

'I'll make a list of those to avoid at all costs. Most everyone else in the Tower would listen to a plan – but mind you: there isn't one of them that would risk imprisonment or injury. We've all heard talk of rebellion, and most support it in their hearts. It's their cowardly bodies you have to convince.' Annis took a deep breath. 'Perhaps I could mesmer one of them to bring us the crystals.'

'No.'

'It would minimise—'

'No,' Morgan said again. 'I'm doing this to free us, not enslave us further. I don't like what we had to do to Friedrich, but he was already being used; we just ensured it wouldn't be effective. I won't do the same to a fellow prisoner in this place.'

Annis looked sad, and she also looked wary. 'Lass, I don't think you understand. You were born out there, wild in the world. We are like birds who've never known but a cage. We see the world through our windows, but I fear if you threw our doors wide open, we might be afraid to leave.'

'But you'd have the choice.' Morgan touched the collar around her neck. 'Freedom doesn't mean you have to leave. It means you choose. It isn't done for you.'

Annis slowly nodded. 'All right. I'll visit the workshop. I'm sure I have a friend or two there.'

'Be careful,' Morgan said. 'We're going against Gregory now.

And he's already killed one Obscurist. He won't hesitate to kill more to hang on to his power.'

Annis winked at her. 'I've run circles around that little shite since we were both your age,' she said. 'I'll be back soon. Oh . . . almost forgot. *Presta atención.*'

She left, taking the food tray with her; Morgan felt the tiny snap of power as the listening scripts were activated again. She was tempted to follow, but she knew Annis was right; the Obscurist had eyes on her at all times, and the only safe place was here, in the rooms they searched daily for new intrusions. *The crystals would be a fine way to spy on someone at a distance*, she thought. Until that moment she hadn't thought of it, but now that she had, she wondered if there might not be a second use for the crystals, after making contact with Eskander.

Knowing what Gregory might be up to . . . that could be valuable.

Annis didn't return for a few hours, which made Morgan pace the floor in worry, but when she finally did, she had a man of about her own age in tow. In fact, he had his hand around Annis's waist and a smile on his face that quickly faltered when he saw Morgan in the room.

Annis shut the door. '*Silencio*. Morgan, this is Pyotr. An old, old friend of mine.'

Pyotr was a man who'd aged well; his hair had silvered, and his strong face – never pretty, Morgan guessed – still looked striking. He nodded to her cautiously. 'Hello.'

'Hello, Pyotr,' she replied, and sat down on her bed.

He stared at her in confusion, then at Annis. 'Forgive me, love, but . . . I must have misunderstood.'

Morgan realised that Annis had coaxed him here with a promise of something a great deal more intimate than a conversation, and had to stifle an uncomfortable laugh. Of all the things she didn't want to think about, Annis's love life was top of the list. Annis was the first to admit that it was quite colourful.

'You didn't at all,' Annis told him cheerfully. 'I lied dreadfully, but if you're a patient man, I might just keep all my promises. Make yourself comfortable, Pyotr. We've got something to discuss with you.'

Annis's instincts proved to be as good as ever; Pyotr, it turned out, had been dragged to the Iron Tower against his will when he was almost fifteen and had never stopped wanting to find his way out again. 'You're the one who escaped the Tower,' he said. 'Twice.'

'I did,' Morgan said. 'More than twice, actually, but once I came back without anyone the wiser. And I came back this time under my own will again.'

'Gregory says you were dragged back.'

'He would,' Annis said sourly. She sat on her bed and patted the spot next to her. 'We've got a long story.'

'Short, really,' Morgan said, as the other man sank down beside Annis. 'How badly do you want to get out of the Iron Tower? Not just as a fugitive. As a free man, no collar around your neck. Free to come and go as you please.'

He blinked. He'd been here a long time, and for a moment she was afraid that it had been too long for him to remember the rebellious, angry boy who'd been brought here fighting. But then he said, 'If you can promise such a thing, I'd fight for it. And I'm far from the only one. But don't say it if you can't do it. Lives will be lost.'

'I know,' Morgan said. 'And I promise you that this *will* happen. I am here to make it happen.'

'You're alone,' he pointed out.

'She's not,' Annis said quietly. 'And you aren't the first we've talked to.'

A lie, but a small one, and it seemed to reassure Pyotr that they were serious. 'Still. Rebellions have been tried before. What makes you any different?'

'We're going to have the strongest Obscurist in the world on our side,' Morgan said.

'Gregory?' he laughed out loud. 'Don't be stupid.'

'Gregory was never the strongest,' Annis said. 'Keria was the *second* strongest. But you know who outshone them all.'

Pyotr turned and looked at her with naked astonishment. 'The hermit? That's ridiculous. He hasn't even been heard from since Keria's death. He might be dead himself in there, except he still accepts meals!'

'He isn't dead,' Morgan said. 'I can . . . I suppose the best way to say it is that I can *feel* him. Like heat against my skin. I think he's biding his time.'

'Until what?'

'Until we get the stomach for a real fight,' Annis said. 'You remember how he was. Of all of us, he never accepted this. Never accommodated to it. When his door opens, everything changes.'

'First we have to convince him to try,' Morgan said. 'And that's where you come in.'

It took half an hour to convince Pyotr of their sincerity, but by the time he rose to leave, he seemed a different man: stronger, taller, full of purpose. 'Now, be careful,' Annis cautioned him. 'I know you're putting yourself at risk, but be as careful as you can be. We can't afford to lose you, my sweet.'

'I know how to do it,' he said. 'The scripts we apply to the crystals often shatter them. I'll simply substitute broken crystals for a good pair. No one will notice. But the scripts rarely work, you know. I myself only have a success rate of forty per cent, and I am the most successful.'

'Then we'll do it together,' Morgan said. 'Thank you, Pyotr. Thank you for trusting us.'

'You, I don't know. Her?' He laughed and, in a move so practised that it seemed rehearsed, gathered Annis into his arms and kissed her soundly. They parted laughing, and the delight in her eyes flashed like fire. 'Her, I know. And trust. I will be back.'

'One moment,' Annis said, and ruffled his hair into a disordered mess and disarranged his clothes. 'No one would ever believe you'd been here if you came out so neat.'

He laughed and kissed her again, and was gone, striding like a man with a purpose.

'You didn't have to, ah, promise him . . .' Morgan started awkwardly. Annis rolled her eyes.

'Child. I am the mistress of my own body. It's well known in the Tower that I enjoy what pleasure I can find. You're not compromising my honour or any such nonsense. Pyotr and I have a long-standing, cheerful little arrangement.'

'Do you love him?'

'No. Not in the way you probably mean, at least. Keria and Eskander – they had that kind of love. But me? I've never found it, nor do I feel the lack.' Annis's gaze seemed far too sharp. 'In the Tower, we've never had the luxury of weddings and marriage and growing old together. You'll need to decide for yourself what your life is like outside of it, I suppose. For me, this suits well enough.'

They were fundamentally different in that, Morgan decided, but she had to admit that Annis seemed completely at peace with her life here . . . but perfectly willing to risk it, at the same time.

Pyotr proved to be as good as his word; he appeared back

at their door two hours later and produced two small quartz crystals. 'Not tuned yet,' he said, and handed over the written script to Morgan. 'This is the formula. We keep tinkering with it, but the crystals are always slightly flawed, and that makes it impossible to know how the power will flow through both. Statistically, one of them cracks half the time.'

Morgan rewrote the script with a tiny change, and Pyotr set the crystals atop it, and took in a deep breath and held out his hands, touching both. Morgan set her own fingers over his, and together, they bled power slowly into the crystals. Pytor was strong, but he'd never attained the kind of fine control that Morgan had been born with, and she guided and smoothed the power he imbued through every pen stroke of the script.

It flashed through the crystals in a simultaneous burst that left a burnt smell in the air, and a strange hum; when Morgan opened her eyes and pulled her hands back, she saw that both crystals were intact.

And both were glowing, very faintly, along the cloudy fault lines within.

'What did you do?' Pyotr asked. 'I've never seen it so perfectly aligned before, not even with a successful match.'

'You have to think of the cracks and faults inside the crystal not as flaws, but as features,' she said. 'You're matching two unlike things together, and each has different weight, different features, different alignments. But at the smallest level, they are the same. Don't think at the top. Think at the bottom.'

Pyotr gave her a long, considering look and then nodded. 'I see what you mean, I think. But I don't think I could have done that without you.' His eyes widened. 'You don't look well, child.'

She didn't feel well, either. This wasn't the drug still coursing through her system; that had very specific uses and triggers. No, she had just poured a great deal of power out, and in a manner that her body was no longer capable of replacing in the way that Pyotr could. The drug and the collar didn't shut her down because what she was doing was in no way an aggressive use . . . but at the same time, her own body had a way of punishing her.

She felt the hollow darkness inside, and a growing desperation. *I'm empty. I need . . . I need fuel.* But not food, not rest, nothing that innocent.

She held out her hand to Annis and noted the faint, dark lines forming beneath her flesh. 'Take me up,' she said. 'To the garden.' Because the alternatives were impossible. She hadn't extended herself so far before, not since coming here, and the Iron Tower's walls muted her ability to draw from outside. Out in the world, she could have taken a little from a lot of things around her, and none would be the wiser. But here . . . there were few things she could reach to drain.

And all of them would notice.

Annis led her quickly out of their rooms and to the lifting chamber, which swept them upward level after level, past the rooms she'd once had, past another floor where her friends had been imprisoned. As she passed it, she felt a dark surge of need overtake her, and it was all she could do not to reach for Annis's hand again.

Instead, she shrank into the corner, shivering, and when the doors opened, she plunged out into the rich foliage of the greenhouse.

There were people here. *No no no* . . . She stumbled away to a secluded alcove veiled by ferns and flowering bushes and sank down on the ground. The earth here went deep, and when she blinked, she could see the life pulsing through the stalks of the flowers, the plants, the leaves, the roots.

'Get back,' she said to Annis. 'Leave!'

Annis flinched and pulled back, and Morgan couldn't control her need any longer. She plunged her fingers into the loose, black soil . . .

. . . and killed.

The flowers near her wilted first, all their colour fading. But she couldn't stop there. She pulled life from the stalks, the leaves, down to the roots. Then one thick shrub. Then the next. Then a willow tree. Worms boiled to the surface, and she ripped life from their writhing bodies.

She heard Annis gasp in horror and told herself to stop, *stop*, before it was too late . . . and somehow, with all the strength in her, she pulled her hands out of the now-sterile soil, and crawled backward. Dry branches rattled. Dead petals and leaves rained down, dry and desiccated.

She blinked back tears of relief and rage and horror and saw what she'd done. A portion of the garden ten feet all around her had turned brown and brittle.

It would never grow anything again.

Annis backed away from her, hands at her mouth, as Morgan wearily rose. Tears glittered in her pale-blue eyes. 'What are you?' Annis asked. It was barely a whisper.

'I don't know,' Morgan said, and she meant it. 'I'm hoping Eskander can tell me.'

CHAPTER TWENTY-THREE

It must have been a crisis for Annis, but Morgan hardly noticed; she was too busy fighting the enormous need to keep drinking in the life buzzing and hissing and pulsing around her. The bright sparks of flying insects. The hum of a beehive. The warning call of birds, fleeing to the farthest branches.

The bright blurs of Obscurists. They were blinding to her, and desperately burning with just the energy she needed.

She shut her eyes and concentrated on deep, steady breaths until the emptiness inside began to recede. The howling vortex slowed and then stopped. *I am not empty. I'm not.*

When she opened her eyes again, she felt better. More herself. And realised that she was stumbling along, half-dragged by Annis; just as she realised it, Annis got her out of the lifting chamber, and Morgan foggily realised she was now on their residence floor.

'I'm all right,' she told Annis, and pulled free. She had to brace herself against the wall, but she *would* be all right. No matter what. Annis seemed glad to let go, because she moved a sharp three steps away and watched her carefully. 'I'm not a mad dog, Annis. Not yet.'

'You *destroyed* things,' Annis said. 'I've never in my life seen an Obscurist do that. We channel life. We don't destroy it.'

'Not here,' Morgan said, and forced herself into a normal walk, with only a slight pressure of fingertips on the wall to keep herself upright. Once they were back in the room, she saw that Pyotr was gone but the crystals remained, humming and gently glittering along their faults.

Annis still left a good distance between them. Morgan looked down at her hands and spread her fingers. The dark streaks were gone. And she felt almost herself again.

'*Silencio*. Now,' Annis said. 'Explain.'

'It . . . it's difficult. I used too much power, too quickly, when I was too weak; I didn't have a choice, I was trying to save lives by making things grow faster . . .' Her voice faded out. It sounded like a threadbare defence, even to herself. 'It all went wrong. The plants died. Insects. Animals. Everything. I was told that if I rested, took good care, I might improve again. But it would never be the same for me. The connection I had to power . . . it's distorted. Twisted. And sometimes I need . . .' She gestured helplessly upward. 'You saw.'

'You need things to die to make you live?' Annis said.

'You consume living things in every dish you eat.'

'It isn't the same!'

'It is,' Morgan said. 'But if you want to leave and never deal with me again, I understand that. Just . . . don't betray me. Please.'

Annis shook her head and sank down on her bed, head in her hands. She looked her age in that moment, every year of it; then she wiped the tears from her face and took a deep breath. 'I always said I'd deal with the Christian devil to win freedom for those who wanted out of here. Like Eskander. I suppose you're near enough, at that.' She swallowed. 'Could you kill Gregory the same way? Just . . . draw the life out of him?'

'Not before he'd kill me. That's why I haven't. That, and . . . I don't want to do that. Not that way.'

'Why? It would solve everything.'

That evil taste on her tongue. That howling emptiness. She couldn't describe *why*, except to say, 'Because if I kill that way, I think . . . I think it will destroy whatever's left in me that's still good. And you'll have something much worse than Gregory to stop.' She looked up and met Annis's eyes. 'Will you help me? Get me to the air duct?'

It was a long moment, and then Annis said, 'If you're up to it.'

'I am.' *I have to be.*

CHAPTER TWENTY-FOUR

Getting to the proper level meant bypassing four separate security measures, but those were minor issues, far too reliant on the wards and scripts and common knowledge that the area was off-limits. There was one guard present, on a roaming schedule, but Annis had noted down his routes, and they slipped by him without notice. He was bored and tired and had likely never had an alarm in all his time inside the Iron Tower.

The air-circulation hub was a vast open core, drawing in air from the outside of the building, filtering it, running it through a complex series of devices to heat or cool as needed, and then blowing it back out through a series of branching ducts.

'Constructed by Artifex engineers,' Annis said, and pointed to the etched letters beneath the rows and rows of grilles. 'And helpfully labelled as well. But we won't be able to take these covers off, you know.'

'Doesn't matter. Can you tell which one goes to Eskander's rooms?'

'Which room do you prefer?'

'Sitting room,' she said. Talking to him in the privacy of his bedroom seemed . . . presumptuous. Annis nodded and led the way through a twisting, confusing maze of corridors that must be used only by maintenance engineers, and only very occasionally. 'Here,' Annis said, and pointed to one particular grille. 'That's the one.'

'You're sure?'

'I'm sure. It's the same number that appeared in the plans for the vent. Engineers like things to be specific.' Annis winked. 'I met one of them once who was assigned here to install the lift and the new electrical lights. Well, *met* isn't quite the right word. But I did like him.'

'Very helpful,' Morgan said, and pulled one of the crystals from the pocket of her robe. Even wrapped in the thick layer of padding she'd tied around it, it was a small thing, only about the size of her finger, and nearly as slim, and it fitted easily through the grate. She set it down carefully.

'The question now is, how do we ensure it gets to the far end—' Annis began, then checked herself as she heard the steady roar of the air system begin. 'Of course. It's light enough. The air will take it to the other end of the duct, all the way to the grate.'

'We hope. Move.'

They wedged themselves into an alcove meant for this purpose, holding tight to handholds put there, as the huge fan set in the centre of the open middle spun up with an increasing roar, and fresh air blew through every grated opening around the circle. It was deafeningly loud, which was amazing, since Morgan had never thought about how the air moved through this sealed tower . . . or why she rarely heard the sound of it. *There must be sound suppressors on the grates of some kind.* Oh no. No, no, no . . . that might destroy this plan before it could start.

But no. She calmed her racing heartbeat. The most effective way wouldn't be to put that suppression on the grille inside a room, but here, where the noise was the loudest . . . and when the fan spun down again, and the hurricane-force wind died, she ventured out to the grate to peer inside. Good, the crystal was now gone . . . and as she ran her fingers over the grate, she could feel the script that had been woven through the metal to quiet the noise.

She broke it with a sharp snap, took out the other crystal from her pocket, and said, 'Obscurist Eskander? Can you hear me? Please answer if you can hear me. I will be able to hear you on this end.'

She held the crystal to her ear and, to her surprise, heard music – a harp, she thought, but she wasn't certain; the sound quality wasn't that sharp. Whatever it might be, it stopped abruptly, and there was nothing for a long moment. Long enough that she wondered if she'd imagined the sound at all.

Then a man's voice, shockingly close, said, 'Who are you? How is this possible?'

'My name is Morgan,' she said. 'Morgan Hault. I knew the Obscurist – I mean, the old one, Keria. And I know your son, Christopher Wolfe.'

He didn't answer.

'I came back to the Iron Tower to find you, sir. And to get your help.'

'Didn't they tell you? I don't care. And I don't help. Leave me alone. That's all I ask.'

'Keria died to save your son, sir. I was there. I saw.' Morgan heard her voice shake, but she didn't know if he could. 'At the end, she chose his life over her own. And she saved us all. I know how much that must have hurt—'

'You don't know *anything* about her, or about me,' he said. 'I told you. Leave me alone.'

He could have stopped this with a snap of his fingers, Morgan thought; he could have broken the crystal any time he pleased.

But he hadn't. And she had to believe that deep inside, he *needed* to talk. And to be useful in some way. Self-imposed exile was a harsh, inhuman sentence; how long since he'd had a visitor, after Keria? How many people even remembered he was here?

'He needs your help,' she said. 'Your son. The Archivist has him in his prison. He plans to execute him.'

Silence, still. She wished that she'd worked out a way to *see* this man, to know if she was getting through to him at all.

Annis said, 'Morgan. The fan will start up again soon. We have to move!'

Morgan shook her head and twined her fingers into the metal grate. 'Eskander, *please*! Your son saved our lives. He is a brave, brilliant man, and *he needs you*. I'm begging you, please help!'

'I can't,' Eskander said. It sounded hollow.

'You can; you know you should be the Obscurist! Take what's rightly yours! Stop Gregory, and lead us *out of this tower*!'

'Lives would be lost.'

'They're being lost *now*. Gregory killed a boy in front of me, just to prove a point! Do you think he cares about any of us? He only cares about his own greed! You must have known him, before you shut yourself away. You must know I'm telling the truth!'

'Morgan!' Annis sounded desperate now, and when Morgan glanced back, she saw the woman's robes fluttering in the wind that was already starting to form. The gigantic fan was starting its next cycle. 'Morgan, *we have to go*! We can come back!'

Morgan knew instinctively that if she stopped here, short of convincing him, it would all be for nothing. He'd refuse to answer again. He'd break the crystal. 'Go! I'll hold on here!' she shouted over the gust of wind that pushed her against the grate. 'Just go, Annis!'

'Annis?' She could hardly hear Eskander over the building roar, but she pushed the crystal harder against her ear and hardly felt the cut that opened. 'Is Annis with you?'

'Yes! She's here! She's helping me, and she said if Keria was still alive, she'd be the first to go against Gregory! But he killed her, and now *you have to be the one*!'

She didn't hear his reply. The fan spun up to a shattering roar and threatened to tear her loose, and she had to drop the crystal and watch as it shattered on the metal grate before it was blown away into the darkness. She grabbed at the mesh with her left hand and tried to cling with all her might; she felt muscles trembling and pulling and tearing, and her robes tore in the battering. Her hair came loose. It felt like threads of steel cutting her face to pieces, and she struggled to breathe against the intense pressure on her back. *How long does it last?* She wasn't going to make it. Her fingers were bleeding and cramping, and what breath she had was lost in a scream of pain as her right hand lost its grip, and she felt the wind shear her sideways, felt something pop in her arm, and then her left hand was loose and she felt herself lifting up, twisting wildly. She couldn't think how to use her power, or on what to focus; there was just panic, terrible and awful panic . . .

And then a hand grabbed her and dragged her down. Annis. She'd stripped off her robe and tied it to the handhold, with the other end tied tight around her ankle. The thin shift she wore flattened against her body in the wind and sent her wild hair flying like a flag, but she held on and pulled Morgan into her tight, unyielding embrace and held her against the storm as they both twisted and hovered in the blast, until its weakening dumped them back down to the metal floor, and both fell still holding each other.

Annis was the first to get her breath, and she used it to laugh. A raw, half-terrified sound, but it was still laughter, and against her will, Morgan joined her until they rolled on their backs, exhausted.

'Did it work?' Annis asked, and finger-combed her wild hair out of her face as she sat up. Morgan's was no better, and she tried to twist it back into a rough queue to keep it from her eyes. 'Is he with us?'

'The crystal broke.' Morgan's laughter turned to ashes in her mouth, and she swallowed hard against a sudden, weightless feeling of horror. 'I lost him.'

She looked utterly ragged, she realised as Annis helped her up; at least Annis's robe had survived the storm with only minor distress, but Morgan's robe would hardly pass a glance without drawing attention. *Do I dare?* She'd already expended more power than she wished, and she couldn't tell how much more she had left before the emptiness set in. But she tapped a trickle of it, whispered a formula under her breath to guide the work, and the tears knitted back together. Imperfect, like a child's mending, but it would have to do.

'We should hurry,' Annis said. She'd seen the work but said nothing beyond a slight compression of her lips. 'I'd not put it past Gregory to have someone besides me checking on your whereabouts.'

'What are we going to say about the garden?'

'I've no idea at all. Do you?'

'Tell the truth,' Morgan said. 'That you don't know what happened. And I won't tell him, either. Let him puzzle it out, unless he already knows that an Obscurist can go . . . dark. If he does, he might see me as more valuable yet. I imagine he'd like an assassin to order all his own.'

'Or he'd kill you,' Annis said archly. 'A paranoid choob like that wouldn't see you as useful. Only dangerous to his rule.'

'Can't help that. We were seen there. It's a good chance he'll hang on to me even harder.'

Annis wasn't happy with that, but she fell silent, and they hurried back through the winding maze of metal corridors. A brief wait for the bored guard to pass, and they dashed for the stairs. Easier to go down than up, but then they called the lifting chamber to take them up.

Morgan didn't even notice anything out of the ordinary, so sunk was she in the sense of failure, until Annis said, 'The devil?' and pushed buttons again. 'Missed our stop.'

It's Gregory. He's got us trapped. He's taking us where he wants us. Morgan readied herself for whatever was coming as the lift slowed and stopped. She exchanged a look with Annis, and they both stepped out on the landing. No guards. No Gregory.

Then Annis said, in a voice that Morgan had never heard before, 'Oh.'

She turned to look where Annis was staring, down the hall, where a door was standing open.

They took two tentative steps in that direction before a deep male voice said, 'Still falling for that old trick, Annis? After all this time?'

Annis squealed, half in shock, half in delight, and a man stepped forward that Morgan hadn't noticed at all; it was as if he'd wrapped himself in shadows and become part of the wall. Now he'd stepped into the light, and Morgan had only a second to take him in: an older man, silvered hair cascading over his shoulders, clean-shaven, with dark eyes and skin of dark amber.

'Barbarian!' Annis cried, and threw herself on him. He seemed unprepared for that, but only for an instant, and then he embraced her like he might never let her go again. 'Oh, my dear. My dear. Is it really you?'

'Really me,' he said, and finally pushed her to arm's length. As he looked her over, Morgan began to see the resemblance to Scholar Wolfe, especially the frown that grooved between his brows. 'I swore I'd never open that door again, you know.'

'I know,' Annis said, and fit her hand to his cheek. 'But I also know that you'll not abandon those who so desperately need you. Not you, Eskander.'

'Won't I?' The bitter smile was wholly like Wolfe's. 'You have a short memory. I abandoned Keria. And you.'

'No. You never did.'

'I didn't save her when she needed me.'

'She didn't call on you. Keria never was one to cry for help. She fought her battles alone, and she'd be happy to have died in one of them.'

He was like Wolfe in another way, Morgan thought: his unbreaking devotion, because she could see the grief and loss. She'd known Keria Morning, the old Obscurist, only as a frightening, cold, powerful woman until the last moments, but he had known her as someone completely different.

Someone to be grieved.

When Eskander's gaze fixed on her, Morgan felt exposed . . . every fault and flaw showing. Another thing that Wolfe had inherited from his father, this intense, judgemental stare. 'You're my son's student? Morgan?' She nodded. Wasn't sure if she could speak. 'Keria spoke of you, the last time I saw her. She thought you were a rare talent. She'd never said that before.'

Morgan wasn't sure what to say to that, except, 'I'm honoured.'

'You shouldn't be. Talent makes you a target. Talent makes you their weapon.'

'I'm not theirs.'

He smiled faintly. 'Good. Then take that off.'

He wasn't wearing a collar. It hit her with a sudden shock that he didn't wear the standard robes of a Tower Obscurist; he had on a loose black shirt, plain trousers, comfortably distressed boots. A belt that held what looked like a High-Garda-issue pistol. Add a Scholar's robe, and his likeness to his son would be uncanny.

It hit her a second later what he was actually saying. 'Take what off?' She thought he meant the robe.

He touched his fingers to his throat, and she mimicked him and put her hand to the collar. 'I can't!'

'I can,' he said. 'If you will permit me . . . ?'

'He'll know,' Morgan said.

'Of course he will.' This time, the smile was dark, and full of menace. 'I'm looking forward to it.'

She nodded. She didn't believe he could do it until Eskander stepped close to her, put both hands on her collar, and pulled.

She felt the harsh flash of broken scripts. Not broken: shattered. Destroyed. The power it took was immense, and it took her breath away.

The golden collar hung loose as he moved back, and he left it up to her to take hold of it, pull it free, and let it drop to the floor with a harsh metallic ring. She felt the vulnerable, raw circle where the collar had been and felt a rush of tears first, and then something else, cleaner, sharper: *freedom*.

'And me?' Annis asked quietly.

'And you,' he said, and easily broke hers, too. 'Don't be afraid, Annis.'

She let out a shaky laugh and took the collar off. Instead of letting it drop, she looked at it. Turned it over and over in her hands, running her fingers over the incised symbols, and then crouched and put it carefully down. The skin it had covered all these years was ghostly, and at the edges, ridged with scars. 'I've not been without it since I was a wee lass,' she said. 'A child. I never knew how heavy it was.'

'They'll know,' Morgan said.

Eskander smiled. 'No. They won't. Not until I'm ready for them to know. Now, let's begin.'

EPHEMERA

The creature is finished. I understand why you desire new automata; I understand that new improvements are necessary to respond to ever-growing threats and keep the population respectful of our power. It's certain that this does convey that as nothing before ever has, not even the statues of the gods.

The technical challenges have been considerable, and while I know that it's taken five years beyond our original estimates, your new automaton is finally ready to be tested.

I hope you know what you are doing. I don't scare easily, but this . . . I am scared of this.

And we all should be.

It could end everything.

PART NINE

JESS

CHAPTER TWENTY-FIVE

There was a new uneasiness in the air in Alexandria. Even Jess could feel it. He woke early – middle of the night, actually – and had spent his time after washing and dressing in sending messages out in family code. He owed an explanation to Red Ibrahim. The name *traitor* had been thrown at him along with Greek Fire, and he didn't much like either of them.

Morgan still hadn't written, but that would have to remain a mystery; he knew time was running out, and fast. The Alexandrian newspaper was tightly censored by the Library, but there were other sources of news, and now that he was finally trusted by the Archivist – though, honestly, he knew he couldn't count on it for long – he'd left to seek the gossip out well before dawn. He didn't bother about the trailing High Garda eyes assigned to him, because he simply went to the local bakeshop and bought breakfast and thick, hot coffee and engaged in quiet conversation with the other patrons.

'I heard that Spain has completely broken free,' one old man said, leaning close. 'There's some treaty between the rebel countries, too. Like they'll be marching on us. High Garda will put a stop to it.' But he hadn't sounded confident. Others told him of rumours of some great invention, but they were uncertain what it could be. Most assumed it was a war machine of some sort.

He thought it likely to be the whisper of Thomas's press. Those whispers reaching Alexandria meant the speculation had to be a roar already on the borders, as tight as the Library locked down the flow of news here.

He found out when an anonymous woman wearing librarian robes took a seat at the counter next to him, ordered pastries, and left a printed piece of paper in her wake. It could have been dropped by anyone, but Jess had seen the expert dodge, and he retrieved it before anyone else could see it.

The printing was vastly inferior to the quality Thomas had achieved; the block type was clumsily lined up, and the spacing terrible. But it was a fresh-printed page with ink that still smudged when he rubbed on it, and it said THE LIBRARY IS LYING TO YOU. A LIFE IS WORTH MORE THAN A BOOK. The symbol on the bottom was a new one, but he thought it had a passing resemblance to the flames the Burners used to sketch on their handwritten flyers.

Anit, he thought, had wasted no time in arranging for the construction of a press right here in the city . . . and taking payments from the Burners to upgrade their propaganda leaflets. There was a little touch of satisfaction, but it was quickly chased away by the memory of the Archivist's warning.

The Archivist wanted to exclusively direct the use of Thomas's invention. He wouldn't take kindly to the news that upstarts were already taking advantage and the invention he was paying so heavily for was already spreading without him.

Jess folded the paper small and put it into his pocket for disposal somewhere safe . . . but then, he didn't need to, as the next young man who slouched at the bar muttered, 'You have a message for His Excellency?' Spanish. To confirm it, the man signed, under cover of the counter, *Scrubber*.

'We really need a new word,' Jess said. He took the paper from his pocket and a pen, and wrote on the back, *Find out where my other friends are. Tell them things are moving quickly. The Archivist is bound to move up the executions.*

He passed the folded paper on, and the young man claimed his morning roll and coffee, and sauntered off looking like he had not a care in the world.

Jess wished he could be as relaxed.

As the sun began to blush the eastern horizon he headed back, and had just stretched out on his bed when the knock rattled the door. The new High Garda Elite had a heavy hand.

'You're up,' the man said, and sounded a bit unhappy about it. 'All right. The faster we go, the faster we're finished.'

'And what is it we're doing?' Jess didn't expect an answer and in fact, didn't get one. Their commander was already striding away, and Jess had to hurry to catch up. There was a full team of soldiers in the street, and more in two different troop carriers lined up. The commander whistled, and made a quick hand signal, and the soldiers waiting for her began to pile into the remaining carrier. This early, traffic was light on the street, though Jess saw a few nervous residents peeking through windows and around doors to see what was causing a stir. Seeing three lorries full of High Garda likely didn't reassure them, but then again, they had good reason to be worried.

They all did, now.

The commander clung silently to a handhold as the carrier hissed and clanked down the Alexandrian streets with alarming speed. Still not talking. 'Are we going after smugglers again?' Jess asked her. 'I hope this time you brought a proper army.'

The captain didn't seem even mildly amused. 'Not smugglers.'

That seemed . . . odd. And strangely ominous. 'Then what value are you expecting out of me, Captain?'

'Out of you? Not much. But the Artifex said you could identify what we were looking for.'

'Which is?'

She didn't bother to answer him, and he supposed she didn't need to; the Artifex had put this squarely on his head, no doubt at the orders of his fellow in corruption, the Archivist Magister.

Jess had no doubt whatsoever that today was going to be a very bad day, but he consoled himself that at least it would be far, far worse for whoever would be on the receiving end of this visit. Having fifty High Garda knocking on the door would ruin anyone's breakfast.

He couldn't see out, and so he didn't recognise the street until he exited the carrier – last, since none of the soldiers seemed inclined to give way for him. But then he did, and it was only an instant before memory caught up to instinct, and he knew they were standing on the street where Red Ibrahim lived.

Red Ibrahim was an old, dangerous man, but even the most dangerous men could be brought down. He'd survived sixty years or so in a business where ten years was considered astonishing; he'd done so right under the very noses of the High Garda and the Archivist. It took a particularly hard and brilliant person to accomplish that.

So how had they found him now?

There was only one answer.

My father has sold out his oldest friend and business ally. Just as he'd sell his own sons for a tidy profit if the opportunity presented itself.

Jess had no idea what Brendan would have done in this

situation; he only knew that he owed Red Ibrahim and Anit, and he couldn't be the cause of their murders.

And how exactly are you going to prevent it? That was definitely his brother's caustic voice in his head. *You can't. This has gone beyond you. You just have to keep up with the avalanche now. The priority is to save your friends and save the Library. Saving smugglers isn't part of it.*

The commander turned to him and pointed at the house.

Not Red Ibrahim's house. A modest stucco home sitting two doors down, guarded by an old fountain and a gate with weathered old boards that needed a fresh coat of paint. Jess had never noted the place before, never even glanced at it. It looked like the nondescript house of a well-off librarian, or a low-level Scholar. *I'm out of practice*, Jess thought. He'd have spotted such a thoroughly unexceptional house in minutes, back in the day, before the Library had made him lax about such things.

Someone didn't want to be noticed.

The soldiers obviously had their orders; they silently moved away, each intent on getting to his or her position. There was a breach team who swarmed over the wall and quietly opened the gate; one even took the precaution of oiling the hinges first. Jess followed the captain to the front door. Unassuming or not, it was a stout barrier, but the captain gave a silent hand signal. Her Greek Fire expert took a flask and funnel and poured carefully measured drops of the liquid into the crack of the door to dissolve the lock, then stepped back with a brisk nod.

The first soldier opened the door quietly, and to no significant drama, though Jess had expected some kind of violence to erupt. One by one, the team he was with filed inside, and he was nearly the last to enter, though the soldiers stood aside to let him move up to the captain.

They were in a small, shabby room, with a worn carpet on the floor and two chairs, a single lamp, and a bookcase. Nothing of note, though Jess strode to the bookcase and looked through the titles. They were all in Library binding, of course, and he pulled one at random to leaf through it. Nothing suspicious. It all seemed in order, but then, the best smugglers made sure it did.

He let his eyes unfocus and regard the shelf as a whole. Nothing at all suspicious . . . and then, because he wasn't overthinking it, his gaze sharpened on a single book. No different, no larger, no smaller, but there was something about it . . . ah. Discoloration on the top edge of the binding, as if this book was often retrieved . . . and yet, none evenly along the spine. It had been removed. Not read.

It would have taken someone with his practised eye to see it, but once seen, it was unmistakable. If this had been smugglers, or even collectors, he might have kept all this to himself . . . but not this time. This time, they were looking for Burners, and whether they'd invested in a printing press or not, they were still enemies.

As Jess considered his next step, he heard a soldier report back. 'We've been through every room, Captain. Nothing suspicious. No one here.'

'They're here,' Jess said. 'You just can't see them.'

The captain turned slowly to stare at him. 'Meaning what? That they're invisible? Ghosts? Speak sense.'

For answer, Jess reached out and tipped the book, then back in.

They all heard the *click*. Soldiers fanned out, but Jess didn't move. He knew where it was. No point in helping them, though. They'd surely work out that this house didn't have space for any hidden rooms of any size.

Not unless they were below.

He bent and pulled back the rug. Even with the cover gone, it was cleverly done; the sides of the trapdoor were almost invisible, flush with the wooden floor. There was one piece of wood of an odd size, as if it had been added as a replacement or fit; he pushed on it, and one end flipped up to form a handle.

'Ready?' he asked softly.

The captain formed up the troops and then gave him a brisk nod.

He pulled the trap up in one fast motion, and the soldiers plunged down the steps. They went quietly, and the quiet remained for two or three heartbeats . . . until the sound of shots exploded. Shots, cries, shouts, screams. Flashes of light. Jess stepped back as the battle intensified and the sharp smell of gunpowder and blood hit the air. He had no High Garda armour, and putting himself in the thick of it would do no one any good. Besides, it seemed from the slowing gunfire that he wasn't needed.

In the brief pause between one spate of shouting and the next, he heard the unmistakable soft click of another latch being released.

Jess stepped back, careful to be as silent as he could, and angled to see into the next room. A bedroom, with a small, flat bed that was swinging silently upward. Clever. He had no weapon, but he took a heavy soapstone statue of Horus from the bookcase and waited.

The Burner who emerged stopped and took a bottle from her pocket. Greek Fire, sloshing in her shaking hand. She shouted, 'A life is worth more than a book, you Library ghouls!' and tossed it down the steps. Jess heard it shatter and knew the captain would order her people back out through the other trap.

The Burner turned to run and saw him blocking her path.

She was older than he was, but not by much. A year, maybe two. African extraction, with a sharply triangular face and skin as dark as burnished ebony.

And she didn't hesitate to attack.

He saw her lunge and draw the knife at her belt in the same motion, and he used the statue to deflect the stab that would have surely gutted him. 'Stop!' He tried to keep it as low as he could. 'Stop, I'm not your enemy!'

She didn't believe him, and why would she? He'd come here with the High Garda. And truthfully, he was no friend of the Burners, either. She came at him again with the knife, and this time she scored a shallow cut along his ribs with it before he swung the statue and connected hard with her head.

She dropped. Not out, but not conscious enough to escape, either, and now it was too late even if she'd had a planned exit; High Garda troops were coming up through the other trapdoor at a run, and the captain spotted him. 'You! Brightwell! With me! You two, get that Burner and put her in with the rest we've got.'

Jess set the statue down and went to the captain as the Burner was dragged to the front door and out towards the troop carriers. More of her companions were being led up, or carried, from the rooms below. Jess counted a dozen of them before the last was out, and the captain grabbed his shoulder and shoved him towards the steps.

'I'm not going down there,' Jess said. 'She's thrown Greek Fire.'

'It's out,' she said. 'We have suppressant. Go on. I need your expert opinion on what I'm looking at down there.'

'Expert?' he asked, brows arched. 'Really?'

'Shut up and move.'

He descended carefully. The room was smoky but lit by

still-burning glows, and though the acrid, thick mist made him cough, it didn't seem to be actively dangerous. The ceiling was higher than he'd expected; it had taken a lot of work to dig out this large room. Multiple exits, too. He spotted at least three other trapdoors, all open. 'Did anyone get away?' he asked.

'We don't think so, but it's possible,' said one of the other soldiers. 'There's a tunnel in the back we're following. This place is a warren. It's dug under half the houses on the block.'

Including Red Ibrahim's? No, not bloody likely. He'd avoid that, at all costs. And what possible alliance could he have with Burners?

But he knew the answer to that the instant his eyes fixed on the structure that had been built in the centre of the room. It was crude, and poorly aligned, but the plan of it was familiar. Stacks of raw paper sat against the walls, ready for pressing. Jess thought of the flyer he'd used as notepaper to send to the Spanish ambassador. It had almost certainly come from this press.

'You know what it is?' the captain asked. 'It seems to be some kind of . . . ink machine.'

Jess looked around and found a printed page in a corner; it was smeared and poorly aligned, but legible. He handed it to the captain and watched the stages of realisation hit in turn. Confusion, first. Then dawning wonder. Then unease, as she realised the implications. He could tell that this captain wasn't someone who tended to think of the immense possibilities . . . only the dangers. But then, that was why she'd had risen to her current post . . . and likely no further.

'It prints duplicates,' Jess said. 'Ink on paper. No Obscurist required.'

'It's a machine that makes Burner lies look true.' The captain crumpled the paper up and threw it with force against the wall.

It bounced and rolled, and she stomped it flat. 'And they can blanket the street with them. It's obscene.'

'It's a tool,' Jess said. 'And it can do a great deal of good, in the right use.'

'*Good*? If anyone can decide what is right and wrong, then we are *lost*, Brightwell! No unity, no sanity. It's an abomination.'

Jess imagined that was what the first Archivist to destroy one of these machines had said. It had been the excuse for cutting the throat of the Scholar who invented it, too. 'Perhaps,' he said. 'But just think for a moment what the Library could do with it.'

'If even one of these things exists, there *is* no Library, don't you understand that?' The captain turned and walked back to the steps. 'Gold Squad! Get down here. I want this thing destroyed. Not one scrap of it should remain when you're done, do you understand? Make a list of all the materials that go into it. We will want to track purchases.'

A swarm of High Garda came down into the basement and began dismantling the press with hands, hammers, iron bars – anything they could find. They'd make short work of it, Jess thought.

But it didn't matter. It wouldn't be the only one in Alexandria. If the Burners had discovered how useful it was, and they obviously had, then Anit would have built several of them; this one she'd sold to the Burners, but there would be bigger ones. Better ones. Red Ibrahim had access to money and talent that the Burners couldn't dream of, and he would see the astonishing possibilities where the High Garda captain would only see the threat.

Not that he was wrong, of course. There was no more dire, direct threat to the Great Library's power than the machine the soldiers were so busily dismantling. But the jinn was long out of the bottle by now; print machines were being thrown together in all corners of the world. The revolution was disorganised, but it was inevitable. The Archivist was riding a blind horse towards a cliff, and someone had to stop the inevitable disaster.

That wouldn't be done by destroying this machine, or any of them, or all of them. It would be done by remembering what the Library was, at its heart: a defiant outpost of courage, built by those who made knowledge something to be cherished, not destroyed.

People like this captain – who saw only danger from progress, while paying lip service to a tradition they didn't understand – were the largest obstacle to that goal. For generations, they'd placed all their worth and trust in the Library being the *only* source of knowledge. And they'd cling to that with everything they had.

But being the only source had never been the Library's founding purpose. Only preservation, and protection.

Jess didn't argue; the captain wouldn't listen and saw him as hardly better than a Burner anyway. Jess sat deep in thought on a barrel of ink, paging through the records of what the Burners had already printed and distributed – a shockingly high number of leaflets – when the captain snatched the notebook from his hand and stuffed it into her own pocket next to a personal journal. *I miss my journal*, Jess thought, and was strangely surprised to feel a little pang of grief. He'd not written down a thing that had happened in his life for such a long time; he'd broken the habit and custom without a glance backward the instant he knew the Library might be reading the contents. But he was surprised to realise that he missed it. Maybe, once this was over, he could write about what had happened. That might help this strange, grey mood that had taken him over.

You can take it apart, but you can't destroy the idea, he wanted to tell the captain, but he'd be wasting his time.

'Well?' the captain snapped. 'Are you staying here to wait for the Burners to come back and tear you apart, or are you going with us? Either way is fine with me.'

He couldn't help but ask, 'You mean, you'd let me stay?'

The woman shrugged. 'Stay if you like. But it'll be the end of you if you do.'

'What are you talking about?'

'I was told to withdraw. You should do the same, if you want to live.'

'Captain?'

She walked away, and Jess trailed up through the house, to the street.

'Last time,' she said. 'Are you coming, or staying?'

'Staying,' Jess said. Since he'd been given the choice, which was baffling. The captain stepped into the carrier, and it sped away, leaving a cloud of white steam behind it. The next two carriers followed close behind.

And then they were gone.

They'd left him behind. Free. That hardly seemed right, and he was trying to decide what the hell was happening when he heard the alarm sound from the Lighthouse.

It was legendary, that sound: an eerie, shrieking rise and fall that pierced the ear and woke a deep, anxious terror inside. Monsters screamed like that. The alarm at the Lighthouse had last sounded two hundred years ago, when a huge storm had threatened the city; it hadn't been activated on a clear day, like this one, in hundreds of years before that.

Jess stood rooted to the spot, listening, and saw people stepping outside of buildings and homes around him. Red Ibrahim's door opened, and a cluster of servants came out, nervously wiping their hands on aprons. No sign of the man himself.

'What is it?' asked a large square woman in a white headscarf. A chef, he thought, pulled away from the morning's food preparations. 'Do you know?'

Jess shook his head. 'A test?'

'I've never heard it tested before. Wouldn't they announce it in advance?' She rocked back and forth, silent for a moment, then burst out, 'I wish they'd shut it off!'

She'd had to speak loudly to be heard over the wailing, and as soon as she said it, as if she'd wished it done, the shriek of the alarm cut off. Echoes rolled through the streets, and a profound, uneasy silence settled. Nothing moved – nothing except speeding troop carriers, moving out from the High Garda compound. Dozens of them, spreading out to different parts of the city.

And with them, the loping, shining forms of automata.

Jess felt sickness curl deep inside. *Something is happening. Something bad.*

Then the amplified voice of the Archivist rang out. What Obscurist magic it was, he couldn't fathom, though Morgan likely would have known, but the voice of one man reached an entire city, and it was clear and eerily calm.

'Citizens of Alexandria, this is the Archivist of the Great Library. Be it known to you now that no Burner shall be left alive in our great and ancient city. No criminal smuggler shall be left alive to deal in forbidden books. No quarter will be given those who seek to destroy the safety and security of thousands of years. We have been merciful. I tell you now, we *will not be merciful again.*

'To that end the High Garda is now marching on hidden sites in our city to rout Burners and criminals from their holes and destroy utterly any trace of their existence. There will be damage. There will be innocent lives lost. But we believe in the greater worth of the Library. *Knowledge is all!*'

As Jess heard those around him devoutly repeat it, he saw that one of the troop carriers, with a phalanx of running automaton lions, was heading in their direction.

He turned to the servants. 'Get out of here!' he shouted, and grabbed the chef's arm as she started to obey. 'Wait. Where's Red Ibrahim?'

'Who?'

'Don't waste my time, woman. Where is he?'

She gave him a long look, and he felt something sharp prick his stomach. He looked down to find a wickedly well-used knife resting there. 'Take your hand off me. The master of the house is gone. There's only us inside.'

'Then leave,' he said. 'And warn him. Tell him to go to ground, *now*—'

The words died in his throat, because he caught something from the corner of his eye, and turned his head to look. There was still a knife threatening to gut him, but in that moment, it no longer mattered. Cold filled his veins, froze his spine, and he heard the chef whisper, 'What in good Heron's name is . . .' She fell silent, then let out a scream, backed up, and ran.

Jess didn't move. Couldn't. His brain struggled to make sense of the *size* of it, the eerie beauty of it, as the sleek, serpentine shape rose on beating wings. *That isn't possible.*

They'd built a *dragon*.

The entire city was screaming. He heard the panic coming in waves as the dragon rose and circled in lazy spirals, banking and turning. It was a nightmare. It was deeply wrong. It was beautiful.

And then it came down.

The part of his mind that was frozen, clinical, trying to understand . . . it noted that this monster descended like a hawk, a swift, brutal, eerily silent descent. It had claws and talons, and it landed on the street at the end of the block. And the *scale of it* . . . he had never imagined anything could be built so large, so vividly and horribly *swift*. A snake-like neck stretched up as high as a three-storey building to support a head shaped like that of an ancient, brutal dinosaur, if such had been made of clouded steel. Spiked, razor-sharp teeth. And the body: a hissing, whispering marvel of interlocking-plate scales, iridescent in the bright sunlight.

Its eyes glowed dark yellow, and there was no mercy in them. No thought.

Everyone near him was gone now, running for their lives. Houses had emptied. And the dragon's talons clashed on stone as it lowered its head and breathed down a thick, green fog into the street.

Jess had time to taste that bitter, poisonous tang in the back of his throat before his lungs convulsed into coughs, and he found himself falling to his hands and knees trying to find clearer air. *That's the stench of Greek Fire.* He'd seen that mist build up in Philadelphia, clouding the air until it all ignited at once . . . and then he realised that the Library had taken note of it, too. *First the mist, then the fire*, he thought, and lurched up to his feet again to run. He couldn't see where he was going; the rancid fog stung and blurred his vision, but he knew he was still on the road, feeling cobbles under his feet. He could hear the metallic hiss and clank of the automaton behind him, but *how far, where* . . .

Instinct told him *Run, just run, it doesn't matter, run!*

Jess ran, blinded, as fast as he could go, until he tasted clearer air, and then he dashed a hand over his eyes and tried to see where he was.

He'd come dangerously close to falling over a kerb and impaling himself on an iron fence, but he was near the farther end of the street now, and he dared to slow down and try to look back.

Just as he did, a spark ignited in the cloud, and for an instant he'd never forget, the fog of Greek Fire glowed like beautiful, fragile network of green lace, suspended in the air . . .

. . . and then everything in it exploded.

The houses. The street. Fences. Fountains, weeping flames.

A green bubble of hell.

Stones melted. Houses collapsed. If anything lived inside that fog, it was incinerated to the bones. *The servants? The chef? What about the others on the street? Did they get out in time?*

Jess let out a raw scream, because he was in Philadelphia again, seeing the bombs fall and lives lost, and it was happening *here, in Alexandria*, and for what? *For what?* To punish the Burners? Red Ibrahim?

No. To terrify. To show the city that the Archivist would not allow any opposition.

The wail of the alarm started again, and from inside the inferno came a chilling, answering roar, and the dragon launched itself up. It trailed streamers of fire behind it, nightmarish curls that writhed and twisted into black smoke. The automaton was streaked with soot and ash, but it was intact. Eerily alive.

It circled the sky over the city, and the threat was as clear as the sun in the sky: *you are all one breath away from death now.*

Jess found himself sitting now, clinging to the iron fence; it felt hot, and he realised that his clothes were giving off little curls of wispy smoke. His skin felt dry and hot, and he wearily got to his feet and walked on through falling ash and the eerie wail of the alarm until he saw the troop carrier that had been headed towards his street.

It was parked at the top of the hill, and four automaton lions waited, pacing.

Nowhere else to go, he thought, and kept walking. He coughed and tasted the bitter aftertaste of the fog. Spat out a thick mouthful of greenish phlegm and nearly collapsed with the force of another convulsive series of coughs.

When he finally straightened, the lions had surrounded him, and as one, they growled and showed teeth when he tried to move forward.

'I wouldn't,' said a light, calm voice. 'You're Jess Brightwell, are you not?'

For a split second, he nearly answered *yes*, but he caught it just in time and said, 'For the thousandth time, no. I'm his twin, Brendan, and for God's sake, can't you get that into your thick skulls? What the *hell* was that thing?'

'Take him,' the voice said. 'He's the one we want.'

CHAPTER TWENTY-SIX

Jess didn't bother to ask where he was being taken. He assumed that he would be taken back to his cramped little prison, to wait there on the Archivist's pleasure, but he couldn't shake the horror of what he'd just seen. War was one thing; it was horrible and brutal, but there were rules, at least there should be. He'd been trained as High Garda. Where was the duty and honour in what had just happened? Where was the benefit to knowledge? Had any of those people ever threatened the Great Library? This was the Library's own city. The Archivist was making war against his own people.

He didn't recognise any of the soldiers who sat silently around him. They wore the uniform of High Garda Elite, which he supposed wasn't surprising. He wondered how many more the Archivist had in reserve. And he wondered if it would do any good to tell them just how faithless the man was whom they were so faithfully obeying.

The soldier sitting next to him coughed and sent him a scowl. 'You stink,' the man said. 'Smells like Greek Fire and cat piss.'

'Quiet,' said a commanding voice from down the row. 'You've smelt worse than that on many a day, and I doubt you have his excuse. Leave him alone. He'll get what's coming to him soon enough.'

The soldier subsided, but the look he was giving Jess was

pure loathing. Jess hardly even noticed. In every blink of his eyes he saw that street aflame, and the bodies in it. His hands were shaking and suddenly the stench that the soldier had commented on was all too real and suffocating.

He didn't much notice the trip at all, but suddenly he realised that they'd stopped and soldiers were pouring out of the open door. The hostile soldier next to him grabbed him by his shackled wrists and heaved him up; Jess was forced to rise or have both shoulders dislocated. He didn't much mind the pain. At least it gave him something to focus on.

This wasn't his little house. He recognised this bare courtyard, with its view of the Lighthouse in the distance. It was a rally point for High Garda troops, and the huge sweep of the Serapeum rose into the sky above them. The whole courtyard was full of soldiers. Some wore the Elite uniform, but most wore the same as the one he'd worn with such pride just months back. Loyal men and women. Jess wondered who they had been told they were fighting. Burners and rebels most likely. He wondered if any of them harboured any doubts.

As before, he was led through a maze of tunnels. He recognised part of it, but that part had belonged to another route before. It confirmed what he'd suspected – that the building itself was an automaton in some sense. Its defences started with the confusion of its ever-changing corridors, a defence Jess wasn't sure he understood or could outwit, at least not yet. Right now, there was nothing in this world he wanted more than to be out of here even if there was nowhere else to go. He was too heartsick to play games and too angry to pretend any longer. If he had the chance he intended to kill the Archivist any way he could. It might not stop that dragon from flying again, but at least it was something.

He was in the mood for murder.

Neksa was at her desk in the outer office, and she looked nervous and disturbed. She fiddled with the Library band on her wrist in a way that he was sure he'd never seen before. She avoided looking at him directly, and that was when he was sure that something had gone very wrong.

In the Archivist's office, there were two people standing and one on his knees. Guards as well, of course, lurking in the shadows along with the waiting automaton gods. Jess's mind reeled, and for a long moment he was sure he had gone insane. This could not be right. Could not be happening.

But then his brother Brendan shook his head and said, 'Sorry, Brother.' It was the brisk tone that made Jess take a step back and realise he wasn't imagining things. His brother really was here.

And then the man kneeling on the carpet looked up. His hair was a matted, greying mess, and he looked paler and more wild than Jess had ever seen him, but it was Scholar Wolfe. Bruised, and from the look in his eyes half-mad, but alive.

'Scholar?' Jess moved towards him, but before he could get more than a step, his brother grabbed his elbow and pulled him to stop. 'Let me go. What's been done to him?'

The third man in the tableau was the Archivist, of course. He was standing behind his desk, but with no sense of calm about him. His hands were clenched behind his back, and his colour had an unhealthy reddish tone to it. 'Nothing has been done to him. Not yet. In fact, Christopher has done me a great favour. I don't suppose he meant to do so, but that doesn't change the fact that you have been lying to me all this time. And we're going to find out exactly how you managed that.'

'I already told him that you drugged me and took my place,' Brendan said. 'And that Father had no choice but to play along if he wanted to get his bargain. Once he realised the game was up, he sent me as a sign of good faith to finish the deal. And I will. I'm sorry, Brother. It was never going to work for long.'

'You think he really intends to give Father any bargain?' Jess almost laughed. Besides the awful taste of chemicals and death, he tasted something even worse: defeat. 'Don't be stupid. He has both Callum Brightwell's sons. He can get what he wants without paying a *geneih*. Unless you think that Father is even more heartless than I ever thought he was. Why did you come here? He'll kill us both.'

'My fault,' Wolfe said. His voice sounded rusty and hollow and haunted. 'Why didn't you tell me what you planned? Because you knew I'd never let you take this risk? Jess . . .'

'Too clever by half,' the Archivist agreed. 'It's the clever ones that get caught in their own traps. If you'd only told the Scholar what you intended, he wouldn't have come to me and told me a lie that turned out to be true. He told me you'd taken your brother's place. And of course it was what I suspected from the beginning, but you did an excellent job of putting my suspicions to rest. I intend to spend some time with you to find out exactly what you've been up to. You didn't do this alone. You had help, and I intend to pull every name out of you and send every one of your allies screaming into the afterlife. I admit you were bold. We'll see how bold you are at the Feast of Greater Burning.' He suddenly opened the Codex on his desk and scribbled a note.

'No need for that,' Jess's brother said in a deliberately calm and careless tone. He was the master of making it seem he didn't care. 'Just send the boy home. My father will still hold to the bargain, as long as Jess is safe.'

'Your father will do exactly what I tell him. He's going to lose a son. Take care he doesn't lose two. Your brother's written his own fate, and his own very unhappy ending. If you're as smart as I believe you to be, you'll stand aside and save your family and your fortune. No point in losing everything, is there?'

'Don't believe him,' Jess said. 'He'll kill all of us. Some of us will just die later.'

Brendan shrugged. 'I don't see that I have much choice,' he said. 'And I don't see that you do either. You started this, Jess. And you know the consequences. The Library always wins in the end.' He turned towards the Archivist and bowed slightly. 'You understand that I had to try to save him. He's my brother. But one thing about our family: we put business first. My da will understand what had to be done. I brought you the plans. And that makes us square for our end of the deal.'

The double doors opened, and Neksa stepped inside. She shot an involuntary look at Jess, then Brendan, before she settled her gaze on the Archivist. 'Sir,' she said and bowed.

'Come in, my dear,' he said, and smiled. Jess didn't like the look of it even though the Archivist took a seat and tried to seem welcoming. 'Do you recognise these young men?'

'Of course,' she said, and she sounded baffled. 'The two Brightwell brothers. But I thought only one was here.'

'Did you.'

Jess caught the tone, and he knew his brother did as well, but neither of them moved. The guards, responding to some signal he hadn't seen, had drawn weapons and moved closer. Whatever was about to happen, there was no way to stop it.

'You rented a house to one of them, I believe,' the Archivist said. 'Or have I been misinformed?'

'I—' Neksa seemed caught off guard. She bit her lip and tried again. 'I did, sir. Some time ago now. But that was long before there was any hint that his brother would turn against the Library. I can only beg your understanding and assure you of my loyalty.'

'Did you help?' the Archivist asked.

'I don't understand, please, sir, I have never betrayed you in any way, if that is what you are saying. I never would. You are the Archivist, and I would never betray my oath.'

The Archivist looked at Brendan. There was a hint of a smile on his lips, and it chilled Jess to the bone. 'Is that true?'

Brendan returned the old man's gaze for a long moment before he said, 'She rented me a house for money. I was here to check up on my brother while he was in High Garda training. Then I left. I hardly exchanged half a dozen words with her.'

'Hardly an impassioned plea for her life, young man,' the Archivist said. 'Do you want her to live?'

Jess heard a muffled gasp from Neksa, but he couldn't look away from his brother's face. Even now Brendan didn't betray any anxiety or any fear.

'I don't much care,' Brendan said, and turned to look at the young woman with the same indifference. 'Please yourself, I suppose; she's your employee, not mine.'

It was a ploy, Jess realised, and a good one; even knowing his brother he would've believed that Brendan didn't care either way. And it was the only way that Neksa still had a chance of walking out alive. If she reached the outer office, he could only hope she had the sense to run, because the Archivist wouldn't forget, and he certainly wouldn't forgive.

The Archivist nodded. 'It's true,' he said. 'She's never given me the slightest hint that she might be anything but loyal. She's bright, efficient, and a tireless servant of the Library. I could never find anyone half as competent to take her place. She knows my secrets. And that's why this is such a loss.'

Brendan knew, in that instant, and he began to move towards her, but it was already too late. The statue of Horus stepped from its alcove and, in one terrifying, fluid motion, drove the spear it carried through her back with so much force it emerged from her chest and buried itself in the floor. Jess shouted, but his voice blended with the sound of his twin's scream. Brendan reached her just as the automaton withdrew the spear in a spray of blood and stepped back into its alcove. He caught Neksa as she fell forward and wrapped his arms around her as he eased her to the floor. She was still alive. Jess tried to get to her and to his brother, but in the next instant he was shoved down on his knees next to Wolfe, and there were guns at the back of both of their heads. *Don't*, Jess thought wildly at his brother. *Don't try it.*

And if it entered Brendan's mind at all, his brother dismissed the idea of killing the old man because he was trying to stop the rush of blood from Neksa's wounds. It was useless, and no one could've saved her, not even the most skilled of Medica, and Jess closed his eyes and tried not to listen to the words his brother was whispering to the woman who was dying in his arms. It was private. It was heartbreaking.

He knew she was gone when his brother went quiet. Brendan's back was to him, and his brother was still, but there was something forming under that stillness that was very, very dangerous.

Brendan eased Neksa back to the carpet and closed her eyes with bloodied fingers.

Then he went for the Archivist.

Jess timed his move precisely; he threw himself forward, hit his brother in mid-lunge, and knocked him sideways to the floor. They tangled together and rolled, and then Brendan's fingers were around Jess's throat and there was no way he could defend himself except to try to writhe free, and his brother's eyes were wide and dark and wholly mad with fury . . . and then they went blank, as the High Garda soldiers dragged him off and forced him to his knees in the spreading pool of blood from Neksa's fallen body.

'You two, settle down,' the Archivist said. He hadn't moved from where he'd been sitting, and he still had a calm, remote look on his face. Jess had always hated him. He'd never hated him so much it felt like physical pain before. 'It had to be done, of course. The girl couldn't be trusted, and that's deeply unfortunate. And now I find I can't trust either of you. Much as I'd hoped that your father and I could reach a lasting agreement, it seems he's no more trustworthy than any other criminal. For the protection of the Great Library, I have to remove all contaminants from our society. Rebels. Burners. Criminals. And you . . . you are guilty of at least one of those things, if not more.' He nodded to the High Garda captain. 'Take them back to the prison. Remove the body for funeral rites. She deserves that from us, at least.'

'I'm going to kill you,' Brendan said. His voice held all the rage that Jess had swallowed, and more. 'You evil old bastard, you're going to pay for this if I have to crawl out of hell to bring you the bill.'

'Save your breath,' Jess told his brother. 'He's not worth wasting it.'

The Archivist smiled and shrugged. 'Wolfe? No threats from you, then?'

Wolfe kept silent. His dark eyes were half-hidden under his wild hair, and he didn't look capable of much, weak as he was. But somehow, Jess thought that was more frightening than his brother's raw, wounded fury.

'Take them out of my sight.' The Archivist sighed, and took up his pen. 'I have to find a new assistant.'

They took Brendan out first, and Jess was glad of that.

It meant his brother was spared the sight of the girl he loved being rolled into the spoilt carpet and taken away without ceremony, or even a last look from the man who'd killed her.

CHAPTER TWENTY-SEVEN

The corridors had shifted again, and Jess grimly memorised this configuration, too; he was starting to see a pattern to it, but he'd need more data to finish the puzzle. Not likely to get it in the time he had left. He had the feeling he'd been to this office for the last time.

Brendan's hands were shackled now, and his ankles, too; as Jess was pushed down into the carrier seat, he got the same treatment. So did Wolfe. No chance of using their numbers to take down the six High Garda soldiers crowded in with them, though Jess had considered it as an option for a flash. Brendan sat silently now, as still as an automaton. He was half-soaked in Neksa's blood, and Jess could imagine how that felt cooling against his skin. If he'd ever needed more of a reason to see the Archivist dead, he had it now.

'Bren,' he said quietly. And when he got no response: '*Scraps.*'

'Don't,' Brendan said. 'Just don't.'

'Leave him,' Wolfe said from Jess's other side. 'Jess. Is Santi—'

'I don't know,' Jess said. 'But I'm glad to see you alive.'

'Are you?' Wolfe had recovered a ghost of his usual acerbic tone. 'That's mystifying, considering the horror I unleashed on you just now. Both of you.'

'My fault,' Jess said. 'Dario and I, we thought . . . we thought you'd tell Santi what we planned, and Santi would put a quick stop to it. I hated not telling you, but . . .' He shook his head. 'It wasn't worth what you've been through, Scholar, and I am sorry for that.'

'Don't take the world on your back. I don't need your guilt, Brightwell. I need your mind working. We're not finished.'

It looked like they were, Jess thought, but he kept that silent. At least Wolfe wasn't broken to his core. Not yet. But Brendan . . . No, he couldn't be. His twin bounced; he didn't break. He never cared enough to be hurt the way that others could be. Or at least, he never showed it if he was.

'Not sure how we're getting out of this, sir,' Jess admitted. 'My plans didn't include . . . this. Any of this.'

'I suppose it would be asking a great deal if they did,' Wolfe said. 'But there's all the time in the world to feel defeated.'

'Shut up, the lot of you,' growled one of the soldiers. 'You're going nowhere but into the cells, and into the ground.'

Hard to argue that he was wrong . . . except that the carrier, which had been hurtling along at a fast clip suddenly decelerated, and threw everyone's weight towards the front.

'Blessed Isis, learn to drive, you mongrel—' shouted the same soldier who'd first spoken, and he pushed his way up to the front to bang on the driver's compartment. 'What's happening?'

No answer. The carrier continued to slow down, and Jess looked over at Wolfe, then at Brendan. Brendan's eyes were shut, his face tense and still, but Wolfe seemed more than aware of things. 'Be ready,' the Scholar whispered, and Jess nodded. Ready for what, he wasn't sure; with ankles and wrists pinned, it wasn't likely he could do more than flail at random. But anything out of the ordinary was something that might, *might* be useful.

The carrier ground to a hissing stop, and a brisk, businesslike boom sounded three times on the door. 'Come on, soldier, we don't have all day,' barked a bored voice. 'Orders and papers. High Commander's orders.'

'Talk to the driver!' their guard commander shouted without opening up. 'He's got the clearances!'

'He says you've got them.'

'We're transporting prisoners on the orders of the Archivist, you idiot. Can't you see the Elite seal on the vehicle?'

'Word is, some faction's stolen two of those very things. I'll need to inspect before I can open the barricades.'

'What's your rank, soldier?' the Elite guard barked.

'Lieutenant, sir. And yours?'

'I outrank you. *Open the barricades*!'

'Show me your orders and it's yours.'

'Damn your soul to the crocodiles—' The commander backed up and drew his sidearm, and around them, his soldiers followed suit. 'Be ready. I don't like this.'

'Lieutenant?' More bangs on the door. 'If you force me to crack this can, I'll have your head, superior or not!'

He sounded like an annoyed, tired High Garda officer, Jess thought, and that must have decided the Elite commander, too, because he unlatched the door and slid it open, just enough to thrust his Codex out. 'First page,' he said. 'And then I'll want your name. You can expect to be cleaning toilets in my barracks by—'

He stopped because he was coughing . . . and in a second, they all were: helpless, racking coughs, though Jess couldn't see any smoke. In the next seconds his eyes filled with burning tears, and he felt, rather than saw, soldiers stumbling blindly towards the door, retching.

Then the three of them were alone, struggling to breathe in the toxic atmosphere, until the door slid fully open and brought in a gust of bracing fresh air that Jess sucked in with real relief. He was lying on the floor, with Wolfe half on top of him, and as he blinked the burn from his eyes, he saw someone pulling Wolfe out by the feet into the glare of daylight.

He was grabbed and dragged next, and caught by a second pair of hands before his head could hit the ground.

'Move!' the same voice barked. 'We have a minute, maybe two, and we'd best be gone!'

Jess craned his head as he was being carried past and saw a pile of unconscious High Garda Elites next to the troop carrier, which was idling and billowing steam in the road. There was an official-looking barricade, but no one manning it now.

He was being carried by two men, and as he looked up at the one holding his shoulders, he put the upside-down face into the right orientation. 'Tom? Tom Rolleson?'

Troll grinned. 'Welcome back, Jess,' he said. 'Hell of a mess you've got us in.'

Jess found himself – between coughing fits – unceremoniously loaded into another carrier, and as his irritated eyes adjusted, he realised he was, finally, among friends. Santi's company, to be specific: the voice that had demanded credentials from the other vehicle had been Centurion Botha's, and as the man applied the Library key to the manacles on his wrists, then his ankles, Jess had to grab for a handhold as the vehicle lurched into motion. 'The gas,' he said. 'Yours?'

'A little invention we took off some Burners a while ago,' Botha said, and unlocked Scholar Wolfe's cuffs. 'We thought it might come in handy sometime.' He started to apply the key to Brendan's restraints and then checked himself and sat back, looking from Jess to his twin. 'Two of you is too many, Brightwell. Assuming I've let loose the right one?'

'You did,' Jess said, at the same moment his brother said, 'No, you didn't,' and thrust his restraints back out at Botha.

'Ease off, Scraps,' Jess said. 'We're among friends.'

'You are. I don't know where I stand.' Brendan sounded better. Not good, by any means, but at least calm, and no longer ragged with rage. 'What kind of friends? Because these look like your type, not mine.'

'I see the resemblance is more than skin-deep,' Botha said. 'What's your name, other Brightwell?'

'Brendan.'

'Brendan, I am Centurion Botha. If I remove these, do I have your word you will not make me kill you over something stupid?'

Brendan shrugged. 'For all that signifies.'

'Go ahead,' Jess said. 'I'll take responsibility for him. Do anything stupid, and I'll throw you out for the Elites to find.'

'You would,' Brendan said. He said nothing else as Botha unlocked his restraints, and settled back without any troublemaking.

Which left Jess free to hear Scholar Wolfe say, 'Do you know if Nic is—'

'He's well, sir,' Botha said immediately. 'You'll see him soon. I promise that.'

Wolfe took in a deep breath and sat back to put his head in his hands. 'I hate for him to see me like this,' he said. 'But he's seen me far worse. Where are we going?'

Botha cast a raised eyebrow towards Brendan. Jess shrugged. 'For better or worse, he's got nowhere else to go,' he said. 'Safe enough to tell him.'

'We're going to a safe place,' Botha said. 'It belongs to a friend of yours.'

'Of mine?' Jess asked, and frowned. 'I'm not hip-deep in those these days.'

'You'll see,' Botha said. 'You have more than you think.'

They emerged into a large, dark space, with light cascading in sharp squares from skylights above. This was clearly a military storage area, and kitted out for vehicles like High Garda troop carriers; there were four more parked nearby, but in the dim light Jess couldn't make out the insignia, except that it wasn't the Horus eye of the Library. Militarily neat, and for a moment he had the strange sensation that they'd somehow found a safe space in the middle of the High Garda compound . . . until he realised that the signs posted to keep the space clear, and keep weapons locked, were in Spanish.

His suspicions proved right when Botha led them through an enclosed hallway without windows and into a large, gracious tiled courtyard with ornate fountains and a garden that looked nothing like ones usually found in Alexandria. This one was unmistakably European, and olive trees grew in ropy spirals around the edges, topped with pale, dusty leaves and dark fruit. Orange trees sprawled in massive pots.

And waiting in the courtyard stood the Spanish ambassador, Alvaro Santiago, but Jess spent only an instant in recognition before he took in the people standing beside him.

Thomas, with a thick scruff of golden beard and hair curling down to his collar. Glain, next to him, lean and immaculate in a High Garda uniform. Khalila, framed by a wine-red dress and matching hijab. Dario, as resplendent as his cousin's closet could provide. And, on the end, in plain black, stood Captain Santi.

Khalila was the first to rush forward and, without hesitation, fold Jess in an embrace, then kiss him on both cheeks. He pressed his forehead to hers and smiled. 'I thought you'd slip a knife in my ribs.'

'Oh, I would have, for a few days after your dramatic departure,' she said. 'You beautiful fool. I forgave you at least an hour ago, as soon as I knew I might see you again.'

He was almost shaken by that. He hadn't realised until she was here, *real*, how much he'd missed her explosive brilliance and calm energy. She released him and stepped away, and the next was Dario, who offered only a grave handshake. 'Still alive, after all,' he said.

'And I see you've already found yourself a decent tailor,' Jess said, and pulled him into an embrace. Dario returned it briefly, but with real feeling. 'You had to tell your cousin your nickname for me.'

'Of course,' Dario said. 'I tell everyone to call you scrubber. And as for my tailor, one must keep up standards.' Dario's tone was light, but he was taking in Brendan's bloody clothes, and Wolfe, who was staring motionless at Santi. Taking in all information, as he usually did, even if he came to the wrong conclusion half the time. Well, that was unfair. A quarter of the time.

Dario stepped aside, and Glain gave him a grin and a one-armed, briskly martial hug before stepping back.

That left Captain Santi, who was moving straight for Wolfe, slowly, as if he couldn't believe his lover wouldn't vanish . . . and Thomas.

Thomas stood where he was and made Jess come to him. *He looks different*, Jess thought. He'd grown a thick, golden scruff of beard, and his hair had grown long and wild to his collar. And as glad as Jess was to see him, the careful expression in Thomas's eyes made him slow down.

Then he understood why. *The last time he saw me, I was lying to him. And it hurt.* Khalila and Glain had forgiven him, for their own reasons; Dario had already known. But Thomas . . . it had cut Thomas deep.

So the first thing Jess said was, 'I'm sorry. Truly sorry, Thomas.'

Thomas nodded, and they stood there staring at each other, with an awkward, uncomfortable space between them . . . and then Thomas jerked his chin towards Wolfe and Santi, and Jess turned to look.

Wolfe extended a hand to Santi. It trembled badly, until Santi grabbed it and pulled Wolfe into his arms, and the sound he made came deep from his soul, a raw sound of relief that seemed to echo through the air. When they parted, it was only to arm's length, and Santi looked at Wolfe, *into* him, and said, 'I should have been with you. I would have been with you.'

'You were,' Wolfe said. 'Every moment.'

Then they were kissing, and Jess looked away, back at Thomas, who was smiling a little now. 'Good to see that,' Thomas said, and the smile faded when he focused back on Jess. 'You left us. You left us thinking – God knows what we were thinking. But I nearly killed you, and I am *not* sorry for that. It was the right thing to do, at the time.'

'What I did was the right thing to do,' Jess said. 'At the time. But I'm still sorry.'

Thomas sighed. 'I suppose it will have to do, as an apology.' He pulled Jess into a hug, slapped his back so hard it stung, and then pushed him back. 'Talk later. We have things to do now.' He frowned then, and stopped Jess from moving with a hand on his shoulder. 'Something's wrong.'

'Obviously,' Jess said. 'But we're not going to solve it standing here.'

Thomas nodded, and slid a look to Brendan, who was still standing where Jess had left him. 'And him? Is he all right?'

Jess shook his head but didn't try to explain; Brendan wouldn't want anyone knowing his grief, at least, not here. Not now. That was why he had a slight smile on his face and empty eyes. It was a mask, and sooner or later, it would have to come off . . . but if it helped now, so be it.

'Ambassador.' Jess moved to Alvaro Santiago and bowed. He made sure it was profound, even though it hurt. 'Thank you. I assume we're safe here . . . ?'

'For now,' Santiago said. He didn't seem quite as light-hearted as before. 'As safe as anyone is in this city at the moment. But the moment is changing, and I think you know that.' He raised his voice. 'Everyone, welcome. Come inside. I've set aside rooms for you, baths, clothes, meals. When you're rested, we will meet to discuss our futures.'

Somehow, Jess didn't think the ambassador's future would run quite the same path as his own, but for now, at least, it was enough.

Trouble came when Jess was in his room, stripping off his chemical-soaked shirt with real relief; he was naked to the waist when a knock came at his door, and he sighed and threw on the soft white shirt that had been provided for him before he opened the door.

Niccolo Santi grabbed him by the throat and walked him four brisk steps backward to the nearest wall. The impact drove the breath from Jess's chest, and he tried to gasp out a question, but Santi's hand tightened. The captain's hand was brutally strong, and his eyes were cold. 'No,' he said. 'You don't talk. I talk, Brightwell. Do you know why? Nod if you do.'

Jess jerked his head awkwardly up and down. He'd seen Santi in a killing mood, but never aimed at *him* . . . and this was very definitely personal.

'You took him,' Santi said. His voice was low and calm, the one they all knew was the most dangerous sign of his temper. 'You ripped him away and handed him to the Archivist. You had no way of knowing what they would do to him or what hole they'd throw him into. And you – you, of all of them, *knew* what he'd endured. You sent him back to hell, boy. And I do not forget that, even if he walked out of it alive.'

Jess felt his face growing thick and red, and what little air he could painfully pull in wasn't enough. All it would take was one spasm of Santi's hand, and he'd be unconscious. On his way to an ugly death.

Fight back, his instincts told him. He had a chance. Santi was so focused on his rage that he could hurt him, break free, and escape . . . but he held himself still with a huge effort. He wouldn't fight back.

He was guilty of what Santi accused.

Santi let him go a second later and pushed himself backward. Surprised, Jess thought, at his own violence. Santi was a trained soldier, and he was a man who was in command of himself at almost all times . . . but not now. They exchanged looks. Santi was staring at him as if he didn't know him, and Jess gasped for breath and put a hand to his painful neck.

'Sir,' Jess managed to say. 'I'm—'

'I don't care,' Santi said. 'I don't care if you're overflowing with regret. I don't care if this was Dario's harebrained idea, as I suspect it was. I don't even care that you brought him back to me, because we both know Wolfe could have died there, alone, and that I will never forgive, Jess. I want to send him out of here, away from all of this, and never let him come back. The only reason I won't is I know he wouldn't go.'

'Sir,' Jess tried again. 'It's my fault. I know that. I should have told him, and you, before we set it all in motion.'

'If you'd told me, *stronzo*, I would have knocked your heads together until you came up with a better plan.'

'I know. I didn't tell you because I knew you'd stop us. And I knew Wolfe would have agreed, but told you. Same outcome. It wasn't easy, Captain. But it's my responsibility, and I'll try to earn your trust again.'

'You're lucky I'm not twenty years younger,' Santi said. 'I'd have killed you.' He sighed and rubbed his head in frustration. 'But you're just a boy, and you made a mistake, and I should know better myself. I'm sorry for putting my hands on you, Jess.'

'You wanted me to fight back.'

Santi's glance at him told him it was true. 'And you didn't.'

'Because I know you'd kill me in any kind of a fight, Captain. I can outrun you. I can't outfight you.'

He watched the captain pull in a deep breath, hold it, and then let it out in a rush. 'Promise me you won't put Christopher in that kind of danger again. Not that. Not ever.'

Jess nodded. 'I swear, I'll do everything I can.'

'Am I such a child that I need a lover and a student to decide my own life for me?'

That sharp voice stopped them both in their tracks. Santi turned, and Jess looked past him to find Scholar Wolfe in the doorway, arms folded. He looked tired but clean; his colour was still too pale by half, but his eyes were bright, and the temper in them was all too familiar.

Santi winced. 'Chris—'

'Oh, no, by all means, choke the young man half to death

for doing exactly what I would have done in his place. And yes, of course, decide my life. Pad me in cotton like a fragile bottle of Greek Fire. *Nic*. I am here. I am standing. I am sane. And much as I love you, much as I will always love you, don't ever assume I can't, or won't, think for myself.' Wolfe's voice softened, took on a warmer timbre. 'My love, I know you're blaming him because you failed to see it coming. Don't. They fooled me as well. Fooled me so well I betrayed *him* earlier today, and almost got him and his brother murdered. For my troubles, I am responsible for the cruel death of a young woman who did absolutely nothing to deserve it, so if you're angry with him . . . be just as angry with me.'

Santi went to him and folded him in his arms, because he – like Jess – had heard the tremble in the man's voice. And Wolfe let out his breath and sank into that embrace with real gratitude. 'I'm sorry,' Santi whispered. 'I shouldn't have taken it out on Jess. But seeing you like this – it rips me to pieces. You know that.'

'I do,' Wolfe said. 'But I am mending. A broken bone heals twice as strong, remember?'

Santi laughed. It sounded unsteady and half-desperate. 'I remember. I remember everything. That's the curse of it, isn't it?'

'That's the beauty of it,' Wolfe replied. 'Come. Leave Jess to rest. He's as exhausted as I am, I think.'

Santi exchanged a look with Jess, and Jess nodded. Santi meant what he said: he wouldn't forget Jess's betrayal. And Jess would have to earn back any kind of trust. It was a lot to understand from a single look, and yet completely clear. He might be forgiven by the others, and easily, but for Santi, he'd have a long road back.

And that was fair.

Jess locked the door again, took off his clothes, and stepped into the luxury of the Spanish embassy's shower. He stayed in it for far too long, until the water began to run cold and his skin pebbled into gooseflesh; the feeling of being *safe* was something he didn't want to give up, and as soon as he switched off the spray, dried himself, and dressed again in the High Garda uniform provided, he was back on guard. Alvaro Santiago, as he was sure they all knew, was an ally, but not a friend.

They had no friends in Alexandria. Not now.

Downstairs, he found most of the others gathered in a small library; it was richly decorated, and the chair Jess sank into with a sigh was the most comfortable thing he could imagine. His aching body craved sleep, but comfort would have to do for now.

Everyone stopped talking when he took a seat and stared at him. 'What?' he asked.

Dario shook his head. 'I'm still amazed you're alive,' he said. 'You are an unbelievably good liar, Jess. Better than I would have imagined, if you survived this long. I find that your best quality.'

'Shut up, peacock,' Jess said. 'If you have a best quality, I'm still struggling to find it.'

'Boys,' Glain said. 'Don't make me separate you. By which I mean, heads from bodies. We've got this far. Stop squabbling about the size of your—'

'Glain!' Khalila said.

'Talents,' Glain finished. Her voice softened. 'Have you talked to your brother?'

'No,' Jess said. 'He doesn't want to talk.'

'How do you know?'

'Twins,' Jess said. 'I don't want to, either, and I didn't just watch the girl I loved . . .' His voice trailed off, because suddenly he imagined Morgan in Neksa's place, and the spear driving through her body into the floor. Her blood warm on his hands.

'*Mein Gott*, Jess, is that what happened?' Thomas leant forward, and the large armchair he sat in creaked as if struggling under the strain. 'Were you there? What happened?'

It was an innocent question, but Jess suddenly felt even more tired. 'The Archivist had her killed,' he said. 'By an automaton. No reason except to make a point. I thought we were next.' As soon as he said it, he knew that was true. He'd been pushing that awareness away all this time, had denied it while he'd been on his knees in front of the Archivist, but yes. He and Brendan had been on the raw edge of death, close enough to feel it. And see it. A shudder worked through him, and he closed his eyes. 'I think my brother truly cared for her. So I don't know, Thomas. I don't know how he is now. I just know he doesn't want to talk about it.' *And neither do I*, he thought, but didn't say. Thomas was a good enough friend to know it.

He opened his eyes when he felt Khalila take his hand. She didn't speak, and for that he was grateful. They all sat in silence for a while, before Glain, always to the point, said, 'How safe are we here?'

'On a scale of absolutely not at all?' Dario shrugged. 'Somewhat, for now. My cousin's a good man, and he'll do what he can to help us, but he is at the mercy of my *other* cousin. The royal one. And if the Archivist decides to expel all ambassadors from the city, as he might . . .' He raised a hand and let it drop. 'It's possible he could evacuate us along with his staff. But that hardly gets us closer to our goal.'

'Maybe our goal can't be reached without an army,' Glain said. 'Didn't you clever foxes think of that? Or did you expect to simply trick the Archivist into writing his own execution order?'

'Now there's a thought,' Dario said. She sent him a dark look. 'But not a serious one. We have the start of an army, don't we? Santi's company is here, with us. And Santi's sent messages to other captains he trusts. Add them up, and . . .'

'We have enough to lose, and badly,' Thomas said. 'Alexandria can be taken. The Serapeum? From all I've seen and heard, that would be much, much harder. The Curia has only to seal themselves inside it, and wait. The remaining High Garda forces, the automata . . . these can't be overcome for long.'

'You're right,' Jess said. 'I've been in and out of the Archivist's office several times since I've been here, and each time, I entered and left different ways. The hallways move. The entire pyramid is a vast clockwork that the Archivist can reorder any time he wishes. It's a death trap for an invasion. They could hold it for ever, and we'd be cut to pieces.'

'What's the mood in the city?' Khalila asked. She stood up and poured herself a cup of water from a pitcher sitting nearby, and Jess followed suit. He hadn't realised how thirsty he was until he saw her drinking it. It tasted clear, pure, and wonderfully cool. 'Scholar Murasaki in Cadiz has been contacting senior Scholars all over the world, and her word is certainly influential. More and more outposts of the Great Library are declaring themselves neutral and refusing to allow High Garda soldiers through their Translation Chambers. It makes things much more complicated for the Archivist if he has to move troops slowly, through foreign lands and waters. Especially now, with more countries abandoning the treaty every day.'

'Unsettled,' Jess said. 'But the news isn't reaching people here of much of that, and what is, is being dismissed as panic and rumour. The Burners are spreading word, though, and recruiting on it. And they have presses to print up their messages; Red Ibrahim must have installed a few across the city already. Have you spoken to him?'

'Not exactly,' Khalila said, when no one else volunteered. 'We left that relationship at a bit of an awkward point, in that Red Ibrahim wanted to sell us to the Archivist, and we did not wish to be sold. I don't *think* Anit took it personally. Why, haven't you spoken to him?'

Jess shook his head. 'If I'd tried, I'd have led the Elites right to his door. I let my father do any communicating, but since it's my da, I don't know what he's been saying, either. He's tried to change the deal two or three times already. I'd not put it past him now to tell Red Ibrahim to sell us out. He likely considers both his sons lost.'

'Just like that?' It was Glain who said it, and unusually for her it sounded quiet, and almost compassionate. 'Not much of a family you have, Jess.'

'No,' he said. 'Not much. I'd have thought you'd figured that out by now.'

He hadn't meant for Brendan to hear it, but when he looked up he saw that his twin was standing like a shadow in the doorway. 'I didn't mean you,' he said. It sounded false, and awkward, and his brother said nothing. He poured water, gulped it, and poured again.

'So how do we kill him?' Brendan asked.

Silence for a moment, before Glain said, 'You mean the Archivist.'

'I didn't mean the man who runs the falafel concession. How do we kill him?'

They all looked at one other. Of course, it would have come to this question eventually, but Brendan had gone right to the core of it. *We're assassinating the most important man in the world*, Jess thought. *What other choice do we have, if we want to save anything now? Anyone?*

'The Feast of Greater Burning is our chance,' Dario said. 'The Archivist will be there—'

'And very well protected,' Glain muttered.

'—and so will his Curia. He's demanded Scholars and librarians all over the city to attend. For all we know, he's summoned Scholars from all over the world. He intends this to be a brutal display of his power.'

'Which is exactly why it's the wrong place to try to kill him,' Glain argued. 'He'll expect it.'

'Doesn't matter,' Brendan said. 'Anyone can be killed. You just have to stop caring about surviving it.'

Khalila looked at him, then at Jess, worry clear on her face. Jess just shook his head. 'We want him to step down,' she said at last. 'If we can make it impossible for him to continue . . .'

'Dying makes it impossible for him to continue.'

'Scraps—' Jess said.

'He has to be killed,' Brendan said, as calmly as if Jess hadn't spoken at all. 'He'll never give up power on his own. And besides, all the harm he's done, the death he's ordered here and everywhere . . . he doesn't deserve the breaths he's drawing right now.' He turned and met Jess's eyes. 'Am I wrong?'

'You're angry,' Jess said. 'You feel guilty. But no. You're not wrong. I'm sorry, Khalila, but he isn't. I've been here. You haven't. I've seen – seen the lengths he's willing to go to keep his power, and the Library's. Maybe my brother's right.'

'Then it can be done,' Glain said. 'I'm a good shot. Santi's even better. If we plan this properly—'

'Always plans with you,' Brendan said. 'Never action.'

He put his cup down and walked towards the door. Jess got up and followed, and stopped him just before he made it out. 'What are you going to do?' he asked.

'I'm not staying here,' Brendan said. 'And I'm not relying on your too-noble friends, either. Let me go, Jess.'

'No chance,' Jess said, and he meant it. 'You go, I go. Together.'

'You can't go,' Khalila said. She'd got up, and though she hadn't approached, it was clear she wanted to. 'Jess! You're safe here. At least rest for the night! Tomorrow—'

Jess was listening, but he was looking into Brendan's eyes, and he knew what he was seeing there. He slowly shook his head. 'What are you thinking, Brother?' he asked.

'I'm thinking that all the honourable intentions in the world won't make the Archivist listen to a word your friends have to say,' Brendan said. 'You and I, we know people who aren't so honourable.'

That was all true. And Jess knew that whatever Ambassador Santiago might personally wish, he was a politician . . . and they couldn't be relied on for long because their will was not their own. Criminals, on the other hand, tended to be more straightforward. 'If you're talking about our most prominent cousin, he might not be so well disposed towards us right now.'

Brendan shrugged. He clearly didn't care about such details. And Jess recognised the smile that smoothed across his lips. It was deeply dangerous. 'Then we'll be charming,' he said. 'Come on, brother. Just this once. Let's uphold our family honour and do the wrong thing.'

'Jess!' Khalila's voice was pleading.

'She's right, my friend,' Thomas said. 'You should stay here.'

'No. We need a backup in case Spain fails us,' Jess said, and let a grin that matched his brother's slide into place. 'Brendan's right. It's time to do the wrong thing.'

'We'll be back,' Brendan said. 'And if not, don't look. You won't find us.'

With that he was gone, and Jess moved fast to follow.

CHAPTER TWENTY-EIGHT

Getting out of the embassy without being noticed wasn't going to be easy. He and Brendan both agreed that going out the front would walk them right into High Garda custody in short order; their only chance of getting out clean was to make their own way. Besides, it felt good to exercise all his athletic skills again. Brendan, for all his usual lack of enthusiasm for action, was strong and lithe; he found handholds up to the roof and gave Jess a lift and together they lay flat on the warm clay tiles and watched the guard patrols until they found a gap. Not much of one, a narrow window that required skill and speed to take advantage of it, but then they were over the wall and into a no-man's-land of empty space before another tall fence, one with outward-curving spikes appeared twenty steps down the hill.

'Don't like this,' Jess said. 'The ambassador isn't stupid. He'll have some kind of defences—'

They both heard the barking at the same time, exchanged a look, and raced for the outer fence. This one was smooth iron bars set close together, the only crossbars at the bottom and top, well above their heads.

A pack of sleek black dogs crested the hill, spotted them, and began baying furiously as they came on.

'On my shoulders!' Jess shouted, and grabbed the bars for

support. Brendan vaulted up and stood, and Jess grabbed his brother's ankles. 'Lifting!' He put his hands under his brother's heels, and pushed, panting against the tearing strain in muscles unused to this particular move. It worked. His brother scrambled up to the top, slung a leg over the crossbar, and reached down.

Jess backed up and took a running leap, and Brendan's hand slapped around his wrist. Jess braced himself against the fence and tried to take some of the strain as his brother pulled . . . and then his fingers curled around the cross brace, and he was able to get up and over, and make the leap down with Brendan to the other side just as the dogs crashed to a furious, foaming halt against the barrier, leaping and barking and snarling.

Brendan kissed his fingers to the pack, rolled the strain from his shoulders, and said, 'You know where to find our cousin?'

'He won't be happy to see us, I can almost guarantee that.'

'Like I said: we can be charming. Come on, Jess. Sun's almost down.'

Jess's High Garda uniform made it easier for him to blend in, especially in the late afternoon crowds near the docks; he stole his brother a hooded jacket, the better to cover up their unmistakable resemblance, and took him through the shadier parts of the port, to an old, tumbledown tavern with a creaking sign painted with the face of a gorgon. The Medusa was one of the first places Jess had learnt to visit; it was a favourite of sailors, traders, smugglers and criminals, and he wasn't surprised to find it open when most of the port's more respectable establishments were starting to shutter their windows and doors.

The mood in the city was hushed and grim, and no one – except the proprietors of the Medusa – wanted to take chances this evening.

Jess pushed his way in, and immediately his uniform brought stilled conversations and appraising looks. He scanned the room and saw the broken-toothed old man – by all appearances, a drunk who'd nearly grown himself into the table at which he sat – and eased in across from him. His brother squeezed in beside him and pulled back his hood.

'We need to talk to our cousin,' Jess said, and the old man ignored them. His glass was empty. Jess looked at Brendan. 'You've got *geneih*?'

Brendan dumped a handful of golden Library coins on the table, which brought a greasy young man in an apron immediately at the sound of ringing currency. 'Gentlemen,' he said. 'What have you?'

'What he's having,' Jess said. 'Four of them.' He pointed to the drunk. 'He'll have two.'

Like a magic trick, the cash was gone; it seemed the server had never come close to the coins, but they vanished all the same. Jess leant forward and tried to see if the man was even conscious. His eyes were open and he was breathing, but when Jess passed a hand in front of the wrinkled old face, he got no response.

'This is your plan?' Brendan sounded impatient. 'I'm not here to drink myself senseless. Or even sensible.'

'Wait,' Jess said.

The drinks arrived, and two of them were set down firmly in front of the old man, with one apiece for Jess and Brendan. Neither of them touched the stuff. Jess arranged the glasses in front of the old man into a rough triangle and said, 'A life might be worth more than a book, but a book is worth more than your life if they catch you with it. You've got three on you right now.'

The old man wasn't drunk. His eyes suddenly, sharply

focused on Jess's face, and there was nothing vague about their grey depths now. 'What do you want, Garda?'

'I'm not Garda,' Jess said. 'I'm a Brightwell.'

'I'm not drunk enough to see double,' the man said. 'You're the twins. You'd best get yourselves home to cold England if you know what's good for you. You've got no family here.'

'Oh, come on, even the best family wants to kill each other half the time,' Brendan said. 'We want to see him. Now.'

'No.' The old man bared rotten teeth, and Jess leant back to avoid the smell of his breath. 'He doesn't want to see you. Ever. You helped destroy one of his operations and *burnt his house down*. You killed ten of his people. You're lucky I don't spill your guts right now.'

'I didn't kill anyone. I was a prisoner. And the dragon almost burnt me along with the house.'

Brendan leant forward and locked gazes with the old man. 'You want to see your guts first?' And Jess was suddenly aware that his brother held a knife under the table, pressed against the old man's stomach – probably the man's own knife, at that. Brendan always did have fast hands. 'No more conversation. Get us to him or your last drink ends up on the floor the hard way.'

The man who was assuredly *not* a drunk stared at him a moment, then looked past them and whistled. A high, sharp sound that echoed through the room and cut conversation dead. All around them, dangerous-looking men and women pushed back their chairs and rose, and Jess sent his brother a glare. *Just had to push it, didn't you?* 'These young men want to go to the temple,' the old man said. 'Let them make their supplications. It's a night to get right with our gods, I think.'

Before either of them could draw breath, much less put up a

fight, there were cloth bags jammed over their heads, and Jess felt a heavy blow and sharp, lancing pain at the back of his head . . . and then nothing.

He woke up with the bag being dragged off. The smell of dried lentils from the bag's former contents made him sneeze, and that woke a headache the size of the Serapeum behind his eyes. *Stupid*, he thought, and tried to move his hands. Tied, of course. But as he pulled, he felt the bonds being sliced apart, and he was pulled to his feet. He found his balance and blinked away bleary tears.

He hadn't expected to find himself actually *in* a temple, but that was where he was: the temple of the Roman goddess Laverna. Not a very well-frequented temple. Small, dusty, kept up more for appearances than for actual rites. He'd never visited it in Alexandria and was a little surprised to even see the goddess included here. He looked around and found Brendan standing next to him. The man who'd cut his bonds had moved off and was somewhere in the columned shadows behind them.

'Strange, isn't it?' said the man standing a few feet ahead of them on the tiled floor. He was facing the graceful marble statue of the goddess, with a knife in her right hand and coins in her left. 'The Egyptians never had a god of thieves. The Romans, on the other hand, not only had one but honoured her as goddess of thieves, cheats, plagiarists . . . and they even had a gate for her in Rome. I've seen it. Perhaps I'll go to Rome after this. It's a city that welcomes our brothers.'

He turned to look at them, and Jess knew him as his vision finally sharpened: Red Ibrahim. Anit's father. The head of criminal enterprises, including book smuggling, here in Alexandria. He was a native of the city, and he had the shaved head of someone who might even aspire to be a priest . . . but his religion was more along the lines of the worship of Laverna. He was a hard man. A man who'd survived and flourished in the hardest place on earth to practise his trade. He'd lost two sons to it.

Before, Jess had faced him as a business ally, if not real family. But here, now, the feeling was very different.

'You shouldn't have come to me,' Red Ibrahim said. 'I have no mercy for traitors.'

'Hear us out,' Brendan said. 'Please, Cousin. Our father—'

'Your father wants you home, immediately. Both of you. No more deals with the Archivist. No more playacting. Your place is with your family, and not here. Do you understand?'

'I'm going to kill the Archivist,' Brendan said. 'And you are not stopping me.'

Red Ibrahim didn't answer. He shook his head and turned to Jess. 'Your brother is a fool, and he's angry. I hope you are clearer of mind. I will see you taken to a ship and sent home, and you can forget about this place for ever. The Archivist will win tomorrow, or not; your friends will achieve their goal, or not. But you will not be here to see it. I'm closing my operations in this city. Already, most of my people have set sail, or will today.'

'Rats,' Brendan said. 'And the ship's not sinking. It's being set back on course.'

'We're not going back to England,' Jess said. 'Not until this is over. Run if you like. But first you're going to help us.'

'Help you *what*? Overthrow the Archivist Magister of the Great Library? I'm not a fool, and you're not a hero, young man. You should remember that, especially now. It will keep you alive.'

'Alive isn't enough.'

Red Ibrahim shook his head. 'Then this won't matter. I'll

tell your father I tried. But he'd rather you never come home than you spill what you know to the Library. And I agree. You are princes of our underworld kingdom. And you can't be taken alive.'

He reached under the flowing Egyptian robes he wore and came out with a High Garda pistol. Jess watched him thumb the selector switch from *stun* to *kill*, and time seemed to slow to a trickle as his senses expanded. There was another exit from this shrine, behind the goddess's statue; he could see the glimmer of it on the dusty tiles. It meant going through Red Ibrahim to get to it, but that would have to be done. The accomplice behind them cut them off from that escape, and Jess could feel him moving up. He didn't look, but he knew that man, too, would be armed. He was heading for Brendan's back.

And Red Ibrahim was taking aim at Jess's head.

Jess dropped just before the shot came, and felt a hot burn along his scalp as it only just missed. His brother was moving, too, a blur in the air beside him, and he instinctively rolled to his right to put room between them. Red Ibrahim would think he'd hit his target, at least for an instant, and Jess used that instant to set his feet and launch himself straight at the man.

He hit Red Ibrahim squarely, and the gun tumbled free as they both fell backward to the floor at the feet of the statue. Jess reached for it, but it put him off-balance, and quick as a striking cobra, Red Ibrahim flipped him on his back and pinned him there with a sharp right knee on his upper arm and a left knee compressing his chest. The older man caught Jess's left hand as he launched it in an attack and twisted it down at a painful angle. The gun was out of reach now for both of them; Red Ibrahim would have to shift his weight to get it, and Jess was alert for any hint of that.

But Ibrahim simply drew a knife and reached to cut Jess's throat.

The scream and shot came simultaneously, and for a confused second Jess was sure that the statue of Laverna had moved and punched a red hole through Ibrahim's skull . . . but that wasn't right. Ibrahim's eyes went wide and surprised, and then blank. His weight slithered bonelessly to fall heavily away, and Jess finally put the pieces together: the spray of blood on the white marble of the goddess's statue, the shot, the scream.

And he turned his head towards where the gun had been and saw Anit kneeling there, trembling, as the gun fell to the floor. It bounced close to him, and he grabbed for it and came up to his knees just in time to see that Brendan was against a column and the man holding him was about to stab him in the heart.

Jess fired, and the man staggered back and sprawled full length on the floor. He crawled for a few seconds, then went still.

Brendan looked up, panting. His face was bloody, and his knuckles dripped crimson, but he nodded to Jess, and Jess nodded back.

What did we just do?

Brendan pulled Jess to his feet, wiped the thick track of blood from the side of his face, and went to Anit, who was still on her knees, hands resting limply on her thighs. The girl – child, really, she was far from old enough for this – stared at her fallen father, and then she looked up at the two of them with tears shimmering in her eyes. 'I couldn't—I . . . he was going to—' She suddenly covered her mouth with both hands, and a wail burst out of her, only a little muffled by the cover. 'No, no, *Father*—'

'Anit?' Jess got her attention, slowly. 'Anit, why . . .'

Her hands were trembling badly. When she lowered them from her mouth, he took them in his. Cold as ice. But when she answered, her voice was steadier than he expected. 'He betrayed you,' she said. 'He betrayed your father, too; he took the money from the Archivist. He broke the oaths. I had no choice.' She swallowed. 'He would have killed you both. I couldn't—' She shook her head, and didn't finish, but Jess understood.

He understood what they owed her.

'We can't leave her,' Jess said. 'She'll have to come with us.'

'Come with us where, exactly? Whatever protection Red Ibrahim could have offered, it's gone now; his men will be fading into the night as quickly as they can, if they don't come looking for us to settle the score . . .' Brendan's calculations finally added up to what Jess's already had, and he looked at Anit with new speculation. 'Or . . . we take her with us. She knows the operation. She has her father's codes and secrets. And however loyal his men are, they won't attack if we have her.'

Much as Jess didn't like to think about it as keeping Anit hostage, his brother was right. Besides, leaving Anit for her father's guards to discover would be cruel. She'd confess in a heartbeat, and they'd kill her for what she'd done . . . at least, unless she found her centre and power very quickly. Right now, that seemed unlikely. She needed time to recover and regroup.

Jess helped the girl up. 'Come on, Anit,' he said. 'We'll take you somewhere safe.'

'I killed my father. Do you think there's safety from that?'

'We'll keep you safe until you're ready,' he said, and she turned and looked at him. The glassy shock over her eyes cracked, and what bled through was fury.

'I wish I'd never met you,' she said. 'Any of you!'

'You're not the first to say that,' Brendan said. 'But you're the one who killed your da, not us. You should be thinking of yourself. Do you have somewhere else to go?'

She broke free of Jess. For a second he thought she meant to take the gun, and he quickly switched it to stun; he had no desire to kill her, no matter what she might do. But she just pulled away and ran back to her father.

Jess glanced at his brother, and Brendan returned it, but neither of them followed her. She knelt down and posed her father's body: arms crossed on his chest like the pharaohs of old, legs straight, robe perfectly neat. Last, she unwound the red silk scarf she wore around her throat and placed it over his closed eyes.

'We don't have time for this,' Brendan muttered.

'Make time,' Jess said. 'She saved my life, and I saved yours because of it.'

Anit prayed for a moment, then kissed her father's still lips and said, 'Anubis, guide him to his rest. Forgive me, Father. But you were wrong. You have been wrong since you betrayed what we believe for the Archivist's gold.' She reached into the fold of his robe and came out with a red velvet case. Then she stood up, turned, and looked at both of them. 'Come on,' she said. 'I saved your lives because it suits my purposes. No use if all of us die here.'

There was already something different about her, Jess thought. Something stronger, and more dangerous, than he'd seen before.

'What's in the case?' Brendan asked as she led the way to the back door of the temple.

'Keys,' she said. 'To the kingdom.'

PART TEN

KHALILA

CHAPTER TWENTY-NINE

Captain Santi, when he heard of the Brightwells' escape, was grim but silent. It was Scholar Wolfe who lost his temper.

'And you didn't stop them?' he shouted at the rest of them, and for a moment Khalila felt like a student again, caught short and feeling the burn of his contempt.

'How?' Dario spread his hands wide. 'You know Jess. His brother's just as bad. What were we supposed to do, sit on them? Tie them up?'

'If necessary!' Wolfe spat the words like nails and stalked away. Without his Scholar's robe he looked less majestic but more lethal, Khalila thought. A man who'd endured much, and survived more. There was an edge to him that was honed almost to breaking. 'Do you know where they've gone? Tell me it isn't some wild plan to kill the Archivist.'

None of them replied to that – presumably, Khalila thought, because they all knew that was exactly what the two young men were about. Jess knew better, but he was also willing to forget that to protect his brother.

'There's nothing we can do about them now,' Khalila said, and got the full, dark force of Wolfe's attention. She didn't flinch. 'But there is something we can do, and it's more important. We must get the Scholars, especially the Research Scholars, on our side. Most of them have to see how dangerous the Archivist has become; they only need some assurance that we are sensible to join us. Scholar, you know many of them, if not all of them. Which of them do you think we should approach?'

'I can't approach anyone. I'm under an instant death sentence if they find me in the streets, or had you forgotten that?'

'No, I hadn't,' Khalila said. 'And you should stay here. I doubt the captain will allow you out of his sight again, in any case—'

'True,' Santi said. 'And no, Chris, it isn't up for debate.'

Khalila hurried on. 'But Dario and I . . . we are far less well-known. Scholar Murasaki has already arrived at the Lighthouse from Cadiz, and she is doing her part for us. Give us names. Let us go to the most influential of them tonight.'

'Not alone,' Glain said. 'I'm your escort, and don't bother to argue about it.'

'Why would I?' Khalila said, and smiled. 'You see? We're well protected. But we should do this, sir. Now.'

'You'll be recognised.'

'Not here. Young women in hijabs are common. I'll blend in. Dario . . . might have to amend his wardrobe, however.'

'What's wrong with it?' Dario asked.

'You look like a Spanish noble.'

'I *am*.'

'And do you think there are dozens of them roaming the streets here tonight?'

'I get your point,' he said, and sighed. 'I'll change.' He paused on the way out of the door to look at Wolfe. 'Scholar, she's right. She usually is, of course. Give her the names. We'll need every advantage if we intend to do anything meaningful tomorrow.'

Wolfe glared, and it was a hot enough look to burn stones . . . but then he stalked to a small desk in the corner of the library and took up a pen. 'Give me a moment,' he said. 'I'm writing individual letters. Hopefully, they will help open minds to what you have to say.'

It took half an hour, more or less, and Khalila helped slip each of the letters into envelopes and write the Scholars' names on them. 'You signed these,' she said. 'You realise that if all this fails, these are proof you were bent on undermining the Archivist's authority.'

'Do you really think that matters, if this fails? Proof or no proof, we'll all be in the ground.' He paused and signed the last letter. 'Khalila, if you let yourself be taken while you're out tonight, it's not likely we can save you. You might end up in the same jail I just escaped. You understand that.'

'Of course,' she said. 'Don't worry, sir. We'll be back.'

'Do that,' he said, and for an instant she was sure she saw something kind in his eyes. Something warm. Rare, to see such vulnerability in this man. 'Well, at least you. Santiago and Wathen, now . . .' He handed her the last letter, and Khalila smiled and looked towards Glain – who seemed to be sleeping, and wasn't, of course.

'Nice of you to think of me,' Glain said without opening her eyes or adjusting her relaxed posture. 'I'll come back just to spite you, sir.'

Dario was just a few moments later, and with him came the ambassador. 'My esteemed cousin Alvaro would prefer it if we do not vault the fence and draw unwanted attention, like our thieving friends,' he said. 'He's arranged for a carriage. He's also insisted on a disguise for me.' He spread his arms, and Khalila had to cover a laugh, because Dario was wearing, of all things, a Christian monk's robe. 'Should you be asked, I am Brother Ferdinand, a poor Franciscan monk.'

'Is there a real Brother Ferdinand?'

'Sometimes,' Alvaro said, without a flicker. 'But he's hardly ever the same person, and no one remembers monks, anyway. The driver of the carriage is a loyal retainer of mine, but I warn you: if you compromise yourselves or are otherwise identified, he'll have to drive away without you.'

'Understood,' Khalila said. 'Thank you.'

'Don't thank me. I have other news, I'm afraid. I can only extend the safety of this embassy to you until tomorrow morning. I've received orders from Madrid. The king has ordered this embassy closed and all of our staff withdrawn; he's arranged for a ship to be waiting in the harbour to take us to a neutral port. I fear this means he's planning something more than waiting to see what happens.'

'Meaning?' Wolfe asked.

The ambassador shook his head. 'Even if I knew, I couldn't tell you. My hospitality is one thing. My loyalty is quite another. I tell you this because when you leave the safety of these gates tomorrow, you will have nowhere left to return. I'm sorry for that.'

'You've done more than could be expected,' Santi said, and offered his hand. The ambassador took it in a firm shake. 'We're grateful. And if this goes right tomorrow, perhaps the embassy might stay open.'

'Perhaps.' There was something in Alvaro Santiago's voice that indicated he doubted it, though nothing showed on his face. 'May my God and yours hold us close in the hours to come.'

That hung a pall in the air, and Khalila turned to Dario and said, 'Well, Brother Ferdinand, we had best be about our business.'

'It's the Lord's work,' he said, deadpan, and bowed her through the door.

CHAPTER THIRTY

'Divide and conquer,' Dario said as the carriage rolled through the eerily quiet streets of Alexandria towards the port and along the curving drive that went towards the Lighthouse. 'Am I to convince these Scholars to fight, or only to not support the Archivist?'

'You're not to convince them of anything,' Khalila said, 'because I know you, Dario. You will frighten or infuriate them into entirely the wrong thing. Just present the case as I laid it out for you and tell them that they must make their own decision.'

'I don't like you splitting up,' Glain said. 'I can only watch one of you.'

'Half the time will be spent in the open. It's worth the risk. Naturally, you'll be watching Khalila,' Dario said. 'Brother Ferdinand can take care of himself.'

'And I can't?' Khalila raised her eyebrows and watched his discomfort grow as he realised the trap he'd put himself inside. 'Very well. Glain will stay with me. And you, *Brother*, had best carry your God as your sword and shield.'

'Or this,' Dario said, and eased a High Garda pistol from his heavy sleeve. 'Courtesy of Lieutenant Zara. I think she likes me.'

'At least someone does,' Khalila said, and then relented and kissed him, very quickly, as the carriage began to slow. 'Dario. If you're taken . . .'

'I won't be,' he said. 'Until later, madonna.'

'Until later,' she said. He opened the carriage door as the vehicle halted, and as he started to get out she was seized by a very real surge of dread. 'Dario!' She grabbed his hand, and he froze, one foot on the step down. She swallowed a sudden lump in her throat and said, 'The answer is yes. It was always yes, by the way. But I thought I should make you wait a while, since you seemed so confident.'

It took him only an instant to realise what she was saying, and the look on his face, in his eyes – it took her breath away, and it definitely did *not* belong on a monk. 'You do me the greatest honour I will ever receive,' he said, and it didn't sound like a glib, facile line; it sounded like something raw, and very real. He pressed her fingers to his lips, and she caught her breath at the intense heat of his mouth against her skin. His eyes never left hers. 'I will live my life to be worthy of it.'

He stepped down, and Khalila took in a deep breath. Glain said, 'What the hell was that?'

'Dario asked me to marry him just before we were taken in England,' she said. 'And I just agreed. Am I insane, Glain?'

'Absolutely,' Glain said, and gave her a full, wide smile. 'He'll make you happy. And if he doesn't, just tell me, and I'll end him.'

Khalila smiled back, and then Brother Ferdinand was helping her down from the carriage with all due respect, as fine an example of a monk as she could imagine, and she turned to face the Lighthouse.

Her smile faded, and all the anxiety she'd pushed aside began to buzz in her veins.

Now is our test.

And this, most of all, they could not fail.

There were, strangely, no High Garda soldiers at the Lighthouse this evening; the sunset was spreading red across the sky, and down at the base of the tower night had already spread a dark blue shadow.

But there were automata, and Khalila moved quickly to avoid a roaming sphinx. There were crowds of people in the vast courtyard, many of them Library assistants seeking transportation home; even here, their voices were muted and quiet, the mood dark. Khalila used the exiting workers as cover and hoped Glain would do the same; Dario had already slipped through.

Once inside the Lighthouse's tower, she caught her breath and tried to slow her pounding heartbeat. Glain joined her just a moment later, and they took the winding stairs up to the first of their Scholars, a Medica named Parker. She was a commanding older woman with sweeping walnut hair, eyes the colour of the open sea, and an attitude that Khalila could best liken to that of an angry, wounded lion. She took Wolfe's letter, ripped it open with a sharply pointed fingernail lacquered crimson, and read the contents once rapidly, then twice slowly before she spoke. 'Close the door,' she said without looking up. 'Is he serious?'

'I assume you know Scholar Wolfe,' Khalila said. 'Have you ever known him not to be?'

'Fair point. The man has the sense of humour of a corpse.' Scholar Parker drummed her fingernails on her polished black desk, then folded the letter again. 'I heard that Wolfe had been thrown back into prison.'

'He's free,' Khalila said. 'That's all I can tell you.'

'Do you know what's in this?' She tapped the folded paper, and Khalila shook her head. 'I've known Christopher Wolfe for ten years, and I've never known him to make wild claims, but he says he's seen the Black Archives. That's insane enough, but then he says—'

'That the Archivist ordered them burnt,' Khalila finished quietly. 'Tens of thousands of original, irreplaceable books. Yes.

327 SMOKE AND IRON

He's telling the truth. I was there too. I saw it happen. And it's a horror I'll never forget.'

'You're one of his students.'

'Yes, Scholar.'

'So strange. I never thought Wolfe had the patience to teach, and if he did, that he'd be a terrible influence. But you seem more or less sane.'

'More or less,' Khalila agreed. 'Scholar, I am not here to ask you for anything but an open mind. Scholar Wolfe has no doubt written what he believes; I know what I do. And if you believe that the Library is facing the worst moment of its existence . . . then please think on which side you'll stand tomorrow. Think what you believe in, and what you want the Great Library to be not today, but tomorrow, and the day after, and for the next hundred generations. Because Scholar Wolfe and I don't believe that it can continue down the path it is on. And if he's written to you, I think he knows you don't believe it, either.'

Scholar Parker said nothing, and there was no reading her expression. All it would take, Khalila thought, would be for that well-manicured hand to press the gold button on her desk and summon Lighthouse security, and this would end quickly, and badly . . . but Parker finally opened a drawer and dropped the letter into it. She closed it with a firm *click* of a lock engaging. 'Do you know where I was born?' she asked, which seemed an odd question. Khalila shook her head. 'I'm from the American colonies. We have a tendency to question authority. You may tell Scholar Wolfe that I'll think about what he's said . . . and tell him I wish him safety. Now you should go. I don't imagine it's very safe for you here.'

'It isn't,' Khalila agreed, and got up from where she'd taken a seat. Glain was still beside the closed door, looking every inch a crisp, cool High Garda soldier. 'Thank you.'

'Who else are you seeing?'

'I don't think I should tell you that.'

Parker nodded. 'Quite right. But if Scholar Yang is on your list, take him off. He's been spouting the Archivist's rhetoric for some months now, and it wouldn't end well.'

Khalila felt a little hint of a chill. 'Thank you,' she said again, and moved to the door.

As soon as they were in the curving hallway, Glain said, '*Is* Scholar Yang on your list?'

'Not mine,' Khalila said. 'Dario's. Go tell him. Go *now*.'

Khalila forced herself to trust that Glain would find him, and delivered her other ten letters, spending only a few moments with each recipient; a few she received immediate and positive indications from, and a few an alarming and glacial silence. Most were somewhere in the middle, cautiously noncommittal. *If these are our best and most influential friends, then Allah protect us*, she thought. She felt sick that she'd missed prayers, and hoped that he would remember and understand her need. But soldiers didn't pause in battle to pray, and neither could she.

As she left the last Scholar's office on the fortieth floor, she consulted the Codex directory and found Scholar Yang's office was only one floor below; she took the winding steps down, and as she opened the door to the hallway she listened for any trouble.

She heard nothing. Nothing at all.

Scholar Yang's office was sixteen doors down. He was a historian by inclination, or so she'd understood; surely a historian would understand better than anyone the risk of the Library hurtling blindly forward down this course. *He would understand*, she told herself.

She raised her hand to knock on the door, and as she did, she smelt something odd, and oddly familiar. The smell of sea air and stone, those were completely right, but that sharp, metallic scent . . .

She looked down and saw blood on the floor in a circle the size of her head. Hand-shaped smears of it, too, on the wall just to the right. The hem of her dress had fallen in the still-liquid pool, and as she stared, a thick red stain began working its way up through the fabric.

She stepped back with a gasp.

The hallway was silent. Whatever had happened here happened long enough ago that the prisoner – *or body* – was already gone, and only this silent evidence left.

She went back to the stairs and hurried down another flight, then another, with her heart beating so fast she thought she might fly apart . . . and then, with intense relief, she saw Glain rounding the lower floor and heading up towards her.

The relief didn't outlast the look Glain gave her. They met on the landing, and Glain didn't pause. She took Khalila's arm and said, 'Go, go, we have to go *now*.'

'Dario—' No. Not Dario. It couldn't be.

'They have him,' Glain said. 'Nothing I could do. I have to get you out before they lock the whole building and send sphinxes up to sniff us out. *Move!*'

Khalila wanted to protest. Wanted to argue. Wanted to stay.

But she knew Glain was right, and she knew that Dario would say the same. 'Is he dead?' She didn't want to know that answer, but she asked. She had to ask.

'No,' Glain said. 'But we will be, if we don't keep moving.'

PART ELEVEN

WOLFE

'They'll be all right,' Santi said, and Wolfe thought he sounded certain of it. Half an act, surely, but Wolfe nodded in agreement without entering into it. Nic had a rare talent for reading him, especially when his nerves were so raw. All he could do was hope the others weren't as perceptive.

Not that there were any others left. Jess had hared off after his wild brother; Thomas had gone with the ambassador to look at the workshop facilities he'd been promised earlier. Glain, Dario, and Khalila . . . all risking their lives out there in the night.

And though he knew where Morgan was, he didn't know *how* she was. Or if she'd made any progress at all towards her goal of taking the Iron Tower out of the Archivist's arsenal. If she managed it – an enormous variable – then it would truly change the game completely. But so far, there'd been no word, no sign. The Codex and Blanks continued to carry on with their mundane tasks; out in the streets, word was that automata still roamed, stalked, and flew.

The one bright sign, according to Alvaro Santiago, was that the Translation Chambers seemed to be malfunctioning from Alexandria outbound. That, at least, was keeping the Archivist's plans to seed his troops in Serapeums at a standstill . . . and if that was all Morgan accomplished, it was still a great deal.

So it was him, Santi, and Santi's lieutenant Zara, who'd come to roost in the reading room in the chair that Khalila had left empty. She seemed confident, too. Perhaps it was a special class they taught at the High Garda officers' school.

'Tell me everything that's happened,' Wolfe said. 'Seeing as the children aren't here, you don't have to feather the truth.'

'I wouldn't anyway,' Zara said. 'And neither should you. They aren't children any more than we are . . . not with as much as they've done and seen. Protect them, certainly. But don't coddle them.'

'And I'll thank you to *not* tell me how to behave around my own students.'

'They *were* your students. Not any more. Now they follow you because they hero-worship you, not from any desperate urge to learn from you. You do realise that, don't you?'

'Zara,' Santi said. The tone was a warning. Zara sighed and changed subjects.

'All right. Since you came back here, it seems that the hornet's nest – which had already been kicked by the mess in Philadelphia – only buzzed and stung more. The Burners had been circumspect here, but within days of the news they were organising, recruiting, setting up cancerous little cells around the city. They staged public burnings of their journals, and a few suicides. When the High Garda cracked down, they retaliated with new attacks on the compound. A week ago, inked flyers began to appear all over the town – a few at first, then more and more. Combined with the rebellion in the provinces, the upstart kings and angry Scholars in the field . . . well. The Archivist has been struggling to put out more fires than he can safely handle.'

'Is it true the High Garda Commander resigned?' Santi asked.

'Resigned and turned in his gold band. He left for his family home, so I'm told. The new commander . . . he's the Archivist's ugly little puppet, and if he's told to put the Archives to the torch, I'm sure he wouldn't hesitate, though how many of his men would follow I don't know. Enough, I suppose.'

'Any progress with the other captains?'

'Your name has currency still, and at least three-quarters of the High Garda captains would support you and, at the very least, stand down their troops. But the Elites?' She shook her head. 'No chance. They swear personal loyalty to the Archivist now. Not to the Library. They're five hundred strong, and they'll fight every step.'

'That's better than I'd hoped,' Santi said. 'If we can have most of the High Garda refuse to act . . .'

'That leaves a good few thousand of them willing to cut our throats,' Wolfe finished sourly. 'It's not enough. We can't rely on Scholars to fight our battles, though most of the Research Scholars I know have field experience. And we still have the automata to contend with.'

'Including the dragon,' Zara said. 'I saw it myself. It's a nightmare – breathes toxic gas that catches fire, and it can rend with teeth and claws, too. Armoured and fast. I can't think of anything that could take it down. The sphinxes are bad enough, but this . . .'

Dragon. Wolfe hadn't seen it for himself, had only heard Jess's description . . . but it had sounded like a nightmare, indeed. His mother never would have agreed to such a thing . . . or perhaps she had. Perhaps it had been in the works for a very long time and required only Gregory's eagerness to ingratiate himself to make it a reality.

'We have something that can bring it down,' Santi said. 'Thomas's weapon. The Ray of Apollo.'

'You have it?' Zara's eyes widened. 'I thought it was destroyed in the escape from Philadelphia.'

'He built another one. A better one,' Wolfe said. 'But we had to leave it in England. Unless somehow you worked a miracle, Nic?'

'No chance to,' Santi said, and settled in a chair beside Wolfe. 'We were chained and put on board the ship the same night. As far as I'm aware, Jess's father has the thing, and Thomas's pet lion, too.'

'He might regret that last thing,' Wolfe said. 'I don't think Thomas told it to obey any of them, did he?'

'No,' Santi agreed. 'He didn't. With any luck, maybe they've shut it up in the workshop and not got their hands on the weapon either.'

'We can hope.'

Santi looked at the clock, and Wolfe saw the flicker of doubt. Their children – and he would always think of them as their children, he'd given up on anything else – were late returning, and that was almost certainly not good news. 'I could take a team out and look for them,' Nic said.

'No,' Wolfe said.

'He'd be safe enough inside the carrier,' Zara said. 'I can get a picked team together, Captain.'

'No,' Wolfe said again, and speared Zara with a glare. 'You won't. We wait.'

Santi launched himself out of the chair and paced to the back of the room. He was pouring a glass of wine, but that, Wolfe thought, was just a thing to do instead of arguing.

'You push him, Scholar,' Zara said. She, too, was watching Santi. 'I don't think you understand how much he endures for you.'

'You really think I don't?'

She swung her gaze back at him. As flat and alien as a tiger's. 'I don't think you know how much he hurts for your sake. But . . . he loves you. And needs you.'

'And you,' Wolfe said, though it hurt to say it. 'You keep him moving forward when he wants to turn back. He told me that once. When he thinks too much of me, you make him think about the goal.'

'He always thinks too much about you,' she said. 'It'll be the end of him someday, Scholar. It's up to you to look after *him*.'

Wolfe watched her stand up and leave; he wasn't sure how to respond to that, or if he should. Santi hadn't heard. He came back and settled in the chair he'd left, sipped some of the wine and handed it over to Wolfe. 'What do we do if they don't come back?' he asked.

'We go to the Feast of Greater Burning, and we do what we can,' Wolfe said. 'And tomorrow, we'll probably die. You know that, don't you?'

'I do,' Nic said. Wolfe drank the rest of the wine; it was a thick marvel of a red, better than he'd tasted in years. The Spanish had a way with grapes.

'Did you tell your company to fight with us or to stand down?'

'I told them to act according to their conscience. What else could I tell them? I'm not even their captain, not any more. I have no rank. No career. Nothing.'

'Do you blame me?' Wolfe asked quietly. He put the cup down, and when he straightened again, he had Santi's full focus on him.

'No,' Santi said. A harsh word, but it came gently, and with love. 'I don't. Ever. What I've done, I've done because it needed to be done, and I accept whatever comes of it. *Amore mio*, I'll find a place in the world, if we live through tomorrow. Don't concern yourself with that.'

Wolfe grabbed for his hand and held it, closed his eyes, remembered the horror of the nights in the prison when he'd imagined Santi in such detail, such life, to keep it all at bay. But that fantasy had been nothing compared to the reality of having him here, seeing that smile.

Something tugged at him, and for a second he felt a bubble of panic surface. Some memory clawing to the surface, something from the prison.

Then he remembered, and a flinch ran through him. *I came so close to losing my mind. So close.*

'What is it?' Santi asked, and moved closer. 'Chris?'

'Nothing,' he said. 'I—One night in the prison, I imagined something. Someone, actually. It seemed so real.'

'Someone?'

'Him,' Wolfe said, and could hardly hear his own voice. 'From Rome. Qualls.'

Santi went still. 'The torturer.'

Wolfe nodded. 'I think it was just . . . my brain, playing tricks. He isn't here. He left the Archivist's service, didn't he? Retired far from here.'

'You saw Qualls?'

'No. I imagined him.' Wolfe wished there was more wine left in the glass, but he didn't have the strength to fetch himself more. 'I don't know why I'd imagine he'd want to rescue me, though. Do you?'

They'd talked about Qualls once, and only once, months after Wolfe's release from the Roman prison. Santi had wanted very badly to hunt the man down and rip him to pieces. Maybe still did. 'Do you think he was real?'

'He seemed real. I don't know,' Wolfe said. His hands were shaking, and he clenched them into fists. 'But promise me that tomorrow, there's no prison. No Qualls. If it comes to that—'

'If it does,' Santi said, 'then it comes for us both.'

Their fingers intertwined, and Wolfe leant his head against Santi's shoulder. Odd, that the promise of death would sound so inviting when put that way. 'I'd rather live with you,' he said. 'Let's try for that.'

'Yes. Let's.' Santi's head came up, and he looked at the closed door. 'Did you hear that?'

'What?'

Santi was already up. 'Carriage,' he said, and was halfway down the stairs by the time Wolfe managed to make it to his feet. He followed as quickly as he could and was nearly to the floor of the grand entrance to the embassy when the doors opened and Glain and Khalila entered.

Glain and Khalila, alone.

'What happened?' Santi was asking. Khalila's face showed her distress, and Wolfe's eyes fixed on a heavy stain of blood at the bottom of her skirt. 'Where is he?'

'Taken,' Glain said. 'I'm sorry, Captain. I should have been there. Stopped it.'

'Where were you?'

The Welsh girl straightened to her full height and looked into the middle distance. An automatic, formal reporting stance. 'Sir, I elected to accompany Dario; Khalila asked me to. He sent me to make sure she was all right. When I got back, he'd been taken by the High Garda. We couldn't get to him. I thought the best I could do was make sure she was safe.' Her chin set itself at a more aggressive angle. 'I'll go get him, sir.'

'You won't,' Santi said. 'Does the ambassador know?'

'The ambassador does *not* know, and would prefer you tell him immediately,' said Alvaro Santiago, coming at a brisk walk from what must have been his office. He looked grim, and lines formed at the corners of his mouth and eyes as he listened to the story. 'He was caught with your letters on him, then. A clear sign of treason. I'll file a formal protest, but if they have him, they'll keep him.'

'Can you find out where he's being held?'

'If I go and demand answers of the High Garda, the first question they will ask is how I knew,' he said. 'No. I can't reasonably find out until at least the morning. If they suspect you're hiding here, diplomacy won't save you, and I'd rather not have my entire staff slaughtered to protect you. We wait. Dario may not be especially likable, but I promise you this: he has honour to spare. He'll say nothing to put you at risk. And tomorrow, we *will* find him. All right?'

'No!' Khalila shook off Glain's restraining hand. 'No, it isn't all right. They *hurt him*. There was blood—'

'Not enough for a fatal wound,' Glain put in.

'There was a *great deal* of blood, and I want to go find him! Let me go find him!'

'Khalila.' Santi put his hands on her shoulders, and Wolfe saw the tense fury drain out of her. 'He knew the risk. And if I know Dario, he'll be claiming every royal privilege from here to Spain, and the High Garda will have to take it seriously. They'll send word to the Artifex, and the Artifex will have him transferred to the prison as he considers his options. *We can't get him.* Not tonight. I'm sorry.'

The breath went out of her in a wrenching sound that might have been a sob, but there were no tears in her eyes. 'Where's Thomas?'

'In the workshop,' Alvaro said. 'He asked me for special tools and locked me out. I don't know what he's doing. Is he always so . . .'

'Strange? Yes,' Wolfe said. 'And brilliant. Work will help him. Leave him there.' He exchanged a look with Santi. 'All of you, go rest. There's nothing more we can do tonight. Morning will come soon enough.'

'Has Jess come back?' Glain asked.

'No,' Wolfe said.

And privately, he doubted they'd ever see the boy again.

PART TWELVE

MORGAN

CHAPTER THIRTY-TWO

Somehow, Morgan had never anticipated that getting the most powerful Obscurist in the world on her side would be anything but a total victory. She'd thought of it as a lock to be picked, a door to be opened . . . but now that the lock had fallen and the door swung wide, there was a flesh-and-blood man.

Even though she'd known all along that he had voluntarily exiled himself *for almost forty years*, an act of will that no one she knew could duplicate . . . she'd never imagined he'd be so damned stubborn.

'That's simply a failure of your imagination,' Annis said. They sat together in the reading room, where Eskander had sent them.

'We got him out of his room!'

'We did,' she agreed. 'But you see, you never knew the *young* Eskander. I did. He was wild and impulsive and full of passion. But he's had forty years of strict silence and self-control, and I think you can see that he's no longer a man who makes quick decisions. He heard us out. Now he's thinking.'

'We don't have *time*!'

'We have nothing but time,' Annis shot back. 'Here, in the Iron Tower, that's all we have. Here, read this. Is this what he was looking for? It's well above my ken.'

Morgan took the Blank she held and skimmed the cramped, ancient writing, then shook her head. 'That's a formula to undo familiarity links, but it's too specific. We need something broader.'

Annis rubbed her forehead and wiped the Blank's contents. 'I doubt they'll give us access to something so advanced.'

'The Obscurist special library contains all the research that's needed to write new, highly advanced formulae; they can't leave out things if they expect us to invent properly. It'll be here. And likely look completely benign.'

'Why can't he do this? He knows what he's looking for!'

'Because by accessing the contents here in the reading room, it doesn't track to a specific person,' Morgan said. 'If any of these texts *are* flagged as dangerous, then it's best to have none of our names appearing on any High Garda list, don't you think?'

Annis grumbled but went back to the Codex. 'He might have given us a proper year instead of a range. This could take for ever.'

Morgan understood how she felt, but she knew Annis wouldn't understand the reverse. To the older woman, this was just annoyance and boredom. To Morgan, every minute off the clock was another minute the world turned closer to the Feast of Greater Burning, and she knew that she'd lose cherished lives there if they failed in this.

'We have to go faster,' Morgan said, and Annis shot her a grateful look of agreement.

'It's a pity we can't have the automata search for us,' she said. 'Though I suppose ripping apart heretics is more in line with their mission.'

Morgan paused in the act of turning a page, and her eyes widened. She jumped up and threw her arms around Annis, who seemed shocked, but laughed. 'You're a genius!' Morgan said, and kissed her cheek.

'I have never in my life been told so,' Annis said. 'Why, exactly?'

'The Archives,' Morgan said. 'As newly discovered books come in, there are specially built automata, Scribes, who do nothing but read and transcribe the contents into the record. Isn't that right?'

'Of course. The words have to be meticulously copied into the Archives to become available.'

'And how many Scribes are there?'

'Tens of thousands, back in the earliest days,' Annis said. 'I don't know how many today. Thousands, at least.'

'Pen! I need a pen!' Morgan began pulling open drawers in the copy desks on the sides of the room, unearthing bits of discarded paper, broken nibs, a half-dried bottle of ink . . . and then Annis pressed a working pen into her hand, and Morgan pulled a fresh sheet of paper from a stack.

'What are you doing?' Annis leant forward. Morgan, without pausing as she swiftly, confidently sketched out the formula that she was building in her mind, used one shoulder to bump the woman back. She didn't answer. Didn't have time. The reading room had no windows, but she knew the world was turning fast towards morning, and when the sun reached its hottest, highest point for the day, people would die.

Her pen sketched one last Greek symbol, and then she sat back and ran through it in her mind again. *It should work.* No one had thought of the Scribes as anything but conduits before, and the Archives as the only real repository of knowledge . . . but the Scribes were the vital link between originals and copies.

She put the pen down, took a deep breath, and opened herself to the flow of the energy that bound up the world. This was going to require almost everything she had so carefully hoarded, but it would be worth it.

She touched a finger to the inked symbols, and they exploded into a matrix of swirling, glittering shapes that circled around her in a storm. Moving far too fast. She quickly began to place them in order, until they moved in a tight cylinder around her, and then she closed her eyes and *pushed*. What she was doing was nothing like rewriting the lion automata, which were individual constructions; the Scribes were all connected, stationary, linked by real mechanical wires and tubes of fluids as well as alchemy. They had been constructed so for a reason: to allow smooth, seamless, mindless action.

What affected one of them affected all of them. By design.

She felt, rather than saw, the formula disappearing into the flow, travelling from where she sat to the Archives, and into the first Scribe, who automatically relayed it to the next, and the next, and the next . . .

She collapsed forward onto the desk, gasping for breath, as the last of her energy trickled away and the insatiable hunger set in. *No, no, not now* . . . She felt as if she was smothering, drowning in air that was too thick to breathe. Rescue blazed in glowing, strong lights next to her, and all she had to do was *reach* . . .

But that was Annis, and if she reached out now, she'd destroy a human life. She wouldn't be able to stop.

'Morgan? Morgan!' Annis was shaking her, and when Morgan opened her eyes, she saw the older woman's face was tense with worry. 'Lass, are you all right?'

'Yes,' Morgan said. She wasn't, she trembled all over, and the emptiness inside her threatened to eat her alive. She pictured locking it away, behind door after door after door, until she could draw a breath. It sustained her body, at least, if nothing else. 'Yes. Give me the Codex.'

Annis retrieved the book from the table where they'd been working and opened it in front of her. Morgan picked up the pen. Her hand was unsteady, but she wrote down three words in ancient Greek.

'That's all?' Annis frowned. 'How is that going to get us anywhere? Is that a title?'

'No,' Morgan said. 'It's the words for the Scribes to find. Those three, together. That should tell us which book.'

'You're having the Scribes search for it?'

'Yes.'

Annis sank into a chair. Her mouth opened and closed as she worked it through, and then she said, 'That's *brilliant*.'

'Only if it works,' Morgan said. She was still trembling, but less so with every breath. *I can keep it under control*, she told herself. *I won't give in to it*. But the other side of that coin was that until she did give in and swallow the energy of other living creatures, she would be as powerless as any normal person walking the streets of Alexandria. *Corrupted*. That was what she'd been called, back in Philadelphia, and she had to believe that it wasn't true, that it was something she could overcome. Use carefully.

I will not hurt Annis. I will not.

Annis had no idea of the danger she was in. She put her hand on Morgan's shoulder, and Morgan flinched at the contact. The power she needed was *right there*, hovering just beyond her skin . . .

'Look!' Annis leant closer to the Codex. 'It's writing!'

A single entry was writing in precision-perfect penmanship. Morgan could picture the automaton on the other end making the loops and lines, an unthinking and perfect machine.

'*On the Practical Effects of Advanced, Multiple-Source*

Familiarity Formulae and the Energy Exchange Principle,' Annis read. 'My God, you've found it.'

'I hope,' Morgan said. 'Get it.'

Annis pressed a finger to the title and held a Blank close. As they watched, the empty pages of the Blank filled with cramped, archaic script, a perfect copy of the original volume locked away in the Archives. The product of an obscure, long-forgotten Scholar whose name Morgan didn't even recognise.

As they turned pages, a glowing corner of a page caught her eye, and she quickly flipped to it.

There, on the page, was the answer they'd been looking for.

'The Iron Tower's security keys,' Annis said. She sounded quiet, and almost shaken. 'Morgan. This is the answer. *This is what we need to open the doors, remove the collars*. To let us all . . . leave.' Annis's eyes filled with tears, and she looked lost now. 'I thought – until this moment, it was just an idea, you understand. A puzzle to solve. But this . . . this is real. This is . . .'

Morgan heard the footsteps approaching before Annis did, and quickly wiped the Blank and cleared the Scribe's writing in the Codex. The other books weren't incriminating but this one . . . this was.

'Oh, hello,' said Bjorn, a lean older man with a sharply pointed face. Morgan knew him slightly, but he wasn't someone she came into contact with on anything like a regular basis. *Maybe it's nothing*, she told herself. Bjorn's energy flooded the room, far brighter and more compelling than Annis's, and she felt the locks breaking on her resolve. *If I just take a little . . .*

No. As desperate as she was, as empty, she knew she wouldn't be able to siphon just enough. She had no idea how it would feel to another Obscurist, but she thought it would be painful.

Agonising, very possibly. And she couldn't do that, not to an innocent person.

'Hello,' Annis said. She, at least, seemed instantly at ease. 'Well, if it isn't my favourite musician. I haven't heard you play in weeks. What on earth has kept you away? Please tell me it's not a new lover.'

'You know you're the only one for me,' Bjorn said, and winked at her. His smile seemed wrong to Morgan, but then, everything did now. She was fighting her own darkness, and it seemed to crowd in from everywhere. 'No, I've been on a special project, my crimson witch. The new master wanted something special done.' He shrugged. 'Some sort of new flying automaton. Don't really see the point, honestly.'

'Flying?' Morgan forced herself back into some sort of focus. 'Is it a new model completely?'

'Don't know and don't care. My part of it was just the gravitational formulae. Devilishly tricky, by the way. I must have destroyed a hundred scrolls before I got it right, and then it had to fit with all the others.'

'Others?'

'Navigational, and some kind of fire formula. Specialist work, all of it. Oh, Gregory supplied a rough master formula, but believe me, it took weeks to get the details—'

A new automaton, just in time for the Feast of Greater Burning. Morgan felt sick and dizzy and most of all, *out of time*. She looked half-desperately at Annis, who couldn't have understood the half of what was going through her mind, but Annis was, if nothing else, emotionally perceptive. She walked to Bjorn, took his arm, and said, 'Why don't you tell me all about it, my love, over a tall glass of something that will make the evening better?'

'Well, that's a better option than reading myself to sleep,' he said. 'Which was what I was about. And after the drink?'

'Depends on whether or not you're at all awake,' Annis said. She walked him to the entrance. 'And whether or not you put me to sleep with the boring details of your project.'

As she pulled the door shut she sent Morgan a last look with a roll of her eyes. *The things I do for you.*

Morgan felt the dusty stirrings of a laugh, but it died quickly, and not even a ghost stayed on. She quickly restored the Blank's contents, found the page, and marked it with a scrap of paper before she slipped out of the reading room and down to Eskander's private suite.

When she knocked, he answered. 'In,' he said. 'Quickly. Were you seen?'

She shook her head. 'No. I was careful. I found—'

He was already taking the book from her hands, and when he did, their fingers brushed, and the incandescent *power* of the man broke through every lock, every door, every semblance of control she had in her. She was trembling with emptiness, and he had so much life in him, so much to spare. The dark hollows inside her where her power had been echoed with the screaming need to be filled.

She'd only take a little.

She grabbed his wrist and began to draw his life away.

'No.' Eskander wrenched free, and she felt the flood of power break with a crystalline shock. 'This only makes your problems worse, don't you see that? The more you siphon from other living things, the more narrow and twisted your pathways become. You've already damaged yourself. Don't finish the job. You'll end up blackened, like Gilles de Rais. Mad and murderous and dangerous, or don't they teach the warnings any more?'

Morgan didn't answer. She wasn't certain she could.

Eskander finally sighed. 'We're so tied to the Tower now that few have the chance of ever expending their power to the level of real damage. You're the first I've ever seen who's capable of it, other than Keria.'

'And you,' Morgan said. Her voice was barely a thread.

'Yes,' he agreed. 'And me. I was so desperate to escape this place, to save Keria from it . . . and we almost achieved that. We came so close, before—before the child was born. But I pushed too far. I broke the wards, but in doing so, I burnt myself black inside, just as you have. It's why I walled myself away. I could *feel* the life burning in everything around me, whispering to me to claim it. It was driving me mad.'

His image blurred, and she realised that her eyes were burning with tears; she knew exactly what he was saying, exactly how it felt to be so empty, so desperate, so *broken*. She'd felt it in Philadelphia, and though she tried, she had never fully healed. She didn't know how.

'I don't want to be this,' she whispered. 'I don't *want it*.'

'Did you want to be an Obscurist?'

'*No!*'

Eskander's wavering image smiled. She blinked, and felt the heavy slide of tears down her cheeks. He reached out and wiped them away with his thumbs, then fitted his hands around her cheeks. 'Neither did I,' he said. 'But where you are now, that is worse. That will lead you into madness.'

'I don't know how to stop it!' She heard the desperation in her voice, and the fear too. 'How – how did you?'

'I had help,' he said. 'I had Keria, who scoured the Archives for treatments, and came here even though I told her to leave me alone. I was afraid for her, but I think she was more afraid to lose me. She showed me how to become myself again.' Eskander paused, and looked from her to Annis. 'There are two ways. One is slow and gentle. The other – the other is fast, but painful.'

'Fast,' Morgan said. Wounded as she was, damaged, *broken*, she could do great harm to their enemies . . . but she could do it to those she loved, too. She knew the stories that Eskander had referred to; she'd looked them up in the Codex after coming here. Stories of madness and murder. At a certain point, an Obscurist severed from the natural flow of energy in the world was a parasite . . . and predator. She could feel those urges inside her, begging her to survive at any cost. 'I want to be healed. Annis is right, and there isn't much time. How can I do that?'

'I can't show you,' he said. He took both her hands and said, 'What I will do is remake you. This is not alchemy, Morgan; this is not potions and incantations and phases of the moon. This is pure, elemental power. And it is going to hurt.' He smiled, but there was no warmth in it now. 'It certainly hurt me when Keria did it to me. I won't lie to you; it might not work, and if it doesn't, you will be . . . less than you are now.'

'But if it works?'

'Then you will be restored. More than restored; I sense the potential in you to surpass me, in terms of your power. You will be a force to be reckoned with, either way. But only one of those outcomes means anything good for you.'

Morgan drew in a breath. This, she sensed, was a huge risk, but she didn't see any other direction to go but forward. 'Yes,' she said. 'Please. Do it.'

She felt the incredible power seething in the man, and now she could also hear the whisper of the Tower itself, containing and muting all of their talents, their powers. What would Eskander be outside these walls? She couldn't imagine.

'I'm ready,' she asked.

'No, child, I don't think you are.'

She didn't even have time to draw breath or brace herself before a wave of agony hit, so intense that it seemed to burn her from the inside out, combust everything inside her and char it black, reduce it to ash and reduce the ashes to nothing. *He's killing me*, she had time to think, in that endless, torturous limbo of pain.

For a moment she floated, anchored to her body by only the thinnest, fraying cord of light . . . and in that moment, the power racing through Eskander exploded out and through her, tracing an intricate web of paths through her body. As each channel snapped to life, another lightning-hot spasm of pain raced through her, but it was a different frequency of pain that resonated more and more strongly inside her, until with a hissing snap, she was . . .

Incandescent.

When she opened her eyes the glow remained, a brilliant golden whisper over her skin that only gradually faded, and with every blink she saw the pulse of the world around her – not only living things, but *everything*, lit in energy and structures like crystalline castles. And below her, around her, the whispering opalescent power that coursed through the air, the ground, stretching through the sky to brush the stars.

Eskander let her go and stepped back. She stared at him in wonder, at the brilliant flare of him, until the effect finally faded, and he was just a man, and this just a room.

She felt . . . new. Completely new.

'What – what did you do?' She could barely get the words out. Eskander picked up the book that he'd set aside and flipped to the marker she'd put inside. He read the passage rapidly and nodded. Turned the page and nodded again, then walked to his desk, where he sat and took out pen and paper.

He wasn't going to answer her, she realised, and she tried again. 'Sir, how did you . . . how did you fix . . .'

'I didn't,' he said. 'I destroyed. I rebuilt the nerves and pathways that your own life force depends upon into their proper structure. You were like a tree struck by lightning; some part of the tree still lives, but the trickle of life isn't enough to sustain it. Neither completely dead nor completely alive. Now you are alive again, and an Obscurist completely. Don't mistake me: you're not indestructible. The power you have must be carefully measured and portioned, and you must learn when, and how, to use it without destroying those paths again.'

'But . . . I only did what I had to do to save others—'

'You are not a god,' he interrupted her. 'Saving lives is something all men and women must do when called on, but never think you *alone* can do it. I'm accounted the most powerful Obscurist in a thousand years. Do you think I can save a hundred lives at a time? A thousand? A city? Of course I can't, because Obscurists are just humans with a better view of the world, and a larger lever with which to move it. Others can act, and must. We are not the saviours of the world.'

It set her on her heels, and in the next moment, she felt angry. Angry that he wasn't willing to step into the full responsibility of his power. 'So that's it? You're not going to help save those people who are going to die? My *friends*?'

'Morgan, if the power we wield was the answer to every question, the Obscurist Magnus would be the Archivist, wouldn't he? But Obscurists are forbidden by law to hold the post. I know this is a disappointment to you, but I'm not the saviour you're looking for.' He never stopped writing while he spoke – quick, certain strokes of his pen, and now he sat back, took the page in his hand, and pulled the symbols off the page and into the representation she was familiar with – glittering, spinning symbols surrounding him. But the ones he'd created were not chaotic. They already had a smooth, humming, complicated path, interweaving and interlocking like gears in a precision machine. 'However, I can help, and I will. The Iron Tower is the fragile point where the Library rests its weight; we always have been since the first Obscurist created the Codex and the Blanks. Could the Library have survived without us? Yes. But not in its current form. It depends on us for almost everything, and that must continue in some fashion. The Codex, the Great Archives . . . these things must remain intact, even as we plan some better future for them. The Translation Chambers I will block once the moment is right. Be careful. Until then, the Archivist will still have an easy avenue of escape.'

'But . . . you said—'

'I said I wasn't your saviour. I never said I wouldn't do what I can.' He banished the formula he'd written with a wave of his hand. 'I can open the doors of this tower. Remove our collars. I can stop Gregory, or at least make him run to the safety of his master. But I can't force any one of these Obscurists to follow you out into the world. Most of them have never set foot out there; like me, they've been caged so long they've forgotten the smell of free air. And none of them are combat ready. We're housecats, not tigers.'

It was a shocking dose of cold water, and for a moment Morgan didn't know what to say to him. He'd said it with such dispassion, such lack of concern . . . as if all this, even the deaths clicking relentlessly towards them, were academic exercises.

'And what about your son?' she asked.

Eskander turned towards her. There was the ghost of Christopher Wolfe in the shape of his face, the bitterly dark eyes. 'My son must save himself,' he said. 'As must we all. There is no single person who can stop any of it. Gregory must be overthrown, and I'll have to step into his place to keep order. My place is here looking after these people, not out there fighting.'

'But—'

'Gregory will leave the Tower in a procession with the Curia. Once he's out of the doors, I'll amend the wards, and he'll never cross this threshold again. Whatever happens to him from there isn't my concern.'

'I thought you were going to set us free!'

'And I will. As soon as I amend the wards, any Obscurists who wish can come and go as they please. Is that fair?'

'No!' she shouted. 'It isn't fair! You have the power to protect *everyone*, not just Obscurists!'

'I couldn't protect Keria,' he said, and it stopped her cold. Not the words, but the tone. The bleak, obsidian-hard reality of it. 'I've learnt bitter lessons about limits. I wish I could be what you all want. But I don't think that's my fate.'

'You *make* your fate! We all do! And if you turn your back on him . . .'

'Wait until sunrise,' he said. 'As for the Iron Tower soldiers, you'll need to deal with them yourself – and you, unlike these other hothouse flowers, are fully capable of doing that. The doors will open for you. After that, you're on your own. May the gods keep you, Morgan.'

'Eskander, you have to help—'

She was talking to his back. Eskander was walking away. He firmly, but calmly, opened the door and ushered her out, and shut the portal behind her. She felt the hot rush of the wards locking back in place. She could see them now, a marvel of precision and intricate planning.

She knew she could break them. But that wouldn't solve anything. Eskander was *so* like his son.

Except that in one important sense, he wasn't like Wolfe at all. Wolfe was a hero. Wolfe stepped forward.

And his father had just disappointed her.

CHAPTER THIRTY-THREE

Morgan stood on a padded bench to look out of the window of their room. It didn't face east, but she was watching the Lighthouse, which would show the sunrise first in a dazzle in the reflective mirrors at its top. The sky had turned a beautiful, delicate blue, something neither morning nor night, and as she watched, it continued to slip lighter. She toyed with the collar clasped around her neck, but it didn't feel like a trap any more. Though it still resonated as active – Eskander's doing – she could unsnap and remove it at any time. Like most of what she was doing in this tower, it was a misdirection. A lie.

'You remind me of Keria,' Annis said from below. She was up and dressed, and instead of comfortable Tower robes she'd put on a pair of thick canvas trousers, a red silk shirt, boots, and a thick belt loaded with the travel case Obscurists carried when sent on missions for the Library . . . something with pens, paper, ink, and Translation tags to carry them back to safety in the event of emergency. The case was beautifully worked leather and embossed with the Library symbol.

'I don't look anything like her,' Morgan said.

'No, of course not, but she liked it up there, watching the sunrises and sunsets. She liked to imagine being out there. And, of course, once she became the Obscurist Magnus she was free to live out those dreams, in some part. But more than that, you remind me of Keria because you're so unhappy.'

Morgan watched the Lighthouse. She couldn't command the sun to rise any faster, but she couldn't look away, either. 'My friends are going to die today unless miracles happen. Why wouldn't I be unhappy?'

'You're unhappy because you feel guilty.'

'About what?'

'That you're worried you're not in love with a young man who's in love with you.'

Now she *did* look away, because that was a truth that lanced straight through her. She instinctively started to deny it – she did love him; she knew she did. The problem was that she wasn't sure she was *in* love with him. Or capable of that kind of feeling. He was as close as she'd ever been to the grand sweeps of emotion she'd seen others take. She wanted to be in love. Jess was everything she should crave: brave, kind, clever, funny, and her heart fluttered and skin warmed when their eyes met.

She swallowed and said, 'How do you know if . . . if he's the one?'

'Oh, that cherished old nonsense. For some people, there's only one, all their life. For others, love comes twice, or three times, or more. For others, none at all. And, well, for me, I'm the latter category, but that doesn't make me unhappy or stop me from enjoying the men – and women, for that matter – around me. You see? Once you know yourself, you'll know how you feel.' Annis's tone shifted. 'It's almost dawn.'

Morgan snapped her attention back to the window and yes, there was a blaze of sun lighting the golden top spire of the Lighthouse and beginning to shimmer on the reflectors.

Morning, on the day of the Feast of Greater Burning.

She jumped down and reached for her robe. Annis's eyebrows arched. 'You're wearing an Obscurist robe? Do you really think that's wise?'

'Not wise,' Morgan said, and pulled the cloth on over the shirt and trousers she wore. 'But I'm tired of hiding what I am.'

There was a polite knock at the door just then, and after a quick look between them, Annis said, 'Yes?'

Gregory opened the door. Behind him stood a full contingent of the High Garda. He wore the formal robes of the Obscurist Magnus, bright-red silk covered with gold and jewelled alchemical symbols, and he carried a staff crowned with the eye of Horus.

'Well,' Annis said. 'Don't *you* look fancy this morning, your worship. Is it your birthday again?'

'You tampered with the formulae written into this room.' Gregory wasn't speaking to Annis. He'd ignored her completely. He tilted his staff towards Morgan. 'I know your barely capable companion hardly has the wits to light a candle, so it must be you who's done it.' The staff slowly moved to point at Annis, who sat up straighter but didn't speak. 'Do I need to make another sacrifice on the altar of your pride?'

'No, Obscurist, I'll confess,' Morgan said. 'I stopped eating the food prepared for me. I stole food where I could. After a day or so, I was able to adjust the formulae you used to spy on me. It's not her fault. She had nothing to do with it.' She swallowed a real taste of dread. 'She's well loved in this tower, and you know that. If you kill her for no good reason, do you really think it helps the rest accept you as their lord and master?'

He didn't like that, and for a second she felt terror he'd actually do it, order Annis murdered in front of her . . . but he must have realised she was being truthful, at least about the consequences. Annis knew everyone, and everyone liked Annis. Many loved her fiercely. If he hurt her, he'd never truly rule here.

'You're coming with me,' he told her. 'I want you to see the end of your Scholar Wolfe, and all your friends.'

'But you'll bring her back,' Annis said. 'Won't you? Safe? Please, Gregory.'

'If she behaves herself,' Gregory said, and glanced back at the High Garda captain, who was standing just at his elbow. 'Hold her.'

Before Morgan could realise which of them he meant, the captain had hold of her in a bear hug that trapped her arms at her sides and lifted her off the ground. Morgan kicked and shouted, but another soldier stepped forward, jammed a metal brace into her mouth, and wrenched it wide open. She tasted iron and blood and let out a muffled scream. She reached for power, but Gregory's was already there, blocking her.

'Hurry it up,' Gregory said. 'She's fighting me.'

The guard poured a liquid down her throat, and she felt it cascade through her like a fall of silk, smoothing out the alarm, the tension, the resistance. Annis was on her feet now and shouting, and Gregory backhanded her contemptuously when the woman came at him. When she tried to get up from the bed where she'd fallen, a High Garda soldier stepped forward and pointed a sidearm at her. 'Stay down,' the soldier barked, and Annis slowly held up her hands.

Morgan couldn't fight back. She felt numb, barely anchored to her body now. As the soldier removed the mouth brace and the captain lowered her to her feet, she hardly noticed the changes. She struggled to keep her thoughts from sliding away like silvery fish in a stream.

Gregory grabbed her chin in his fingers and tilted her head

up. He peered into her eyes, and she felt a snap of power around her but couldn't reach for it. She could walk, and see, and hear, but the path to any resistance was dark and impassable.

She looked desperately at Annis, and Annis stared back at her. The fear and anger in her friend's eyes told her that there was nothing to be done, for now, but submit.

She nodded slightly and hoped Annis understood . . . and then Gregory was leaving, and she was being pulled along by soldiers in his wake, to the Feast of Greater Burning.

PART THIRTEEN

JESS

CHAPTER THIRTY-FOUR

When Anit led them into a deserted warehouse by the port, Jess was all but certain she intended to have them killed. He was considering whether or not it would be wise to draw a weapon when his twin brother took the choice away from him by drawing first and putting the muzzle of the High Garda pistol against the back of Anit's skull as she unlocked the door. 'Let's be clear,' Brendan said. 'If you're planning anything, you die before we hit the ground. And I'm not my brother. I won't hesitate.'

Jess was mildly offended by that, but in all practical senses his brother was right; he did take an instant to weigh the consequences, where Brendan dealt with whatever came, regardless. Odd, because back in their childhoods, Brendan had been the planner, the schemer, the watcher.

People changed. He was only starting to realise how much and how quickly.

Anit didn't so much as flinch. She finished unlocking the door as if he hadn't just threatened her life and swung the entrance open as she pocketed the keys. 'I'll go first, shall I?' From the weeping, guilt-ridden girl at the temple, she'd become something completely different now. Jess wasn't sure if it was a good change, but it was useful for now. She stepped over the threshold, and Brendan followed close behind, while Jess closed the door and engaged the heavy lock, which on this side didn't require keys.

Lights went on, row after row of chemical glows suspended from the tall ceiling, and it seemed to stretch on for ever. Below each band of lights were huge multi-level storage racks loaded with crates and boxes.

Not a soul in sight.

It was a stunning sight, and a testament to Red Ibrahim's wealth. 'Is all this *books*?' Jess asked. If so, it dwarfed his father's own vast operation.

'No,' she said. 'Legitimate trade goods. My father's real business has always been storage and shipping; it's profitable, and it makes an excellent shield for our smaller operations. This way.' She cut a maze-like path between the shelving, and Jess wondered how, exactly, the workers retrieved those crates stacked thirty feet above their heads . . . until he saw the neatly stored gantries along the wall, wheeled platforms with hand cranks to push the height of the platforms up or down as needed. No Obscurist magic here; this was simple, efficient gears and human ingenuity.

'Can't we take a straighter course?' Brendan asked after the twelfth turn, and a zag in the opposite direction, again.

Anit didn't answer, but Jess said, 'Pressure sensitive floor, am I correct? The path has to be perfect.' She didn't answer, but in two more turns, they reached a huge wall of shelves stretching along the side . . . and one small section let out a pressurised hiss and slid inward and off to the side on a track. Anit led the way inside

The hidden entrance sealed itself behind them, and lights flickered on – bright lights, bright as yellow suns, and aimed into their eyes. Jess threw up a hand to try to peer past, and Anit said, 'Stop where you are. Don't move. Brendan, put your gun away.'

Brendan looked prone to argue. Jess said, 'Do it,' and his twin finally complied.

'Clear,' Anit said in a completely normal tone of voice, and walked forward. More lights came on, and the spotlights that had pinned them in place faded; looking up, Jess saw they were odd glass globes with thin metal inside, not at all like the usual comfortable chemical glows. He'd seen something similar before, and it took him a second to place it.

The Iron Tower. Morgan had explained they ran on a forbidden technology: electricity. Somehow, he wasn't surprised that Red Ibrahim had taken advantage of it as well.

The lights coming on in the hall beyond revealed a tight group of men, all armed. They'd been aiming, Jess realised, while he and Brendan were blinded in the glare. Anit could have easily stepped aside and had them shot dead . . . but she hadn't.

'Anit? Is that blood? Are you injured?' A tall man stepped forward. He had a reddish tint to his dark skin, and an accent that, to Jess's ears, placed his birthplace along the African coast. Somalia, or Kenya. A shaved head and gold rings in his ears.

'No, Tadalesh. It isn't my blood,' Anit said. 'It's my father's. He's dead.'

These were Red Ibrahim's people, and all of them took the news as Jess could have expected: angrily. 'Who killed him?' Tadalesh demanded, and took a step forward, aiming the gun at Brendan, who of course raised his, too. 'Was it you?'

'No,' Anit said, and pushed Brendan's arm down. 'It wasn't him.' For a second Jess was sure she was about to confess, and that might get them *all* killed . . . but Anit, guilt ridden or not, had better sense than that. 'If you want someone to blame, forget the hand that pulled the trigger. It's the Archivist who's our real enemy, and theirs as well. We have common cause now. This is

Brendan Brightwell, and Jess Brightwell, and they are cousins in the trade from England.'

'Why's that one wearing a High Garda uniform, then?' asked a hard-looking woman who held a High Garda rifle.

'Because it's safer,' Anit said. 'And because as you well know, not every High Garda soldier is our born enemy. Some of them make our lives easier. Consider him a friend unless he proves me wrong.' She took a deep breath, looked down at the blood on her dress, and said, 'My father is gone. His sons are gone. But I remain, and you answer to me. Serve me well, and I will see you all rich, safe, and happy. Cross me, and I promise that you won't live long enough to regret it. I may be young, but I am not naïve, and I am not stupid.' She looked up again, and her eyes were burning with determination. She looked very much like her father now. 'By the blood of my father, I will see him avenged, and I will carry on his business. If any of you disagree, say it now; for the next minute, and the next minute only, I will allow you to walk away without penalty, but if you go, you will never work for me, or with me, ever again.'

Time ticked by. Red Ibrahim's smugglers – the top ranks of his lieutenants, Jess thought; surely these were his most trusted associates – looked uneasily at one another, and though a few shifted their weight, none of them walked away.

When the minute was up – and Jess was certain Anit had counted it to the second – she said, 'All right. We have an opportunity, and one that won't come again. Come with me.'

'Did she mean that for us, too?' Brendan asked as Anit strode away through the circle of her lieutenants – hers now, not her father's – and down the hall. Jess shrugged and followed. He didn't know what she planned, but he knew one thing, and only one: she was their only ally just now.

And one way or another, they needed to get to the Feast of Greater Burning.

The secret area of the warehouse went down into the rock, tunnels that opened into a warren of rooms, passages, and (or so Jess assumed) entrances and exits. Red Ibrahim had built this place to preserve not just business, but lives; there were rooms where fugitives could live in comfort for extended periods, and even bathing facilities and a small kitchen.

Anit led them past all of it to a large round room filled with books and scrolls. She went straight to a honeycomb of wood that held scroll cases and checked tags and pulled out a leather holder that seemed ready to fall to pieces.

'The cow that came from remembers the first Pharaohs,' Brendan said. Anit nodded, cleared a space on a table, and unrolled the scroll carefully. Tadalesh turned up the lights in the room, and the lieutenants crowded around.

'What is it?' one of them asked, craning his neck to make sense of it.

'The Colosseum,' she said. 'Where the Feast of Greater Burning will be held. Every Scholar and librarian in Alexandria is required to be there. The full Curia will be there. And the Archivist.'

'So . . . we're going to strike the Archives,' Tadalesh said. 'Finally.'

'No.'

'It's the best chance we've ever had to—'

'No,' she said. 'We leave the Archives alone. I've made a deal with the Brightwells. There are cousins of our own going to their deaths in that arena today. And who cares about them? No one but us. We have one objective, and only one: rescue our people.' She smiled, but it was a chillingly cold sort of thing, and it matched the drying blood on her dress. 'If the Archivist or any member of his circle of sycophants stands in the way of that, then I'll pay a fortune for the knife, arrow, or bullet that takes them down. I'll spend my father's fortune to avenge him and to save his people. Is that clear? Profit can wait. Revenge comes first.'

Forgoing profit was almost certainly a completely new idea to the men and women Anit was speaking to; in Jess's family, profit – or at least, avoiding a loss – had been central to every action taken. Loyalty had always been second on the list. From the glances among Anit's people, he could see their experience was no different . . . but revenge was a powerful incentive. These same people had worked for Red Ibrahim for years to be standing here. They had cast their fortunes with him. And even if loyalty came second to profit, it still finished ahead of anything else.

'If you take down the Archivist,' Jess said, 'then I can assure you that the way will be clear to earning profits with those presses you've built in secret . . . and doing it legitimately. But only if the Archivist isn't standing in the way of it.'

'And, of course, the Brightwells get a portion,' Anit said. 'Since they developed the entire technology.'

It was useful for them to grab on to that; it explained the Brightwells' presence here, and they understood business dealings just fine. They wouldn't understand that this was personal for Jess, and now for Brendan, but Anit had given him a perfect opportunity to conceal that.

One by one, the lieutenants nodded. Tadalesh seemed the most reluctant; clearly, he'd been dreaming about getting his hands on books from the Archives for quite some time. But he finally agreed, and bent to look at the plans.

'Trouble will be getting in,' said one of them. 'The main entrance will be well secured, and none of us has Library bands. They'll have automata everywhere, not to mention High Garda.'

'Fewer High Garda than you'd think,' Jess said. 'Word is, they're staying in the compound.' At least he hoped that would be the case, that Santi had been able to convince his friends and fellow captains to refuse the orders. 'And there's another way in. I've been there. I know it.'

'Show us,' Anit said, and stepped back.

Jess put his finger on the door that led down to the oldest parts of the amphitheatre and the unexpected modernity of the workshop; praise the old gods of Egypt, these particular corridors were solid concrete and timber, and they wouldn't be moving like the ones in the Serapeum. 'Get us in there,' he said, 'and I can get you directly to the floor of the arena. We can get your people to safety the same way.'

'You're sure? It looks sealed.'

'It isn't,' Jess said. 'And if you want weapons, that's where they're being made. New weapons. Deadly ones.'

'How do you know this?' Tadalesh asked.

'The Archivist showed me,' Jess said. 'And I'd like to make it his worst mistake yet.'

A sharp sound rang through the room – a bell, ringing in the distance. They all looked up, as if to hear it better, but Anit was the first to react. 'Someone's forced the outer door. High Garda, most likely. Exits,' she snapped. 'Scatter plan. Gather your people and head for the amphitheatre. Bring weapons. I'll join you in the street behind the main entrance.' She turned to Jess. 'Can you get us through the perimeter fence? Take care of the automata?'

'We can,' Brendan said, when Jess stopped to think for a few seconds. 'We'll gather our own forces and meet you there. All right?'

She nodded. 'I'll take you to an exit. From there, you're on your own. Good luck to you.'

'Good luck to us all,' Jess said. 'Anit?' Her gaze caught and held his. 'Thank you.'

He meant it for much more than just the help in escaping, and she knew it.

'It's for my father,' she said. 'And after this is done, we will talk about compensation.' Her smile was brief, and every bit her father's. 'After all, even family gets paid. Eventually.'

PART FOURTEEN

THE FEAST OF GREATER BURNING

CHAPTER THIRTY-FIVE

Thomas

Working was what kept him steady, and so he spent the hours in the workshop of the Spanish embassy. It had been built by a competent engineer, he could see that at a glance; walking into it had made him feel at home in a way few things could these days. The smell of tools, oils, freshly lathed wood and metal.

'I hope this is to your liking,' said Ambassador Santiago. He stood in the doorway surveying the large room, and clearly not much familiar with the tools, presses, vice benches, and materials carefully placed for convenience. 'My artisans use it, as do my soldiers. Is there anything you might need that you don't see here?'

'Yes,' Thomas said. He walked over to a stack of ready-made rifle barrels and checked the alignment by rolling one on the table. Straight and true. That was good. Very good. 'I'll need a diamond. A large one, please.'

'A—' He'd succeeded in putting a Santiago at a loss for words. 'I see. How large, precisely?'

Thomas showed him with a space between two fingers. Not a small space. 'About this,' he said. 'And as flawless as you can find, please. If there are rubies and sapphires, those will also be welcome.'

The ambassador's expression was priceless. Thomas was

mildly sorry that Jess wasn't here to see it. 'Are you . . . making some kind of jewellery?'

'This clearly isn't the time for that,' Thomas said. 'No. I am making a weapon. One capable of bringing down a flying automaton. And I think you would agree, it is something we very badly need.'

'Do you want an assistant? I can send someone—'

He missed Jess, but Jess had other concerns. 'No. Just the gems, please. And if there's food, have someone bring some? I forgot to eat.'

'Of course.' The ambassador clearly thought he was insane, but Thomas paid no attention to that, or to the man's departure. He had only a few hours to do what he needed to do, and much to avoid thinking about. With quick, precise movements he pulled four barrels, checked each one, and then moved on to retrieve the thinnest wire on the shelves. It was expertly drawn and perfectly formed, and as he measured and cut what he needed he remembered the makeshift, laughable device he and Jess had cobbled together out of hope and scraps in Philadelphia. Amazing it had worked even once, much less held together long enough to save their lives.

He'd made improvements on his design since then, and now, as he imagined the three-dimensional plans he'd so carefully constructed in his head, he knew what he was creating was, in its way, as dangerous as the press the Library feared so much. High Garda weapons were deadly, but they had limited ranges.

This weapon – at least, theoretically – could strike any target at any distance, so long as it travelled in a straight line. In theory, if powerful enough, it could cross the distance between stars, the way starlight reached the earth.

Light was the most ephemeral of forces, and yet one of the

most powerful. It had properties of gas and liquid and solid. Pure light, *solid* light . . . that was an astonishing and dangerous thing. And once he had created it and used it in public, where others could see . . . he could not control how it would be used in other hands.

So be it. Just now, he couldn't think of the future, or of anything else beyond what would come when the new day arrived.

One piece at a time, he machined the parts he needed for not one but for four separate Rays of Apollo. He had no written plans, but he didn't need them; he had the image in his mind, and he could spin and enlarge and match pieces to it at will. He worked quietly and surely, building each piece with care, and when food arrived he ate without even looking at what the Spanish had provided him and drank whatever had come with it. His concentration stayed on the plans and the parts, and the quiet, intense satisfaction when a piece fitted perfectly with the next.

At some point the ambassador must have returned, because he turned to see a black leather case on the table beside him and put the carefully assembled weapon – the first of four – aside to open it.

Inside sat the largest, most perfect diamond he'd ever seen. The size of a baby's hand, and when he put it to the light – morning light, he realised, beginning to reflect from the distant golden cap of the Serapeum – the light exploded into perfect rainbows around him. Flawless.

It would do.

Next to it sat five other stones: two rubies, a truly enormous emerald, and two sapphires of unusual clarity. The note with them said, *Spain will expect these returned, Scholar Schreiber.*

Thomas examined and discarded one of the rubies and –

with regret – the emerald, which simply wouldn't fit without alterations he knew the ambassador would frown on. Then he began to add the stones to the weapons, fixing them in place with the mounts he'd added for that purpose.

Now he needed power.

He walked out of the workshop into the embassy, ignoring the polite enquiries of the few staff about at this hour (who were, he vaguely noticed, packing things as if to move). The questions became less polite when he ripped open the control panel he found in a maintenance closet and stripped out the power supply for the chemical glows. The room plunged into inky darkness, except for the rising glow of dawn through the windows, and the questions turned into demands.

He was ripping away the fourth power supply when the guards surrounded him, and a very harried, tired-looking man in a silk robe came into the room, took everything in at a glance before the power went out, and shouted for the guards to hold their fire.

A shot went off, but it missed him, and Thomas shoved his way through and into the embassy entry hall, which had better light from the east-facing windows. Some of the guards and servants were activating portable glows, and the ambassador was speaking to him, but Thomas wasn't listening. He was closely examining the contacts and matching the power flow of these particular units against the requirements of the Ray; they were complicated mathematical calculations, and he truly didn't have time to spare for the man. He hadn't *destroyed* anything. Merely borrowed. Even now, a servant of the residence was plugging in new power supplies and the lights were coming back on.

Though he supposed he could have asked. It was simply that he was so close to finishing his task that communicating with someone else was a waste of time he couldn't spare.

The ambassador, thoroughly exasperated (at least, that was what Thomas gathered from the way he threw up his hands), stalked away to berate Scholar Wolfe, who stood watching from the stairs.

Ja. This would serve. All the calculations fit. He'd need to install some fittings to secure the power supply and make it simple to replace, but it would do until he could spend the time to create something better.

When he finished, it was full light outside. Morning. And as he looked at the four weapons he'd built, the terrible power of them he'd harnessed, the focus broke inside him, and all the things he hadn't allowed himself to feel rushed back in.

He sat down, hard, on a workbench and put his head in his hands. His breath came faster, and then faster still, an engine turning in his chest that he couldn't control.

And he didn't know *why*.

Someone called his name, but he couldn't look up or answer. It wasn't until her weight settled in next to him and he smelt the soft jasmine scent of her perfume that he knew Khalila had joined him. Her hands rested gently on his shoulder and his back. She was saying his name.

He couldn't get his breath. The engine inside him was racing, faster and faster, and he saw black spots now, and his hands trembled like an old man's.

'Thomas, put your head down. There. Slow, deep breaths. In through your nose, then out through your mouth. You're all right now. You're safe. You're safe.'

Whether it was her even, quiet voice or the gentle pressure of her hands, he began to listen, and follow her advice. It helped push back the dizziness, the spots, the panic that had threatened to send him to a very dark place. When his breathing slowed, he sent her a quick, guilty glance. 'I'm sorry,' he said. 'I don't know—'

'I do,' she said. 'You're afraid. We're all afraid. Do you feel a little better?'

He nodded. 'I suppose – I suppose I felt very alone for a moment. When I'm making something, there's nothing else, and then . . . it's gone. And it's only me.' He managed a smile. 'And I am sometimes not quite enough.'

'Because of Rome?'

'Yes.' He didn't want to talk about that yet, though he knew – and Wolfe had quietly told him – that only talking would ease the pressure building inside of him. 'I needed to make something to help us. This was all I could think of. Is Jess—' She shook her head, and he didn't finish the question. 'He'll be all right. He's a survivor, our Jess.'

'Yes,' she said, and her arm slid into the crook of his, holding tight. 'I hope Dario is.'

'Dario?' Thomas blinked. He'd missed something in his preoccupations. He'd been working so intently that he'd ignored everything, and perhaps . . . perhaps he shouldn't have. 'What about him?'

'He was taken,' she said. Her voice remained steady, but he felt the tremor in her. 'He's—I don't know, Thomas. I hope he's alive. I pray he is. If he isn't . . .'

'He is,' Thomas said, and put his arm around her shoulders. She felt slight and fragile, but he knew her strength, too. 'We will all be all right.' To his surprise, he almost believed it. 'We've come so far, and through so much. And if I'm wrong, and today is the end of it . . .'

'I couldn't ask for better friends to have at my side,' Khalila finished, which was exactly his thought. 'I know. I feel the same.' She hesitated a moment and then said, 'Do you want to tell me about Rome?'

'No,' he said. 'I want you to pick up one of those and come with me.'

She slipped off of the bench and took up one of the sleek new weapons. She seemed surprised when she lifted it. 'It's lighter than I thought.'

'Yes. I thought of some improvements. Be careful of the trigger.' He picked up the one on the other end and led her out of the workshop through the back door. The dawn had that strangely magical glow to it, thick with morning dew, a soft and shimmering colour that faded from blazing orange to gold to blue, and to the west still clinging stubbornly to night. The garden they'd entered had a stone wall built around it, and Thomas nodded at the far end of it. 'There. Shoot.'

'I—' Khalila gave him an uncertain look but hefted the weapon competently enough. Wolfe's training, and hard lessons in survival. She sighted, took a breath, and pressed the guarded trigger.

A beam of solid red light poured from the barrel and struck the wall, and the wall simply . . . vanished with a crack and a sudden puff of steam. No, it *melted*. Thomas blinked, and his brain made involuntary heat-transfer calculations, and he looked back at Khalila. 'Is it hot to the touch?'

'Warm,' she said. 'But not too hot, no. I only fired it for a second.'

Thomas nodded, raised his gun, and sighted as well. He fired at the newly shortened wall, and once again, it cracked, hissed steam, and melted into a thick, reddish mass on the ground. As he watched, the melted stone cooled to dull crimson, then black, like lava.

He checked the power reserve gauge on each of the weapons and nodded. 'Good. They should each handle four or five of such bursts. Fewer, if the trigger is held longer.'

Khalila looked glad to hand hers back to him. 'I suppose we need them,' she said. 'But they're—'

'Powerful,' he said. 'Yes. And dangerous. But we need to be dangerous now, don't we? If we want to survive?'

She nodded. And though he didn't want to, he knew they were both thinking of the same question.

At what cost?

Khalila walked with him back into the workshop, where they found Scholar Wolfe standing there. He'd put on a black Scholar's robe, and in all aspects, Thomas thought, he looked mostly unchanged since the first day he'd met them at the train to Alexandria. For all the damage, Wolfe survived.

'These are astonishing,' Wolfe said. 'You did these overnight.'

'I needed to keep busy.'

Wolfe laughed, but it sounded bleak. 'Yes. Obviously. But only Thomas Schreiber could keep busy by perfecting a beautiful death machine like this. Perhaps you should take up cards.'

'We need them,' Thomas said.

'Oh, I know we do,' Wolfe agreed. 'But forgive me for clinging one more moment to the fiction that right will prevail without becoming worse than its opposite.'

Thomas felt something zip through him, like a high-tension wire breaking, and he didn't know he was angry, *truly* angry, until that moment. 'You want to let them continue to do what they did to us? To thousands before us, and after? Do you really think it will stop, if we don't stop it?'

'I'd like to believe that even now, there is some argument that avoids a bloodbath.'

'Then make it,' Thomas said. 'But I won't let them do what was done to me, and to you, to Dario or Khalila, or anyone they've taken.' He took one of the rays and held it out to Wolfe. 'It's time to decide, Scholar. Are you talking, or fighting?'

Wolfe glared at him and at the weapon; Thomas knew he was thinking about Santi, who would never have hesitated.

He took the ray and said, 'I can do both.'

'Then let's be ready,' Thomas said. 'Because it won't be long now.'

CHAPTER THIRTY-SIX

Santi

From his perch on the roof of the Spanish embassy, Santi watched the procession wind past the Serapeum. He'd borrowed a pair of field glasses from the Spanish commander who'd been more occupied with loading weapons, armour, and valuables into the convoy of trunks set to depart shortly; the embassy staff would be going with it, and the ambassador, too. To his credit, Alvaro Santiago truly didn't want to go, but he was sensible enough to know that should the Archivist come out of this day on top, Spain would be next on his list to crush, and the embassy would have all of the safety of a globe of Greek Fire.

'Well?' Zara asked. She was at his shoulder, as still as a lounging cat. 'Anything?'

'High Garda Elite companies,' he said, and lowered the glasses. 'Not a single High Garda banner. I think you're right. The High Commander closed the compound.'

'Or, just as likely, he's no longer the Lord High Commander,' she said. 'Given how popular he wasn't with his peers. They'll sit this out. But that might not matter. The Elites are enough, especially with the automata out in force and that beast up there.' She nodded towards the Serapeum, where the metallic shimmer of the dragon sat coiled around the top of the pyramid, awaiting its orders. 'That has to go first, or we'll end up like pigs turning on spits.'

'Nothing from the Iron Tower?'

'Nothing except that the Obscurist has left it, along with a solid contingent of the guards assigned there. That's him, in the red. The automata are still working. Nothing's changed. Whatever your girl was doing in there, she's failed.'

'I wouldn't count her out.'

'Or in,' Zara said. 'We have our company. We have whatever's left of your Scholar's students. We have . . . what else, exactly? Nic, this is a fool's errand. The odds aren't even high; they're zero. If we go out there, we will *die*. And they will win, for ever. Is that what you call victory?'

He didn't answer her. He took up the glasses again and tightened the focus. It was far to the road where the procession was taking place, but he thought that walking just behind the Obscurist was someone in a white robe. Someone who might have been Morgan.

If he's taken her from the Tower, what does that mean? That she's won? Or that she's lost? He couldn't know, and Zara's points were irritatingly right. There were a few failure points, and thus far, all of them seemed to have crashed in on themselves. Jess and his brother were missing, gone off on some revenge mission. There was no indication that any of the Scholars that Wolfe had approached – or any from the distant Serapeums – would offer their support. The automata remained a danger, and the Obscurists showed no sign of turning on their master.

And Dario was missing. Taken, and perhaps dead, and of all of these things, Santi felt that the keenest. The loss of any of these young, brilliant minds was something he, like Wolfe, didn't want to face. And as unlikable as Dario might be at times, he'd changed. He'd become something better.

He deserved a chance. So did those prisoners who were being

marched now in that procession towards the amphitheatre.

'There's no cheering,' he said.

'What?'

'There are crowds along the street, but they're all silent. Do you hear anything else?'

Zara listened, then shook her head. 'So? The common folk of Alexandria are going to rise up for us? You're dreaming, Captain.'

'I might be,' he said, and turned the glasses back to the glimmering scales of the dragon. 'First, we have to take that creature down. Ideas?'

'It's a *dragon*. It *breathes Greek Fire*.'

'You're usually better than this.'

'And you're usually better than to throw yourself into a useless fight,' she replied. 'Unless something dramatic happens . . .'

Something drew Santi's attention down to the open drive in front of the mansion. Four shapes, fanning out at equidistant points in the middle of the road. He recognised Wolfe's robe blowing in the morning breeze an instant before he heard Thomas's deep voice say, 'Now,' and four beams of light – one red, two blue, one a shattering white – drew lines from the four humans straight to the dragon at the top of the Serapeum.

The shrieking, grating scream that came out of the dragon was loud enough to shatter windows, and down on the street below the Serapeum the procession scattered as the dragon unfurled its wings and launched itself upward.

It wasn't flying evenly. When Santi lifted the glasses and focused, he saw that along one side – the side that had been facing the embassy – half of its heavy, plated scales were gone, revealing cables, gears, wires, tubes that were slashed open to expose ropes of green liquid cascading out.

He removed the glasses and threw himself down on the edge of the roof to shout, 'Again! You hit it! Keep hitting it!'

Wolfe looked up, and so did the other three faces. Khalila, Thomas, and Glain. 'Again!' Wolfe shouted, and the beams sliced out again. One missed completely as the dragon banked, but three found marks. Thomas's – the white beam – sheared off one entire wing of the creature and sent it spinning heavily off to crash somewhere down into the city. A cloud of screams rose. 'Keep firing!'

The dragon was making a clumsy attempt to keep aloft, but as the rays fired at it again, it marked its enemies and, in an awkward corkscrewing motion, turned its fall into a lunge.

God save us, it's coming straight for us.

'Up! Get up!' Zara was dragging at his arm, but there wasn't any point; they'd never get off the roof, and the four down below weren't running. They were holding down their triggers, sending continuous blinding pulses of light at the automaton as its enormous, shredding jaws cranked open and it fell towards them.

It was Wolfe's shot that cut the head from the beast. It hit at just the right angle, cutting clean through a gap in the melted, blackened scales and into the body of the creature; the weight of the head ripped it free and sent it tumbling down in a rough spiral to crash into the iron fence that ringed the compound, where it was impaled down to the ground on the spikes.

The body fell limply out of the sky. It hit just past the fence and skidded to a stop, hissing steam and leaking Greek Fire that caught the entire metal skeleton on fire and slowly, steadily began to melt it down. The barbed tail of the thing continued to twitch, but that, Santi thought, was just the heat burning through the metal cables.

Wolfe turned to look up, and Santi found himself smiling. No, grinning. He saw the matching, vulpine expression on his lover's face.

'Now,' he said, 'we have a chance. Come on, Zara, let's get—'

He rolled over and started to rise, and checked himself when he realised that she was holding a pistol on him. Her dark eyes were wide and very steady.

'No, Captain,' she said. 'Not this time. I'm not letting you kill yourself. Not for him. I've watched you drag yourself through hell for him, and you can't do this, Nic, *you can't*. You swore oaths. This is wrong.'

He got up slowly, eyes on hers and not on the gun held between them. When he reached out, he was reaching out to her. 'I would go to the lowest depths of hell for him,' he said, and put his hand on the gun. 'Zara, if turning my back on him is the price of loyalty, you'd better shoot.' He could have taken the weapon, and they both knew it. She could have fired, and they both knew that too.

Zara let the gun drop to the roof between them, reached up, and ripped the rank and insignia from her High Garda uniform. She opened her hand and let that fall between them too. Her eyes were full of tears and rage, and she just shook her head and walked away.

He wanted to tell her something better . . . that he valued her, that he would miss her, that she was worth more than this. But in the end, he stood quietly and let her leave. It would be unkind of him to lie to her, even as a kindness. He would never choose her over Wolfe. Best she understand that now, at the end of all of this.

He left her gun and insignia where they had fallen, and once he was sure she was gone, he went down to find Wolfe, throw his arms around him, and say, 'They'll be here soon. We need to go. Now.' He pulled back and looked at Glain. 'Get Botha. Tell him he's promoted to lieutenant. Find Troll; he's my new second. You're promoted to sergeant, and head of the Blue Dogs.'

She saluted as smartly as he could ever have hoped. 'Thank you, sir. It's a start.'

He returned her salute, open hand over heart, and as she ran off to find his company, Wolfe said, 'She's going for your job, Nic.'

'After today, she can have it,' he said. 'And may God help anyone who gets in her way. She didn't miss a single shot, did you notice?'

'I was trying not to be roasted alive. It tends to erase the details.'

Santi pulled his lover close, and in this quiet moment before everything began, and ended, he was happier than he'd been in years.

CHAPTER THIRTY-SEVEN

Glain

Finding Botha and Tom Rolleson took only a moment: Santi's company was camped under a large camouflage tent in the back. Though Botha seemed surprised, Troll didn't; whether or not they valued promotions on a day like this she couldn't say, but both seemed calm and ready. The whole company did. They were ready to move on a moment's notice. *We have five hundred soldiers*, she thought. *Against the same amount of High Garda Elite and a small army of automata.* She didn't mind a hard fight, but she had to admit that even after removing the dragon from the equation, the maths was still unforgiving.

But it was better than it had been before Thomas had stepped out of the workshop with those weapons.

Still, Glain was happy to surrender the strange gun back to Thomas after running to rejoin him and Khalila; not that she didn't value the pure destructive power of the thing, but there was a skin-crawling *ease* to it that made her feel a little ill. Killing – and though this time they'd only aimed those beams at an automaton, surely the time was fast approaching where it would be searing human flesh – killing ought to be more . . . difficult.

Thomas checked each one and opened three out of four of the weapons to knock out large, shining stones.

'Are those . . . jewels?'

'Yes,' he said, but he was engrossed in the last weapon. 'Interesting. The diamond drew the least power, perhaps because of the size of the stone, or the refraction, or . . . I'll have to examine the power consumption rates more closely.'

'Where did you get them?'

He glanced at her, and the fog lifted in his eyes for a second. He put two warm blue stones and one very warm red one into her hand. 'Give these back to the ambassador,' he said. 'Tell him I need the loan of this last one a little longer.'

'Oh, I'll take the guns as well,' said the ambassador himself, and Glain kicked herself mentally for not seeing the man approach. He was a quiet one, Alvaro Santiago. 'Please.'

'No,' Thomas said.

Santiago raised both eyebrows. He wasn't dressed like a royal ambassador now; he looked like a common sailor. The only thing that didn't fit – and would change the instant he left these grounds, Glain thought – was his accent, far too refined for the rest of him. 'Perhaps I should rephrase my request,' Alvaro said, and a brace of Spanish soldiers – both in common clothing, too – stepped out of concealment behind the columns and levelled guns on the three of them.

Glain revised her objections to the power of the weapons, but it was too late now, and she was late even drawing her sidearm. Next to her, Khalila began to step forward and, no doubt, deliver a powerful speech; Glain stopped her by the single expedient of throwing out a solid arm to halt her in her tracks, and looking to Thomas.

Thomas flipped a switch on his Ray of Apollo and calmly raised it and pointed it at the ambassador. 'No,' he said again. 'After today, these will be destroyed. I'll send your diamond to you.'

'The diamond is not half so valuable as what you hold in your hands, and I'm sure you know this,' Alvaro said. 'Thomas. You are a brilliant young man, an Artifex worthy of the best days of the Great Library. Don't be stupid. I would hate to extinguish such a light.'

'If I shoot,' Thomas said, 'there won't be enough of you left to bury. I'm grateful for your help and your workshop. But I won't give you these guns. And I won't make more for you, or for anyone. There are no plans. The secret dies with me.'

Glain eased her sidearm out of its holster. She took up a High Garda shooting stance and aimed at the ambassador's head. 'So say we all,' she said.

For a long, tense moment she was certain the man would order them killed; she was not at all sure Thomas intended to carry out his threat. But then Alvaro turned to his men and gestured, and they lowered their weapons. 'Very well, Scholar, I understand,' he said. 'But you must also understand that sooner or later, someone else will make one, and that person will be less moral than you. It wasn't worth your life.'

'It was to me,' Thomas said. He pointed the Ray down at the three discarded, de-jewelled weapons, and with one short pull of the trigger reduced them to smoking, melted wreckage. He checked the gauge on the weapon. 'Interesting. Still two more shots. Don't make me waste them.'

Santiago shook his head and said, 'Use them to free my cousin. I do care about the wretch. I'd stay if my king didn't order me home.' He gave Glain a respectful nod and she put away her gun. Khalila earned a full court bow. 'I will be seeing all of you again, I hope.'

'If you do,' Khalila said, 'I hope you don't bring an army with you. Tomorrow, this is still the Great Library, and it stands.

If we win, we will keep it safe against anyone – even friends – who tries to take what isn't rightly theirs. You should be on your way. The fall of that dragon will bring Library troops.'

'I expect no less. *Hasta luego*, my friends.'

And then they were gone, disappearing into the shadows of the columns, and when Glain advanced to follow, she found the whole entry hall deserted. By the time she reached the back doors, she found them locked and the convoy already moving away. For a rich, spoilt royal, he knew how to move with military precision and speed; she had to grant him that much.

Botha joined her at the windows and said, 'I assumed we should let them leave without starting a fight. Was I wrong?'

'Not that I know,' she said. She shot a glance towards the lieutenant's calm, unreadable face. 'Do you think—'

'I don't think,' he said. 'It's not useful before the fight. Only during it.' He turned, and Glain followed a second later, as the others came into the room. 'Sir. We're ready. The High Garda Elite carriers can hold fifty, if we're friendly, but the rest of the company will have to be on foot.'

Santi nodded. 'The Blue Dogs, the Harpies, Shadow Team, and Mars One for the vehicles. Arrange them as you prefer. Split the company into four units. Stay away from the main routes. Third and fourth units are covering fire. Use the heights.'

'Sir.' Botha saluted, and said, 'You'll be in the vehicles?'

'Yes,' he said. 'All of us. Glain, Thomas and Khalila in one, me and Wolfe in another. And Lieutenant? Library engagement rules. You don't kill unless you must, but if you must, you get it done. Protect the Scholars and librarians down on the killing floor. Let us handle the rest.'

Glain opened her mouth to protest, then shut it with a snap. Santi's orders were precise and calculated. He wasn't mounting a High Garda rebellion. He was showing that they were committed to the Library's principles. And that was noble.

Just very possibly suicidal.

Glain claimed herself a proper rifle and a healthy supply of ammunition from the armorer, who was loading up the extra guns and supplies in the rear of the carrier, and as she crowded into the carrier with Khalila and Thomas and the door hissed closed, she thought she ought to by all rights be afraid. They had little chance, after all. The might of the Great Library was against them, along with history, tradition, and her captain's own scruples.

She met Khalila's eyes as the carrier rattled through the streets, speeding towards the amphitheatre. Held up her hand. Khalila clasped it. Then both their hands were swallowed up by Thomas's.

'Together,' she said.

'Together,' they both echoed.

The Blue Dogs – Glain's squad – howled. The Harpies let out their weird, unsettling keening cry.

It was war.

CHAPTER THIRTY-EIGHT

Jess

'Down,' growled Tadalesh, when Jess inched up to peer over the edge of the roof. 'If you want to gawk, go stand with the crowds on the road.'

'Any sign of Elites?' Jess ignored Anit's lieutenant and got his own good look. The street below seemed clear.

'No. The Elites are inside the fence, and that way.' Tadalesh jerked his sharp chin towards the main street, where the procession was pouring in towards the amphitheatre. It was almost finished; the Scholars and librarians had gone first, a parade of fluttering robes conducted in silence. Then a tall, stalking row of automaton Egyptian gods, the largest of which – Horus, easily identifiable even at this distance – carried a huge, sharp sword. The Curia – the heads of the Library's major disciplines, including the Obscurist Magnus – were proceeding now, and with them, under a huge cloth-of-gold covering, the marching honour guard of Elites, with the Archivist carried on a sedan chair in the centre of the pack.

There was no cheering. Nothing but silence from those gathered along the route. Jess wondered if the Archivist felt as uneasy about that as he did.

That was when the dragon, coiled around the Serapeum, let out a shriek that seemed to shatter the sky, and Jess saw the flash of solid beams of light slice into the thing for just a flash before they cut off.

Thomas. Thomas built a Ray of Apollo. No, more than one; that much was clear as the dragon launched itself into the air and began to clumsily beat towards the source of the attack. It had lost its grace, but none of its power.

And then the ray weapons flashed again, and pieces rained from the sky. Scales the size of troop carriers. A sheared-off wing, spiralling to slam through the roof of a building. And then the head came loose, and the whole terrifying automaton slammed down into the ground with an impact that Jess felt through his entire body before the sound of it rolled over them. The Greek Fire inside the thing began to burn in pale green flames, and for a second Jess couldn't process what had happened. Then he had a mad impulse to shout, to leap to his feet and punch the sky in triumph.

That had been an impossible task, and *Thomas had done it.*

'Your friends?' Tadalesh asked.

'Yes,' Jess said.

'You think they will sell us those guns?'

'No.'

Tadalesh shrugged. 'Maybe we take them anyway.'

'Maybe they kill you first,' Jess said. He rolled over on his side and gestured to Brendan, who climbed down from the roof and joined the massed hundred or so men and women Anit had assembled. They were a hard rabble, and heavily armed. He liked the discipline and rules of the High Garda, but for some things, a gang of thieves was just . . . better.

The cutter acted quickly at the fence, opening a section with judiciously applied Greek Fire wide enough to allow five to pour through at a time. They'd timed it between the loops of the automata sphinxes, but even so, they'd be spotted in seconds, and from then on it would be a real fight.

Tadalesh was sliding over the edge of the roof, and Jess followed. He found hand- and footholds and jumped the last ten feet to land in a roll and come up running, and he was halfway to the fence when the first automaton sphinx spotted the breach and let out a harsh metallic cry. It flapped metal wings and glided towards Anit's people, claws unsheathed and ready to rip into flesh.

Brendan slid into its path and it dropped onto him, pinned him to the ground, and opened its needle-toothed mouth to bite. Brendan twisted, reached, and jammed his rifle between the jaws, forced the head up, and found the switch.

The sphinx froze in place, and Anit pulled him free as two others tipped the statue over with a crash. Brendan got to his feet and yanked his rifle free, and Jess shoved through the thieves' army to make it to his brother's side.

'Stupid!' he shouted. Brendan was hurt. He could see the blood soaking into his shirt.

'Effective!' Brendan shouted back, and grinned. 'It's nothing. Get us in – more are coming!'

The workshop entrance was locked, but Jess and the cutter got it open in seconds, and Jess took the lead, grabbing a glow from the wall and calling up the path that he'd taken to the Archivist's workshop. Another pair of doors, these thicker. Behind them, the sphinxes would be swarming and killing as many as they could reach. Getting trapped here in the corridor was deadly.

It took a costly half a minute, but the doors finally slammed open, and Jess was one of the first onto the balcony where he and the Archivist had last stood. The railing had been newly repaired, and the metal was still shining. The workshop below was well lit but empty of any workers or guards. Just the silent, still forms of automata under construction.

Jess wrapped a rope around the rail and slid down, and more ropes joined his. Anit was still on the balcony and ordering men to hold the door; that wouldn't hold for long against automata, but maybe long enough.

And then the doors flew open, knocking Anit's people back, and High Garda poured through. Jess raised his rifle and aimed, then realised who was in the lead. 'Don't fire! Don't fire!' He shouted it as loudly as he could, and Anit echoed him up on the balcony.

It was Niccolo Santi, and Scholar Wolfe beside him, and Jess saw Thomas's golden head towering above the crowd.

The two factions faced off, a neutral space between them, and Jess grabbed the rope he'd slid down and climbed, vaulted over the rail, and pushed into the empty centre where Anit and Brendan were already standing.

'Captain,' Jess said. 'Good to see you.'

Santi nodded. 'Same.'

'You followed us.'

'We thought we'd let you lead the way.'

'How many with you?'

'Fifty now. The rest coming,' Santi said. 'We'll have cover fire from high points nearby, but this will be a ground fight. You understand.' He looked at Anit. 'Why are you here?'

'To get our people back,' she said. 'Same as you.'

'Common cause?'

'For now,' Anit said. 'Until it isn't. I think we'll know that moment.'

It wasn't perfect, but they didn't have time for perfect. Just movement. The High Garda moved forward, and a team sealed the door behind them with fast, effective welders. Jess left his brother with Anit and joined his friends.

Naturally opposing sides, but for now, Santi was right: common cause.

They coursed through the workshop, moving past the tables, the dead automata, the curtain-covered, half-finished machines. Jess ripped down the curtain at the back of the room and found another dragon lying dormant on the ground. It looked ready to fly. *We should destroy that*, he thought, but the truth was they didn't have time. Up on the balcony, the doors were shaking under a relentless assault.

The back of the workshop was an enormous rolling door, and as they shoved it away on its rails they were standing on a wide, up-slanting ramp. Jess ran towards the top of it and found another door, large enough to easily accommodate that dragon, or a horde of elephants, or a full-scale ship. There were controls on the wall. A simple push of a button, and they would be in the amphitheatre.

Santi and Wolfe paused next to him. Anit, flanked by a hard crowd of her lieutenants. Khalila, Thomas, and Glain.

And his twin, who nodded and said, 'Go.'

No going back.

Jess hit the button, and the door opened into the Feast of Greater Burning.

There was no one to rescue. No one on the floor of the amphitheatre. No automata, no prisoners, *no one*. They rushed out, and slowed, and Jess turned in place to look at what they'd just done.

The stands were full of Scholars. Librarians. In the gilded central box sat the Curia of the Great Library, all dressed in their formal robes, and standing at the railing were two people. The Archivist, dressed in heavy, jewelled robes, with a crown with the eye of Horus towering on his head.

And the Artifex, his closest ally and friend, wearing the robes of his office. He held a golden whistle in his hand, and he was smiling.

'Back!' Jess shouted, but it was too late. The doors were sliding shut, trapping half of their people in the tunnels. A hundred of them had made it through – a mix of Anit's thieves and Santi's High Garda. Instinctively, the thieves spread out, and the High Garda bunched together in a cohesive, protective formation.

He caught a look at Santi's face, and his heart stopped for a moment. That was the face of a man who knew it was over. Who knew they'd lost.

'Did you really think I'd have brought you to that workshop without a reason?' the Archivist asked him. 'I knew you'd betray me, whichever Brightwell you proved to be. You did exactly what I wanted you to do. You delivered my enemies.' He gestured, and another door opened. Jess's heart thudded back to life, and he took better hold of his rifle. *Shoot whatever comes out*, he thought, but what came out was a young woman in a white Obscurist's robe, and it was Morgan, who staggered a few steps and then dropped to her knees.

He broke ranks to run to her, grabbed her and hauled her to her feet again. She was gasping for breath, and one glance at her face was enough to tell him that she was in no shape to help anyone, not even herself. 'It's okay,' he told her. That was a lie, but it was all he could give her now. He got her safely back to the High Garda lines, where Khalila took her and said, 'What's wrong, Morgan? Morgan?'

Morgan tried to speak, but she couldn't seem to. She ripped away her collar and threw it onto the sand that covered the arena floor, and finally managed to say, 'Drugged. Trying.' She grabbed for Khalila's hand. 'Together.'

'Yes,' Khalila said, and looked desperately at Jess. 'We're together now.'

Another door opened, and two High Garda Elites came through dragging another limp form. They left him on the sand and retreated. Khalila gasped, and this time she was the one who dashed forward. Glain was a step behind her, and together they towed Dario Santiago back to whatever safety this was. He'd been beaten and bloodied, but he managed to give Khalila a broken smile and say, 'Hello, madonna,' before turning to Jess and holding out his hand. Jess thought he was meant to take it, but Dario impatiently shook that off and said, 'Gun, Scrubber. Give me a gun!'

Glain passed her sidearm over.

'Now,' the Archivist said. 'You're all present. I would have included Red Ibrahim with you, except that he was found dead yesterday. I wonder which one of you killed him. Not that I intended to let a single smuggler live after today, but it would have been a nice symbol, having him here. At least we have his heir. Anit, is it?'

She stepped forward, all of fourteen and as old as the stones of the city, and made a startlingly rude gesture up at the box. 'Remember the name, old man,' she shouted back. 'We'll spit on your funeral fire!'

He shook his head. 'You are stones in the shoes of history, and you will be shaken out. No more tolerance. No more black markets, Burners, rebels. The Library will continue, and you will not.' He raised his voice into a shout. '*Knowledge is all!*'

The Scholars and librarians repeated it. No great shout of affirmation, Jess thought; it was almost a prayer, instead. *They're waiting*, he thought. *They need something to show them there's hope.*

Jess spun, raised his rifle, and fired straight at the Archivist.

The shot hit an invisible shield, and the bullet hung there a foot away from the old man's face, vibrating. The Archivist nodded to Gregory, who gestured, and the bullet dropped to the sand.

No one spoke. Jess changed targets and fired at the Artifex, then Gregory. None of the shots made any difference.

Santi reached out and pushed his rifle down. 'Save your ammunition,' he said. 'This is only just starting.'

The Artifex raised the whistle that Jess had noticed to his lips, and it made a high, thin trilling sound.

Above them, the sky filled with birds, launching out of hollows in the top of the amphitheatre. Circling and catching the light of the sun on metallic wings.

Jess felt a strange impulse to laugh. *Birds.* They'd brought down a dragon. He wasn't going to fear a few sparrows.

But it wasn't a few. It was thousands. They continued pouring up, blackening the sky, circling in a vast whirl . . . and then the Artifex whistled again.

And the birds dived.

CHAPTER THIRTY-NINE

Morgan

She could hardly keep her feet under her, but she felt the black energy of the birds circling overhead. Automata: small ones, light and simple, without much complexity in their formulae. One of them, ten of them, easily crushed.

Thousands of them shifted and came down in a deadly dive.

One narrowly missed her, burying itself in the sand, and as it did she realised that the beaks were long and sharp, like flying knives . . . and another sliced the skin of her upper arm as it arrowed down.

Next to her, a High Garda soldier was looking up, and a bird buried itself in his eye. He staggered, opened his mouth, and then simply died.

All around her, the birds were falling in a dead rain, stabbing and cutting and killing. And there were thousands more, and thousands more.

They were going to be cut to pieces.

Morgan fell to her knees and pushed. The drug that Gregory had poured down her throat numbed her, and she fumbled clumsily for anything, *anything* to stop this.

She felt something responding. Something whispering and ghostly, and with an effort that made her gasp and reel, she caught hold of a thin trickle of power, shaped it, and thrust it at the bird hurtling down towards Jess's unprotected head.

It veered. It spread its wings and flapped to gain altitude. It circled, flitting among its diving fellows. She saw the script now. It was blindingly simple.

She changed one symbol, and the bird banked, gained speed, and folded its wings.

It ripped through the golden cloth that covered the Curia's box and buried its knife-sharp beak into Gregory's ear, all the way to his brain. She knew he'd lacked the imagination to build that barrier in a circle. He only saw a shield.

And now he staggered, screaming, flailing, and she grabbed for another bird. Another. As the Curia members scrambled out of the way, Gregory tried to protect himself, but it was too late, far too late, and when the last bird arrowed into his eye, he slumped back down to his chair in a fluttering heap of red robes.

It felt like someone had opened the door of a cell in her mind, and she pulled in a deep, clean breath as the numbness and fog rolled away. The world exploded into light and fire and power.

And the birds began to fall, smashing down without direction.

Dead. Thousands, hitting the sand, but not another one hitting the people standing in the arena.

She felt the paths inside her, the ones Eskander had so carefully recovered, scorch in painful streaks. *Too much.* She'd just wielded more power than anyone should at once, and when she tried to reach to stop the rank of Egyptian gods that stalked from the tunnels into the arena, each four times the height of a human . . . she failed. Her powers slid off them like oil from water, and she felt a wave of pain and nausea send her reeling to her knees.

'Morgan?' Khalila was beside her.

'I can't,' she gasped. 'I can't!'

Khalila took Jess's sidearm from his holster and began to fire at the goddess Bast who approached them with relentless speed, crushing the lifeless automaton birds under its feet. It wouldn't help, Morgan wanted to tell her. It would take power greater than hers to stop even one of these things.

'Scatter!' she heard Santi yell, and the High Garda troops exploded into motion, weaving between and around the gods. Some were caught. The giant figure of Isis swept up a soldier in its hand and crushed him, then reached for another.

The Scholars and librarians had come to their feet now, and the Archivist was shouting something and pointing at Morgan, specifically at Morgan. Jess shoved her behind him as Bast kept coming. 'Khalila! Take her!' he shouted, and Khalila tried, but Morgan's legs had gone numb now, and she couldn't run.

The three of them fell under the shadow of the god. Its cat-face showed no emotion as she raised a flail; it was razor-sharp, and would cut them apart with one blow. Khalila continued to fire, though she must have known it was useless.

Jess wouldn't leave.

He wouldn't leave.

And that was the moment she knew, after all her doubts and worries, that what she felt for him was love, because the strength of it took her breath away. She reached for him, and he took her hand and stepped back beside her. Khalila held her other hand. None of them spoke, because there wasn't any need. *They'll remember how we die*, Morgan thought. *Maybe our fate isn't to change the Library. Maybe it's to die to show them how to continue.*

She was almost, almost at peace with that . . . and then she heard shouts coming from the stands, from the Scholars and librarians, and she looked past the automaton and saw that a new column of people had walked into the arena, this time from the door that had admitted the gods.

Eskander, in a blindingly white Obscurist robe, led his people into the arena, just as he'd led them out of the Iron Tower, and next to him, looking entirely different from the smiling, happy woman Morgan knew, was Annis.

Eskander raised his hands, and the Obscurists raised theirs, and Morgan felt the breathtaking rush of power blast through the arena. The gods swayed, slowed, and turned towards the Obscurists.

And then, one by one, they knelt.

It wasn't one man's power, Morgan realised. It was *all of them*, blending and combining into an unstoppable flood. No wonder the Obscurists had been penned up in the Iron Tower, where the walls muted and confined them.

Together, and free, they were far more dangerous than anyone could have known. A dying breed, but a powerful one to the last.

One god didn't kneel. Just one.

Horus.

It stalked towards the Obscurists, and some of them broke and ran. Then more, as the automaton approached and raised its huge sword capable of mowing all of them down.

But some stayed, and Eskander directed their power, amplified it, and Horus began to slow.

But it didn't stop.

'Fire!' Santi shouted, and all around the arena, Anit's people and Santi's company poured bullets into the machine. The golden skin began to dent, but it wasn't enough.

None of it would be enough.

'Jess!'

Thomas's voice rang across the amphitheatre, and for the first time Morgan realised with a shock that the young man was down, one leg at an ugly, broken angle. But he heaved himself up to a sitting position, and with all the strength in his upper body, he threw the Ray of Apollo towards them.

Towards Jess, who dropped his rifle, lunged, caught the falling weapon, and came up on one knee to aim and fire.

He cut Horus in half, a long, slanting cut from left shoulder to right hip, and the top half of the god slipped sideways, tumbled, and rolled on the sand.

Dead.

The Archivist and the Curia stood silently now. Shocked, and only just realising how badly this trap had gone for them. Around the arena, automata raced from opening tunnels: Spartans armed with spears. Lions. Sphinxes, large and small. All deadly, all intent on killing.

But they're losing, Morgan thought. She didn't take her gaze from the Archivist as Jess stood and raised that Ray of Apollo again. The shield that had protected him had died with Gregory, and she doubted it would have stopped Thomas's solid light . . . but when Jess fired, nothing happened.

The weapon was empty of power.

He dropped it, grabbed his rifle, and fired once, but he missed as the Archivist finally realised his danger and raced for an exit.

'Stop them!' Shouts went up from both Santi and Anit, but also from Scholars who were coming to the railings and vaulting down into the arena. Joining them. *Scholars were joining them!*

Morgan felt tears burn her eyes as she watched the Archivist and his Curia driven together into the centre of their golden box by a ring of Scholars, High Garda soldiers, thieves. Santi's troops were quickly and competently destroying the automata; there were losses, but fewer and fewer. A lion bounded at them, and Khalila moved in front of it, stepped under the slashing paws, and turned it off with a single, accurate slap of her hand.

Khalila climbed up on to the back of the thing balanced on the snarling head and shouted at Santi. 'Captain! Don't kill them!'

Santi relayed the order to his people, and when Anit's thieves didn't seem inclined to obey they were thrown out of the box back to the arena with quick, efficient violence. The alliance, it seemed, was coming to an end.

That was when she saw Jess climbing into the box.

No, it wasn't Jess. Jess was here, with her.

It was his twin.

Brendan.

CHAPTER FORTY

Jess

Jess saw his twin climb the railings, but he didn't have time to wonder why; he was too busy slipping under the spear of a Spartan and finding the switch to stop the thing. It had already killed a few people, by the smears of blood on it, and he felt a surge of bitter triumph as it froze in its crouching lunge.

Then he looked for Brendan.

His brother avoided Lieutenant Botha's outstretched hand and went straight for the Archivist.

Yes, Jess thought. *Kill him*. As long as the Archivist lived, there wouldn't be peace here, or progress. Killing Gregory had been a good start, but only a start. He knew Khalila didn't approve, and likely Wolfe wouldn't either . . . but he'd watched Neksa die.

Fitting, that his brother should be the one to end this.

He saw a shadow behind Brendan, and then as his brother grabbed for the Archivist, he saw his twin stumble.

He felt the knife, somehow. Its phantom shadow slid into his back, and he felt its cold presence tear his heart in two.

No. NO!

Jess must have shouted it, must have screamed, but he didn't hear himself doing it; he was too far away to get to his brother, but he ran, dodging the claws and spears of automata, launching himself up to grab the railing, and when he landed on the floor of the box the Archivist was being pushed towards an exit that had opened in the floor. A trapdoor.

The black shadow was a High Garda uniform without insignia, and she was hurrying the old man into the escape hatch. As she looked back, her gaze caught Jess's.

Green eyes. A sharp, pale face.

In her hand, a bloody dagger.

Zara.

Anit lunged for the opening, but it slammed shut before she could reach it. Santi leapt over Gregory's fallen body and reached the trapdoor a second later, but it was seamless from this side.

'Find the exit!' Santi shouted. He'd gone sickly pallid, and Jess knew he'd seen her, too.

Zara Cole had betrayed all of them.

Zara Cole had murdered his brother.

Jess didn't watch the rest. He grabbed Brendan from where he'd fallen. His twin was still breathing, but his eyes were already blind and wide, as if he was trapped in a dark, dark room searching for an exit.

'Jess?' he whispered. 'Jess?'

'I'm here, Brother,' he said, and grabbed Brendan's trembling hand. No blood on Brendan's front. The wound was in the back, invisible. Deep. Deadly. 'Medica! I need a Medica!'

'Jess,' Brendan gasped. Blood on his lips. Foaming from his mouth. 'Jess, tell Da—'

And then he was gone. Just . . . gone. Brendan lay heavy in his arms and just a moment ago, seconds ago, he had been vital and alive and *his brother*.

'Brendan!' Anit was by him now. And Santi. Santi tried to take his brother away, and he shoved the man backward, hard.

'Leave him alone!' Jess shouted. 'Get me a Medica!'

'It's no use, son.' That was Scholar Wolfe, grim and bloodstained and holding one arm at an awkward angle, but there was bitter compassion in his eyes. 'Jess, a Medica can't save him. I'm sorry.'

'I don't want your sympathy. I want *a Medica*!'

'Jess.' Morgan's hands fitted themselves to his cheeks and made him turn towards her. She looked exhausted, bloody, and her face was wet with tears. 'Jess, he's gone. *He's gone.*'

It wasn't true until he let Scholar Wolfe take the weight of his brother in his arms, and then he knew it was true, because Brendan had never been so limp, so quiet, so *empty*.

'She killed him,' Jess said, and swallowed. 'Zara killed him.'

'I know,' Wolfe said. 'We'll find them. I swear that to you.'

Jess collapsed into a seat – the Archivist's seat, he realised – and looked down at the blood that covered his chest. Morgan was with him, but he felt very, very alone.

Tell Da . . .

There was nothing to tell his father. Nothing at all.

He'd succeeded in what he'd come here to do.

But he'd failed at the one thing that mattered.

CHAPTER FORTY-ONE

Khalila

The amphitheatre was a roaring sea of confusion. Only a few automata still roamed the sands, and they were being dealt with; Khalila forced herself to put the death and the loss aside and take stock of what was around her.

Someone needed to take control of this. If no one did, she thought, there would be nothing left of the Great Library by sunset, and Alexandria would be easy prey for what was coming.

She found the tall Obscurist in white robes – stained with blood and dirt now – and shouted, 'Who are you?'

'Eskander,' he shouted back. 'Where's the Archivist?'

'Gone! Can you quiet this crowd?'

'I'm not a magician. I'm an Obscurist.'

He was, she thought, a great deal more than that, but she didn't say it. She said, 'Then can you make me heard? To all of them?'

The red-haired woman standing beside him unsnapped a leather case on her belt, took out pen and paper, and sketched out a quick series of symbols. She handed it to him. He nodded, pressed his finger to the paper, and said to Khalila, 'Talk. They'll hear you. Whether they pay attention or not is your affair.'

She took a deep breath and ran to the same lion she'd climbed before. It felt hot under her shoes, and she realised she was cold now, even in the heat of the baking sun. Panic raced through her, and then it was gone.

'Scholars! Librarians! Listen to me!'

The roar faded, purely from surprise, she thought, and she saw faces turning towards her up in the stands. She wondered what they saw: a slight young woman in a bloodstained robe and hijab? A fellow Scholar? She had no way of knowing. But she continued. There was no choice.

'You were brought here to see the Archivist's enemies destroyed,' she said. Her voice rang from the stone, echoed, and it sounded like it belonged to someone else. Someone with real power. 'You were to be witness to his power and his triumph. But that is not our Library. That is not our spirit, or our soul, or our purpose. We are not here to be powerful. We are here to protect and spread knowledge. The Library has survived tyrants and kings before, and we stand here today together, to say *we are not this*. Not kings. Not tyrants. Not rulers. *We serve.*'

She had their attention. No one moved. No one spoke. The last automaton had frozen in place.

'The Archivist made us into an ugly thing,' she said. 'A thing that used fear to control the world. But we are not what he made us. We are more. We stand, unafraid. And together. *Because we are the Great Library!*'

The shout came back from thousands of them. Scholars. Librarians. Obscurists. Soldiers. It echoed from stones that had seen death and destruction, beauty and grace.

'We endure,' she said. 'And now we will choose a new Curia, a new Archivist, and we will bring our light back to a world we left in darkness. Do you agree?'

The shout was a full roar now.

Khalila Seif lowered her head and listened to the Great

Library being reborn. Fragile, hopeful, perhaps too innocent to survive in this changing world.

But new.

'Then each of the specialties, gather. Elect your new leaders to come forward. And let a new Archivist be chosen to lead us before we leave this place today.'

She hopped down from the lion and felt a kind of wave wash over her; when she reached Eskander, he said, 'I stopped the amplification. You can speak normally.'

Her throat felt oddly raw and dry. She coughed, and as she caught her breath, the red-haired woman pressed a metal flask into her hand. It contained water, thank Allah, and she gulped thirstily. 'Fine speech,' the woman said. 'I don't think the Obscurists need a meeting to know that the man who brought us here is our Obscurist Magnus, like it or not.'

'Not,' Eskander said. 'But I will accept until someone better comes.'

Khalila studied him for a moment and then said, 'You seem familiar, sir.'

He ignored her and walked away, and as he came face-to-face with Scholar Wolfe, she realised who he was.

Jess had lost his family today. And Wolfe had found his.

My father. Uncle. My brothers! Khalila gasped and flinched at her horrible thoughtlessness; she raced to find Santi, who was having his wounds treated by a silent Medica. 'The prisoners!' she said. 'Where are they?'

'I've sent the Blue Dogs to free them,' Santi said. 'They were never taken out of their cells. It was all a feint, to get us here. And it worked.'

'Not for the Archivist.'

'Our success may be temporary. He's alive. And he's got

plenty of allies willing to help him take back his throne. Let's not forget, the Spanish will be coming; they're no longer bound by a treaty, and though they might claim to be coming to protect us, once they get a foothold, the Library will never be independent again. The Burners will see us as vulnerable. God knows who else.' He looked past her, to where Wolfe and Eskander were quietly talking. 'But I suppose this will do, for today.'

'It will have to,' she agreed.

'You don't have a specialty yet, do you?'

It seemed an odd question. She shook her head. 'I left before I chose one.'

'Maybe one's chosen you,' Santi told her. 'You were born for this, Khalila.'

'For what?'

'To lead,' he said.

She laughed, half in horror. 'I'm no one. There are Scholars far older and wiser than I am.'

'That's true. But soon enough, I think you'll be rising up among them.' Santi closed his eyes for a moment, then opened them. 'I'm proud of all of you. But most especially of you.'

She didn't know what to say to that. *Thank you* seemed too little. Before she could find the words, he heaved a sigh and stood up, to the Medica's evident annoyance. 'Come on, then,' he said. 'We have work to do. Whatever happens tomorrow, we're a wounded beast in a world full of wolves. And we had better learn to use our teeth before it's too late.'

She followed Captain Santi into the crowds, to begin the hardest work of all.

Survival.

EPHEMERA

Text of a letter from King Ramón Alfonse of Spain to the Archivist of the Great Library of Alexandria. Available in the Codex.

Respectful greetings to the new Archivist of the Great Library. Long may you hold the keys of this great and ancient institution and uphold its true purpose throughout the world.

However, I remain concerned that the Great Library stands in such peril and turmoil, given the rebellion of the former Archivist and one-third of the High Garda and a full five hundred of its Elites. Please do not bother to deny these facts; I am well aware of what occurs within the city, and indeed within the Serapeum itself.

Your Curia is new and untried. Your Obscurists are demanding new freedoms in exchange for operation of the most basic of services and causing great disruption in what we have come to depend on out in the world.

One can only assume, now, that your weakness leaves the greatest treasures in the world – your Archives – to the strongest and fastest at your gates. And that is unacceptable to those who, like you, value and wish to preserve such knowledge from destruction.

To that end, the combined navies of Spain, Portugal, the American colonies, Russia and Japan sail for your port, and our forces will come to you as friends, not as conquerors. I pray you stand down your armies and allow us entry.

If not, I pray for us all, and the dark days to come.

SOUND TRACK

As always, music played a huge part in getting me into and through this story. Enjoy the songs? Please buy them from the artists and support their work.

'Go to War'	Nothing More
'Who We Are'	Nothing More
'Wonderful Wonderful'	The Killers
'Under Your Spell'	The Sweeplings
'Ahead of Myself'	X Ambassadors
'No Roots'	Alice Merton
'Who We Are'	Welshly Arms
'Revolution'	The Score
'Be by Our Side'	The Sweeplings
'Wrong Side of Heaven'	Five Finger Death Punch
'Bloodfeather'	Highly Suspect
'Champion'	Fall Out Boy
'Becomes the Colour'	Emily Wells
'Cold Blood'	Valen

ACKNOWLEDGEMENTS

Special thanks to Zaheerah Khalik, Fauzia Ali, and Zahdia Anwer for their invaluable assistance.

To librarians and teachers everywhere, who operate without funds, without support, without even basic acknowledgment much of the time: you inspire me, and so many other people. You touch lives and create hope. You connect our past to our future. Don't forget how important you really are.

ACKNOWLEDGEMENTS